STONE SPRING

STONE SPRING

NORTHLAND: BOOK ONE

STEPHEN BAXTER

GOLLANCZ

LONDON

The right of Stephen Baxter to be identified as the author of
this work has been asserted by him in accordance with the
Copyright, Designs and Patents Act 1988.

First published in Great Britain in 2010 by Gollancz
An imprint of the Orion Publishing Group
Orion House, 5 Upper St Martin's Lane,
London WC2H 9EA
An Hachette UK Company

A CIP catalogue record for this book
is available from the British Library

ISBN 978 0 575 08918 1 (Cased)
ISBN 978 0 575 08919 8 (Trade Paperback)

1 3 5 7 9 10 8 6 4 2

Typeset at The Spartan Press Ltd,
Lymington, Hants

Printed and bound in the UK by
CPI Mackays, Chatham ME5 8TD

The Orion Publishing Group's policy is to use papers
that are natural, renewable and recyclable products and
made from wood grown in sustainable forests. The logging
and manufacturing processes are expected to conform to the
environmental regulations of the country of origin.

www.stephen-baxter.com
www.orionbooks.co.uk

For Robert Holdstock

NORTHLAND
c. 7300 BC.

MODERN COASTLINE
ANCIENT COASTLINE
RIVERS

N

ETXELUR
First Mother's Ribs

ALBIA

MOON SEA

NORTHLAND

World River (Elbe)

Great River (Ouse)

(Thames)

GAIRA

(Rhine)

THE CONTINENT

ETXELUR
c. 7300 BC.

North Island

Middens

Causeway

Flint Island

ETXELUR BAY

The Seven Houses

R. Little Mother's Milk

D-S '10

N

Dunes
Houses

ONE

1

The comet swam out of the dark. Its light bathed the planet that lay ahead, reflecting from a hemisphere that gleamed a lifeless bone-white.

Vast ice caps covered much of North America and central Asia. In Europe a single monstrous dome stretched from Scotland to Scandinavia, in places piled kilometres thick. To the south was a polar desert, scoured by winds, giving way to tundra. At the glaciation's greatest extent Britain and northern Europe had been abandoned entirely; no human had lived north of the Alps.

At last, prompted by subtle, cyclic changes in Earth's orbit, the climate had shifted – and with dramatic suddenness. Over a few decades millennia-old ice receded north. The revealed landscape, scoured to the bedrock, was tentatively colonised by the grey-green of life. Migrant herds and the humans who depended on them slowly followed, taking back landscapes on which there was rarely a trace of forgotten ancestors.

With so much water still locked up in the ice, the seas were low, and all around the world swathes of continental shelf were exposed. In northern Europe Britain was united with the continent by a bridge of land that, as it happened, had been spared the scouring of the ice. As the thaw proceeded, this north land, a country the size of Britain itself, became rich terrain for humans, who explored the water courses and probed the thickening forests for game.

But now, in the chill nights, eyes animal and human were drawn to the shifting light in the sky.

The comet punched into the atmosphere. It disintegrated over North America and exploded in multiple airbursts and impacts, random acts of cosmic violence. Whole animal herds were exterminated, and human survivors, fleeing south, thought the Sky Wolf was murdering the land they had named for him. One comet fragment skimmed across the atmosphere to detonate over Scandinavia.

In time the skies cleared – but the remnant American ice caps had been destabilised. One tremendous sheet had been draining south down the Mississippi river system. Now huge volumes of cold water flowed through the inland sea that covered the Gulf of St Lawrence, chilling the north Atlantic. Around the world the ice spread from the north once more, and life retreated to its southern refuges. This new winter lasted a thousand years.

But even as the ice receded again, even as life took back the land once more, the world was not at rest. Meltwater fuelled rising seas, and the very bedrock rebounded, relieved of the weight of ice – or it sank, in areas that had been at the edge of the masses of ice and uplifted by its huge weight. In a process governed by geological chance, coastlines advanced and receded. The basic shape of the world changed around the people, constantly.

And to north and south of the rich hunting grounds of Europe's north land, generation on generation, the chill oceans bit at the coasts, seeking a way to sever the land bridge.

2

The Year of the Great Sea: Winter Solstice.

The day of Ana's blood tide, with her father missing and her mother dead, was always going to be difficult. And it got a lot worse, early that very morning, when the two Pretani boys walked into her house.

Sunta, Ana's grandmother, sat with Ana opposite the door. Ana was holding open her tunic, the skin of her exposed belly prickling in the cold air that leaked in around the door flap. Sunta dipped her fingertips in a thick paste of water, menstrual blood and ochre, carefully painting circles around Ana's navel. The sign, when finished, would be three big concentric circles, the largest spanning Ana's ribs to her pubis, with a vertical tail cutting from the centre down to her groin. This was the most ancient mark of Etxelur, the sign of the Door to the Mothers' House – the land of ancestors. Later this painting would be the basis of a tattoo Ana would carry through her life.

Thus they sat, alone in the house, when the two Pretani boys pushed through the door flap.

They looked around. They just ignored the women. There was snow on their shoulders and their boots. Under fur cloaks they wore tunics of heavy, stiff hide, not cloth as the Etxelur women wore. The boys dumped their packs on the floor's stone flags, kicked at pallets stuffed with dry bracken, walked around the peat fire in the big hearth, tested the strength of the house's sloping wooden supports by pushing at them with their

5

shoulders, and jabbered at each other in their own guttural language. To Ana it was as if two bear cubs had wandered into the house.

For her part Sunta didn't even look up. 'Pretani,' she murmured.

Fourteen years old, Ana had only a blurred memory of the last time Pretani had come to Etxelur, a memory of big men who smelled of leather and tree sap and blood. 'What are they doing in our house? I thought the snailheads were coming for the midwinter gathering.'

Sunta, sitting cross-legged, was stick-thin inside a bundle of furs. She was forty-seven years old, one of the oldest inhabitants of Etxelur, and she was dying. But her eyes were sharp as flint. 'Arses they are, like the last time they were here, like all Pretani, like all men. But it is custom for the chief Pretani to lodge in my house, the house of the Giver's mother, and here they are. Oh, just ignore them.' She continued working on the design on Ana's belly, her clawlike finger never wavering in the smooth arcs it drew.

But Ana couldn't take her eyes off the Pretani. She tried to remember what her mother had told her about them before she died. They were younger than they had looked at first. Boy-men, from the forests of Albia.

Under tied-back mops of black hair, both of them wore beards. The older one had a thick charcoal-black line tattooed on his forehead. But the younger one, who was probably not much older than Ana, had a finer face, a strong jaw, thin nose, high brow, prominent cheekbones. No forehead scars. He peered into the stone-lined hole in the ground where they kept limpets for use as bait in fishing, and he studied the way the house had been set up over a pit dug into the sand, knee deep, to give more room. These were features you wouldn't find in houses in the woods of Albia, she supposed, where nobody fished, and drainage would always be a problem. The younger boy was similar enough to the other that they must be

6

brothers, but he seemed to have a spark of curiosity the other lacked.

He glanced at Ana, a flash of dark eyes as he caught her watching him. She looked away.

His brother, meanwhile, raised his fur-boot-swathed foot and swung a kick at the wall, not quite opposite where the women sat. Brush snapped, and layers of dried kelp fell to the floor. Even a little snow fell in.

At last Sunta rose to her feet. She wore her big old winter cloak, sealskin lined with gull down, and as she rose stray wisps of feathers fluttered into the air around her. She wasn't much more than two-thirds the size of the Pretani, but she looked oddly grand. 'Stop that.' She switched to the traders' tongue. 'I said, stop kicking my wall, you big arse.'

The man looked down at her, directly for the first time. 'What did you call me?'

'Oh, so you can see me after all. Arse. *Arse*.' She bent stiffly and slapped her bony behind, through the thickness of her cloak.

Ana sought for the words in the unfamiliar tongue. 'But then,' she said, 'grandmother calls all men arses.'

The Pretani's gaze flickered over her body, like a carrion bird eyeing up a piece of meat. She realised she was still holding open her tunic, exposing her throat and breasts and belly. She fumbled to close it.

Her grandmother snapped, 'Leave that. You'll smudge the paint.' In the traders' tongue she said, 'You. Big fellow. Tell me your name.'

The man sneered. 'Get out of my way.'

'You get out of my way.'

'In my country the women get out of the way of the men, who own the houses.'

'This isn't your country, and I thank the mothers for that.'

He looked around. 'Where is the Giver? Where is the man who owns this house?'

'In Etxelur the women own the houses. This is my house. I am the oldest woman here.'

7

'From the shrivelled look of you, I think you are probably the oldest woman in the world. My name is Gall. This is my brother Shade. In our country our father is the Root. The most powerful man. Do you understand? We have come to this scrubby coastal place to hunt and to trade and to let you hear our songs of killing. Every seven years, we do this. It is an old custom.'

Sunta said, 'And did you travel all this way just to kick a hole in my wall?'

'I was making a new door.' He pointed. '*That* door is in the wrong place.'

'No, it isn't,' Ana said. 'In all our houses the door faces north.'

The younger boy, Shade, asked, 'Why? What's so special about north? There's nothing north of here but ocean.'

'That's where the Door to the Mothers' House lies. Where our ancestors once lived, now lost under the sea—'

Gall snorted. '*We* have doors facing south-east.'

'Why?' Sunta snapped at him.

'Because of the light – it goes around – something to do with the sun. That's the priest's business. All I know is I'm not going to stay in a house with a door in the wrong place.'

Sunta smiled. 'But this is the Giver's house. It is the largest in Etxelur. If you don't stay here you'll have to stay in a smaller house, and it would not be the Giver's house. What would your father think of that?'

Gall scowled. 'I ask you again – if this is the Giver's house, where is the Giver?'

Ana said, 'In the autumn my father went to sea to hunt whale.'

Shade looked at her. 'He has not come back?'

'No.'

Gall sneered. 'Then he's dead.'

'No!'

'He's dead and you have no Giver.'

'Kirike is not dead,' Sunta said quietly. 'Not until the priest says so, or his body washes up on the beach, or his Other, the

8

pine marten, says so in a human tongue. Anyhow we don't need a Giver until the summer. And even if he returns, even if he were standing here now—'

'What?'

'Even then, Pretani arse, you would do as I say, here in my house.'

Enraged, he ran a dirty thumbnail along the line on his forehead. 'See this? I got this scar when I first took a man's life. I was fourteen years old.'

Sunta smiled. 'If you like I'll show you the scars *I* got when I first *gave* a woman her life. I was thirteen years old.'

Complicated, baffled expressions chased across Gall's face. He was evidently grasping for a way out of this while saving his pride. 'This house is evidently the least unsuitable in this squalid huddle for sons of Albia. We will stay here. We will discuss the issue of the door later.'

'As you wish,' Sunta said, mocking. 'And we will also discuss how you are going to fix my wall.'

He was about to argue with that when Lightning burst in. The dog's tail was up, his eyes bright, tongue lolling, his fur covered in snow. Excited by the presence of the strangers, the dog jumped up at them, barking.

Gall cringed back. 'Wolf! Wolf!' He drew a flint-blade knife from his belt.

Ana stood between Gall and the dog. 'You harm him and I'll harm you back, Pretani.'

Sunta laughed, rocking. 'Lightning is Kirike's dog – oh, come here, Lightning! He chose him because he was the runt of the litter, and gave him his name as a joke, because as a puppy he was the slowest dog anybody had ever seen. And you big men cower before him!'

Shade looked nervous, but he was smiling. 'Pretani don't keep dogs.'

'Maybe you should,' Ana said, petting Lightning.

Gall, trying to regain his pride, put away his knife and strutted around the house. 'I am hungry from the journey.'

'Are you indeed?' Sunta asked. She gave no sign she was going to offer him food.

He paused by the hearth. 'What kind of fire is this? Where is the wood?'

'This is not your forest-world. Wood is precious here. We burn peat.'

'It is a stupid fire. It gives off smoke but no heat.' He hawked and spat on the inadequate fire. 'Come, Shade. Let's find a less ugly old woman who might feed us.' And with that he walked out of the north-facing door. His brother hurried after him, with a backwards glance at Ana.

When they were gone the space suddenly seemed huge and empty.

Sunta seemed to collapse, as if her bones had turned to water. 'Oh, what a fuss. Give me your hand, dear.' Ana helped her back to where she had been sitting. Sunta's seal-fur cloak fell open, scattering feathers and exposing her body; the only flesh on her was the mass that protruded from her belly, the growth that so horribly mimicked a pregnancy. 'All men are arses. Do something about that hole in the wall, would you? The wind pierces me.'

Ana took handfuls of dry bracken from a pallet and shoved them into the broken place. 'You can't be serious.'

'About what?'

'About letting them stay here!'

'Every seven years the Pretani hunters come to the winter gathering. And they always stay in the Giver's house. I am your grandmother, and I remember *my* grandmother telling me how this was the way when she was a girl, and *her* grandmother told her of it when she was a girl, and before that only the sun and moon remember. This is custom, like it or not.'

'I don't care about custom. I *live* here. All my things are here . . .'

'They won't touch you, you know.'

'That's not the point. And why today, of all days?' She felt

10

tears prickle her eyes. Her grandmother didn't approve of crying; she dug the heels of her hands into her eyes. 'It's my blood tide. And now *them*. If only my father were here—'

'But he isn't,' Sunta said. Her voice broke up in a flurry of dry, painful-sounding coughs. She sat back and dipped her finger in the paint once more. 'Now let's see how much mess you've made.'

Ana turned away, breathing hard. She was no longer a child; her blood tide marked the dawning of adulthood. She had to behave well. Deliberately she calmed herself and opened her tunic.

But when she turned back Sunta had fallen asleep. A single thread of drool dripped from her open mouth, the stubs of her worn teeth.

3

As the day wore on towards noon, and with her blood-tide mark still no more than a sketch, Ana pulled on her own sealskin cloak and left the house to collect fish for her grandmother's meal. The fishing boats were due back at noon, and perhaps she could get some fresh cod, Sunta's favourite; if not there was probably some on the drying racks. And if her father had been here, she couldn't help but think, they might all be feasting on whale meat.

Once outside Ana could hear seals calling, like children singing.

The house was one of seven clustered together on a plain of tough grass, just south of a bank of dunes that offered some protection from the north wind. This morning the fresh snow, a hand deep, covered the Seven Houses' thatch of dried kelp; the houses were conical heaps, like wind-carved snow drifts. The adults scraped the snow away from the houses and piled it into banks. They had shovels made of the shoulder blades of deer, big old tools. Children ran around, excited, throwing snow in the air and over each other.

Ana picked her way north, towards the dunes and the coast beyond. The snow crunched and squeaked under her feet. The ground between the houses had been churned to mud, frozen, then blanketed over by snow, so you couldn't see the ridges in the soil, hard as rock, or the places where a sheet of ice covered a puddle of ice-cold mud, waiting to trap an unwary foot. The going got easier as she climbed the ridge of dunes, for here the frost and snow and sand were mixed up, and the long dead grass brushed her legs. Even on the newest snow she saw tracks of rabbits, deer, the arrow-head markings of birds, and here and there tiny paw prints, almost invisible, that were the tracks of stoats and weasels. Ana went at it briskly, relishing the feeling of her heart and lungs working.

As she moved away from the houses the land grew silent, even the cries of the children muffled. Sunta once told her that snow was sound made solid and fallen to the ground, birdsong and wolf cries and the calls of people all compressed into the same shimmering white.

When she breasted the ridge the wind pushed into her face, and she paused for breath, looking out over the northern panorama. Here on her dune she stood over the mouth of a deep bay, which opened out to the sea to her right. On the far side of the bay stood Flint Island, a central pile of tumbled yellow-brown rocks surrounded by a rim of wrack-scarred beach. The tide was high just now, and the grey waters of the bay covered the causeway that linked the island to the mainland, to the west. Above the drowned causeway a flight of whooper swans clattered. On the mud flats further west huge flocks of wading birds and fowl had gathered, their plumage bright in the cold winter sunlight. She recognised wigoes, geese. Seals littered the rocky islets off the eastern point of Flint Island, their bodies glistening, their voices raised in the thin cries she had heard outside her grandmother's house.

All around the bay she could see people working. Down below the dunes the fishing boats had been dragged up onto the beach, and their catch lay in glistening silver heaps on the sand. Further back the drying racks were set up. A thin, slow-moving figure must be Jurgi, the priest, apologising to the tiny spirits of the fish. On the mud flats and marshes people gathered rushes and reeds, and some of the men hunted swans with their spears and bolas. On the island she saw Pretani, bulky dark figures, hovering over a heap of mined flint. There were other strangers here, traders and folk from east and south, gathering at a time of year when, paradoxically, despite the shortness of the days, frozen lakes and snow-covered ground made for easy walking and sled-dragging.

The whole place swarmed with children. They dug in the mud and raced at the sea, daring each other as they fled the frothy waves. Dogs ran with the children, yapping their excitement at the games they played. There were always more children than adults in Etxelur, burning through lives that, for many, would be brief.

Beyond Flint Island there was only the sea, the endless sea. Its grey flatness was matched by a lid of cloud above, though the sun was visible low in the sky, a milky blur across whose face wisps of cloud raced like smoke. More snow coming, Ana thought. She looked to the north, trying to make out the stud of rock that was North Island, the holy place to which she would be taken tonight for the blood tide. But the midwinter daylight was murky, uncertain.

This place, this bay with its island of flint treasures and marshland and dune fields, was Etxelur. And this was the northernmost coast of Northland, a rich, rolling landscape that extended to the south as far as you could walk. Ana had grown up here, and she knew every scrap of it, every outcrop of jutting, layered rock, every grain of sand. She loved this rich, generous place, and its people. Despite the Pretani she couldn't stay unhappy for long, not today. This was her day, the day of her blood tide, the first truly significant day of any woman's life.

And as she walked down the track through the dunes towards the beach, people nodded to her, smiling as they worked. 'The sun's warmth stay with you on the ocean tonight, Ana!'

Little Arga, seven years old and Ana's cousin, came running up. 'Ana! Ana! Where have you been? I want to see your marks. Has Mama Sunta drawn them yet?'

Ana took her hand. 'Let me get out of the wind first. Where's Zesi?'

'With the flint.' Arga pointed. Flint samples, hewn from the lodes on the island, had been set out in neat rows on a platform

14

of eroded rock above the high water mark, sorted by size, colour and type. Ana saw her sister Zesi sitting cross-legged on the sand – and, she saw with dismay, the two Pretani boys loomed over her. Evidently they were discussing the flint.

'Let's show Zesi your blood marks,' Arga said. She was slim, tall for her age, with the family's pale skin and red hair.

Ana hung back. 'She's busy with the Pretani. Let's not bother her . . .'

But now the older Pretani, Gall, touched Zesi's hair, a flame of red on this drab day. Zesi snapped at him and pulled her hair back. Gall laughed and drifted off, heading for the smoking fish, and Shade followed, looking back with vague regret.

Arga said, 'They're gone. Come on.'

The two girls ran hand in hand down the beach, towards the rock flat. Close to, Ana could see how artfully the flints had been arrayed, over the big triple-ring marking that had been cut into the rock flat in a time before remembering.

Zesi greeted them with a grin as they sat on the sand beside her. 'So how's blood tide day so far?'

'A nightmare.'

'Oh, everybody feels that way; it works out in the end. Let me see your circles.'

Reluctantly Ana pushed back her cloak and opened her tunic. Arga bent close to see, her small face intent.

Zesi traced the circles on her sister's belly. 'It's not bad.'

'Sunta's very weak.'

'She'll finish this off for you, she won't let you down.'

'Unless those Pretani idiots mess everything up.'

Zesi let her hair come loose, and shook it out around her head. In the wan daylight the colour made her pale skin shine like the moon. Zesi was seventeen, three years older than Ana, and, Ana knew, she would always be more beautiful. 'Oh, the Pretani! The older one – Gall? – went on about the argument he had with Mama Sunta.'

'I know. I was there.'

'I think they've come here for wives, as well as the seven-year

15

visit and the trading for flint. Their forest is full of their cousins, so they say. They're disappointed father isn't here. They wanted to talk it over with him.'

Ana frowned. 'If there was going to be a marriage it would have to be you with that oaf Gall. And it would be Mama Sunta who would have to agree.'

'Yes, but that's not how it works where they live. There, the men run everything. And, listen to this, I worked it out from what Gall said – if I married him I'd have to leave here and go and live with his family.'

'That's stupid,' Arga said. 'If you get married the man comes to live with you and your mother. Everybody does it that way.'

'Evidently not in Albia.' She sighed. 'They're disappointed we have no brothers, too. They wanted the oldest brother to come back and fight in the forest with them, in the summer.'

'What for?'

'The wildwood challenge. Another every-seven-years thing, hunting aurochs in the Albia forest, everybody seeing who's got the biggest cock. You know what men are like.'

'Arses,' said Arga, seven years old and solemn.

'Not all men.' It was the younger Pretani, Shade. He was coming back, almost shyly. 'I am sorry if my speaking is not good. The traders' tongue is difficult.'

Ana pulled her tunic tight. 'And you've come for another look at my chest, have you?'

He may not have understood the words, but he got the sentiment. He blushed under his sparse beard, suddenly looking much younger. 'I was curious.'

'Where's your brother? Isn't he curious?'

Shade gestured. Gall was with the fishing parties, who were showing off hooks of antler bone and nets of plaited sinew and bark, and telling stories of the sea. 'He is telling heroic tales of his own battles with bears and wolves. A good tale is worth telling. And Gall is loud, and catches my father's ear.'

'Your tunic looks itchy,' Arga said, staring.

16

'It is hide. It is what we wear, in Albia.'

'Not cloth, like sensible people?'

'Cloth?'

'We make it from reeds and bark and stuff. And you're shivering,' Arga said bluntly.

'No, I am not.'

'You are,' said Ana. 'It's because you're wearing that stupid deerskin cloak. We wear those in summer.'

'This is what we wear,' he said miserably. 'It is fine in Albia.'

Zesi laughed, for he was blushing again. 'Oh, come here. Sit between Ana and Arga. They'll warm you up.'

The Pretani hesitated. Perhaps he thought Zesi was playing some trick on him. But he sat, smoothing his cloak under him.

'So,' Ana said, 'why aren't you over there with your brother telling lies?'

'I know little about cod, and fishing. I do know about other things. Flint, and trading.' He picked up a piece from the display before him; inside a remnant carapace of brittle chalk, it was creamy brown. 'This is good quality.'

'It comes from the island,' Zesi said, pointing. 'Flint Island, we call it. But the best pieces we have are much older. We don't usually trade them. Sometimes they are used as tokens in the Giving feasts in the summer.'

'Why older, I mean, why the best . . .' He gave up his attempt to frame the question in the unfamiliar language.

Ana pointed to the centre of the bay, to their west. 'The best lode of all is out there. That's where the good old stuff came from. The sea covered it over.'

He frowned. 'Like a tide coming in?'

'It wasn't a tide,' Ana said.

'I know nothing of the sea.'

'No, you don't,' Ana snapped. She felt oddly resentful of his questions.

But Zesi seemed amused. 'Ask something else.'

'What does *this* mean?' He indicated the design etched into

17

the rock flat, the three circles of grooves and ridges, the straight-line tail that slashed to the centre.

'You'll see this all over Etxelur. Some say it's a kind of memory of the Door to the Mothers' House. Which is the old land we came from.'

Arga said seriously, 'We lived there without dying. But when the moon gave death to the world we had to leave.'

Shade stared at the mark. 'So,' he said, turning shyly to Ana, 'why are these circles drawn on your belly in blood?'

'It isn't just blood,' Ana said. 'There's water and ochre and honey and other stuff.'

Zesi said briskly, 'This is the blood tide. After a girl becomes a woman, at low tide in the next midwinter she is taken out by boat to North Island, which is north of Flint Island. The moon is death, ice. Ana's new body is a gift of warmth and life. We must show we defy the moon, and the tides she draws . . .'

'Still sitting with the women, brother?' Gall approached. He held an immense cod in his left hand; he had bits of bone and scaly skin stuck in his beard, and Ana could smell the wood-smoke on him. His traders' tongue was guttural, coarse. 'You'll turn into a girl yourself. Come on, let's go back to that Giver's hovel and see if we can persuade that old crone to cook this for us.'

Ana jumped to her feet. 'You leave her alone. She's ill.'

'Not too ill to lash me with her tongue, was she? Well, if she can't do it, you'll have to.' He threw the cod in the sand at her feet, belched, and looked down at the circles on the rock. 'I heard you wittering about this scratch. Yak, yak, yak. You'd get more sense out of those seals on that island. I'll tell you the bit I like.' With his booted toe he traced out the tail that cut through the concentric grooves and ridges, and he leered at Ana. 'Straight and hard and thrusting up into the belly.'

Zesi got up, her expression icy, and picked up the fish. 'I'll cook your food. Just you leave Mama Sunta alone.'

'Hah! Come on, little brother, let's put some flesh on your bones.'

Shade stood, expressionless, and followed his brother and Zesi towards the dunes.

Arga sat with Ana, watching them go. 'Arses,' she said.

4

Late in the day Sunta told Ana that the boats were waiting for her, on the north shore of Flint Island.

It was dark when Ana emerged from her house, ready for the long walk around the bay to the island. At least the threatened fresh snow hadn't appeared, and the cloud cover was thin enough to show a brilliant moon. The snow carelessly piled up by the people with their reindeer-bone scrapers had frozen again, hard enough to hurt if you kicked it.

The moon's face was surrounded by a ring of colour. This was said to be a crowd of the spirits of the dead, falling to their final destination in the moon's icy embrace.

But tonight Ana wasn't bothered so much by the dead as by the living, who had come drifting out of the Seven Houses. Many of the people of Etxelur, friends and family, had turned out to walk with her. But in among them were strangers, come to see the show. The two Pretani boys, with Gall munching on a haunch of whale meat and leering at the women. Traders, jabbering the crude argot that was their only common tongue. Even snailheads – early arrivals of the people from the far south. The centre of attention, she felt as if she was withering with embarrassment.

They wasted no time in the cold. The priest, Jurgi, led the way as he always did on such occasions. As they set off you could see by the moonlight how his mouth protruded, the great incisors of a wolf sticking out of his human lips. Arga solemnly walked beside him, wide-eyed, honoured to be carrying the skin bag that contained the priest's irons.

Ana followed, with Mama Sunta and Zesi. Which was all wrong, of course. Ana should have been walking with her parents, not Sunta and Zesi. But only a year before her mother had died in childbirth, and her father, some said half-mad with grief, had gone sailing off and never returned. And Sunta was so weak that Zesi and Ana had to walk to either side of her, holding her up in her great sealskin coat.

'I feel stupid,' Ana murmured to Zesi over Mama Sunta's lolling head.

Zesi replied, 'Everybody feels that way. Tonight is about you and the moon. If you want to find the right Other, then you must concentrate.'

Ana said bitterly, 'It was easy for you. A good Other chose you, the crossbill. Father was here. And mother.'

'Easy, was it?' Zesi snapped. 'Well, I'm not your mother, and I don't have to listen to you moaning.'

They trudged on in sullen silence.

They crossed the causeway to the island, a stripe of dry land that, when the tide was low, separated bay water from the open sea. Ana looked back over the bay, across the water to the southern beaches. Fires burned all along the shore, the tanners and knappers and fisherfolk working, brilliant human sparks in the drab darkness of the night. The moon's cold white light glimmered from stretches of open water, on the ocean, in the bay of Etxelur, and across the boggy landscape. At times, Ana thought, Etxelur seemed more water than land.

Once over the causeway they headed north towards the islands, following a trail through low, rounded hills that, under sparse snow, were coated with dry, brown, fallen bracken, lying like lank hair, with here and there the stubborn green of grass. As they broke out at the shore the wind hit them, a hard steady gust coming off the sea, and white-capped waves growled. They clambered down the last line of dunes to the beach. Their boots crunched over gravel eroding from the dunes, fringing the level sand. On the beach itself the tide was low, and rock formations glistened, exposed to the air, dark with clinging weed and

21

barnacles. There was much wrack gathered up in bands, strips and tubes of seaweed, bits of driftwood pushed high up the beach, relics of a winter storm. Ana's footstep stirred the blanched, disarticulated remnants of a crab.

They came to the middens. These were heaps of mollusc shells and fishbone and other detritus, tall and long, each curving gracefully like the crescent moon, as if embracing the sea. Windblown snow was piled up in the lee of the middens. The boats that would carry Ana to North Island were waiting here, cupped by the middens.

But first the priest carried his charm bag to the crest of one of the middens. Here he set out his branding irons, bits of the hard, rusty stuff that, it was said, had fallen from the sky – unimaginably rare pieces, more valued even than the priest's scraps of gold. These pieces were used for nothing but marking the people with the symbols of their Others, be they otter, fox, snow hare, pine marten – most precious of all the seal, most unwelcome the owl. One of these would be chosen to mark Ana that evening, in a flash of fire and pain, after it became clear what her Other must be.

Jurgi seemed to hesitate. Then he beckoned to Ana. She made her way after him up the midden. Loose shells slid and cracked under her feet, and there was a rich, cloying smell of salt and rot.

The priest had laid out the equipment for the fire, bits of false gold and flint to make a spark, scraps of dried moss for kindling, blocks of peat for fuel. He took out the wolf jaw that filled his upper mouth. 'The fire must be built,' he said gravely, his toothless speech slurred. She understood; the brand had to be heated in a new fire, started from scratch, not from an ember of some old blaze. 'This is a role for a man from your house. Your father, your brother . . .'

'I have no brother. My father is—'

'I know. Still the fire must be started.'

'I will do it!' The call came from the Pretani boy Shade. Without waiting for permission he scrambled up the midden, slipping on the unfamiliar surface. His brother hooted and laughed, and called out insults in his own tongue. 'I will do it,' Shade repeated breathlessly, as he reached the crest of the mound.

Ana glared at him. 'Why must you push your way in like this? You aren't my brother or my father. You aren't even from Etxelur.'

'But I am living in your house. And I am good at starting fires.'

Ana frowned. 'There must be another way. Custom decrees—'

The priest tried to look grave, then laughed. 'Custom decrees that we are allowed a little imagination. Trust me. But can I trust you, Pretani?'

'Oh, yes.' But Shade was distracted. 'This place is so strange, this hill. I don't know the word.'

'Midden,' said Ana heavily. 'It's a midden.'

'A heaping-up of shells . . . So high and so long – a hundred paces? I will measure it out. Many, many shells.'

The priest nodded. 'It has taken many generations to build these middens. They are holy places for us. We bury the bones of our dead here. But, can you see, the sea is taking back the land . . .'

The ends of the midden arcs where they cut to the coast were eroded, worn down by the sea.

Shade held out his arms along the line of the midden. 'Still, they are two bits of circles. Like those on your belly, on the stone flat on the beach, and now here in the ocean. This is how you know yourself. Circles in circles.'

Jurgi said dryly, 'Maybe you should be a priest.'

'Oh, shut up,' Ana said. She'd had enough; this was *her* night. She started to make her way down the midden. 'Let him build his stupid fire. Come on, priest, let's get to the boats before the tide turns.'

A little fleet of boats pushed off from the island's sandy shore, paddles lapping at the chill black water. The boats were frames of wood over which hide was stretched, dried and caulked with tallow.

Ana travelled in one boat, which was paddled by the priest and by Zesi in the place of her father. Mama Sunta sat in another boat with her daughter Rute, Ana's aunt, and Rute's husband Jaku. Ana's eyes were used to the dark now, and she could see them all quite clearly in the misty moonlight. The paddlers all wore heavy fur mittens to protect their hands from the cold. Out on the water in the dark Ana felt small, terribly fragile, yet she had barely left the land. But her father, if he lived, was out on the breast of the wider ocean in a boat not much more substantial than this.

Nobody spoke as the boats receded from the shore. Indeed it had been a long while since Sunta had said anything; she was just a heap of sealskin, with her crumpled white face barely visible beneath a hat of bear fur. Ana was glad of the silence, compared to the clamour and the foolishness that had plagued the day since the arrival of the Pretani boys.

Lost in her thoughts, she was startled by a noise coming from the dark, beyond the waves' lapping, a kind of shuffling, a snort of breath. The priest stopped paddling and put his finger to his lips. Then he pointed ahead.

Suddenly Ana saw a black shape like a hole cut neatly out of the moonlit sky. This was North Island, a scrap of rock only exposed at low tide; already they had reached it.

And on its tiny foreshore a bulky form stirred. It was a seal, a huge one, a bull.

The priest dipped his paddle in the water and, almost noise-lessly, swung the boat around to bring Ana alongside the seal. Only paces separated them. The seal, clearly visible now in the moonlight, was looking straight back at Ana, quite still, its eyes pools of blackness. She could make out no colours in its pelt.

The priest smiled at her.

She understood why. The seal was the best Other of all. The seal was a survivor of the days before death had come to the world, when humans had lived among the animals, and had shifted forms from one kind to another as easily as ice melts to water. That had ended when the little mothers made their lethal bargain with the moon, and so had saved the whole world from starvation as the undying animals ate all there was to eat. But just as humans and animals now had to die, so they could no longer share each other's forms. A human was for ever a human, a dog a dog. The seals, however, had been too busy playing to hear of the little mothers' bargain. And so they had become stuck in a middle form, neither of the land or the sea, with faces like dogs and bodies like fish, and there they had remained ever since, relics of a better time.

Ana couldn't look away from the seal's deep, heavy gaze.

But then, without warning, it slid off its rock, slipped into the water and vanished. The priest frowned, and Ana felt a stab of disappointment. Was the seal not to be her Other after all?

The boats, quietly paddled, drifted towards the island.

Jurgi nodded to Ana. 'It is time.'

She shucked off her cloak and opened up her tunic. Zesi helped her pull her boots off her feet. Then, uncertainly, the ring-symbol of Northland painted on her bare belly, she stood up in the boat and faced the island. The ice cold air was sharp on her flesh.

The priest turned to the second boat. 'Mama Sunta . . .' Sunta, in the place of Ana's mother, was to stand now, and drop into the ocean a rag stained with Ana's first woman-blood, now dried and rust-brown. All this was to be performed in the light of the moon, the goddess of death, as a defiance of her dread legacy.

But Sunta didn't move. Rute, her daughter, reached over and touched her shoulder. The old woman seemed to start awake, but her eyes were unseeing. She clutched at her belly, at the thing growing inside her. Ana, standing in the cold air, smelled an acrid stink of piss and shit; Sunta's bowels had emptied. Then she fell back, limp, and sighed like a receding tide. Rute shook her. 'Mama Sunta!' But Sunta moved no more.

And a clatter of wings came from the island. Ana, startled, would have fallen if Zesi had not helped her. She saw an owl, unmistakable, lift from a rocky ledge and make for the mainland, beating its great wings, its eerie flat face held before it.

Ana sat, shivering, and Zesi put her arms around her. 'The owl,' Ana said. The owl that dared hunt only at night, in the domain of the moon, the goddess of death. The owl that had flown into the air just as Sunta had died, bringing death to this unique moment of life. 'The owl. My Other! No mother, no father, now this . . . Oh, Jurgi, can't you help me?'

The priest leaned forward. 'I am sorry. The Other chooses you . . . Come, Zesi, put a cloak around her.'

From the other boat, in the dark, came the sound of Rute sobbing.

5

Far around the curve of the world – to the west of Etxelur, beyond Albia's forest-clad valleys, beyond an ocean flecked with ice and a handful of fragile skin boats – there was a land where the sun had not yet set. And a boy was crying.

'Dreamer, what's wrong with him?' Moon Reacher plucked at Ice Dreamer's sleeve. 'Stone Shaper. Why is he crying?'

Ice Dreamer stopped walking and looked down at Moon Reacher, the girl's red, windblown face, her tied-back nut-brown hair, her shapeless, grubby hide clothes scavenged from the bodies of the dead. Moon Reacher's words seemed to come from another reality – perhaps from the Big House where your totem carried your spirit when you died. Words were human things. Ice Dreamer wasn't in a human world, not any more.

This world, the land of the Sky Wolf, was a place of ground frozen hard as rock under her skin boots, and air so cold it was like a blade sliding in and out of her lungs, and, to the north, only ice, ice that shone with a pale, cruelly pointless beauty, ice as far as she could see. The only warmth in the whole world was in her belly, her own core, where her new baby lay dreaming dreams of the Big House she had so recently left. And Ice Dreamer didn't even like to think about that, for when the baby came, who would there be to help her with the birth? All the women and girls were dead or lost, all save Moon Reacher, only eight years old. Maybe it would be better if the baby was never born at all, if she just stayed and grew old in the warmth and mindless safety of Dreamer's womb.

27

Yet here was Moon Reacher, still tugging at her sleeve. 'Dreamer! Why is Stone Shaper crying?'

Mammoth Talker loomed over them, massive in his furs, his pack huge on his back, his treasured spear in his fist.

And beside him Stone Shaper was indeed crying again, shuddering silently, the tears frosting on his cheeks. His medicine bag hung around his neck. Even wrapped in his bearskin cloak Shaper looked skinny, weak; he was nineteen years old.

They were all that was left. The four of them might be the last of the True People, anywhere.

Mammoth Talker growled, 'He cries because he is weak. Less than a priest. Less than a woman, than a child. That unborn thing in your belly, Dreamer. Shaper is less than that.' Talker was somewhere over thirty years old, perpetually angry, irritated to be stopped yet again.

Dreamer shot back, 'If he's so weak, Talker, *you* should have taken the medicine bag when Wolf Dancer got himself killed. Reacher, I think he's crying because he thinks this is his fault.' She gestured. 'The cold. The winter. He thinks he isn't saying the right words to make the spring come.'

'That's silly,' Reacher looked up at Shaper, and took his hand. 'The winter's bigger than you will ever be.'

Shaper looked down at her, taking gulping breaths.

'She's right,' said Dreamer. 'And you shouldn't be wasting your strength on tears. Have you still got the fire safe?'

'Of course I have.' He held up his medicine bag.

'Then you're doing the most important job you have.' She looked around. The world was a mouth of grey, the sky featureless, the tough grass on the ground frozen flat, the sun invisible. Trying to get some relief from the north wind they had been heading roughly east, skirting a bluff of rocks, soft brown stone worn by the wind into fantastic shapes. She turned to Mammoth Talker. 'How late do you think it is?'

'How am I supposed to know? Ask him. Maybe the answer lies in the track of his tears.'

'Oh, shut up.' They were all tired, however early or late it was. Glancing across at the rock formation, she saw there was a kind of hollow under a ledge of stone, with a drift of soil underneath it. There was no source of water she could see, but there were old snow drifts in shadowed crevices above that lower ledge, ice they could melt. 'Look at that. Maybe we could make a shelter for the night.'

For a heartbeat it seemed Talker might refuse. His huge fist opened and closed around his spear, with its precious point bequeathed by his father, a blade as long as a man's head, finely shaped, elaborately fluted. In his eyes he was the only hunter left, a hunter trailed by a gaggle of a woman, a boy-priest, and a child. He always wanted to go on, go further. But they had nowhere to go. 'All right. Make your shelter.' He shucked his pack off his shoulders and dropped it on the ground. 'I'll go find us something to eat. Take care of my spear points.' He hoisted his spear and stalked off towards the south.

'Watch out for the Cowards. And bring back wood if you find it,' Dreamer called after him, but if he heard he showed no sign of it.

'I'll set the traps,' Moon Reacher said. She took off her pack and dug into it, looking for the snares, loops of bison-sinew rope with sharp bone stakes to stick into the ground. 'I bet there are jackrabbits around these rocks.'

'Look out for running water, a spring. And be careful.' Moving cautiously, trying not to strain the muscles of her belly, Dreamer lifted her own pack's strap over her head, and let it fall to the ground beside Talker's. 'Come on, Shaper. Let's see what we can make of this place.'

Shaper unpicked Mammoth Talker's heavy pack, which, aside from his carefully wrapped bundle of spear points, mostly consisted of skins, enough for a small house.

Dreamer crawled under the ledge, exploring. At the front the space was high enough to kneel, but it narrowed at the back. Dry, dirty soil had been piled up here by the wind, along with dead grass and a handful of bones. There were animal scuts, small pellets, maybe gopher droppings – with any luck Moon

29

Reacher would turn out to be right about the jackrabbits – and bigger turds, maybe from the scavenger that had brought the bones in here. She scraped the scuts and grass and bones into a heap. All of these would burn, but if Talker didn't come back with wood it wouldn't be enough.

As she scraped up the dung her baby, some six months since conception, kicked her hard. She winced, and had to rest.

She had a sudden, sharp memory of her own childhood, when she had been younger than Moon Reacher, and the houses, six, seven, eight of them, had stood by a lake where trees dipped into the water. That had been a place somewhere far to the south of here, south and east. She could surely never find it again, for the people had been walking away from it since before she had become a woman. All gone now, she supposed. Oh, the lake and the grassy plain would still be there. But now, if anybody lived there, it would be Cowards in their swarming numbers and shabby huts, and they would know nothing of the people who had gone before. And here she was burning turds, and melting snow to drink.

Stone Shaper clumsily lifted a hide sheet over the mouth of the hollow, dropped it, and bent to try again. With a sigh Ice Dreamer crawled out of the cave to help him. They used loose rocks to hold the hide in place, and shut out the breeze from the little cave. Once back inside, Dreamer scraped a pit in the sandy ground to make the hearth, and lined it with flat stones gathered from the back of the hollow.

Stone Shaper reverently unpacked his medicine bag. In with the precious stones, herbs and strange old bits of curved tooth was an ember of last night's fire, wrapped in moss and soft leather. He made a bed of dry moss and bits of grass in the hearth, laid down the ember, and blew on it gently, adding shreds of moss one by one until a tiny flame caught. This he sheltered with his hands, and Ice Dreamer helped him, feeding the flame with dried grass from the cave. When the fire was burning they sat back. It gave off light but little heat; for that

30

they would have to wait for Mammoth Talker's return with some decent fuel.

'Mammoth Talker is right,' said Stone Shaper. He loosened his tunic at the neck, and sat with his legs stretched out. 'I am no priest. I am no man. I am shamed by my tears.'

'Well, Talker isn't much of a man himself to say such things. You're the only priest we've got.'

'I never wanted to be a priest.' He flexed his hands. 'I am Stone Shaper. That's my name, that's what I should do.'

And, she thought bitterly, I never wanted to be Pregnant Woman, far from my grandmothers and aunts. 'This is the pattern of our lives, Shaper. Why, do you think Wolf Dancer wanted to be a priest either? The last *true* priest was Eagle Seer, before the split . . .'

It had been fifteen years since the True People had abandoned the houses by the lake and walked north in search of hunting lands free of the presence of the Cowards. Eagle Seer had been raised on the march. But the priest before *him*, who Dreamer remembered as a tired old man called the Coyote, had made sure Seer had been trained the way a priest should be trained – from boyhood, from the moment it was clear the spirits had chosen him.

But there had been a split. When it began to seem that nowhere was free of the swarming Cowards, the hunters had started arguing among themselves. Dreamer remembered the long nights, the desperate men posturing and shouting, the women and children, hungry, exhausted, sitting at their feet and trying to keep warm. In the end the men could only agree to do what Ice Dreamer had always thought was the worst choice of all: to split up. Most had turned west. Some, including Mammoth Talker and Horse Driver, who was to become the father of Dreamer's baby, chose east. The women and their children had to follow their men. Dreamer had said goodbye to her sister, her aunt, her mother.

And the only priest, Eagle Seer, had chosen to go west. Talker's group could not survive without a priest, without a

31

door to the world of the spirits. There was no time for Eagle Seer to raise a new priest in accordance with custom. But Seer did his best. Talker and Driver and the other men had chosen Wolf Dancer, and Seer worked hard to train that young man in the arts of healing and weather lore and talking to the dead. He even made Dancer a new medicine bag and filled it with treasures from his own – to much hostility from those he would walk with, who thought he was diluting their own protection.

Well, since the split Ice Dreamer had heard nothing of those who had gone west; even if they lived they were dead to her. One by one her own party had dwindled, as the old and the young failed to keep the pace, and anybody who fell ill was quickly lost. She had been dismayed to find herself pregnant.

And then had come the night of the flood. It had been Horse Driver's fault, Driver who insisted he had seen caribou in the shadow of a grimy glacier that scoured down from an eroded mountain. He had led them to the shore of a chill lake at the glacier's foot, and left the women and children to make camp while the men hunted shadows. Nobody had wanted to be there. They believed that glaciers were the claws of the Sky Wolf, who had smashed the good earth, making it dark and cold and wiping the land clean of game. Driver would not listen.

Well, the Sky Wolf had stirred in his sleep that night. A great piece of his glacier-claw broke away, and a wave of slushy water washed over their poor camp. Only four had survived, or five if you counted the child in Dreamer's belly: Dreamer herself, Mammoth Talker, orphaned Moon Reacher, and poor Stone Shaper, who the hunters had thought was too weak to go with them, and who had found the dead priest's medicine bag.

Now Shaper, exhausted, hungry, stared into the fragment of flame. He fingered the bits of curved tooth in his bag. 'I was thinking about our totems,' he said. 'Here are the three of us, named for the bare bones of the world, ice and stone and moon – and Mammoth Talker, named for a beast nobody living has seen. Have our totems abandoned us?'

Ice Dreamer shifted, trying to find a less uncomfortable

position. 'Whether they have or not, it is up to us to behave as if it is not so.'

He nodded gravely. 'Maybe *you* should be the priest.'

That made her laugh.

Moon Reacher pushed her way into the shelter. 'Oh, it's cosy. Not very warm yet. Why are you laughing?'

'Because we're alive.' Dreamer could smell the blood. 'You caught something.'

With a flourish, Reacher produced a jackrabbit from behind her back and held it up by the ears. The snare still dangled from its leg, and Reacher had broken its neck.

Dreamer leaned forward and kissed her on the forehead. 'You are a great hunter. Come on, let's get this cooking.'

The three of them worked together. Dreamer quickly detached the animal's head and sleeved off its skin. Dreamer and Shaper butchered the jackrabbit quickly, and Reacher used her own small obsidian blade to cut the meat fillets finely, so they would cook faster on the small fire.

When the meat was sizzling on a hot stone, Mammoth Talker pushed into the shelter. He let the cold wind in, and they all had to huddle around the fire to make room. 'I found no prey,' he growled. 'But I did find this.' He dragged in a bundle of wood, dried, old.

They eagerly piled it on the fire. Bark curled, the wood crackled, and smoke began to billow. For the first time that day Dreamer began to feel warm.

'You can have some of my jackrabbit,' Reacher said brightly. She handed Talker a leg.

He gnawed it, crunching the delicate bones. 'And I saw Cowards. Many of them.'

The mood in the shelter immediately turned cold again. Dreamer asked, 'Are we safe here until morning?'

'Yes. But listen to me. The Cowards have killed bison. They drove them into a valley . . . You should see it. Many animals. More bison than Cowards, I think.'

'What have Cowards and their bison to do with us?'

'Don't you see? There is more meat than they can eat, even if every man, woman and child gorges until the meat rots. More than they can carry away. *Meat for us.* All we have to do is take it.'

'But it's the Cowards' kill,' Shaper said. 'They hunted these beasts. We will be scavenging, like the dogs of the prairie.'

Dreamer could see that Talker, the proud hunter, hadn't allowed himself to think that way. 'You should applaud me. Not peck at me with these questions, peck, peck, peck. I will sleep outside this hovel.' He grabbed a handful of Reacher's jackrabbit fillets, more than his share, and pushed his way out of the shelter.

'Don't be a—' *Fool.* Dreamer bit back the word before she could say it; it would do far more harm than good.

Talker left a skin flapping loose. Stone Shaper crawled over to shut out the cold.

6

Mammoth Talker woke them all not long after the dawn.

If he had been uncomfortable in the night, huddled alone in the cold protected only by his cloak, he said nothing of it. But Dreamer thought he looked paler, his eyes that bit darker. Even his great strength was not infinite, and he was a fool to waste it on displays of temper.

He pointed with his spear. 'The kill site is that way. South. Not far. We will leave our stuff here.'

Moon Reacher wasn't happy. She was a child who in her eight years had seen almost everything taken from her, her whole family destroyed by the glacial flood, and now she had a habit of clinging to what was left.

Dreamer squeezed her hand. 'Don't worry, Reacher. We will be fine, our stuff will be safe here.'

Stone Shaper objected too. 'I will take the medicine bag, and the fire, even so.'

'By the Wolf's teeth – fine, fine, just make sure you bring your blades.' Mammoth Talker hefted his spear. 'Everybody had a drink and a piss and a shit? Anybody got anything else to say? Then let's go.'

So they walked south. As soon as they were away from the lee of the rock bluff the wind from the icebound north bit at their backs. The country seemed lifeless, with only dead grass and scrub at their feet. Once Dreamer saw a cloud of dust on the horizon, far to the east. A crowd of large animals – bison, perhaps, or horses, or deer.

Talker was right that it wasn't far to the Cowards' kill site. The morning was not much advanced by the time they saw threads of smoke rising, and Dreamer began to hear noises: a general lowing, deep screams of pain, high-pitched human calls.

Confidently Talker led them towards a bluff of layered, eroded rock. It was clear he had done his scouting well. They climbed, and on the feature's flat top they lay down on their fronts. This was awkward for Dreamer, who tried to favour her belly. They inched forward until they could see.

From here the land sloped downward gently to a valley incised sharply into the ground and littered with shattered rocks. People clustered in knots around fires that burned on both sides of the valley.

The valley itself was dry, as far as Dreamer could see. But it was not empty. The narrowest part of the valley, she was astonished to see, was full of squirming animals.

They were bison, no doubt about that, many of them, heaped up on each other. The living tried to stand on the backs of the dead below, wriggling and tossing their heads. Blood splashed everywhere, and there was a lingering stench of ordure, mixing in the morning air with the smoke from the fires. The air was full of heart-rending bellowing.

She could see where the herd had been driven into the trap. On one side of the valley the dusty ground was churned up by the hooves of stampeding animals, who had evidently crashed through a concealing screen of brush and tumbled down the steep valley wall.

And the hunters worked, Cowards with their strange spiky hair and dense tattoos. As Dreamer watched, a carcass was hauled out of the pit and dragged to a fire, where it was efficiently butchered, the skin slit and dragged away, the limbs detached, the guts spilled, haunches cut off the carcass and hung on racks or thrown straight on the fires. This was going on all around the valley, and the ground was marked by the remains of butchered carcasses, bloody masses that looked as if the animals had been dropped from a height and splashed open.

Some of the Cowards danced for fun around the terrified, furious animals, jabbing with spears, mocking, keeping well back from hooves and horns. There was plenty of meat; there was no need for everybody to work.

Talker murmured, 'It was like this before dark. It must have been going on all night. Look at them prodding the wretched animals with their stupid little spears. Look how they sprawl on the ground, asleep in the middle of the day.'

Dreamer made a rough count. 'I see a dozen fires. There must be a hundred hunters here – hunters and their women and children.'

'The Cowards always hunt in packs,' Talker said dismissively. 'Like dogs. They like to stampede their prey. They set fires and holler and chase.'

Shaper said, 'But some run in front, directing the beasts to the trap they want them to fall into. We call them Cowards. It must take courage to run ahead of a stampede.'

Talker dismissed this. 'It takes courage to face the animal whose life you will take for the sake of your own. To look it in the eye, to see its spirit vanish. Not like this. And look how wastefully they are butchering the beasts. Taking only the best fillets.'

'They can afford to,' Dreamer murmured. 'Anyhow, Talker, what's your plan?'

'There's plenty of meat down there. We could haul away a dozen prime bulls and they wouldn't know the difference.'

'No matter how much they have they won't share with us.'

'They won't know anything about it,' Talker said. 'Not if they don't see us.'

Shaper said, 'We could wait for night, and then sneak up.'

Talker said, 'Have you ever tried butchery in the dark? No. We will go in while there is still light. I'm a hunter. I can sneak up on a deer. I can certainly get close enough to those animals, with the noise and the stink of them, without disturbing the dreams of fat, lazy Cowards.' He pointed. 'See that part of the valley, away from the circle of fires? If we head that way we will be concealed by the slope of the land, and can get to the herd where nobody is working.'

'It's a risk,' Dreamer said. 'If we're seen—'

'If we're seen we run,' said Talker with supreme confidence. 'Those Cowards with their bellies full of meat will never catch us. And then we'll wait for another chance.'

It looked terribly dangerous to Dreamer, who had been on hunts herself, and knew how to read a landscape. 'Let's wait and see if a better chance offers itself.'

'If we wait we'll be discovered. I told you, I scouted this out, I know what I'm doing. You people do nothing but argue, argue. Now we act.' He got on his haunches, preparing to move. 'Follow me. Step where I step. Don't kick a pebble, don't break wind – don't make a sound.' He glared at them until they all nodded, even wide-eyed Reacher.

Talker moved out of the shelter of the bluff. In the open he kept low, running in a crouch.

Dreamer's heavy belly made it difficult for her to copy him, but she did her best, and, padding in his footprints in the dust, stayed as silent as he was.

They came to a kind of tributary, just as dry as the main valley. They crept into this, and then scrambled to lie flat behind a worn boulder that hid them from the kill site. The smell of blood and ordure was strong here, and the noise of the animals was a continual lowing wail. With great care Talker levered himself up until he could see around the boulder. He dropped back, grinning. 'Get your blades ready. We are only paces from the animals, but we must be a hundred paces from the Cowards and their nearest fire.'

Dreamer frowned. 'Really, as far as that?' She tried to remember the land as she had seen it from the bluff.

'Don't argue with me,' he snapped. 'I will go first.' He dug into his wrap and produced a cutting tool, a block of flint with a single sharp edge. He held this in his right hand, and hefted his spear in the left. 'I will take as much meat as I can. Then I will come back here, and we will decide what to do next.'

'I'm not sure—'

'Woman! Do you want to eat? Then do as I say.' And with that, silent as a cloud, he crept around the rock and was gone.

'We are closer than a hundred paces to the Cowards,' Shaper whispered, quietly enough that Reacher couldn't hear. 'I am no hunter but I have a good sense of place.'

Dreamer didn't reply.

For an unmeasured time they huddled behind the rock. Dreamer strained, trying to hear Talker's butchery, or his returning footsteps – or the tread of a Coward band. The hunger and the strain began to make her feel light-headed, and she felt the tension winding up inside her, coiling her guts.

It was too long. She had to see.

She got up to a squat and slowly, carefully, lifted her head above the lip of the stone. She winced at every blade of dead grass that rustled under her legs.

Reacher and the priest-boy watched her wide-eyed.

There was Talker. Beyond him she saw the bison struggling in their heap, dead or dying. Talker had walked just a few paces down the valley slope and cut open a dead animal. Its innards were spilled, a haunch of liver lay on the ground beside him, and there was blood around Talker's mouth. He hadn't been able to resist taking the rich delicacy immediately, the traditional prize of the successful hunter. Too long, Talker, you are taking too long, she thought desperately.

She shifted a little so she could see further along the length of the valley – and there was the nearest fire of the Cowards. She was shocked; it could be no more than fifty paces away. In his courage or stupidity Talker had indeed lied, and was taking a much greater risk than he had admitted—

Movement. She saw them clearly, two, three, four, five – four men, one woman – sneaking through broken ground at the lip of the valley. Even on this freezing day they went naked. They wore their hair stiffened with dust into spikes, and

39

painful-looking jagged tattoos had been incised into their cheeks. They bore no spears or knives, but they each hefted rocks, as you would use to drive a dog away.

They knew Talker was there. They thought he was a scavenging dog or coyote. And meanwhile Talker dug his hand deep in the innards of the dead bison. Perhaps he was looking for the gall bladder; she knew he relished that morsel. He had not heard the Cowards, who were nearly on him.

She stood up. She yelled, 'Talker! Cowards!'

Without waiting to see what happened, she ducked back down. 'They know we are here. Go!'

Stone Shaper did not hesitate. He didn't even pick up his medicine bundle. He ran back the way they had come, keeping to cover, heading for the stone bluff where they had hidden.

But Moon Reacher clung to Dreamer's arm. 'I won't leave you.'

Dreamer could hear the jabber of the Cowards, only paces away. 'Come, then.' And she ran, clutching her heavy belly, the child hanging onto her arm.

She risked one glance back. She saw Talker standing – not running – facing the Cowards. 'I am Mammoth Talker,' he yelled. 'Mammoth Talker! Remember me!' And he hurled his heavy spear with his fluted blade straight at the lead Coward. The spear, heavy enough to bring down a charging bison, smashed into the Coward's chest, and heart and lungs were torn out of his back before he was pinned to the ground.

The Cowards hesitated; they were armed only with rocks. But now Talker had only his stone meat-cutting blade. In a heartbeat they were on him.

Dreamer turned and ran harder. Maybe even now they might make it, if she could get them to a bit of cover where they might hide out—

It felt as if a huge fist grabbed her heels, pulling them out from under her. She went down hard, face first, her nose slamming into the dirt. Tasting blood, she looked down to see rope wrapped around her legs, a throwing rope weighted with stones.

The shouts of the Cowards were loud.

Reacher was still here, dragging at her hand. 'Get up!' she screamed. 'Get up!'

Dreamer, stunned, unable to talk, tried to push the child away.

Hands grabbed her, her shoulders, legs, hair. She was dragged back along the ground, and the pain of her scalp made her scream.

Then she was hauled to her feet and turned around. She saw the men around her in a blur. Before she got her balance the punches came, one in her face that jarred her jaw, another in the pit of her belly. She tried to double over to protect the baby, but the hands pulled her up. She could smell the men, the meat and blood and sweat and smoke from their fires, all around her, she had no control, could do nothing.

There was a respite from the blows. She found she was being held before Mammoth Talker. He dangled, held up by his hair. His chest and face had been smashed inwards so they were like caves of blood and bone. They had killed him with their fists and their stones, the last hunter of the True People. But he had fought, and done some damage. One man stood before her holding up a gashed arm, his face a tattooed mask. He screamed at her in his own tongue.

She hawked and spat blood and dust in his face. Again they fell on her with punches and kicks, and she went down again.

Somebody began to jabber commands. They got her on her back and began to drag at her skins, and somebody took hold of her ankles, forcing her legs apart. She heard them calling, and more men came running to join in. She struggled and spat and bit, but the punches rained down, and she was weakening fast.

And, as if through a bloody haze, she remembered Moon Reacher. She forced her head to left, right, and there she was. A man held the girl up in the air with one big paw around her wrists, and with his other hand he was pulling away her skins like peeling a berry. Reacher's leg was injured; blood streamed down from a wound in her thigh.

41

Dreamer stopped fighting. She looked around until she found the single Coward woman. As naked as the rest, and as garishly tattooed, she stood away from the men, nursing a bruised arm. 'Please!' Dreamer yelled until the woman looked at her, and met her eyes. 'Please – the little girl – she is only a child – you're a woman, help her—'

The woman could never understand her words. The language of the people and of the Cowards had nothing in common. But she shared some basic humanity. She stepped over to the man with Reacher. She slapped him until he let the girl go, and she gestured at Dreamer, on the ground. *Take what you want over there.* She dragged Reacher away, out of Dreamer's sight.

The men were getting organised. One held her arms up over her head, another two, crouching, held her legs open. A younger man, not much more than a boy, ran his hands over her big belly and her milk-swollen breasts, as if fascinated. Then the men started clapping, and another approached her, a huge bull of a man with a swirling blood-red tattoo on his belly. He was already erect, she saw, his penis like a spear shaft, tattooed along its length and with what looked like a splinter of bone through the glans. He leaned over her and grinned.

She worked her aching mouth, summoning up one more mouthful, and spat blood and mucus in his face. That earned her a punch in the head, and the world fell away.

7

The Year of the Great Sea: Spring Equinox.

A few days before the Spring Walk, Jurgi the priest decreed that Mama Sunta's time of laying-out was done. He came to speak to the sisters in their house, the house that had been Sunta's, and now belonged to Zesi, as the oldest surviving woman of the family.

Zesi's house it might be – but the house was full of the Pretani boys, their sprawling beds of bracken and moss and skins, their spears and nets. The Pretani evidently liked it here at Etxelur. They'd stayed as winter turned to spring, and now they were even talking of staying all the way to the summer solstice and the Giving. So, after months and months, they were *still here*. To Ana's nostrils the house stank of their filthy deerskin tunics and their meat-laden farts, and the acrid smells of their maleness.

Then there were the fights. Once Gall had tried to bring a woman to his bed: Pina, a young widow known to be generous with her body. Zesi had flown into a rage, and had hurled Gall's bedding out of the house: 'Get that slack-uddered cow out of my home!' For days afterwards Gall had pulled down his lower eyelids every time Zesi passed, evidently a Pretani sign for jealousy.

And rare was the morning when he wouldn't clamber out of bed naked, stretching, displaying an erection like a stabbing spear.

Sometimes Ana dreamed of burning it all down – or, better yet, she imagined the house being smashed by some great

43

storm, or a tide from the sea. She feared that this was the voice of her Other, the owl, the death bird; she feared this was the darkness that had been discovered inside her the night Sunta died.

Certainly this polluted house wasn't a place where she wanted to discuss the details of her grandmother's burial.

But the priest, composed as ever, picked his way through the Pretani debris without a murmur or a glance, and sat with the women by the warmth of the night fire. He began, 'I know it seems a long time since Sunta's death, at the solstice full moon—'

'We remember when it was,' Zesi snapped.

'My point is, the wait has been long. The months after the solstice are the coldest of all, when even the processes of a sky burial run slow. Some say even this is a blessing of the little mothers, for it gives time for the children of winter to be given up to the sky.' Every winter took its cull of children; the ceremony of interring their little bones was a sad mark of each spring. 'But Sunta is now ready for you to collect her. You understand this is a man's role – if your father were here—'

'But he isn't.' Zesi folded her arms. Her face was set, her eyes clear, her red hair scraped back from her head in a practical knot. 'Well, I'll do it. Although the mothers know I've enough to do already, with the Spring Walk only days away. The low tide isn't going to wait until we're ready, is it?'

This was how Zesi had been since Sunta's death. With her father's continuing absence Zesi had taken on the roles of both the family's senior woman and senior man. For all her complaints about it, Zesi seemed filled with energy by the burden of her dual role.

But Ana became aware that the priest hadn't replied.

'I did wonder,' Jurgi said slowly, 'if Ana might be the one to bear Mama Sunta's bones to the midden.'

'I'm capable of doing it,' Zesi said. 'And I'm older.'

'Of course you are capable. But custom doesn't dictate that the oldest should do this.'

Zesi sounded sceptical. 'Then what does custom dictate?'

'That whoever was the last companion of the dead should be chosen. Ana, Sunta was with you on the night of your blood tide. You should be with her now.'

Ana knew that Zesi didn't like to be away from the centre of things. But after a long pause Zesi said, 'Fine. That's fitting. I've got plenty to do anyhow.' She stood, unwinding her long legs, and grudgingly kissed the top of Ana's head. 'Say goodnight to Mama Sunta for me.'

So it was decided.

The next morning, just before dawn, the priest called again at the Seven Houses. Glimpsed through the flap of Ana's house, he was a silent, spectral figure, with his deer-skull mask hanging eerily at his neck and his charm bag slung at his waist, a fold of ancient seal hide.

Ana had barely slept. The thought of what she must do today filled her with dread. Perhaps that was the owl within her, battling with her spirit. But she slid off her pallet, pulled on her skin boots, and wrapped her winter sealskin cloak over her shoulders.

She glanced around the dark house. Gall was asleep, flat out on his pallet, face down, mouth open, nose squashed out of shape, snoring. The hair sprouted thickly on his bare back, and in the dim light of the fire Ana saw an infestation of bugs stirring through that greasy forest.

Zesi was awake, however; Ana saw her eyes bright in the firelight.

And Shade rolled out of bed. She saw that he had his boots and cloak ready by the side of his pallet.

'What do you think you're doing?'

'Coming with you,' he whispered back. 'To the midden.'

'Oh, no, you're not.' She glared at the priest, beyond the door flap. 'Is this your doing, Jurgi?'

The priest spread his hands. 'We need somebody to dig. Shade said he'd do it. Would you rather do it yourself?'

'Please,' Shade said. 'I knew Sunta too.'

Jurgi beckoned. 'We'll discuss this outside. Don't wake the others.'

But of course, once they got outside, all three bundled up in their winter cloaks, and Jurgi had handed Shade his shovel made of a deer's shoulder bone, there was no point debating it any more. Ana stomped away, with bad grace.

The laying-out platform was set up on a dune matted with marram grass. It was a frame of precious driftwood, taller than a person, long enough for three adults to be laid end to end – or several infants.

The priest and Shade stood by while Ana climbed a step up to the platform. Here was Mama Sunta, a bundle of ragged deer-skin and bones and bits of flesh. At least there was no sign of the growth that had eaten her from within. The bones were cold and shone with dew.

From this slight elevation, Ana looked around. It was still not yet dawn; the sky was a high grey-blue, scattered with cloud. The air was very cold, and the dew was heavy. Mama Sunta had lived out her whole long life in this place, and Ana saw traces of Sunta's long life and her work wherever she looked. From here the Seven Houses were all visible, and Sunta's own home was a mound of kelp thatch the deep green of the sea. The ground between the houses was thoroughly trampled. On the landward side, downwind from the prevailing breezes, was a waste pit and racks where early-season fish were drying. Sunta had always been the best cook. A rubbish tip was full of broken tools and bits of old bone and stone, hide and cloth. Sunta had always emphasised to the children that nothing was ever discarded here, just put aside until it came in handy. A space trampled flat and stained with old blood was used for butchery, and in a smaller area nearby stone was worked. Both places had been barred to the children by Sunta, for fear of their bare feet tearing on flint shards or bone scraps.

A dormouse scuttled past Ana's feet, fresh out of its

hibernation, busy already, early in the year, early in the day. In a world without Sunta.

The priest was watching her. 'Are you all right?'

'You know, I often come out like this. Before the dawn. Just to walk around by myself.'

'I know you do. You probably shouldn't be alone.'

'But people . . .' People shunned her, sometimes subtly, sometimes not. 'People can see the owl in me. I'm bad luck.'

'I don't think you're bad luck. That midwinter day was Sunta's time to die, as it was your time for the blood tide. I know it's affected you. But just because two things happen at the same time doesn't mean they're linked.'

She wrinkled her nose. 'That's a funny thing to say. I don't remember the old priest talking like that.'

'Well, I'm a funny sort of priest. You must give people time, Ana. A chance to know you, now you're a woman. And you need to give yourself a chance to get over this – to get past your grandmother's death. Why do you think I insisted it must be you who buries her today?'

'For Sunta's sake.'

'No. For you.' He touched her arm. 'Come now, we should get to the midden before the sun is too high.'

So Ana lifted Mama Sunta. Most of the joints had lost their ligaments, and as she lifted the skeleton it broke up, and Sunta's skull rolled backwards, revealing empty sockets where worms moved sluggishly in a kind of black muck.

Shade, watching her, said, 'In Albia we hang our dead in the branches of a tree, an oak if we can find one. And when the birds and the worms have done their work we plant the man in the ground, and put an acorn on top of him, so a tree will grow and hold his spirit.'

Ana understood by now that Shade's language had no word for 'woman', no distinction between 'his' and 'hers', as if women were an inferior sort of men.

'But our great men, like our father when he dies, we will plant a whole tree on top of him. I mean, we dig it up roots and all, and make a hole in the ground, and put the living tree over him . . .'

Ana ignored him as she worked. Gently but reverently she wrapped the bones in a parcel made of the remains of Sunta's clothing.

Carrying the body – it was shockingly light – she stepped down from the burial platform. With the priest and the Pretani boy to either side of her, she began the long walk around the bay. In the uncertain light it was sometimes difficult to see the track. But she glimpsed frogspawn massing in the dense water, and crocuses thrusting green shoots out of the dead brown earth. She could feel the change in the world, feel the spring coming, like the moment of the turning of a great tide. And yet her grandmother, in her arms, was dead.

They walked silently. Jurgi, beside her, was an extraordinarily calming man, Ana thought, with his open, beardless face, his blue-dyed hair tied back in a tail, and those sharp brown eyes that seemed to see right into her spirit. He was one of the few who had never recoiled from Ana because of her dread Other.

None in Etxelur was more important than the priest, who was the people's bridge between the world of the senses and the world of the gods. But Jurgi was quite unlike the last priest, Petru, a capering fool with wild hair who always hid his face behind his deer-skull mask. Finally he had danced himself to a frenzied death at a midsummer Giving. Jurgi was already twenty-five, she realised. Few people lived much beyond thirty; Sunta had been unusual in living to see her granddaughters grow up. Jurgi might not have many more years. Ana would miss him when he was gone.

They trudged over the causeway to Flint Island, the going still soggy from the last tide, and walked on, passing around the island's north coast, until the great middens stood before them. The edge of the sun had already lifted over the sea's eastern horizon, which was clear of cloud.

The boy grinned, strong and confident, and hoisted his scapula shovel. 'Where shall I dig?'

The priest clambered up the innermost midden, and paced its length. 'Here.' He pointed to a spot on the midden perhaps a third of its length along. 'This feels right.'

The boy climbed up the midden slope, the shells crunching under his heels. 'And if I disturb old bones—'

'It doesn't matter. Just be respectful.'

Shade knelt and began to dig his blade into the midden surface, crunch, scoop, crunch. He was soon done, and stood back.

The priest looked down at Ana. 'Are you ready?'

'Let's get it done.' She clutched Mama Sunta closer to her chest, and climbed the midden slope, stepping cautiously on the uncertain surface, determined not to stumble.

She stood awkwardly on the lip of the pit the Pretani had dug. The hole was neat and round. Glancing into it she saw a gleam of white, perhaps an exposed bone, picked clean by whatever creatures lived here, feasting on the dead. There was a smell of fresh, salty rot. 'I don't know what to do.'

'Just place her in the pit.'

She leaned down, and placed Mama Sunta on the rough floor.

Jurgi nodded. 'Good. Now we wait. We will seal the pit as soon as the sun clears the horizon. But first I will speak to Sunta.' He shifted his deer mask from where it hung on his chest and fixed it over his face. It was just a skull with antlers still fixed, and holes crudely cut to allow his human eyes to see.

But when he shifted his posture, and wrapped his deerskin cloak tighter around him, it was as if his Other, the deer, had taken his place.

'In the beginning was the gap,' he said. 'The awful interval between being and not being. The gap stretched, and created an egg, out of nothing. Its shell was ice and its yolk was slush and mud and rock. For an unmeasured time the egg was alone, silent. Then the egg shattered. The fragments of its shell became ice giants, who swarmed and fought and devoured each other as they grew.

'From the slush and mud of the yolk grew the first mother.

49

She gave birth to the three little mothers, and the sun and the earth serpent and the sky bird of thunder.

'But still the giants fought, until they fell on the first mother. Her own body, torn apart by the giants, became the substance of the earth, and of animals, and of people. The world became rich.

'But when the land became too full of mouths, the little mothers and the sun came to a concord with the moon, a terrible pact, and death was given to the world.

'Now, Sunta, by lying in these broken shells, you are returned to the egg from which all creation emerged . . .' He shook his head, as if dizzy. He began to speak other words, words so old nobody but the priests understood them any more.

Somewhere a sea bird called, welcoming the day. Ana saw how the low, pinkish sunlight glinted from the shells of the midden, tens of tens of tens of them, the labour of generations. It was unexpectedly beautiful, the sparkling shells, the sweeping curve of the middens. She would not cry, she told herself. Not today.

Shade the Pretani touched her shoulder. 'I am your friend, Ana. I think we are alike, you and I. If you would like to talk of your grandmother, or your mother or father—'

She could smell his sweat. She turned away. She didn't even look at him again, as the priest completed the ceremony, and the sun, mistily visible, at last hauled its bulk clear of the sea.

8

In the days that followed, far to the west of Etxelur the last of the True People in the land of the Sky Wolf struggled to stay alive.

And far to the east, beyond a continent of rivers and forest, a man walking alone approached a place where people lived in a huddle of mud bricks and stone walls.

Chona was not prone to fear.

This morning he walked alone, as he preferred, with his pack of dried meat and trade goods on his back, his worn walking staff in his right hand, his left hand hanging loosely by the blade hidden in a fold of his cloak. He had walked up from the Salt Sea to this river valley, its banks thick with woodland, reeds and papyrus, a green belt in this arid country that led him north towards the town. Skinny to the point of gaunt, the skin of his face made leathery by years of sunlight and wind, the soles of his feet hard as rock, Chona knew he looked elderly, at nearly thirty years old. No threat to anybody. Easy to drive away, even to rob of his precious pack of goods. Well, he was not so weak, as would-be robbers had found to their cost.

He had travelled further than anybody he knew, even among the loose community of traders who met at the harbours and river estuaries and confluences, key nodes in the natural routes that spanned the Continent. He believed he had seen as much of the world as anybody alive. He spoke a dozen languages, knew many more in fragments, and was a master of the crude, flexible traders' tongue that people spoke from one end of the Continent to the other. He was clever and resourceful, and he was without fear – almost.

But he was afraid of Jericho. And he could already see the pall of smoke, fed by dozens of fires, that hung over his destination. His belly clenched.

Following a trail well defined by the feet of animals and people, he climbed away from the river and up towards the higher ground, heading north-west. It was close to noon, and the morning clouds had long burned from a blue shell of sky. Away from the river the ground was dusty and the air was dry as a dead man's mouth.

He heard a murmur of voices, a clatter of hooves, a rattle of stones. Ahead of him on the trail a group of boys were herding goats. They carried long sticks to prod the animals as they bleated and jostled. The rattling Chona heard came from wooden gourds, each containing a pebble, hung around the neck of each goat.

Even this was a strange sight to Chona. They were only boys, but he found his footsteps slowing. Goats were for hunting, or for chasing down for milk when you needed it. Why *gather* them? Why fix gourds to their necks?

He always felt like this. He could turn back, head down south to the communities of fisherfolk around the shore of the Salt Sea, where his bone harpoons and elaborate lures always ensured him a welcome.

'Chona.' Magho came striding down the dusty slope to meet him. He clapped the trader on the shoulder. 'So you came.'

'Yes, I came. But—'

'But you nearly turned back.' Magho boomed laughter. 'I know you, my friend, and that's why I came to fetch you. Once I have a fish on the hook I don't let him get away!' He was a big, burly man, grown fat on the produce of his wheat meadows. He had a heavy bull-like jaw and fleshy nose and thick, tied-back black hair, and his luxuriant beard was turning to grey. He wore a skin tunic, but tied around his ample waist was a belt of green-dyed spun yarn.

If Magho had been keen enough to haul his ugly bulk all the way out to the river trail to meet him, he must want Chona's goods rather badly, and Chona, an instinctive trader, began to smell a deal, and his fear receded. 'You know me well enough, Magho. Only the promise of your hospitality lures me on.'

'You have the obsidian.'

'I have it.'

Magho's grin widened.

As they walked on, Magho kept up a steady flow of chatter. Chona had no family, no children, and preferred not to talk of his life, which consisted of walking to places Magho had never heard of, to make deals with people he didn't want Magho to know about. So he let Magho speak of his own family, his wife, their home, their three children, of whom the eldest boy Novu was such a disappointment. It was all a tactic to keep Chona on that fish hook, of course, but Chona endured it politely.

Now, following a track that curved around to the north-west, they were passing through the gardens that surrounded the town. They were a patchwork of shapes, lopsided circles and rough squares marked out by wicker fences. Here women and many children laboured, bent over, plucking weeds from the meadows of wheat and barley and pulses. They didn't look up at Chona and Magho.

The men passed a field where bricks of mud and straw had been laid out in rows to dry in the sun. Another extraordinary sight.

And as they neared the town that pall of smoke spread a dirty brown stain across the sky ahead, and Chona could already smell meat roasting, and human ordure.

Then, approaching from the west, the trail led them over a bluff, and at last Chona saw Jericho itself. It sprawled across the landscape, a mass of round, brick-built houses pressed together in a plain of dirty mud. Beyond lay the river valley and its reed beds, brilliant white and yellow. Even in the heat of the day smoke seeped up from the reed-thatched roofs of the houses, for the people of Jericho were always busy, busy.

But even stranger to Chona was the wall that faced him, standing in front of the town at its western end. Built of stone pressed into dried mud, the wall ran for dozens of paces, cutting the town off from the country to the west, and looping around like a moon crescent to enclose the buildings, though the loop was not completed. The people of Jericho, or their ancestors, had built this wall to save their town from floods and mud slides from the western hills. Strangest of all was the 'tower' that had been built against the wall, a round structure like a vast tree trunk, wider than it was tall, and likewise made of stone blocks pressed into mud. Chona had seen this before. The tower was so wide you could walk inside it, and climb steps up to the top.

As far as Chona had travelled he had never seen such a structure as this. He believed it must be unique in all the world. Why, even the 'tower' only had a name in the language of Jericho itself, a word that was needed nowhere else. Yet the wall was very ancient; you could see how the stones were worn and cracked, and the wall itself looked half-buried by mud drifts and accumulated garbage.

They walked on, rounding the wall, and the crammed-in houses of Jericho were revealed. Chona recoiled from the crowd and the clamour, and the rank stench. But Magho led the way boldly, treading between the piss puddles, ignoring the stinks and the shouts of children and the bleating of goats, shouting greetings to friends or relatives.

A mob of people crushed through narrow, tangled lanes, some carrying baskets of grain or heavy bread loaves. Children, skinny, pale creatures, ran everywhere, playing and yelling as children always did. And there were animals in with the people: goats, hairy, long-legged sheep, even cattle, adding to the filth around the houses. Birds hovered overhead, gulls roosting on the house roofs or swooping down to feed on heaps of waste.

Chona was always overwhelmed by the sheer number of people you saw in this place. And yet many of them looked so unhealthy, the women with their gappy teeth, the children with their stick-thin limbs and pock-marked faces, the men worn down by the constant work.

In some ways this place wasn't unique. Who didn't have a favourite hazel tree? Who didn't try to keep the weeds out of a favourite mushroom patch? People even built walls and dug ditches to take away the rainwater. But nowhere else, in all Chona's travels, had these habits been driven to the extremes you saw around Jericho. Nowhere did you see the *obsession*, the bent backs and anxious eyes. Nowhere else did people live crushed in together like this, though Chona had travelled as far as anybody else in this empty world, east until you came to the deserts where the camels and horses ran in huge herds, or to the far west along the great river roads until you came to the grey ocean. Nowhere save here: Jericho.

The deep human core of him recoiled. But the trader in him was drawn back here again and again, like a fly to a turd. And so he walked on with Magho, pushing his doubts and fears deep down inside.

9

Chona had no idea how Magho found his way through the muddle to his home; all the houses looked the same to him, just heaps of mud brick rising up in the midden-like town like ugly brown poppies.

Magho brushed aside a gap in the wall covered by a mat of reeds, and led Chona down earthen steps into a kind of pit dug down beneath the level of the ground. Rush mats had been scattered on the ground. A fire burned in a central hearth, banked up and not giving off much smoke, but even so the air was dense and hot. Most of the daylight was shut out, and the house was like a cave. The faecal stink outside was alleviated a bit, but in here there was a more complex aroma of stale food, farts, baby milk, sweat, and a disturbing, almost sweet smell of profound rot.

Two women sat, cross-legged, tying knots in some kind of twine. They wore smocks dyed bright green, with their legs left bare. Chona knew one must be Magho's wife, but he couldn't tell which. And three children were here, one older boy who sat sullen against a wall with his legs drawn up against his chest, and two little ones who played with toy mud bricks on the floor. All this Chona glimpsed in the light that leaked through the reed thatch roof.

Magho clapped his hands. 'Out! Come on, I need to talk to my friend here. Not you, Novu, you little snot,' and he pointed a finger at the older boy, who didn't look up.

The women, looking weary, rolled up their twine, gathered their toddlers, and pushed past Chona. The second was much

56

younger than the first, perhaps a younger sister. She was a plump little thing with bare legs, wide innocent eyes, and full breasts whose weight showed through her loose smock.

He felt a stir of interest in his loins. He had been on the road a while. Jericho was a place where the ancient balance between man and woman, of which he had witnessed all manner of variants in his travels, was tipped firmly in the man's favour. Here a woman hardly dared even speak without a man's permission. And certainly the body of a female relative would be within Magho's gift. It would depend how badly Magho wanted Chona's goods, of course, and how protective he felt of the girl. He might even have his eye on her as a second wife himself – Chona couldn't remember, nor did he care, what the marriage rules were here. If so, Magho might not want her spoiled. And spoiled she would be, Chona thought, indulging in a faint reverie, if he got his hands on her. As with all things in the human world, it just depended who wanted what, and how badly. Those innocent eyes . . .

For now he had to concentrate, as Magho was beckoning him to the mats. 'Sit down, sit down.' Magho offered him food. 'Here, have some meat, this is pickled and spiced, have some bread.'

Chona dropped his pack by the door and propped his walking staff up against a wall. He kept his blade hidden at his left side, however. Magho was a harmless sort, but you never knew, and he didn't much like the look of the boy sitting against the wall. He stepped cautiously through the house's clutter of clothes and bits of food and clay pots, making for Magho on his mats. Niches had been cut into the dried mud of the bricks in the wall, and small artefacts stood here, like sculptures of human heads, with bulging eyes and flaring nostrils and protruding tongues done in bright ochre paint. Chona knew from his previous visits that these were in fact real heads, the flensed skulls of honoured ancestors coated in mud and painted. Chona never liked to meet the eyes of these ancients, who he imagined might know the deals he was trying to strike all too well.

57

Magho cracked open one of his loaves, digging big earthy fingers into the thick crust, and tore off a piece to hand to Chona.

The trader bit into it. This 'bread', another word Chona had learned here, did fill your stomach, but it was like eating dry wood, and he knew that the coarse gritty stuff wore your teeth down if you ate too much of it.

Chewing, he sat on the mat Magho had indicated, crossing his legs. But something pale pushed out of the dirt before his mat. It was a skull embedded in the ground, its jaws gaping, dust sifting in its eye sockets.

The boy saw him flinch, and laughed. He was perhaps sixteen. He was wearing a robe not unlike his mother's, not of hide but of woven vegetable fibre, dyed a bright green. 'Nothing to be afraid of, trader man. It's just another grandfather, wearing his way out of the ground. We bury our dead in the ground under our houses where the worms can cleanse their bones. So you're sitting on a big old heap of corpses. No wonder it stinks of rot in here – that's what you're thinking, aren't you?'

'Shut up, Novu,' his father said. Chona was startled at the change in his voice. Where he had treated the women with indifference, there was real hatred in his tone towards the boy.

But Novu kept talking. 'The last trader we had in here was just the same. He threw up in the piss-pot—'

Magho leaned over and punched the boy in the side of the head. Novu went sprawling. 'I told you to shut up! And if you did what I told you, you wouldn't be in this plight now, would you?' Magho took a deep breath, his massive chest expanding. Then he sat up and turned to Chona, his smile returning. 'Don't worry about that. I caught him above the hairline. The bruise won't show.'

Chona watched the boy rise, cautiously, rubbing his head. He wondered why the father thought Chona would care. And why, if the boy angered his father so much, he was keeping him here in the house during this meeting. 'He doesn't bother me, Magho. He's just a child.'

'A child? A child-man, and that's all he'll ever be, I fear. The gods know he's a difficult one. Here, try some of this tea.' He handed Chona a clay bowl of hot, steaming green liquid. 'We've business to do.' He glanced over at Chona's pack. 'I take it you have what I want.'

Chona allowed himself to smile. 'I wouldn't be here otherwise, my friend.' He leaned over and unfolded his pack. In with the bits of sky-fallen iron and shaped flint and fragments of reindeer bone carved into elusive fish and lumbering bears, he had tucked small parcels wrapped in the softest doe skin. He made a show of unwrapping them slowly. Magho all but drooled.

Small, precious items, bartered across the Continent, were Chona's stock in trade. Not for him the heavy work of trading meat or grain, or sacks of unworked flint. What he liked to carry were treasures valuable far beyond their size and weight – and the further from their source you took them the more valuable they became. The fragments of obsidian he unwrapped now, taken from sites in a mountain range far from here, were among the most valuable of all.

He handed Magho one of the smaller pieces. Magho turned the black, shining rock over in his hands, his eyes wide, his mouth a dark circle. 'I take it you have better examples,' he breathed.

'Oh, yes. All from the finest source in the known world. And all yours, if—'

'If I can pay.' Magho let out his throaty laugh. 'I do like you, Chona. Well, I like all traders. At least you're honest, which is more than can be said for most people in this wretched world.'

'That particular piece would make a fine axe-head,' Chona said. 'Or perhaps something more abstract. An amulet—'

'Oh, I'll leave that to the experts,' Magho said. 'There's a man on the other side of town, called Fless, very old now, about forty and half-blind, but he works stone as you wouldn't believe. My way is simply to give him such pieces as this, and let *him* see what lies within the stone, see with his cataract-blighted eyes, and then tease it out, flake by flake with his bits of bone.' He mimed a fine pressing. 'Marvellous to see him work, with those twisted-up hands and his milky eyes. Yes, he's the man. *If* I can get his time, if somebody hasn't stolen him away.'

Chona took back the obsidian scrap, and handed him another piece. 'I'm sure what Fless makes of these pieces would dazzle your friends like rays of the sun . . .'

This was the odd part of trading with the men of Jericho. Everywhere in the world you found men, and sometimes women, of power, who accumulated wealth – maybe trinkets, maybe more functional items like tools or food. But everywhere else you showed off your power by giving your treasure away: the more you had to give, the greater you were. In Jericho's elaborate, layered society men strutted and showed off what they *owned*, be it women and children, goats and stores of grain – and pointless, purposeless trinkets. Your status came from what you kept to yourself, not what you gave away.

Well, Chona didn't care. He never judged a man he traded with. Magho could wipe his arse on his precious obsidian for all Chona cared – as long as Chona got a fair price first.

But the boy, Novu, still nursing his head, snorted his contempt at Chona's manipulation.

Magho handed back the stone. 'Let's do business. How many pieces?'

'A dozen. I'll show you the rest when we have a deal.'

Magho nodded. 'Very well. So let me show you what I have to trade . . .' He produced a figurine of a pregnant woman, carved of the tooth of some sea creature, quite fine. And a whistle made from the bone of a bird, delicately carved, so small you would need a child's fingers to stop its holes, and yet fully functional, Magho assured him. And a bit of iron, small but one of the purest pieces Chona had ever seen. Magho evidently knew

Chona's preference for small, portable treasures, and with one piece after another he built up an array on the rush mat.

Chona kept his face like stone, merely nodding politely. Some of this was impressive, and in the loose map of the Continent he carried in his head he calculated where he might make a decent profit on each of these pieces. Still, when Magho was done arraying his treasures Chona was disappointed. He would win out of the deal, of course, but not as much as he had hoped.

'I have to be honest, Magho. I'd love to do business with you, you know that. But I'd have to haul away a sack full of pieces like these to compensate me for my obsidian.'

Magho's face fell, but Chona wasn't fooled; Magho, while clearly wanting the obsidian, was an experienced trader too. 'Perhaps we could come to some arrangement. If I could choose the best four or six of your pieces—'

'I wouldn't want to break up the set. That way, if I need to take it elsewhere in the town, I'll have a much better chance of a sale.' That was true enough, and a subtle threat to take the hoard to one of Magho's deadly social rivals.

'I know what will make him cough up the obsidian,' said Novu, the son, still cradling his head, but speaking slyly. 'I saw the way he looked at Minda. Give him a bit of time alone with her and—'

This time the blow he received from his father was to the back of his neck. The boy recoiled, obviously shocked.

'I apologise again for the boy,' Magho said. 'But . . . Minda.' He grinned at Chona. 'You couldn't help noticing her, and I couldn't help noticing *you*. Fifteen years old and sweet as a peach. Virgin, of course.'

'Your wife's sister?'

'Niece, actually. Promised to another. I couldn't help you there, my friend. And besides I already owe my wife's brother, her father, a favour.'

Chona shook his head. 'I have no interest in the girl,' he lied, but he hoped it didn't show. 'We were speaking of trade.'

'Yes, yes.' Magho eyed him, and Chona realised he was about to come to the nub of his offer. 'I do have one more item for you to consider. Something unusual – I merely ask you to have an open mind.'

'What item?'

Magho stood, heavily. And he reached over, grabbed his son by the scruff of the neck, and hauled him to his feet. 'This!'

Novu, obviously dizzy from the blows he had taken, whimpered, staggering. 'Father? What are you doing?'

'He's no use to me,' Magho said. 'Far more trouble than he's worth. But in the right hands he could be invaluable.'

'I don't take slaves.' Chona was confused by the whole situation. 'Invaluable how?'

'He can make bricks,' Magho said, almost proudly. 'You've seen them being baked on the hillside yonder. There's something of an art to it, you know, getting the right proportion of mud and straw and water, mixing them just so, drying them. Get it wrong and they crumble in your hands. Get it right and they last for ever, nearly. This boy has the knack of doing it. Ask anybody, it's a gift of the gods, it's nothing to do with me. I mean, he's useless at everything else.'

Chona snorted. 'Bricks might seem valuable to *you*. But this is an unusual place, where bricks are prized. You know that.'

'But not unique. Come on, man, I've heard you talk. There are towns in the north and west—'

'Far from here. Many days' walk.'

'You're not going to have to carry him there, are you? You can walk him to wherever you want to sell him. He can even carry your pack for you.'

'Why do you want rid of him, Magho?'

Magho glared at the boy. 'Because of an incident that won't make any difference to you. *He's a thief.* He took a jade piece I particularly treasured, and hid it. I won't have a thief in my house. I can't afford it. A man in my position in this town—'

Novu protested, 'You told mother you forgave me for that!'

'So I lied. You're no son of mine. You don't have to sell him for making bricks, of course. He's not bad looking, and he's still young.' He pinched the boy's biceps and thighs. 'You can see that. Feel for yourself. His balls have dropped.' He cupped the boy's groin; Novu flinched. 'And he's a virgin, of course, except for his close relationship with his right hand.'

'I don't run slaves,' Chona repeated.

Magho heaved a sigh. 'You strike a hard bargain. Suppose I had a word with Gorga. My wife's brother. If I could persuade him about Minda, you know . . . A night with her?'

'Well . . .'

Magho clapped him on the shoulder again. 'Just don't ruin her for her husband, you bull. Look, I'll leave you with the goods. I'll come back after I've seen Gorga. And you,' he said, pointing a finger at his son, 'show some respect or I'll break every tooth in your head, no matter what it does to your selling price.'

He stalked out.

The boy sat again, shivering. But he stared defiantly at Chona. 'He set it all up, you know. My father.'

'Set what up?'

'Minda. Do you think it was an accident she was here when you came?'

'You know this, do you?'

He snorted. 'I know my father. I know how he works. Why, once, my mother, his own wife, he made her—'

'Shut up. I don't want to know.' If Magho had set up Minda as a way to swing the deal then he was a better trader than Chona had imagined. But again he felt the blood surge in his loins. Breaking the girl would do him good. Magho had a deal, he decided. An unusual deal, but a deal.

'Get dressed to travel,' he said to the boy. 'Pick out your best clothes. I know places where such clothes will fetch a good price. I've some old skins that will do for you on the trail.'

The boy stared. 'You're taking me? You can't be serious—'

63

As Novu protested, Chona leaned over and absently picked at the edge of the boy's smock, fascinated by the detail of how the fabric had been woven.

And he coughed suddenly, a deep rasping cough that came out of nowhere and tore at his throat.

10

This morning they were to begin the Spring Walk south to the oyster beaches of the Moon Sea. It was only a few days before the equinox.

Etxelur was inhabited by six extended families, including Zesi's, some tens of tens of people, all of whom Zesi knew by name. More than half of the people who lived here would be travelling today, men, women, and many, many children, walking south across the hills they called the Ribs of the First Mother to the rich coastline of the Moon Sea. Those left behind included the very young and their mothers, the old and ill, and others with urgent jobs – fisherfolk who needed to patch their boats and mend their nets ready for the new season, others who were already out hunting the grey seal who came ashore to breed, or climbing the sandstone cliffs further along the coast in search of nesting sea birds and their eggs.

The people started to gather early on the dunes overlooking the Seven Houses. Zesi heard the children playing in the long grass even before she first emerged from her house, carrying the buckets full of the night's piss to empty into the stone-lined fuller's pit. And by the time she and Ana and the Pretani boys had prepared their travelling kit, the dunes were crowded. All here because of Zesi.

As the discussions about the Spring Walk had firmed up, it had been Zesi who had taken a leading role, Zesi who had drawn out agreement, Zesi who had settled small disputes – Zesi around whose house the walkers now gathered, eager for the off. Her missing father had left a big hole in the community.

In Etxelur women owned the houses, and made many fundamental decisions. But men made day-to-day choices, about whether to go fishing this month or hunt inland.

After half a year of making decisions on behalf of her vanished father, Zesi sometimes felt exhausted – wrung out, chased. But she admitted to herself she was having fun playing this dual role, of man and woman. Sometimes, when a boat was sighted coming in from over the horizon, a flurry of excitement would whirl around the settlements: could it be Kirike returning at last? The look of painful hope on poor Ana's face on such occasions was distressing. But Zesi was beginning to think her own feelings about her father's return were much more complicated – and when she felt that way guilt stabbed at her.

She kept her patience as everybody fussed, but the sun was higher than she would have liked before they were ready to go. At last she nodded to Jurgi. The priest stood high on a dune with his bull roarer, a bit of bone on a rope he whirled around his head to make a tremendous screaming noise that had the smaller children running to their mothers and the adults cheering.

And then they were off, with Zesi in the lead and Jurgi walking in his place just behind her, both of them singing the ancient songs of the land ways – and each quietly reminding the other which way to go where the path wasn't clear. The people chattered loudly, and some of the children sang a song in praise of the little mother of the land. The two Pretani boys, who wouldn't let themselves be excluded, whooped and hollered aggressive hunting songs of their own.

Zesi thought she could feel everybody's relief to be off on this adventure after the long winter. Even the dogs ran and yapped in excitement, even Lightning who had spent the winter pining for his owner, Kirike.

They headed south, making for the valley of the river they called the Little Mother's Milk. Away from the coast the land rose and became a sandstone fell, bleaker and more exposed. In places huge layered rocks lay tumbled, as if dropped by giants.

The sun was bright, but a spring mist hung in the air, glowing with light, masking the plains of the far horizon. To either side of the trail, littered with loose, pale sand worn free of the soft underlying rock by footsteps human and animal, the heather had begun to grow, thick and short and green. Zesi found some hawthorn as she walked along, and absently plucked the buds, still early, bright green. They had a rich, nutty flavour when she chewed them. And the first pileworts were out, a bright and early flower with shining yellow petals. She pointed this out to the priest, for it was a good treatment for piles, and worth collecting.

But the country was troubling her, as she sang her songs with the priest. It had been some years since the last walk, and while the trail was easy to find it seemed to Zesi that in some places the ancient songs of the land, with their lists of landmarks and directions, did not match what she saw before her eyes.

The ground was boggier than it used to be, and new ponds pooled in hollows. Here was a stand of trees she remembered playing in as a child. Now the birch were leafless and dead, though a couple of alders survived, and where she remembered fern and grass there now grew samphire and cordgrass. When she dipped her finger in the muddy water that pooled around the surviving alders, she tasted salt. Very strange.

At last the path led them down into the valley of the Milk, steep-sided and cloaked with wood. The pace slowed as people spread out to look for water or to hunt, or bled the birch trees of their sap for resin for rope-making, or inspected fallen trees for flint nodules dragged up out of the earth by the roots.

Zesi was relieved when Gall ran off into the first dense bit of forest they came to, stabbing spear in his hand.

The younger Pretani, Shade, however, stayed close by, walking with her. He was taken with the holloways they followed, paths close to the river that had been worn into the earth. They were channels choked with debris, plant growth, tree roots, last year's leaves, and pools of brackish water. The people kicked them clear as they walked.

67

As the sun started to go down they stopped to make shelter for the night, close to the river. People worked busily, collecting wood for lean-tos and for the fires.

Zesi sat at the edge of a pond and set to work using a flint knife to dig out a stand of bulrushes. Later she would char their thick stems on the fire, and they would suck out the starchy interior.

Shade was still close by, as he had been all day. He had an endearing awkwardness, as if he was never quite sure what he should be doing.

They spotted hares chasing each other through the long grass. Two big animals faced each other, their long black-tipped ears bristling, a male and female, and they stood up on their back legs and boxed with their front paws – mad with lust, Zesi thought, for it was that time of year.

Watching the hares, Shade spoke to her shyly. 'This land is very old,' he said. 'So old your feet have worn tracks into the earth.'

'We follow the tracks our ancestors made when they first walked here, following the little mothers as they made the world. Where's that brother of yours? He's been gone a long time.'

'He is a great hunter. Sometimes, at home, he is away for days, alone. He won't come back without a kill. You'll see . . . The walk is useful.'

That word made her laugh. 'Useful? How?'

'The children are learning how to live on the move. In the forest. As your ancestors might once have lived. They are learn-ing old skills, that might be needed again.'

She grunted. 'You sound like our priest. He likes to say how useful things are. You sound like an old man, not a kid.'

His cheeks burned under his sparse beard. 'I am older than your sister!'

She tried hard not to laugh. 'Does Ana treat you like a kid?'

'She treats me badly. I don't know why. I—'

'I can tell you why.' The voice was Gall's. Suddenly he was

here, a massive presence silhouetted by the low sun. Zesi saw that he had something heavy and limp draped over his shoulders. He was breathing hard, his tunic bloodied. 'Because you're a skinny runt. Here, little boy, I bought you a present.' And he threw his burden to the ground.

It was a deer, a young female, and pregnant.

'Be a man,' Gall said. 'Finish it off. This is your chance to show cold-faced Ana you've got balls – and I don't mean those shrivelled-up nuts she sees you washing every morning, hah!'

Zesi could see the swelling of the doe's belly clearly against its slim form. Panting, salivating, exhausted, obviously terrified, it tried to stand. But the backs of its legs were matted with blood, and every time it rose it fell back to the ground.

There was something fascinating in the deer's agony, Zesi found herself thinking. And the power Gall had over it.

Gall was watching her, amused.

'This is not how we hunt, Pretani. A quick kill, an apology to the beast's spirit – that's our way. Not this, not a half day of agony for a creature like this, all to play a kind of joke on your brother.'

But maybe Gall saw something darker in her, under her bluster. He winked. 'Fun, though, isn't it?'

She turned to Shade. 'Go and get the priest. The deer is his Other.'

Shade ran.

Zesi got to her knees beside the frightened doe. She stroked its neck and held its head. 'There, there. I am sorry. It will be over soon. Soon, soon.' The deer seemed to calm, its eyes wide.

Gall scoffed. 'I think we're more alike than you want to admit – what a beauty you are when you are bloody—'

'Out of my sight, you Pretani savage.'

He held his place for one more heartbeat. Then, growling obscenities in his own tongue, he walked away.

11

They climbed out of the valley of the Milk, and crossed higher, hilly land.

It took days to cross the First Mother's Ribs. But by the fifth afternoon you could smell the salt in the air, and hear the cry of the gulls. The children clambered up ridges and climbed trees, competing to be the first to spot the water.

The sun was low in the sky when the group broke through the last line of trees, and the Moon Sea lay open before them. Here the rocky ground tumbled down to a shallow beach. The tide was low, the beach of this inland sea wide and glistening. Far off to the west Zesi saw movement – probably a seal colony. And even from the treeline you could see the oysters like pebbles on the beach, the promised gift of the moon.

The day had been unseasonably hot, and adults and children alike, worn down by days in the forested hills, dumped their packs, threw off their heavy cloaks and ran down the slope towards the water. Some folk made their way along the coast to an area of salt marsh, a place of thick, sloppy, grey clay, cut through by a complicated network of creeks and channels and small islands, all washed regularly by the tide. Here they spread out, inspecting sea aster, golden samphire, glasswort: plants that liked salt and fed on what they trapped from the tidal flows.

Shade stood uncertainly with Zesi at the head of this beach. 'We have walked from sea to sea,' he said.

'The people who live hereabouts have legends of when this wasn't a sea at all, but a lake. Fresh water. Then the salt gods pissed in it, and everything died, until the fish swam in from the sea . . .'

Shade was only half-listening. A boy of the forest stranded out in the open, once more he looked out of place. Zesi felt she had warmed to him after the incident of Gall's deer. 'Come. Take off your boots. I'll show you what to do.'

She took his hand, and pulled him across the beach.

They reached wet, muddy sand that sucked at their bare feet, slowing them. Shade stared at the exposed seabed, where worm casts glistened, and the shells of oysters jostled. 'You timed this walk,' he said. 'You wanted us to get here when the tide is low.'

'Not just low but at its *lowest*, as it is at the equinoxes, in spring and autumn.'

'This is your victory over the moon.'

'In the end she will take us all to her cold bosom. But today, just today, we can steal her treasures . . . Here. What a beauty!' She picked up an oyster, wider than her outspread fingers. 'Look. It's easy when you get the knack. You place it on a rock, like this. Flat side up. Then you take your knife and work it into the hinge, and just prise it open. Careful! You don't want to lose any juices.'

He stared at the animal exposed inside the opened shell. 'Then what?'

'You eat it!' She picked up the oyster and sucked it into her mouth, letting the salty juices flow after. 'Here. Find another one, and try yourself.'

He was good at the manual art of opening the shells, but the first he tried to eat made him gag, and the juices ran down his face. The second he swallowed, but pulled a face. By the third he was smiling. 'It's salty. It's strange – it's good. The first splash of salt, and then the flesh, it bursts in your mouth, it's almost sweet.'

'It's best not to eat them much later than this, not until the autumn. They spawn in the summer, and the flesh can be white and tasteless . . . Oh, look! Your brother is trying one.'

Jurgi the priest had taken it on himself to teach Gall. With bold gestures Gall tipped up his shell and sucked down the meat, only to spit it out on the ground. 'Urgh! Are you feeding me your snot, man?' Gathering up his blade he stomped off up the beach.

'Don't laugh,' Shade murmured to Zesi.

'I wouldn't dream of it. You really aren't much like your brother, are you?'

'Do you think that's good or bad?'

'What do you think?'

He sighed. 'Well, you're right. I'm not like him. That won't do me any good at home. Gall is stronger, a better hunter. Smarter in some ways. More cunning. More decisive.' He grinned, and stood up. 'I never ate an oyster before, but I have been swimming. I can hold my breath like a seal. Watch me.' He ran off into a sea that was soon lapping over his legs, and then he dived forward and began swimming with strong strokes.

The priest came over, sand clinging to his bare torso, his blue hair wild. 'He likes you.'

She shrugged. 'I'm just not as hard on him as his brother is. Or Ana, come to that, who I think *he* likes.'

'Ana has her problems. Perhaps now your grandmother is safely in the midden – we will see. The day has gone well. The weather is mild, and we arrived at the time of the low tide.'

'The gods have been kind to us.'

He grunted. 'Kind with the weather. The timing is thanks to you and your planning. The gods offer us gifts all the time. It's up to us whether we are capable of taking them or not. Look over there.' He pointed along the beach, to the west.

The sun was low, there was heat haze, and it was difficult to see. She made out movement. She had noticed it before; she thought it was a seal colony. It wasn't. 'Oh,' she said. 'People.'

'Yes.'

'I never heard of us meeting people on this beach before, at this time.'

'I asked Kano the knapper to go and have a look. You know

he's a fast runner. He says they're friendly enough, and speak the traders' tongue.'

'Who are they?'

'Snailheads. From the south. Many of them.'

'Snailheads! Why aren't they at their own beaches?'

'I don't know. There are snailheads coming to the Giving feast in the summer. Maybe we can ask them about it . . .' He sounded distracted; he was staring out to sea.

'What are you looking for?'

'Shade. I saw him thrashing around before. He went a long way out. Now I can't see him at all.'

She frowned. Save for a few children playing at the water's edge, the sea looked empty. 'He said he could swim well. He could hold his breath.'

'He's a forest boy. Do you believe him? Perhaps he was trying to impress you.'

'Oh, for the love of the mothers . . .' She stood and quickly shucked off the rest of her clothes. 'You'd better go find his brother, priest. Men! There's always something.'

And, without looking back, she ran down to the sea.

The beach sloped shallowly, even beyond the water's edge, and she had to cross perhaps fifty paces of clinging, tiring, muddy sand before the water was past her knees. Then she threw herself forward into water that shocked with its chill, and began to swim, heading out the way she had seen the Pretani boy go.

At first the water invigorated her, but she was fighting the current of the incoming tide and soon tired. She stopped and trod water, and wiped the salt water from her eyes and mouth, her hair clinging to her neck. The sea around her glimmered in the low sunlight, and the shore seemed a long way away. 'Shade! Shade, you Pretani idiot!'

'Yes?'

The voice was so close behind her ear that it startled her and she lost her tread. She fell back in the water and got a mouthful of brine that made her cough.

Shade took hold of her under her armpits and steadied her, laughing. 'Are you all right?'

'No thanks to you. You worried me.'

'I told you I was a good swimmer.'

'Well, I didn't believe you.'

'And I can hold my breath. Look—'

'Don't bother.' They were holding hands now, circling. 'How does a boy from the wildwood of Albia get to be a good swimmer?'

'It's a joke of the gods.' He was smiling, his face and beard clean of dirt, his smooth skin marked only by the hunting scar on his cheek. 'A swimmer in the forest. You may as well give a salmon legs. But I don't mind. I suppose I'll never be able to hunt like my brother, or lead men in battle, or boss women around. But at least I can swim.'

His hands were warm in hers, his eyes bright. Their legs tangled, and they moved closer together. She could feel the warmth of his thigh between hers, and then she felt his erection poking at her stomach.

He pulled back. 'I'm sorry—'

'Don't be.' She pulled him to her. His face filled her vision, shutting out sea and shore and people. The world seemed to recede, taking with it all her responsibilities, her mixed-up sister, her fretting over her father, the workload she guiltily enjoyed. All that existed was the water, and this boy.

She took his shoulders and lifted upwards, clamping her legs around his waist. With a gasp he entered her, and their lips locked.

12

'Hungry,' Moon Reacher whimpered. 'Hungry!'

'I know, child,' said Ice Dreamer. 'So am I. We will stop soon.'

Soon. For now, they walked.

They walked east away from the setting sun, which this late in the day cast a pink glow the colour of Dreamer's piss when she squatted. To the south, their right, was the forest's scrubby fringe, birch and pine and a dense undergrowth now shot through with spring green. And to their left, the north, stretched a plain of grass and scrub and isolated stands of trees, where raccoons and voles ran, and sometimes you would see deer or bison or horse in distant herds. Some days it almost looked pretty, with scatters of early spring flowers.

And there were people, fast-moving, elusive hunters on the grass, and enigmatic shadowy foragers in the green depths of the forest. These weren't Cowards. Dreamer and Reacher had walked far from the Cowards' range. But they weren't True People either. They were other sorts of strangers, folk Dreamer had never seen or heard of.

Dreamer kept them heading east, following the boundary between the southern forest and the northern plain, looking for a place where there were no people at all, nobody to drive them away. They walked as they had for uncounted days, while the world washed through its cycle of the seasons, and winter slowly relented. The child with a wounded leg that had now stiffened and smelled of rot, so she had to lean on the woman to make every step. And the woman with burdens of her own, the baby growing lustily in her belly, the pack on her back that

75

weighed her down, the enduring ache in her torn thighs and her lower belly. They walked, for there was nothing else for them to do.

A faint breeze stirred from the east, lifting Dreamer from her numb self-absorption. She stopped, and Reacher stumbled against her, panting hard. Dreamer pushed back her deerskin hood and sniffed the air. For a moment she thought she tasted salt. Another lake ahead? But then the breeze shifted around to the north, to be replaced by the richer, dry, almost burned smell of the grassland.

Leaning heavily on Dreamer, Reacher tugged her sleeve. 'Hungry!'

'I know, child.' Dreamer glanced around. The light was fading and they needed to find shelter. They were on the fringe of a dense clump of forest. She could detect no sign of people, smell no smoke, see no markings on the bark. She decided to take the chance. 'Come on,' she said to Reacher. 'Just a little further.'

They limped together into the shade of the trees. They were mostly pine, tall old trees sparsely spread. It had rained recently – that was going to make it harder to find dry wood for the fire – and there was a rich warm smell of green growth and the rot of the last of the autumn's leaves.

They came to a fallen tree that had ripped a disc of shallow roots out of the ground, leaving a rough hollow shaded by the root mass, a space that might give a little shelter. A little way away she saw a glimmer of open water. This would do. She dropped her pack with relief.

She spread a skin over the damp ground and helped Reacher lie down, favouring her bad leg. Reacher curled up like a baby, knees tucked up to her chest, and seemed to fall asleep immediately. Dreamer longed to rest herself, but she knew that if she lay down she wouldn't be able to move again.

So she collected branches from the fallen tree, dragged them back to the root hollow, and leaned them against the roots to make a roof over Reacher's body. She shook out more of her skins and laid them over the branches, then piled up bracken and leaves and dirt. This crude shelter would keep out any rain, and seal in the warmth of the fire – if she could get it started. She tucked the rest of her kit inside the shelter to keep it dry, the bag with the nuts and dried meat, the remains of Stone Shaper's medicine bag.

Then she pulled out their traps and set them carefully around the forest floor, driving stakes of splintered bone into the ground. Maybe they would be lucky tonight. As she moved, she picked up bits of branch and bark, the older-looking the better; everything was wet, but last season's falls would at least be dry inside and might burn.

At last she took a skin sack and filled it with water from the brackish pond, and crawled inside the shelter.

Reacher slept, still and silent. Dreamer carefully took her ember from the medicine bag. She placed it on a strip of bark, and began to feed it with dried moss, blowing carefully.

While the fire was taking, she dug with her fingers into the dirt, looking for worms and grubs.

Every time she built the fire she remembered their first night, after Mammoth Talker had led them into the kill site of the Cowards.

When the men had done with her they had walked back to their meat and their fires. Dreamer, half-conscious, naked, her body a mass of pain, could barely move.

An unknown time later Reacher had joined her, as naked as she was, the blood streaming from that gash on her leg. Reacher had helped her up, and they had hobbled away. Later Dreamer found she had slung Stone Shaper's abandoned medicine bag around her neck. She didn't remember picking it up. She hadn't seen Stone Shaper since, and didn't imagine she ever would again.

Nor did she remember how they had got back to the shelter under the rock ledge, where the rest of their stuff waited, untouched. That first night they had been able to do no more than huddle together under a heap of skins.

The next morning Dreamer was woken by the baby kicking.

She was flooded with a strange mixture of relief and fear. Her baby was alive, but could her ruined body stand the birth? And, when it came, who would help her? She had wept then, her tears mingling with the blood on her hands.

Reacher had stirred, and, waking, cried out with pain. When Dreamer pulled back the skins that covered her legs, the stink of her swollen wound made Dreamer recoil. Dreamer knew little medicine; that was the priest's job, and the senior women. But she should have cleaned the wound before they slept, maybe sucked out the poison. She would always regret that she had not tried to treat Reacher's wound on that first night.

The priest's ember had not survived the night. It had not been until the fourth night that she had finally succeeded in building a fire, with a roughly made thong bow. The ember she carried now was a relic of that first blaze. With its help, they had survived the long days and nights since.

Now, as the fire's warmth built, Reacher tried to get up. Dreamer handed her the water skin. Reacher drank only a little, looking as pale as the moon for which she had been named. 'I am hungry,' she said. 'Are you hungry?'

'Me and the baby.' Dreamer dug in her pack. Reacher rarely spoke about anything but food – food and pain. She never asked where they were. It didn't matter, Dreamer supposed. They were nowhere. 'I set the traps. Maybe we'll have squirrel tomorrow. In the meantime, here are the snails. Do you remember when we caught them?'

She set a couple of snails on a stone before Reacher. The girl watched them dubiously. The snails barely stirred in their shells. Dreamer had carried them for three days; you had to starve a snail before eating it, to let any poisonous plants it might have eaten work through its system. Dreamer hammered them with a rock, and the shells crunched. Reacher started pulling away smashed shell from moist, sluggishly squirming flesh.

'And worms,' Dreamer said. 'Fresh and warm, out of the ground.' She dropped the creatures on Reacher's stone.

'Do we have any walnuts?'

'We finished those days ago.'

Reacher put a worm in her mouth. 'I'd like meat.'

'I know.'

'Hare would do. Deer, or a steak from a bison.'

They might get hare or gopher or vole, but there would be no deer or bison. She forced a smile. 'Imagine it's deer. Remember the way Elk Tracker used to make her stew?' This old woman had had a way of boiling the meat in a big bowl chipped from stone, with dried herbs she collected, and the juice squeezed from the gall bladder of a young horse, an addition that brought out the flavour like no other. Reacher looked at the worm curling on her palm. 'Close your eyes and imagine. Mmm. Thank you, Elk Tracker.'

'Thank you,' whispered Reacher.

That was that for the food. Reacher didn't even finish what she'd been given.

'Come on,' Dreamer said. 'Let's take a look at your leg, and then we'll sleep.' She put a wooden cup of water over the fire to heat up, and shifted so she could get to Reacher's injury.

'How is the baby?'

'I felt her kick today. She kicks *hard*. I think she likes to play.'

A ghost of a smile touched Reacher's face. They had somehow decided between them that the baby would be a girl; Reacher would be disappointed if it wasn't. 'Does she laugh?'

'I— Yes, she laughs. I can feel it . . .'

Dreamer lifted back the hide wrap from the wounded leg and scraped away the sphagnum moss she had applied that morning, now a bloody mass. The flesh around the wound was black, greenish in places. Away from the wound itself the leg was swollen from hip to ankle, the skin a bruised purple.

Dreamer went to work cleaning the wound, with a bit of cloth dipped in the hot water.

She remembered how, when she had been small, younger than Reacher now, there had been a hunter with a wound like this; he had been alone in the forest for days. The priest, grim-faced, hadn't tried to treat the wound at all. He had made the women hold the hunter down, and he had used a special long saw, a deer shinbone studded with many tiny flint blades, to cut away the leg altogether, from a little below the hip. Would that save Reacher's life? Could Dreamer, alone, make such a cut – and how would she treat the wound afterwards?

Reacher was sleeping again. Her breathing was scratchy and shallow, and a thin sheen of sweat stood on her brow.

Dreamer slept lightly, as always.

Once she heard something come by the shelter. A deep rumble, a heavy tread, a brush against the shelter as if a huge man had walked by. Perhaps it was a bear. It did not return, and she slept again, fitfully.

When the dawn light poked through the gaps in the shelter roof, without disturbing Reacher, she clambered out to make water. She always tried to do this out of sight of Reacher so the girl wouldn't see the blood in her piss.

It was a bright morning, with a bit of warmth already in the low sun. There was a slight rise, only a few paces further on; she vaguely remembered it from the night before. She walked to the ridge and climbed it, the long grass sweeping over her bare legs.

And the country opened up before her, to reveal a lake, wider and deeper than any she had ever seen in her life, glittering blue water that reached the horizon and spanned the world from north to south. She had gone as far east as she could; there was nowhere left for her to walk.

13

It was the middle of the day before Heni returned from his latest walk down this strange shore to visit the Hairy Folk.

Kirike, sitting by their upturned boat, saw him coming from the south, walking along the shingle just above the tidal wrack. Heni was carrying his boots slung around his neck, and his big bare feet made the stones crunch. In one hand he carried a folded skin, heavy with gifts from the Hairy Folk. He looked dark and solid in the brightness of the day, the light of the sea.

Kirike had kept the fire going with logs from the dense pine forest just above the beach. Now he threw on a couple more of the big clams that were so common here. He had a little bowl of mashed acorn, gathered from the oak groves further south; he sprinkled some of this on the flesh of the opening clams for flavouring. The clams were huge oceanic beasts like nothing at home. He was collecting the shells, a heap of them on a string to take home, to make Ana and Zesi marvel.

Heni rolled up, panting hard, and dumped his pack by the fire. He stripped off his coat, cut from the fur of a bear. The lighter skin tunic he wore underneath was soaked with sweat.

'Urgh! By the moon's shining buttocks you stink,' Kirike protested.

'There's heat in that sun. It will be a hot summer, I tell you. At least it will be *here*, wherever we are.' Heni threw himself down. He gulped fresh water from a skin, took a shell and scooped up a big mouthful of clam flesh.

Heni was Kirike's cousin, a little older than Kirike at thirty-four. His head was a mass of thick black hair and beard, and his nose was misshapen from multiple breaks – he was an enthusiastic fighter but not an effective one. They had grown up together, playing and mock-hunting on the beaches of Etxelur. At first Heni had been the leader, the guide, at times the bully who forced Kirike to learn fast. As Kirike had grown he had eventually overtaken Heni in maturity, and now Kirike, as Giver, relied on Heni as his closest ally. Kirike couldn't pick a better companion to have got lost at sea with. But today he did stink, and Kirike pulled a face.

Heni grunted and took another oyster. 'Well, you'd be rank if you had to sit through another blubber feast with those Hairy Folk.' You always had to eat with the strange dark hunters down the beach before they'd consider a trade. 'Mind you, the turtle soup was good, in those big upturned shells.' He winked at Kirike. 'And that little woman with the big arse caught my eye again.'

'Oh, yes?'

'This time she submitted to a little tenderness from old Heni. We snuck off into one of those funny little shacks they have.' Houses made of skin stretched over the ribs of some huge sea beast. 'We didn't get to threading the spear through the shaft-straightener, if you know what I mean, but—'

'You sure which hole was which under all that hair? You sure it's even a woman? I'll swear she's got a better beard than I have.'

'Yes, but you've got bigger tits as well. She's not that hairy. They just wear it long, that's all. Gives you something to grip onto.' Heni lumbered to his feet, stood over their boat, rummaged in his leggings, and with a sigh of satisfaction pissed over the skin of the hull. When he was done he lifted the boat by its prow so that his urine ran in streaks. The boat was a frame of wood and stretched skin. You could clearly see where they had patched it during the winter months here on this beach, with new expanses of deer hide, scraped and soaked in their own piss. 'Look at that,' Heni said. 'Not a leak.' He eyed Kirike. 'So if the boat's ready . . . time to go home? You've been saying all winter that you'd try to be back for the Giving.'

Kirike looked out to sea. As always when they spoke of going home he felt a deep dread stealing over him. 'Maybe a few more days,' he said. 'Collect a bit more meat. Work on the boat some more while we've got the chance. Put some more flesh on our bones before we face the ice again . . .'

'There's no reason not to leave now,' Heni said bluntly. 'Look. I understand. Or I think I do. Remember, it was me who went out in the boat with you in those first days after Sabet died.'

Sabet, Kirike's wife, had died as she laboured to give birth to a dead baby the previous summer. The baby wasn't expected; he had thought that Sabet had put the dangers of childbirth behind her years before, when Zesi and Ana were born, and they were safe. The shock, the sudden end of his long marriage, had broken his heart.

'You weren't much use then, I'll tell you that,' Heni said.

'I know. But I didn't want to be anywhere but in the boat. All those people, the women, Sabet's sister, her mother, the girls . . . If I thought I could have got by in the boat without you I would have done.'

'Well, I was there. And I was there when that storm pushed us west. That gave you an excuse to stay out for a few more days, didn't it?'

'I couldn't help the storm.'

'No. But *then* you said we had to sail north.'

The storm had caused them two days and nights of non-stop bailing: no paddling, no sleeping, no eating, you pissed where you sat and drank and ate one-handed, and with the other hand you bailed. When the storm had blown over they had no idea where they were. They were out of water, had lost their food, their catch and their fishing gear, and the boat leaked in a dozen places. It was obvious they'd been driven west, for that was the way the storm had blown them. *South*: that was the way to go. If they'd headed south they would have hit the shore of North-land, or maybe somewhere on the Albia coast. Then, even if

83

they didn't recognise where they were, they could rest up, fix the boat, and shore-hop east until they reached home.

Instead Kirike had insisted they sail north. 'We went over it and over it,' he said now. 'I just had this feeling we were closer to land to the north than the south.'

'Pig scut.'

'I thought I saw a gull flying that way.'

'Pig scut! There was no gull, except maybe in your head. But I let you talk me into it.'

'We found land, didn't we?'

So they had, a cold shore littered with strange black rocks, where the ice had almost come down to the sea. There had been no people there. No wood either, no trees growing, though they found some driftwood on the strand. But there were seals who had evidently never seen people, for each of them was trusting and friendly right up until the moment the club, delivered with respect, hit the back of its head. They had rested up in a shelter built of snow blocks, ate the seals' flesh, fixed the boat as best they could with sealskin and caulked it with the animals' fat, and then paddled off.

And they headed west, not east.

'The current ran that way.'

'Some of the time.'

'We might have found land. People to trade with.'

'We found ice! We slept on floating ice, and fished through holes in the ice. My piss turned to ice.'

'Nobody ever went so far west before! We were strong, we were healthy. Who could have known what we'd find?'

'All we found was ice . . .'

Over weeks of westward sailing, they had hopped from ice floe to ice floe across the roof of the world. Then the land curved south, and they had passed the mouth of a wide and deep river estuary, ice-bound in the winter. At last they had settled on this shore with the big clams.

Kirike said, 'Maybe this is Albia, but if it is it's like no bit of

84

Albia I ever heard of, even from the traders. If they had clams like these we'd have known about it.'

'We're nowhere,' Heni said. 'A land with no name on the arse of the world. Where the funny-looking people don't speak a shred even of the traders' tongue. Well, we have to go home some time. *If* we can make it back. And what about Zesi? What about Ana? Your daughters don't know if you're dead or alive – or me, come to that.'

Kirike blurted, 'Every time I see them I will think of Sabet.'

Heni nodded gravely. 'Yes. That is true. But do you think your daughters won't be missing their mother too?'

'Sun and moon, it's like talking to a priest.'

'So are we going home?'

'All right! Tonight we'll turn the boat over. In the morning, as soon as it's stocked, if it's not actually storming—'

'Well, about time.'

'So what did you get from the Hairy Folk? Apart from a tit-grab from your bearded lover.'

Heni opened up his pack, to reveal bone and polished stone. 'I traded our last bits of obsidian for this stuff.' He pulled out a fine slate knife. 'Look at the edge on that.'

Kirike picked up an awl made from what felt like a tooth. 'I wonder what animal this came from.'

'They told me. We don't have a name for it. Like a big fat seal, with long teeth that stick down.' He mimed with two pointing fingers. 'And look at this harpoon. See the toggle? Look, you pass a rope through here, it runs out when you throw the spear, and then you can just pull the weapon back.'

Kirike rummaged through the gifts. 'But no food. No dried meat, none of those acorn biscuits they make—'

'Who needs food? Kirike, it's spring, we'll be sitting on an ocean full of fish.' The tooth harpoon was on a loop of cord; he slipped it around his neck. 'Imagine the show we'll make when we paddle into Etxelur with this lot!'

But Kirike, looking over Heni's shoulder, was distracted. To the north, beyond the sandstone bluff that stuck out to sea at the end of this bay, a thread of smoke rose. He stood up. 'Fire.'

'What?' Heni turned to see. 'That's not the Hairy Folk. They're down south, the band we've been trading with anyhow.'

'Then who?'

'I don't know. Makes no difference. Not if we're leaving tomorrow, or the day after.'

'Unless they jump us in the night, burn the boat and steal our stuff.'

Heni frowned. 'Another distraction, Kirike?'

Kirike grinned. 'Call it a precaution. Let's go see.'

Heni grumbled, but he had to give in. They packed Heni's booty and their other gear under the boat, and they each slid a knife of good Etxelur flint into their tunics.

Then Heni pulled on his boots, and they walked north along the beach towards the bluff.

14

'In the beginning the father spirit gave birth to mother earth and father sky. A mud diver made the world from the body of the mother, and set it on the back of a turtle. But another diver dug the anti-world, a wolf thing, out of the body of the father. The father, disgusted, flung the wolf thing away into the sky . . .'

Dreamer lay back against the strange rock panel she had found at the head of the beach, with loops and lines carved into it, an oddly comforting design, brisk and complete. She had banked up the fire early today. Moon Reacher was very cold, and she hadn't stirred, even when Ice Dreamer had poured fresh water from the spring into her mouth, and doused her wound with salt water from the great eastern lake of brine, trying to drown the squirming maggots. Reacher had been just the same yesterday, the face like snow, the purple, bruised lips, the cold limbs. Walking had been impossible for days.

Dreamer cradled Reacher in her arms over her own swollen belly, the two of them, the last of the True People, on the beach before this strange poisonous lake, and she told Reacher the story of the world.

'In those days the world was rich and teemed with game. People crawled out of the sea to populate the land. The People hunted and grew wise and lived long. Even when they died they were born again into this world, for this was the most perfect world there could be. Their most powerful totems were the mammoth, which was like a hairy boulder walking the earth, and the horse, which was a swift runner.

'But then the Sky Wolf, jealous of his banishment from the earth, decided to smash the world.

'When the clouds and frost and the ash had cleared, the great animals had gone, and nothing stirred but stunted creatures barely worthy of the hunt. There was only a handful of True People left, but the earth swarmed with a new race of sub-men who evolved from the cowardly things that burrowed in the ground.

'Now the True People still make their fluted blades, but there is nothing left to hunt. Even when we die we can't return to the hunting ground of the past. The world is dead and we are already dead; this is the afterlife, the anti-world. Even our totems are dead . . .'

She thought she heard Reacher murmur. She held her closer, looking into her hooded eyes. 'You must listen,' she said. 'Listen to the story. For you, Reacher, must tell it to me when I am in labour, and you, child in my womb, must speak it over my bed as I lie dying, for there is nobody else . . .'

Two men were watching her.

The woman sat by a poor, shoddy fire under a shelter made of a heap of driftwood. She was dressed in tattered skins. Her dark hair was a mat of filth and grease, her face streaked with old blood. Bits of kit lay on the ground around her, amid folds of dirty leather. Her belly was swollen, though she was terribly thin; her wrist looked so fine Kirike thought he could have closed his thumb and forefinger around it. She held a child in her arms, a girl, perhaps eight or ten – nothing but skin and bones, and not moving.

The woman had been speaking, murmuring nonsense in an unknown tongue. Now she looked at Kirike with pale, blank eyes, and he suppressed a shudder.

Heni hissed, 'Can you smell that rot? Like spoiled meat.'

'Yes.'

'Do you think she's mad?'

'She's beautiful,' Kirike said. 'Or was. And she's pregnant.'

'Yes. Far gone with it. And look at the kid she's holding. How stiff she is . . .'

Kirike stepped forward cautiously. The woman, watching, didn't move. He crouched and touched the dangling arm of the girl, the wrist. The skin was cold as stone, and he could find no pulse. He moved closer, deliberately smiling at the woman. There was an overpowering stink of filth, of shit and piss and sweat, of stale fish grease – and that dread rot stench. He worked his fingers under the matted hair at the girl's neck, and felt the cold flesh.

He drew back. 'She's dead.'

'Dead for days, I'd say.' Heni leaned forward and cautiously unwrapped the skin around the girl's leg. The limb was swollen to the size of a log, and an open wound swarmed with maggots. He fell back, his hand over his mouth. 'Well, we know how she died.'

'Try not to frighten the live one.' Still smiling, Kirike tried to slide his arms under the girl's stiff body, to take her from the woman. But the woman grabbed the girl back. 'I bet she won't speak a word of any tongue we know. Nobody in this moon-struck land does. It's going to take a while to persuade her to give up that corpse.'

Heni said, 'It's going to take no time at all. We just walk away and leave her to the sea, or the wolves.'

'She's pregnant, man! And she's half-starved. Who knows how long she's been nursing this wretched child? No wonder it's driven the sense from her head. I wonder what happened to her.'

'I don't know, and I don't care. And if she's pregnant, that's another morsel for the wolves. She's not our problem, Kirike. She's not one of ours. This isn't our country!'

'If we can get the body away from her, get some food inside her, clean her up—'

Heni stood over him, arms folded. 'We're going home. You agreed. We leave tomorrow, or the day after. As soon as we fill the boat—'

'Fine. You fill the boat. We'll leave as we said. And, unless she recovers and runs off, we take her with us.'

For a long moment Heni didn't move. 'One day I'll walk away from you, cousin. I'll just walk away, and you'll be dead in a month.'

'But today's not that day, is it? Look – you cover up that stinking leg, and try to lift the body . . .'

The two of them moved towards the cowering woman. Kirike smiled, murmuring soft words in a tongue she could not know.

And then he noticed the design on the rock face on which she was sitting: three circles with a common centre, and a radial slash – the design that had been tattooed into his own wife's belly, the sign of the Door to the Mothers' House – the sign of Etxelur, carved into a rock on the wrong side of the ocean.

15

They walked every day, Novu and his owner, the trader Chona, at a steady, ground-eating pace, following water courses and well-worn tracks, generally following the river north from Jericho. Sometimes they even walked by night.

Generally they walked in silence. In fact Novu got more slaps from Chona, stinging blows on the back of the head, than he did words, for every time he got something wrong, a slap. He quickly learned what was wrong and what was right.

And for the first few days, as he shuffled along in the filthy old skins Chona had given him, a heavy pack on his back, Novu was hobbled by bark rope tied tightly around his ankles.

Novu was a town boy. He had never walked far in his life. He had boots, but his soft feet blistered. Every joint seemed to ache as he shifted the mass of the pack, trying to favour one shoulder and then the other. The hobble made it much worse. He couldn't make Chona's big strides; he had to make two steps for every one of Chona's, and he felt perpetually out of breath. He didn't have a knife, but his hands were free, and he could unpick the knots – but they were tied expertly and he would need time, which Chona, ever vigilant, was never going to give him. But he longed to be free of the hobble, and to be able to stretch his legs.

Sometimes Chona stayed the night with those he traded with. But Novu always had to stay outside, huddled under a skin or a lean-to. Such people didn't live as Novu had in Jericho, but in communities of a few dozen people, in houses that might be shaped like bricks or like pears or like cowpats, maybe with a few herded goats and a scrap of cultivated wheat. They could be very strange, these isolated folks – people who went naked or with feathers sticking up from their topknots, or who tattooed themselves and their children red and black all over, or who stretched their necks or ear lobes or their lower lips, or who wore bones through their cheeks and necks. Chona said it was possible that traders like himself were the only strangers these people ever saw. No wonder they were odd.

It was worse when they stayed out in the country, away from people altogether. Chona carried skins in his backpack, remarkably light and supple, that he would use to make lean-tos in stands of trees. It wasn't long before he had taught Novu how to make a dry and warm shelter.

But when the dark came Novu always found himself curling up in the dirt like an animal in its den. It was not like being at home, snug in the belly of Jericho with the warm bodies of hundreds of people all around him. Here he was *outside*, and there was nothing around him but the wind, and the howls of distant wild dogs – and, occasionally, the snuffling and tread of some curious visitor in the dark. At times even the rope tether by which Chona attached Novu to himself at night was a comfort, of sorts.

Every day he was taken further away from Jericho. But in a way he was glad of it, glad when after the first few days they got far enough from Jericho that there was no chance of encountering anybody who might know him, and laugh at his shame – or, worse, turn away in pity.

After many days of walking they came to a lake. Chona had Novu make camp in a stand of willow, while he sat and bathed his bare feet in the stagnant water at the lake's edge.

'So,' Chona said at length. 'Do you know where you are?' He spoke in Novu's own tongue, his words lightly accented.

Novu had tried to follow the route, with the vague idea of running back home if he got away. After the first couple of days

92

he had run out of familiar landmarks, and since then he knew only that they had kept moving north. He admitted, 'No.'

'Good.' Chona, sitting on the ground, was a slim silhouette in the light of the low sun that reflected from the still water. He looked calm and strong. 'Now, if you ever got away from me, you'd run south, trying to get back to Jericho.'

Novu shrugged. That seemed obvious.

'But if you did flee, I'd run you down easily. Even if you had a day's head start. You know that, don't you?'

'I suppose—'

'And when I did catch you, I'd hamstring you. Do you know what that means? Probably just one leg. You could walk with a crutch. You could still make bricks. But you'd never run any-where ever again. Do you believe me?'

'Yes. Yes, I believe you.'

Chona folded his legs under him, stood easily, and came over to where Novu was sitting. He dug a stone blade from a fold of his tunic. The boy flinched back, but Chona bent down, and held the blade to the rope hobble at Novu's ankles. 'Then we understand each other.' He cut the attaching rope with a single swipe of the blade. 'Get those bands off your ankles, and bathe your feet. Then go catch some fish.' He coughed, wiped his nose on the back of his hand, and walked away.

After that they walked on, still as master and slave, Novu still bearing the bulk of the load. But now at least they went side by side, for Novu, without the hobble, was able to keep up with Chona's long stride, and Chona no longer bothered with the demeaning tether at night.

Novu got less things wrong, and less slaps to the back of the head. Chona helped Novu repair his soft town boots when they started to wear out. He even taught him a few words in the traders' tongue, which he said was spoken from one end of the Continent to the other.

And he began to talk more openly to Novu.

One night he sketched a kind of plan of his world in riverside mud. 'Here is Jericho, at the eastern end of a great ocean that runs far to the west. There are lands to the north of the ocean, lands to the south, as you see. I know little of what lies south, but to the north there are many people, much trading to be done. A vast, vast area. This is the land we call the Continent.'

Novu was used to drawings and plans; they were used all the time in Jericho in building work. But he had no clear idea of what an 'ocean' was, or how far this body of water stretched. It was only when Chona used his thumb to indicate how far they had walked in comparison that he began to grasp its scale.

'That ocean's huge.'

'Yes,' Chona said. 'But I, and other traders, walk its coasts, and have seen the gates of rock in the far west where it opens out into a greater ocean still. Now, I had been thinking of taking you to the north, here . . .' This was a fat peninsula between the middle ocean to the south, and a lesser sea, still a great body in its own right, to the north. 'There are communities that live like you do in Jericho. All heaped up in boxes of mud. There, I am sure, your skills as a brickmaker will be worthy of trading – if your father wasn't lying about you.'

Novu said hotly, 'My father lies about many things, but not about that.'

'But the year is wakening.' He waved his hand over the sketched Continent. 'The trade routes are opening. There are many mountains and forests in the way, but rivers span the Continent east to west, north to south. Trade flows along these great channels, as sap rises in a tree in spring, as the blood flows in a young man's cock. Hah! There are great gatherings *here* and *here*, where the rivers rise or cross, and much business can be done.' The places he indicated with stabs of his muddy finger were dauntingly far to the west. 'These gatherings are soon. I would go there. You can carry my trade goods there, and my bounty back. Then, in the autumn, I will return you to the villages of mud and brick and find somebody who will trade for your skill.'

Novu grunted. 'You use me as my people use cattle, with heavy goods laden on their backs.'

94

'I use you any way I choose,' Chona snapped. 'Anyway, by the autumn you will be in better condition. Less of this flab.' He poked Novu's belly, not hard. Novu flinched back.

In the morning, they walked on.

Day by day, with the steady walking and his sleep deepened by exhaustion, Novu felt his body changing, growing more lean, the soles of his feet toughening, the muscles of his legs tightening. Once he glimpsed his reflection in a flat pond. His face had grown dark in the sun, dark and tough like Chona's.

He wouldn't say he liked Chona; he was too alien for that. But he came to admire the man's self-reliance, his inner strength, his composure, his competence. And now that he was over the shock of his departure he had no desire to go back to Jericho, save on his own terms. He didn't even have any wish for revenge over his father, who, now he thought back, struck him as a murky, worm-like figure, wriggling and jostling with other worms in the crowded, worked-over dirt of the town.

But he was wary of Chona. For one thing he was aware of the way Chona looked at him, at times, when he was washing, or walked ahead. He'd seen Chona's lust for his cousin Minda. The two of them were alone much of the time, sometimes spending days without seeing another human being. Novu had no wish to be the object of that angry passion.

And then there was the coughing. It was getting worse; sometimes it woke Chona in the night, and then Novu. Clearly Chona was growing ill. Maybe he'd caught something back at Jericho. If so, Novu didn't want to share it.

Life could be worse. In many ways Novu's life back at Jericho had been worse than this. But Novu knew that if he ever got the slightest chance he would get away from Chona. If he had to kill the man, he would do it.

16

Some days later they reached the shore of a sea. The strand was crowded with groups of people, but they were fisherfolk, eccentric and inward-looking, and not very interested in Chona's goods.

While they camped by the water Chona had Novu hunt for pretty shells to trade.

At length they reached the outflow of a great river. The estuary with its mud flats, reed beds and threading water channels was densely populated, for it allowed access both to the sea and via the river and its valley to the forests to the west. Chona did not linger here, for, he said, this mighty river was one of the great trade routes that spanned the Continent. So he and Novu headed west, following tracks that paralleled the river.

This was not like the river close to Jericho. It was a broad, rich stream, muscular in its grand flow, and its banks were green, fringed by marshes and reed banks with woodland rising beyond. There was life everywhere, frogs and toads croaking in the shallows, whole flocks of birds nesting and feeding in the reeds, and deer shyly emerging from the forest fringes to drink. Slowly Novu gathered a sense of the huge, rich Continent that stretched to the west of here, on and on, and how this tremendous river drained its very heart.

And there were people here – there could scarcely not be, given how rich the land was, people scattered in small communities along the riverbank and sometimes further inland. They all lived off the land and the bounty of the river. Sometimes Chona would visit them, do a little trading. Some days they rode in their boats, paddled against the river's flow, in return for a few of Chona's shells or bits of stone.

All these people were human beings who had babies and grew old. But apart from those basics they could differ in every detail of how they lived their lives – how they built their houses, how they adorned themselves, how they celebrated birth and death and coming of age, how they arranged their marriages. And, most striking to Novu, they differed hugely in their languages. You could walk for a day along the river to find yourself coming upon yet another community whose tongue was utterly unlike anything you'd ever heard before. He built up a picture in his head of a vast landscape of forests and rivers and grassland, populated by these little communities of people, each of them all but isolated. It was only the traders who travelled far, with their bundles of trade goods, smiling and nodding their way across the landscape.

But nowhere did Novu find a place that was remotely like Jericho. Maybe his father was right in his boasting, that Jericho was something new in the world, and the pride of all mankind.

As the days passed and they headed ever further west the land changed its character, becoming more mountainous. Now the river was constrained by steep banks. The walking was hard work on the sloping ground near the river, and they had to climb to find easier tracks.

Then, one morning, the country opened out, and Novu was treated to a spectacular view of a gorge, deep but narrow. The river cut like a blade through cliffs of pale, banded limestone, coated with ragged forest that in places descended almost to the water's edge.

Chona grunted, shifting his pack. 'This place is called the Narrow, in a hundred tongues. Look, we climb up over this next bluff, and then we'll come to the camp where we'll stay for the night.'

The camp, when they scrambled down to it, turned out to be a roughly flat area by the river where robust-looking houses sat, built on frames of thick tree trunks. All this was in the lee of a steep cliff whose bare rock was covered with odd, fish-shaped carvings. Chona, evidently knowing the place, led Novu in. They were met by the usual gaggle of curious children, and by one or two suspicious stares from the women.

Everyone seemed to be working on fish. The silver bodies were heaped everywhere, fresh caught, or were being gutted or scraped or skinned, or hung up to dry out, or were wrapped in river mud and baked slowly in pits. Wicker baskets and bone harpoons hung on racks and on the walls of the houses. Novu saw boats pulled up on the rocky shore and out working on the river, whose roar was a constant, not unpleasant background to the human noises of the settlement.

Well, it was clear how the folk of this place made their living. After so long by riverbanks and sea coasts Novu had thought he had got used to the stink of fish, but in this place it was ripe and high. There were no dogs, though, and that was unusual.

At last Chona came to a house he recognised, and called a name in another new language. Out came a burly, bearded man of perhaps thirty-five who reminded Novu, oddly, of his father. But this man was dressed in what looked like deerskin, carefully softened, cut and stitched, and he had a hat thick with fish scales on his head, which would have appalled Magho. He greeted Chona with apparent pleasure, but he pulled back when Chona had one of his coughing fits. With gestures, he invited Chona into his home.

Chona turned to Novu, and pointed to the cliff face. 'You're sleeping over there. You'll find hollows and caves and such. No animals; the people use them for winter stores, and I think the children play in there.' He looked around. 'It's a rich place to live. You can see it. They hunt in the forest, where there's deer and aurochs and boar, and then there's the river itself. Fish, the river, it's everything to these people, you know. They bury their dead with their heads pointing downstream, so the river can take their spirits away. And, of course, anybody coming this way, like me, has to pass this point. So old Cardum and his friends can just sit here and let the food and the wealth flow by, and trap it in their nets like salmon. This is no Jericho, but they've been here a long time, and they're rich in their own way. A boy like you might feel at home here. Well – go fix yourself up. Cardum says he'll have his kids bring you supper.'

'Fish?'

Chona laughed. 'If I need you I'll call.'

Novu quickly found a deep, snug cave beneath the cliffs at the back of the settlement, too low to stand up in. It was clean enough, though he did find one dry, coiled turd, maybe left by one of the playing children. He scooped this up in a handful of dirt – it actually smelled of fish – and threw it away. And as he did so he noticed more of those odd fish carvings, this time in the roof of the cave, out of the way of the wind and rain.

He went down to the river and, having drunk his fill and taken a discreet piss, he returned with a bowl of water and an armful of dead branches. At the back of the cave he gathered stones to make a hearth, and dug the ember from last night's fire out of his pack.

As he was nursing his fire, two children peered under the overhang. Both boys, maybe eight years old, they looked oddly like Cardum, both round and jowly with thick black hair. They threw in a parcel of some kind, shouted what was evidently an insult, and ran off, giggling.

'And you're the same!' Novu yelled back.

The parcel turned out to be a couple of plump fish, fresh from the river, wrapped in thick broad-lobed leaves. He had no name for their kind, but he had learned how to prepare fish. He briskly skinned and gutted the fish. He buried the waste, not wanting to offend anybody by throwing it out or to attract rats by leaving it lying around. He dropped handfuls of dirt into his bowl of water, making clay, and plastered it over the fish, moulding a compact lump that he dropped on the fire.

After he'd fetched in more water he sat back, leaning against the wall, waiting for the fish to cook.

His cave looked north, and as the sun set the daylight sank

down to a bare grey-blue. His eyes adapted to the dark, and he saw how the glow of the subdued fire was picking out the carvings on the roof of his shelter. He felt oddly content. Food, warmth, peace. It was a relief, for once, to be alone. The rush of the river filled his head, like the sound of his own blood flowing.

But it didn't last long. Chona came crawling in. He sniffed loudly, making himself cough. 'That smells good. Enough for two?'

'Maybe. And if not, I suppose I'll go hungry again, will I?'

Chona just laughed. He settled against the cave wall, shucked off his boots and pulled a skin over his legs. 'Getting colder.'

'So why didn't you stay in the house of, umm—'

'Cardum? Too crowded. Crawling with kids and farting men and complaining women. Ate my fill of *his* fish, though.'

Novu wondered how much of that was true. That coughing might have something to do with it. Nobody wanted a sick man around their kids.

'Their women aren't bad, if you can stand the smell. I'll swear they sweat fish oil. There's one in there I had my eye on last time, a niece of a niece of Cardum's, I think, plump little thing—'

'Just how you like them,' Novu said dryly.

'Got the impression she was willing to trade a little comfort for a jade bead or a pretty shell . . . Well. She'll be ripe for a couple more summers. How's that fish doing?' Without waiting for a reply he lifted the fish off the fire and cracked open the baked-hard clay. The flesh, tender and steaming, fell apart in the clay fragments, and Chona took healthy handfuls.

Even when he had done there was plenty for Novu, and he ate, ravenous as he always was after a day of travelling.

'So,' Chona said around mouthfuls of food. 'Think you'll sleep well tonight?'

'Why shouldn't I?'

'You've been dreaming, the last couple of nights on the road. You came near to a punch in the head a few times.'

'Sorry.'

'You were worse when we left Jericho, you know. Have to be deaf not to hear you. Thrashing and muttering. All that anger at your father.'

Novu felt resentful at being probed like this. 'Look – you're going to sell me. You take the very food out of my mouth. Have you got to poke at my spirit as well?'

Chona laughed. 'You're developing a bit of fire in the belly, aren't you? That might help when I sell you on. Tell me why your father hated you that much. I mean, the thing about the thieving was just the final excuse, wasn't it?'

'We never got on,' Novu said. 'I wasn't like *him*. Vain and greedy. And on the other hand I wasn't a tough hunter type, like some of my cousins. I played alone a lot—'

'Making bricks.'

'As I got older we started having fights. I'd challenge my father in front of my mother, his brothers. Once he took me to a meeting of his friends. Maybe you know some of them. I think, looking back, he was trying to help me. If I could get to know these people, maybe I could be accepted by them. Be like them some day.'

'Be like *him*.'

'Yes. But they were just a bunch of stupid fat old men to me, with their sea shells and bits of jade and obsidian and gold dangling from their necks and ears. Well, I made a fool of my father. I made them laugh at him.'

Chona grunted. 'He won't have enjoyed that.'

'That was over a year ago. Since then he's been harder on me. You saw it. In turn I played up more. It just got worse and worse. I was stupid to steal from him. Now I can see that he was making plans to get rid of me. Just waiting for the chance.'

'And waiting for the right bit of obsidian to exchange you for.' Chona belched, and lay back on a skin. 'I can see how it went. He feared that you'd become a rival. Position is everything to your father, position among all those other jostling idiots in Jericho. Like goats in a herd, but not as intelligent. That's what I use to sell him stuff, you know. Impress your friends! He feared you were going to undermine all that.'

'I probably would have,' Novu admitted. 'I'd have enjoyed doing it.'

'Well, there you are. So he got rid of you. Brutal, but effective. Bad luck for you.' He settled his head on his arm. 'I've eaten too much. Well, we don't have to walk for a couple of days.' And with that he rolled on his side, loosed a fart that filled the cave with the essence of fish, pulled another skin over his body, and wriggled to make himself comfortable.

Novu leaned back against his wall once more. He tried to ignore the uneven, unsleeping breath of the trader, and listened again to the crackle of his fire, the rush of the river.

The last daylight was all but gone, and as his eyes opened to the dark, he saw more detail in the roof carvings. There were oval shapes, like eggs, chipped into the rock, each about the size of his own head. He thought he saw what looked like a face carved into each egg, circles for eyes, a crescent for a down-turned mouth. But surrounding the face and running down the body were overlapping circles and plates that looked like scales. Half-human, half-fish. Maybe that was how the people of the Narrow saw themselves, their very spirits mingled with the fish that gave them life.

Chona coughed and stirred. He squirmed, his back to Novu, and pushed one hand inside his skin leggings. Novu saw his upper arm working. Novu had seen this before. The trader was a man who, so contained and controlled, hid a powerful lust. He had probably been dreaming of this niece of a niece of Cardum's for days, and was now denied her.

It wasn't long before the trader's body shuddered, and relaxed. Then, at last, Novu was left alone, with the river, and the fish-people of the cave.

17

More than a month after the Spring Walk, Ana had the idea that they should take a party up the valley of the Little Mother's Milk to the old summer camp.

It was a suggestion born out of desperation, after another night of arguments in the house, another night of four-way stresses between herself and her sister and the Pretani brothers, in a house that, despite being the largest in Etxelur, seemed much too small. Ana didn't even understand what was happening any more. Did Gall still want Zesi, or not? And what about his brother? Zesi and Shade barely spoke to each other in the house, but Ana saw the looks that passed between them – looks of guilt and lust, or so she read them. Would Gall stand by and let his little brother have Zesi? It seemed unlikely. And where did Ana herself fit in? She had thought Shade was attracted to her, not Zesi. Did Shade still feel anything for her – if he ever had? Did she care if he did or not? Ana could hardly bear the baffling tension.

What made it worse was that it was still more than a month and a half to the summer solstice, and the Giving celebration. That seemed to be emerging as a major landmark in everybody's mind. It was always the summit of the year anyhow, the longest day, after which the slow run-down to another winter began. And at the Giving the question of her father would come to a head. Although the solstice would be less than a year since Kirike's disappearance, everybody seemed to feel that if he wasn't back by the time of the feast, and Zesi, defying custom, took over his role as the Giver, it would be a kind of closing of Kirike's story.

Ana didn't want to face that. But another part of her longed for the day to come, for the Pretani were going home after the Giving.

A month and a half was too long to wait. And so she suggested a trip up-river as a way to use up some energy. The idea was greeted with a snarl from Zesi, but a day later, after a quiet word from the priest, her sister grudgingly accepted that it was a good idea after all, and the word was passed around.

Not long after dawn, the people gathered around Zesi's house, a few adults and many children, and with soft murmurs and laughter they set off.

It was a short hike from the Seven Houses to the estuary of the Milk, across scrubby grassland carpeted with buttercups. Ana walked with Arga and Lightning, neither of whom seemed troubled by the atmosphere among the adults. The sun rose, the mist burned off with the last of the dew; the birdsong was loud, and Ana was soon warm through. Given all her problems, she felt unreasonably happy.

But it didn't help that both the Pretani boys had decided to come along.

Zesi seemed in a foul mood from the beginning. Burdened with a heavy pack, she set a tough pace, as if the walk was something to be got over with, not to be enjoyed. Some weren't capable of keeping up the pace: the kids, and a young flint knapper called Josu, cousin of a cousin of Ana's, who had been born with a withered leg. Soon the group was strung out, and a couple of the older men quietly moved to the back of the group, keeping an eye on the stragglers.

They reached the river, and by the early afternoon they were following a narrow valley that cut through sandstone bluffs, heading roughly west. Zesi led the tramp upstream, following a well-worn path by the bank of the river.

In places the forest, birch and hazel scrub, came pushing close

104

to the water's edge. The bank itself was crowded with willows, which could grow as much as a hand's length in a month at this time of year, and old alders, trees that liked the damp. The alders' branches were heavy with catkins, some of them as long as Ana's hand. She could see the scars left where wood had been harvested in previous years; the cut trees were recovering, new growths pushing out of their root systems. Alder was useful for the frames of houses, for it stayed supple even after being dried out.

And in the shade of the very oldest trees white windflowers clumped, bluebell carpets shone, and elusive pied flycatchers flitted, spectacular splashes of black and white. People took the chance to gather birds' eggs. It was a rich, charming place.

But Etxelur folk, used to the coast's open spaces, weren't comfortable in the confines of the narrow valley, and Ana thought it was a great relief to everybody when they reached the site of the summer camp.

Here the valley opened out to a wide plain, bounded on either side by low, rounded hills cloaked with grass and forest. The river itself spread out, as if it too was glad to be free of its confinement. The main channel here was shallow and winding, cutting through a floor of turf, heather and scrub, but in places the flow split into two, three or four braids that combined and recombined, and wide marshy areas glimmered in the low sun. All along the valley the green skin of the floor had been eroded back by the changes in the river's course, to reveal bone-white gravel spits.

The old camp itself, set back from the river, had been abandoned since the last visit two years ago. Only one of the houses Ana remembered still stood, a collection of poles leaning against each other with the remains of a covering of skin and thatch. In a few more years, Ana thought, even these ruins would have disappeared into the green, and you'd never know the camp was ever here. People touched the land lightly.

People dumped their packs and began the pleasant work of restoring the camp. Two men chose a site downwind of the houses and close to the forest's edge to dig a fresh waste pit. Another man checked over an old urine pit, lined with stone. He jumped down into it and began raking out dead leaves; later he would seal it up with fat.

Further back was a stand of forest, with an open area where new young trees were sprouting. Ana remembered that this area had been cleared by fire the last time they had camped here, and she thought she saw the pale, wide-eyed face of a deer at the edge of the thicker forest. That was the point of the clearing, to encourage the growth of whippy young hazel shoots and fresh plants, and so to attract the animals.

When Gall saw the deer he immediately sprinted away, spear and club in hand. The deer vanished.

Arga grabbed Ana's hand and Shade's. 'Come on! I'll show you the river, Shade. I bet you don't have rivers like this in Pretani.'

With grudging glances at each other, they both ran with the girl towards the river.

The sun was still high, the summer sky washed out, and the colours of the landscape, blue water and white gravel and green grass, were bright. Lightning, hot, thirsty but full of life, ran at their heels, yapping. Ahead of them a heron, invisible before it moved, took to the air and flapped away, its narrow head held high.

They came to a gravel bank, and the dog disturbed an oystercatcher from her nest amid the stones. The bird rose, red beak bright, peeping indignantly, and flapped away. The dog splashed into the river, shook himself to make a spray, and his pink tongue lapped busily at the cool, air-clear water.

Shade looked down at the ground, puzzled. 'I know the oystercatcher's been nesting here. I just can't see where.'

Arga got to her hands and knees and poked at the gravel. 'Look! Here it is.' She held up a pale brown egg; the nest was just a collection of twigs in the gravel. 'They're good at hiding. I suppose you have to be if you make your nest on the ground.' She popped the egg into her leather pouch. 'You just take one,' she said seriously. 'The little mothers say you should leave the rest. Come on. I'll show you the lagoon.'

They walked further up the valley. Here a lagoon ran beside the river, a crescent of dense, stagnant water choked with reeds and rushes, and surrounded by grass and scrub. Arga, seven years old, enjoying having somebody to show off to, told Shade about the different plants here, the watercress and water chestnut and water lily, and how you used them all. Lightning, his tail wagging ferociously, paddled across muddy ground and stuck his head down among the reeds, trying to get to the water.

Ana knelt, filled a cupped palm with water, and raised it to her face. Tadpoles wriggled, tiny and perfect. She carefully dropped them back into the lagoon's scummy surface.

A sand martin dipped across the water, right in front of her, its wings swept back, darting and swooping in search of insects too small for her even to see. Watching it she found it hard to breathe, as if the bird was dragging her spirit through the light-filled air with it. All the darkness, the winter nights in the unhappiness of the house, the nagging, unhealed wound that was the loss of her father – none of it seemed real or important, compared to the martin's graceful joy.

Shade came to sit beside her. 'This lagoon,' he said. 'It looks as if the river once ran here. See? It curved around in a loop, and joined up down there, somewhere. But at some point the stream cut across the neck of the loop, and left it stranded.' He pointed to the far bank. 'You can see where it's cutting back into the turf, over there.'

His grasp of the Etxelur tongue was now quite good. And she was always impressed by the way he saw patterns in the world. It had never occurred to her that this moon-shaped lagoon might be a relic of the river's past.

He looked around. 'It's odd, however. As if the valley is too big for the river.'

'So it is.' The priest plodded down to the water's edge. Jurgi had got rid of his pack; bare-chested, he carried only his charm bag. He pulled off his boots, sat on the bank and gratefully lowered his feet into the water. 'Ah, that's good. I don't do enough walking; my feet aren't tough enough. In our story of the world, Shade, ice giants made the world from the first mother's body, the land from her bones, the sea from her blood. Later the little mothers finished the job. But the giants' shaping was crude and rough, which is why the world is such a jumble now, with valleys like this, too big for the rivers that contain them.'

'We have a different story. To do with big trees.'

'Maybe all our stories share a deeper truth,' the priest said.

Shade grunted. 'You're a funny sort of priest.'

'Am I?'

'That's what my brother says about you. The priests back home say there's one kind of truth – their truth. If you disagree you get punished. Gall says you're a genius, or mad, or a fool.'

Jurgi laughed out loud. 'Or all three.' Tentatively, he touched Ana's shoulder. 'And how are you?'

Caught between light and dark, she thought. 'I don't know. I wish I was a sand martin.'

'Even sand martins have work to do,' the priest said. 'Digging holes to build nests. Flying far to their winter homes.'

'A tadpole then. Swimming mindlessly.'

'How do you *know* they are mindless? Never mind.' He glanced around, at the people playing in the water, or working at the settlement. 'It was a good idea to come here. Etxelur has not been a happy place this winter.'

'It's because of us, isn't it?'

'Ever since the Pretani boys showed up. Brother against brother, sister against sister.' He sighed. 'Frankly, I think most people wish your father would return, Ana. It is as if we are led by wilful children.'

'It's my fault,' Ana said dismally. 'My Other. I'm bad luck.'

'You've had no control over any of this,' the priest said.

'None of us have,' said Shade heavily.

'If only you'd just go home!' Ana flared at him, her anger surprising herself.

108

'Oh, that's not going to happen,' said the priest. 'Not until this little game of yours is played out, one way or another. Let's hope that these days in the valley will soothe our spirits'

There was a piercing yell. They all looked to the cleared area before the forest. A tall figure emerged, a deer slung over his neck, hand cupped to his mouth.

'Gall's back,' said the priest.

'No.' Ana stood up. 'That's not Gall. That's a snailhead!'

18

That first night they had nothing to do with the snailheads, though they could see the smoke of their fires around the curve of the river.

Gall's red deer, when he returned with it, was set aside for the morning. That night they fed on birds' eggs and young chicks and smaller game flushed out by the dogs, pine martens and a young beaver. The meat was roasted on a fire of fallen branches collected from the forest, the eggs splashed onto hot rocks to be fried and scraped up with wooden spatulas.

The small children, worn out by the walk and the excitement, started to grow sleepy as soon as the sun had gone down and there was food in their bellies. They were put down in the one surviving house; for tonight the adults would make do with lean-tos. It was still early enough in the year for the night to be cold, and Ana took it on herself to check on the children, making sure they were covered with skins and heaps of leaves. Lightning, meanwhile, curled up close to the fire.

The adults and older children got to work at simple jobs, knapping fresh stone blades, repairing rips in house covers with thread made of plaited, greased bark. They had found antlers, dropped by the deer the previous autumn; now they sat around the fire working at the antlers with flint chisels, making awls and scrapers and fish hooks and harpoons with fine, multiple barbs. It was steady, patient, satisfying work, and the priest led them in murmured songs.

They carefully ignored the snailheads.

In the morning, the day began with the butchery of Gall's

deer. It was a big beast, a handsome male. Gall had already removed its antlers. The women took the lead in the butchery, picking up tools from a shared heap as they needed them. But Gall looked faintly disgusted when some of the men of Etxelur joined in – and even more so when Shade picked up a stone blade. Ana knew that in Gall's culture the women did such work, with the hunter sitting around and lapping up the praise for his kill. Maybe Shade was curious about learning a new skill. Or maybe he was just trying to irritate his brother.

The animal's head was removed first, and this was the job of the priest, who used an ancient, lustrous flint tool from his charm bag. He apologised to the deer, closing its lifeless eyes and kissing the lids. Then he cut through the animal's cheek and briskly removed its tongue, severing it at the root; this juicy treat would be his reward.

Then came the skinning. The women made cuts around the hooves and along the inside of the legs; the torso was sliced from throat to crotch. Then the animal was turned over and the skin peeled back, the men hauling, the women crawling around with their blades to chop away sinews and clinging tissue. The skin came away almost intact, and was folded and set aside.

The animal was cut open with heavy blades, and its stomach wall and ribs pulled back. The lungs were torn out and discarded, the guts spilled to the ground. The liver was dug out of the pile of offal and handed to Gall, the hunter, as his prize; he bit into it raw. Then the butchers moved around the carcass, working steadily. The legs were removed and broken at the joints, the ribs put aside, meat sliced from the body. As the animal disintegrated neat piles grew up around it, of meat fillets, big bones to be sucked clean of their marrow, sinews and useful bits of smaller bones, heaps of gut to be chopped up and mixed with blood, salted, fried. Some of the more bitter internal organs would be thrown into the waste pit, which had been placed close to the forest's edge to lure pigs. Only a few scattered fragments were thrown aside, chopped vertebrae, bone fragments.

Before the butchery was finished, Ana went to work with her sister on the skin. They scraped it clean of the last of the blood and fat and sinews, using tools of small stone blades stuck into a bit of bone with resin. It was fine, careful work; you had to get rid of all the waste while not cutting the skin. After they were done here, the skin would be rinsed in the river water and then soaked in the urine pit for a couple of days, after which the hide would be taken out, washed, and put through a process of stretching, rubbing, folding, soaking, until it was quite soft. Meanwhile there were the deer's sinews to work on. These would be scraped with even finer tools. Back at the coast they would be washed in sea water, hung up to dry, and split into fine threads. These would be made soft by working over with scrapers, as Ana preferred, or working through your teeth, as others chose.

In this way virtually none of the deer was wasted, and a proper price paid for taking its life.

Glancing up, wiping a bloody hand across her forehead, Ana saw that four young buzzards were circling overhead, their round wings and tail easily visible. When the people had gone and the birds and worms were done with their feeding, nothing would be left of the deer but a few fragments of bone and broken flint. And perhaps when the river shifted its course again, even those traces would be washed out to sea, leaving the land as clean as if humans had never come here at all.

This was what was best about life, she thought, a little wistfully. Useful labour hard enough to make your muscles ache and your skin glow with sweat. People building their lives together through one small task after another, while respecting the world and the endless gifts the mother gods provided for them.

It was while she was in this pleasant, dreamy, late-morning mood that the party from the snailhead camp approached.

Three came, two men and a woman. None of them looked much older than Zesi. They had no weapons. One man carried

112

something wrapped in a bit of skin that dripped with blood, and a sack heavy with some liquid. The woman carried a bundle that squirmed, feebly – a baby, Ana saw. One man had blond hair; the other man and woman had brown hair, darker eyes.

They looked ordinary, Ana thought, just like the folk of Etxelur. Ordinary save for their elongated skulls, which stuck out behind their heads, and the bone plugs in their tongues that showed when they opened their mouths. Beyond them, the smoke from their camp beyond the river's bend snaked into the sky.

Gall dumped his bit of liver and marched up to the new-comers, fists clenched. 'What do you want?' He spoke in the tongue of Etxelur.

The man holding the bloody parcel faced him. 'Trader tongue,' he said bluntly.

Zesi, followed by Jurgi, came bustling past Gall. 'Trader tongue,' she agreed. 'I speak for these people, not this man.'

'We have gifts,' the man said. He held out his bloody bundle. It was the heart of a deer.

Gall laughed at it. 'What did that come from, an unborn? My left bollock is bigger.'

The snailheads evidently didn't understand all his words, but they caught his tone. The blond man's expression darkened, and Ana saw muscles bunch in his arm. With his heavy frown and his strange, bony, tubular skull, he looked strange, unearthly, frightening.

The priest stepped forward hastily. 'We didn't come here to fight.' He continued in his own tongue, 'And we don't know how many of them there are. Zesi, take the gifts.'

Zesi hesitated. Then she took the heart from the snailhead, bowing her thanks.

The priest took the sack, removed a bone pin from its neck, and drank. 'Blackcurrant juice! Saved through winter!'

The blond snailhead grinned. 'Good?'

'Good!' Jurgi laughed, a bit too loudly. 'Come, sit, have some of my dock tea . . .'

They sat around the embers of the fire, the three snailheads, the priest, Zesi, Ana, Shade, others. Big flat stones and wooden bowls were set on the fire, to cook meat and prepare broths from the deer's entrails. Gall sat a short way away, gnawing on his liver, studiously ignoring the newcomers, yet clearly hearing every word.

Arga and the other children stood by, staring at the newcomers' big heads. Lightning wouldn't be kept away; he came sniffing around the strangers, butting their knees until they rewarded him with attention.

The priest began to make his tea. He took a precious relic from his charm bag: a bowl made from the skull of a bear, brown with handling and polished with age. The visitors looked suitably impressed. Jurgi scooped up water from a wooden bowl and set it on the edge of the fire. Then he took dock and sage leaves, crumbled them in his fingers, and dropped them in the skull bowl.

The blond snailhead man pointed to himself, and his companions. 'Knuckle. Gut. Eyelid.' Their own name for themselves wasn't, of course, 'snailhead', but something like 'the One People'.

The woman called Eyelid smiled and opened up her bundle of soft skin. The baby was sleeping, a thumb in her mouth. Her head from the brow up was tightly bound by plaited rope. She didn't seem to be in any discomfort as her head grew within these bonds, shaped and elongated.

Knuckle pointed at Eyelid's baby. 'Cheek. We camp.' He pointed down the river. 'There.'

Zesi asked, 'How many?'

The traders' tongue was rich in words for numbers. There were over fifty snailheads, men, women and children, just out of sight of the Etxelur summer camp.

This was shocking for the Etxelur folk to hear. The world was *big*, so big that you never had to share your favourite spaces with anybody else, save for happy meetings like the Giving. It was genuinely disconcerting to find fifty snailheads here, as if they had shown up in the heart of Etxelur itself.

'We come here every year or two years,' Zesi said pointedly. 'Our parents before us, and their parents before them.' Her meaning was clear. *This is our place.* 'You?'

Gut shrugged. 'Never been here before. Plenty of room. Plenty of deer for you, for me.' He grinned. Ana saw that his tongue was pierced by a stone plug as fat as her thumb. 'Don't stay here long. Rest, feed, repair kit. Then move on.'

Zesi asked, 'Which way?'

'North.'

'That's where we live,' the priest said. 'Already we saw some of your people. A few moons ago. At a beach. It was strange to see snailheads except at a solstice gathering.'

Knuckle shrugged.

'Why are you here?'

'Need somewhere new to live. We lived south. Beach. Far south . . . Many months of walking. A winter of walking.'

Gall called over, 'So what was wrong with it? Why aren't you still there now?'

'The sea. In the south, our beach. Sea shifts over land.' He mimed a sea's waves, chunks of land falling into it. 'Splash, splash, splash . . .'

'So you couldn't live there any more,' the priest said.

'We walk away. North, east, west.'

'Where will you live?'

'Where there isn't people.'

'Where will that be?'

'We haven't found that yet. We will,' said the man with a quiet confidence.

'They are so strange,' Shade murmured to Ana in the Etxelur tongue. 'Those heads . . . But you have met these people before.'

'A few usually come to the Givers' feast at midsummer. You know how it is. People travel a long way.'

'But not fifty of them.'

115

'Not fifty. And not to come to stay.'

'I think I know of their homeland. Where he means, the far south.' Shade sketched with a fingertip in the dusty ground. 'Albia here, Gaira here. Albia is nearly an island. But Albia and Gaira are joined by the Northland. A neck, like a bird's head to its body . . .'

She struggled to understand. 'Oh.' She pointed to the bottom of his sketch. 'This is north. This is where Etxelur is. The coast.'

'Yes. We are here, a little way inland. But the snailheads come from the other side of the neck.' He pointed to the top of his sketch, the south. Here he had drawn the sea making a deep cut into the land. 'There, a great river flows between cliffs of white chalk. The people live on the cliff tops. Maybe the sea is cutting away the cliffs.'

'Can the sea do that?'

He looked at her. 'The sea drowned the flint beds mined by your ancestors.'

'They can't go home.' The thought horrified her. 'But they can't stay here.'

Gut, the younger of the snailhead men, grinning, was watching them. 'I hear,' he said, in the Etxelur tongue. He held thumb and forefinger a sand grain's width apart. 'A bit. "Can't stay here."'

The priest forced a smile. 'We didn't come here to argue. And nor did you. You have your camp, and we have ours. As to what the future holds, only our gods know that, and yours. But for today and tomorrow and the next day, yes, there is plenty of deer for all, and pig and aurochs, and fish in the river and birds in the air and reeds in the marshes.'

Knuckle nodded, evidently a man as much intent on peace as the priest. 'Yes. Well said. No need to fight, nothing to fight over.' Then a thought struck him. 'Ah! We can share. Hunt together? Catch more that way. The One People are good at hunting deer.'

Gall, looking over, his mouth still stained with blood, grinned

116

dangerously. 'Yes. We'll hunt together. And I'll show you snail-heads how to do it properly.'

Gut looked slyly at Ana and Zesi. 'When we live on your beach we will need wives. I will need a wife.' Mocking, he turned to Zesi and stuck out his pierced tongue. 'Will you be my wife? You look strong. Good babies—'

Gall lunged at him, but the priest saw it coming; he threw himself at Gall and blocked him. He said urgently in the Etxelur tongue, 'Beat him at hunting. That's how you win.'

Gall, breathing hard, eyes bulging, backed off. 'At the hunt, then.'

Gut showed his studded tongue again. He hadn't so much as flinched.

'Good,' said the priest. 'Now – who wants some dock tea?'

19

The hunters were up early the next morning, before the glow of the night's fire had been conquered by the gathering light of dawn.

Ana pushed her head out of the lean-to she shared with Arga. She could make out hunters from the snailhead camp, already waiting by the bend of the river that separated the two camps. Closer by, Shade was pressing his spear point against the ground to test the rope-and-resin attachment of the head to its wooden shaft. Gall was by the urine pit, noisily emptying his bladder over the deer skin. And Zesi was at the edge of the hearth, scooping up grey ash and rubbing it over her face and arms, the better to hide in the shadows of the forest. The snailheads had been surprised that Etxelur women hunted.

When they were ready, bearing their day packs and their weapons, the Pretani, Zesi and a handful of Etxelur folk walked up the riverbank to join the snailheads. The hunters had a soft-voiced discussion about the day's strategy, and then they slipped into the shadows of the trees.

Ana could have gone along. She had chosen not to; a day without Gall, Shade or Zesi would be a relief. She went back to the warmth of her pallet of leaves and soft doe skin, to sleep a bit more.

She heard nothing more of the hunters until the sun was past its noon height.

'*Look out!*'

The single cry in the Etxelur tongue was all the warning they had.

The women from Etxelur had been burning off reeds from the marshy land around the river. A pall of smoke rose high into the air, and the smell of ash was strong. The fire flushed out hare and vole and wildfowl that the children chased with nets of woven bark, and the burning would stimulate new growth.

Meanwhile Ana was on the bank of the lagoon with Arga, collecting club rushes. These were particularly prized plants, for you could eat all of them, their stems and seeds and fat tubers, and would be useful to carry back to Etxelur. Lightning had been digging his nose into their work and running off with tubers, to scoldings from Arga.

When that shout came Lightning reacted immediately, turning to face the forest and barking madly.

And Ana heard a rumble, like thunder, coming from the forest.

Arga tugged her sleeve. 'I can feel it in my stomach. What is it?'

Ana saw shadows in the forest. Heard branches cracking. 'Run!' She dropped her flint blade and basket of rushes. She grabbed Lightning by the scruff of his neck, took Arga's hand, and ran downstream, along the eroded bank.

The animal came crashing through the trees, hooves pounding on the peaty turf, gruffly bellowing its pain. Ana dared to glance back, and she saw it emerge into the sunlight, a huge aurochs bull, thick brown hair, flashing horns, wild rolling eyes, frothing mouth. And she saw a spear dangling from its flanks. The question was, which genius had stampeded it towards the camp?

Then the animal reached the river – the lagoon, where she and Arga had been working only heartbeats before. It crashed forward and fell, landing so hard its head was twisted right around, with a crunch like breaking wood. It struggled and bellowed, but did not rise.

Now the hunters came boiling out of the trees after it, yelling,

119

half-naked, some brandishing spears, Etxelur, Pretani, snailhead together.

'Come on.' The priest was beside Ana. He handed her a spear; she took it by the shaft. 'We'll help them finish him off.'

She glanced around quickly. The children were out of harm's way here. 'Keep hold of Lightning,' she told Arga. The child nodded seriously. Then Ana ran with the priest to the lagoon. 'You'll have a lot of apologising to do today, Jurgi.'

'I'm good at that.'

The hunters and those who had come running from both camps gathered around the fallen bull. The animal, trapped, squirming, was a mass of muscle and fur, tossed horns and lashing hooves, anger and pain and mud and blood and flying water. Ana could smell how its bowels had loosened in terror, and there was a harder rust stink of blood. More spears were hurled at it, or thrust into its flesh.

Then one spear went flying over the lagoon, high in the air, following a smooth arc. Ana watched it curiously, absently. It was going to miss the bull by a long way. The spear seemed to hang.

Then it fell among the snailheads.

A man went down, the heavy spear in his neck. Few saw this, in the chaos of the slaughter. But those near the man reacted and ran that way.

Ana dropped her own spear and hurried over.

It was Gut, the snailhead who had enraged Gall. The spear had got him in the throat, thrown him back and pinned him to the ground. His mouth with that studded tongue gaped wide, full of blood. He was still alive, his fingers feebly thrashing at a spear big enough to penetrate to the heart of a bull aurochs. Alive, but already lost to the world of the living.

Knuckle stood over his brother, face contorted, veins throbbing along the flanks of his long temples. 'Where is Gall? *Where is he*?'

20

Novu and Chona rounded a bluff and looked down on a valley. Under a grey lid of sky it was raining, and their cloaks and tunics were sodden through.

'There,' Chona gasped. The rain hissed on the grass and pattered on the river water, and Novu found it hard to hear what Chona was saying. 'There! By the river – that place. That's where we meet. That's where . . . Come on.' He limped forward, and Novu, laden with their packs, followed.

The river ran over a rocky bed, beside a broad flood plain walled by cliffs of limestone. They had followed the river upstream for so long, they had come so far west, that it was barely recognisable to Novu as the huge waterway they had followed from its estuary, through the Narrow of the fish-people, and across the Continent's rocky heart. Yet here it was, the same river.

And here, Novu knew, Chona had been hoping to find his early-summer gathering of traders, for this place was, uniquely, near the head of several of the great rivers that traversed the Continent, a meeting point of the traders' natural routes. 'Always at this time,' he would say, 'after the equinox, that's when the trading is good. Later, at midsummer, all over the Continent the hunters and fishers gather, doling out food and gifts to each other. So this is the time to catch their leaders, early summer, when the big men start panicking about what gifts they have to give. Oh, the aurochs too fast for you this year? The deer too cunning, the fish too slippery? Shame. Maybe your wife's brothers would be happy with my bits of coloured stone instead . . .' Even traders followed the seasons, Novu was learning, from Chona's increasingly broken talk.

Chona had been desperate to get here. No matter how ill he became, no matter the cough, the pale, blotchy, sweating skin, the feverish broken sleep at night, Chona insisted on pressing on every day, leaning on his staff and on Novu's shoulder. But for days Chona had been watching the sun's arc in the sky, muttering, 'Late. Too late.'

And in the end the illness had slowed Chona down, just enough.

This rainy day the broad plain by the river was all but empty. You could see how the ground had been churned up by many feet, and old hearths lay like black scars on the ground. People had been here, a crowd of them. But now only a couple of houses remained, in the lee of the limestone cliffs, and one of those looked abandoned.

'Too late,' Chona said. 'I told you!' He raised his hand and clipped Novu's head; he was weaker than he used to be, but it still stung.

Novu bore this without complaint. 'It wasn't my fault. You're the ill one. So what now, shall we stand here in the rain?'

'Help me.' A trail, well worn, led from this elevated place to the edge of the water. Chona led the way, though he reached back for support from Novu. 'That house, that one there. With the smoke, and the boat beside it. I think I recognise the design on it, the sunburst on the skins . . .'

They reached the flood plain and limped across muddy grass. Their legs brushed thistles, all that had survived the passage of the traders.

The owner of the house was a big, bluff man who came out and watched their approach, suspiciously.

'Loga!' Chona called, in the traders' tongue. 'Loga . . . It's good to see you, my friend.'

Loga wore a coat sewn together from the black and white pelts of many small animals. 'Chona. You look like shit.'

Chona stood gasping, his eyes concealed by his hood, the rain dripping from his long nose. 'We're soaked. If I can come in—'

'Who's this?' Loga stared at Novu. 'Son?'

'No.' Chona laughed, but it turned into a cough. 'No, no. Trade goods, that's all. Hard worker, good walker, and if you want bricks making . . . Oh, what's the word for "brick"? Never mind, never mind. Loga, if I can just come in and dry off —'

Loga held up a massive hand. 'No. Wife in there, and other wife. Kids. Baby.'

'All right. But look, man – old friend – you can see how I am – this rain will kill me—'

'Cave.' Loga jerked his thumb over his shoulder at the limestone cliffs. Novu saw clefts, vertical, almost like doorways set in the cliff, leading to dark interiors. 'Dry in there. Warm. No bear. We chase out bear. Maybe bear shit. Burn on fire.' Loga grinned. 'Sorry. Wife. Other wife. Baby. Get warm, clean up, we talk.' And he ducked back into his house, sealing shut the skin cover behind him.

It was always this way now. Nobody wanted a sick man near their children.

So Novu led Chona through a cleft in the cliff wall, and into a kind of passageway. It was dark, and Novu wished he had a torch, but the walking was easy, the floor beaten flat by footprints, and the walls were smooth. People had evidently used this passage before.

After a dozen paces the walls opened out to reveal a larger space, a flat floor scarred by old hearths.

'This will do.' Chona slumped to the floor and leaned against a wall. 'Make a fire. Then food . . . Oh, my bones.' He closed his eyes and seemed to sleep immediately.

Novu opened up their packs and spread out their skins. Then he looked around the cave. He picked one of the old hearths to build his fire. He found a little wood piled up at the back of the cave, which he collected, and hard round blocks that might be bear turds; he decided to try burning them later. Before it was dark, he would go back out and collect more wood, and bring it in here to dry out.

He dug out the day's ember, and soon the wood was burning brightly. He got out some dried fish for Chona, and fetched him a bowl of rainwater.

The trader's appetite had been poor for days, but he forced himself to chew. 'Here we are at the heart of the Continent. The beating heart, where rivers like veins flow with trade. And I missed the traders' gathering! I missed it. First time in years. Ten years. More.'

'You've spent ten years as a trader?'

'More than that. My father traded. He showed me the way it works. I walked with him. The way you're walking with me, I suppose. Loga thought you were my son! What a laugh.'

'You don't have a son of your own.'

'No family. No wife. Or a hundred wives.' He cackled, and made a pumping gesture with his crotch. 'The trading, that's everything to me. I saw how my father slowed down when he had his family, it ties you down like a tethered goat. Not for me.'

'Where did you come from? I mean originally.'

'Nowhere you'd know. Nowhere at all.' He spat a bit of fish in the vague direction of the fire, and missed. 'Shut up, boy, you're annoying me.'

Novu brought him another bowl of water. But when he returned the trader had slumped back to sleep, and was snoring loudly.

Left alone, Novu, restless, bored, wandered around the cave. Odd pillar-like formations stood on the floor, and when Novu looked up he could see more pillars dangling from the roof, glistening, damp.

And at the back of the cave more clefts led off, presumably to more hollows deeper inside the rock.

Novu made a torch of a bit of pine branch wrapped tightly with dried reeds. He lit this in the fire, and returned to the back of the cave. He counted four, five, six clefts running off from this chamber, gaps wide enough for him to squeeze through. He picked one and pushed his way in. It was just a little wider than his shoulders, the walls rising above his head.

Maybe the whole cliff was riddled with caves, with clefts and passages everywhere. His imagination ran away. You could get lost. You could wander here for ever! Maybe there were whole tribes of people wandering in the dark, feeding on spiders or rats . . . Oddly he didn't feel frightened by this idea. It would be like a huge, natural Jericho.

The passageway closed in, without revealing anything of interest.

He backed out to the cave, where Chona was still snoring, and tried the next passage along. This was clogged by dried brush that he had to push through. But after a few dozen paces the passage began to open out, the roof rising up, and he found himself in another chamber, longer than Chona's, with tall, smooth, sloping walls. He thought he saw more of those dangling formations on the ceiling. He raised his torch to see better.

A horse bucked at him.

He stumbled back against the wall, nearly dropping the torch, his breath scratchy, his heart hammering. A horse! How could a horse be here? But he heard nothing, smelled nothing. He dared to raise the torch again.

The horse was painted on the wall. It was almost life size. And it wasn't a stick figure, like the art of Jericho; a bold black outline was filled with shading, brown and grey and white, and the hairs of its mane were picked out one by one. He stared, astonished, and he wondered if some god had made this thing. But then, just below it, he saw the mark of a human hand, outlined in red paint.

He stepped up to the horse and touched it. He could scratch away bits of the horse under his nail, just powder, red ochre, black charcoal. When the torch's fire had danced, he had thought that this image, so lifelike, had jumped out at him.

He had never been moved much by the spirit world, never impressed by the priests' capering and gabbling. But there was a sense of age in this cave, age and deep time. If the horse's spirit was still here, it would not harm him now.

A voice, faint, reached him. 'Boy? Boy! I need you . . .'

'Chona?'

The trader stumbled into the cave. His legs were bare, and his erection stuck out like one of the formations on the cave roof.

Novu snapped, 'What are you doing?'

'Taking what's mine. Come on, boy. I haven't had a good hump for days. You'll do. I've watched you, the way you look at people. I know you'd like men as much as women, if you ever got the chance . . .' Chona reached for him. Novu stepped back. Chona stumbled to his knees.

Novu laughed at him. 'You sure about this? You won't be able to sell me as a virgin then, will you?'

Chona knelt, breathing hard. 'You, you,' he said, and his speech was broken by coughing, 'you worthless little turd.'

'And you're too feeble for your own hand tonight. Sleep is what you need.'

Chona fell back onto one arm, awkwardly. The erection crumpled. 'You little turd.'

Novu put one hand behind Chona's head, and lowered him to the floor. The trader's pale flesh shone with moisture. Novu pulled off his own skin-shirt and began to dab at Chona's face. Chona's eyes closed, as if he was slumping back to sleep. Novu wiped a bit of drool from his open mouth, almost tenderly.

Then he pushed the bit of skin into Chona's mouth.

The trader didn't resist. Novu pushed in more skin. Chona gagged, and jerked.

Novu kept one hand over his mouth, and crawled forward so that he knelt over the trader, pinning Chona's chest with his weight, holding down his arms with his legs. Chona twisted now, and bit. But Novu pushed the whole of his hide shirt over the trader's face, and folded his arms before him and leaned forward, pressing down with all his body's weight. Chona couldn't move his arms or his head, but his legs kicked and thrashed.

Novu, his eyes closed, started to count. 'One. Two. Three . . .' He got to twelve, then twenty, then fifty, and then worked his way up to the big traders' numbers Chona had taught him.

Long before he reached a hundred, Chona was still.

When Novu came out of his cave, the morning was dry and bright. Yesterday's rain gleamed on the grass, and pooled in muddy footprints. Novu thought the air felt cleansed. He walked down to the river and took a long, luxurious piss.

When he walked back, Loga was sitting outside his house. Smoke from the night fire seeped out of the house's thatch. Loga was eating something, the baked corpse of some small animal spitted on a stick.

Novu stood before him, and waited.

Loga glanced over at the cave. 'Chona?'

'Dead. The sick— the sickness.' Novu stumbled over the traders' tongue.

Loga nodded. 'Jericho curses. Seen it before. Don't go there myself.'

'Wise.' Novu glanced around. 'This place. Many rivers run from here?'

'Four.' Loga used his teeth to pull the last of his breakfast off the stick, and then started using the stick to sketch maps. This was what traders did, draw maps. 'Four rivers,' he said. 'East. Jericho.' He pinned an anonymous bit of mud.

'The way we came.'

'Yes. South. Middle ocean. West. Great ocean. North. Much land, cold ocean. Four rivers, four ways.' He eyed Novu. 'Alone?'

'Me? Yes.'

'Jericho boy?'

'Not any more.'

'Slave?'

'Not any more.'

'You go home? Go east. Easy down the river.'

'I don't think so. You?'

'North.' He sketched again. 'Big country.' He jabbed the stick to the left: 'Albia.' Right: 'Gaira.' Centre: 'Northland. Big country. Boat, easy on river.'

'Your boat. Big boat.'

'Yes.'

Novu considered. 'I come?'

Loga frowned. 'Why?'

He meant, what was in it for Loga. 'Strong,' said Novu. 'Paddle. And, Chona's goods.'

'Mine now?'

'Some.'

Loga considered. 'Fetch goods. We talk.'

21

Ice Dreamer lay in a heap of furs like a bug in a cocoon. She slept, or woke in a daze that was no different from sleeping, save for the continuing pain of torn thighs, aching breasts, a deeper hurt within.

Somehow, even in her bloodiest reveries, even when she didn't know who she was, Ice Dreamer always knew she was on a boat.

Her world was sky. By day it was either an unbearable bright blue, or was choked with grey clouds. By night there were stars, a silent forest of them. Yet the sky's dark was broken sometimes by sheets of green light that rippled and folded.

And when the rain fell, or the snow, a blanket of skin would be pulled across, enclosing her in a creaking, rocking chamber of leather and wood and smoke, and pale, glimmering firelight.

Other sensations. Water cool in her mouth. Another liquid, heavier, salty and rich, warm, a soup.

The heat inside her. That was the first thing outside herself she was clearly aware of. A warm mass of tissue and blood, it was in her, and of her, and yet not *her*. She folded her thoughts around it, felt its sleeping weight. It was a comfort.

And then the faces.

They hovered over her in the tented dark at night, blurs in the faint yellow lamplight, or they were there in the day, leathery bearded faces framed by hoods of fur, weather-beaten skin pocked by frostbite scars. The faces of men. At first they blurred in her mind, but they gradually separated into two. One older, his face rounder, who eyed her sceptically. The other younger,

129

hair red and tightly curled, nose straight, eyes a startling blue, who looked at her with more complicated feelings. A kind of compassion. But even as he looked at her his attention seemed turned inside, into his own soul.

Men's faces. A memory sharp as a stone blade cut into her mind, of the Cowards' eager faces over her.

In that instant she remembered who she was.

She sat bolt upright.

In response to her sudden movement the boat rocked. The men turned, alarmed, and jabbered in some unknown tongue. Working together quickly and expertly, they stuck their blades flat in the water to stabilise the boat.

It was a bright, clear day, the sun low behind her. She glimpsed sky, and grey water scattered with ice floes. Two men sat before her in the boat, huge in their fur hoods and cloaks and mittens, paddling patiently with big leather blades fixed to poles.

She was suddenly aware of her heavy belly. The baby. It felt *big*, bigger than she remembered; oh, earth and sky, was its time close? And Moon Reacher – she remembered now – she looked around for the girl, but she was not here. Only the two men and herself in this pitifully small boat, alone on the endless water.

The men's breath steamed around their heads as they watched her. They seemed wary of her. The older one, at the boat's prow, stayed where he was sitting. Roundface, she called him. The younger one, Longnose, shipped his blade inside the boat, and, shuffling, came towards her.

She cowered back. Her weight made the boat tip up.

Roundface jabbered, '*Whoa, whoa!*' Longnose leaned back quickly. The boat settled again, rocking and creaking.

Longnose tugged off his mittens, showing dirty hands, and he spoke again. His tongue was like none she had ever heard, not even the Cowards'. He seemed to be smiling, behind that beard.

'My name is Ice Dreamer,' she said, or tried to; her voice was a croak, her mouth dry as dust. 'Ice Dreamer,' she said again. 'Ice

130

Dreamer.' She pointed at her chest. 'And if you come any nearer I'll jump over the side.'

He listened carefully. '*Ice – Ice —*'

'Ice Dreamer. Dreamer.'

'Ice Dreamer.' His accent was thick, almost incomprehensible. He pointed to his own chest. 'Kirike.' And the other man. 'Heni.'

'Kirike. Heni.' They were meaningless names, and too short. Maybe these men didn't have totems. Her throat remained dry. She dipped her hand into the water; she didn't have to lean far over the boat's shallow side. When she lifted it to her mouth the water was so salty it made her gag, and she spat it out.

Heni spoke again. Kirike took a small skin sack and threw it carefully over to Dreamer. It landed heavily, and when she picked it up she could feel liquid slosh inside. Its neck was fixed by a splinter of bone. She opened it, sniffed suspiciously, and then took a sip. It was water, cold, a little brackish, not salty. She drank deeply, letting the cool stuff slide over her throat. 'Better,' she said. 'Better,' more loudly. Her voice was working. She sang a snatch of song, a hymn to the coyote.

That surprised the men. They both burst out laughing. Immediately she remembered where she was, alone with these two men. She stopped singing.

Longnose – Kirike – held his hands up again. He began to speak to her, earnestly, gesturing. He was clearly trying to explain something to her. She just sat and listened. He had a tattoo on his cheek, above the beard, concentric rings and a tail. She had seen it etched in the rocks of the coast, where her walk had ended. He spoke slowly and loudly, as if she was deaf. Heni nudged his back, and they had a short jabbered conversation. Ice Dreamer thought the meaning was clear. '*She doesn't understand, idiot. Try something else.*'

Kirike looked at her, a bit helplessly. Then an idea struck. He rummaged in the bottom of the boat, and he came up with a wooden bowl, covered by skin. He took off the skin to reveal a puddle of some kind of broth. He stuck his finger into the broth

131

and licked off heavy droplets, making a satisfied noise. '*Mmm-mm.*' He held it out to her.

She took it. Cautiously, she dipped in her own finger and tasted the cold stuff. It was thick, meaty, salty, rich. Memories flooded back. Lying half-awake under the furs, she had tasted this stuff, this broth; she had eaten it before. Kirike smiled. He mimed spooning the stuff up into his mouth, then pointed at her. He had fed her.

She couldn't remember it all. Maybe she would never remember, not properly. But she began to work out how she must have got from that barren beach with Moon Reacher, to here, on this huge, limitless lake, in this boat with these men. They must have landed on the beach in their boat. They must have found her. They could have killed her. Instead, evidently, they had taken her onto their boat. And they had cared for her.

She was still heavily pregnant. Her thighs and her crotch and her deep innards still ached from the attentions of the Cowards. But she was not dead. She was not even hungry. Her head was clear. And it was because of these men.

'Thank you,' she said. Their faces were blank. She still held the bowl. She drained it of the last scrap of broth, and handed it back to Kirike, nodding. 'Thank you.'

A grin broke across his face, like the sun breaking through cloud. '*Thank you. Thank you,*' he repeated.

She looked around the boat again. 'The girl,' she said. 'With me, the little girl – Moon Reacher. On the beach.' She desperately mimed – *like me, shorter – I held her like this* . . . She cradled the cold air like a baby.

Kirike seemed baffled, but Heni spoke softly. Kirike nodded. He reached into a fold of his tunic, and produced a lock of nut-brown hair, tied up with a bit of bark rope. He passed the hair to Dreamer, and she teased at it so that it caught the low sun. It was Moon Reacher's, no doubt about it. Kirike spoke steadily to her, his expression grave. His meaning wasn't hard to understand. *The child is dead . . . We couldn't save her . . .* Or perhaps, *She was already dead when we found you.* Dreamer recalled how cold and still Reacher had been, in those last days. Had the child's spirit already vanished from that pale, frail body, even as Dreamer had cradled her, trying to give her warmth?

Moon Reacher, dead like Mammoth Talker and all the others. There was no consolation to be had when the young died. Yet Dreamer felt nothing. Maybe her own spirit had gone, leaving this battered husk of a body behind.

The men were watching her. They were being kind, she saw. They were giving her time, letting her get used to being alive again.

But, behind them, ahead of the drifting boat, a huge mass of ice stuck out of the water like a fist. 'Look out!' she yelled, and she pointed.

The men turned, shouted, and grabbed their paddles. As they dug at water littered with flecks of ice, they snapped at each other and cursed in their own language. Dreamer wondered what strange gods they invoked.

The sun set. Its light made the floating ice blaze pink, though where larger lumps stuck out of the water she could sometimes see subtler shades, purples and greys fading from blue. The men resolutely paddled their boat away from the sunset, heading east – just as she had walked east from her lost home, east until she had run out of country altogether.

As the sun crept below the horizon, the light faded, the cold gathered, and Heni and Kirike shipped their blades. At the boat's prow was a scorched platform of wood, which Heni now detached and stuck in place at the boat's mid-section. It had a worn hollow, and here he set bits of dry moss, wood shavings, and scraps of wood and bone. Then, from a fold of his outer skin, he produced an ember, wrapped up in moss and greasy leather. He set this on the scorched block and blew it until the moss and kindling caught. He nursed the nascent fire, leaning over it to shelter it from the breeze, feeding it one fragment of fuel after another.

A fire on a boat!

The boat's frame was sturdy lime and ash, and its ribs were of bent hazel, tied together with plaited cords made of twisted roots. The outer skin was fixed to the frame by robust stitches, the holes stopped with a mix of animal fat and resin. The People had used boats, on the rivers and the lakes. She had never seen any boat as big or as elaborate as this one. And she certainly hadn't ever seen anybody start a fire in a boat. You'd just put into shore for the night, and build your fire there. If they were so far from the shore, this must be a very wide lake indeed.

Both Kirike and Heni, with glances back at Dreamer, knelt, pulled up their tunics and pissed over the side of the boat. Their urine steamed, thick and yellow. Kirike pointed to a bowl near Dreamer's feet. They must have been keeping her clean. She felt a stab of shame, and clutched her skins closer.

Then, when the fire was crackling healthily, Kirike lifted a pole, a stripped sapling, from the bottom of the boat and set it upright in a socket. He unfolded grease-coated skins and set them up in a kind of tent, tied to the top of the pole and fixed to bone hooks around the rim of the boat. It was low, to get inside you had to crouch down under the shallowly sloping skins, and you certainly couldn't stand up. Dreamer vaguely imagined that if you raised the tent thing too high the whole boat might topple over. But the skins were heavy enough to shut out the wind, and the fire's warmth soon filled the little space.

Once the tent was sealed Kirike and Heni loosened their clothing, shucking off their heavy mitts and boots. Kirike set up a couple of lamps, wicks burning in some kind of oil in stone dishes, and put them at either end of the boat. A soft light suffused the boat – the light she remembered seeing reflected from their faces, in the dark times of her illness.

Kirike and Heni started unwrapping bits of food. Kirike offered her strips of meat, dried and salted. She took them cautiously. The meat was tough, leathery, but she found she was hungry, and it was satisfying to have something to chew.

As they ate Kirike dug out more packets, carefully wrapped in skin. He showed her a collection of big shells, each bigger than

Kirike's widespread hand, that he seemed very proud of. The shells were strung on a bit of rope. And they had tools, stone blades and bone harpoons and spear-straighteners. These looked like artefacts of the Cowards, and she wasn't interested. He had nothing that might have come from the People – none of the big fluted spear points that had once been so prized. Kirike and Heni talked amiably as they picked over their trophies, here in this covered-over boat.

It wasn't like being in a house. It was too small, and the boat creaked and groaned in the swell, and if you put your foot down incautiously you could find yourself stepping in the cold water that constantly seeped through the skin's seams. But nevertheless these two men trusted their boat, as they clearly trusted each other. Dreamer felt oddly safe in its rolling embrace.

There was a bit of comedy when Heni decided he needed a shit. The men bickered, Kirike evidently complaining about losing heat, Heni twisting with agitation as the pressure in his bowels built up. They were like husband and wife, stuck together and too used to each other. In the end Heni got his way and stuck his bare arse out of the boat. Cold air swirled. He strained and was mercifully quick, letting the shit just drop over the side, but when he pulled his backside into the boat Kirike mockingly picked icicles off the thick black hairs coating his buttocks.

After that the men dug themselves down into heaps of furs. Arguing mildly, coughing, farting, blowing their noses into their hands, the men settled down to sleep.

Dreamer closed her eyes and listened to the boat creak, and settled her hands on her belly. The baby was asleep. It seemed content. She thought she could feel its heart beat, feel the heaviness of the blood it drew from her body. As she slid into sleep herself she was troubled, for the baby was very large, and she knew its time must be near, and she had no idea how she could cope. Yet sleep she did.

*

135

In the days that followed she came to learn the routine of the men's strange lives, here in their boat-home.

Whenever they could they paddled, always heading east. Often they would sleep in the boat, as they had that first night, but other times they would push the boat in towards an ice floe, or sometimes even a scrap of rocky land. At one extraordinary shore she saw a huge dome of ice squatting over the land. It thinned towards the coast and she saw dark mountains sticking up out of the ice, their peaks sculpted like a flint core, and rivers of dirty ice flowed between the mountains towards the water. Nothing lived here but birds, and creatures that flopped up onto the ice out of the sea. They did not land here.

When they did find a place to land, the men would drag the boat out of the water, with Dreamer still riding inside, and then help her out. The first time they landed she had trouble standing; her legs felt weak as a child's, and it felt odd to stand on a surface that wasn't pitching and rocking. But Kirike supported her and, holding her arm, encouraging her with a flow of words in his strange language, he made her take one step, two, three. Her heart pumped, and a kind of mist cleared from her head, and she was a little more herself again.

Whenever they managed to get out of the boat the three of them would walk away from each other, sometimes until they became dark specks on a sheet of white. She would squat on the ice and leave runny turds steaming in the cold air, and watch with dismay as urine laden with blood pooled around her feet.

Sometimes they would stay two nights, three, on the land. The men would make minor repairs to the boat, and gather food. They would take the boat out for a morning or afternoon, empty of everything but their fishing kit, leaving Dreamer with the heaps of spare gear. Alone with her unborn child, she waited in a world reduced to abstractions, plain white below, clear empty blue above, and wondered what might become of her if they never returned. But the men always did return, hauling their catch, and they would all bundle up into the little house-boat for another night.

136

Sometimes, out on the sea, she saw creatures like fish, but much greater than fish, accompanying the boat. They would even leap out of the water, their grey sleek bodies massive and heavy, and she flinched. But Kirike laughed at her, and threw fish scraps. These strange companions were just playing, and her spirits came to lift when their graceful bodies broke the surface, with their strange smiling faces and rattling cries.

And then there were the even stranger fish-animals the men hunted, whenever they spotted one. She had never seen their like before. These creatures that could be bigger than a man had bodies like a fish's but faces like a dog's, and they seemed to spend as long sitting out on the ice or rocks as they did in the water. Kirike and Heni hunted them enthusiastically, but with respect, and their butchery was quick and efficient.

Dreamer soon learned that the broth that had kept her alive during her illness was made from boiled meat from the fish-animal. In the process she learned her first word of Kirike's language, through his pointing. 'Seal.'

'Seal.'

More pointing. 'Dolphin. Fish. Spear. Net. Harpoon . . .'

The journey went on and on, until she had long lost track of the days.

Sometimes the weather would close in, and they would be stuck in their tiny shelter for days, and their mood inevitably turned inwards, souring. There was always a tension between the men, she realised, as she learned to read their moods. Kirike was more welcoming; maybe it was Kirike who had wanted to save her in the first place. Heni was much more grudging. She saw something in Kirike's eyes. He was injured within. Somehow helping her helped *him*. She fretted that it was a pretty tenuous reason to be kept alive. Dreamer always tried to stay out of the way of any arguments.

As the days passed, it was the sheer endlessness of the journey that wore her down. How large could this briny lake be? Maybe, she thought, brooding, the lake was not of this world at all. She feared she was the last of the True People. If everybody else was dead, maybe she was dead too. What if these strange men weren't human, but were agents of the Sky Wolf whose rage had destroyed the world?

One day, as the men paddled, with the setting sun bright and pointlessly beautiful in her eyes, she folded her hands on her swollen belly and repeated the ancient priest's words to her child. ' "The world is dead. We are dead, already dead; this is the afterlife, of which even the priests know nothing. Even our totems are dead . . ." ' She folded over and began to weep, deep heaving sobs, though her tears would not flow.

Kirike stopped paddling. He worked his way down the boat to her, and folded her in his arms. But his thick furs were frost-coated and there was no hint of warmth from him, as if he was dead too, the dead embracing the dead.

Heni snorted his contempt. He stayed where he was, paddling gently.

Thus the days and nights wore away. Until the night she woke up screaming in agony.

22

'You're mad,' Heni insisted. 'You can't cut the baby out. Even the priests hesitate to do that. And we're not priests. We're just two idiots in a boat who can't even find their way home.'

'There's no choice. Her waters broke. The baby's coming.' Kirike, more desperate than he wanted to admit, looked down at Dreamer, where they had laid her down in the shelter of the boat tent. Mercifully the sea was calm. It was the first time in many days the two of them had had to handle the woman like this, but after the contractions had started she had soon lost consciousness. He put his hands under her tunic, over the top of her swollen belly. 'But the contractions have stopped. Or they're so weak I can't feel them. And even if she woke up to push . . .' He glanced down at the marks of an obvious and brutal rape. 'She'd be torn apart.'

Heni put his hand on his shoulder. 'Look – you've done wonders. She was nearly as dead as that kid when we found her. You brought her back to life. You gave her these days on the boat. She's even laughed, at times. You gave her that. You can't do any more for her.'

'I've seen this done twice,' Kirike insisted. 'The cutting-out. The first time I helped the priest.'

'How long ago was that? You were a boy! Watching a priest do it isn't the same as doing it yourself, believe me. And the second time—'

'It was Sabet. And, yes, it failed, we lost mother and baby. But don't you think I paid close attention? Anyhow what do you suggest we do? Tip her over the side?'

'Yes. Let the little mother of the sea embrace her, and her baby. It's out of your hands now.'

'Not yet.' He felt his heart hammer. He stripped off his tunic so he was bare from the waist up. 'Give me my best blade, Heni. The big one of the old Etxelur flint. Get an ember from the fire. And the sleeping moss.'

Heni hesitated for a long moment. Then he began to unpack the fold with their few remaining medicines, put together for them by Jurgi the priest before they left Etxelur, for what should have been a few days' fishing and had become a journey of months.

The sleeping moss had been soaked in sap taken from a poppy's seed pod. Kirike lifted Dreamer's chin to tip her head back.

'Just a drip in each nostril,' Heni said. 'Too little, it won't take the pain away. Too much and it will poison her—'

'I know! Shut up, man.' Carefully Kirike squeezed the moss over her nose, delivering the droplets. Then he held his hand over her mouth, forcing her to breathe through her nose. She shifted, stirred, moaned.

He leaned over, pushed his arms out through the tent's flap and dunked his hands in cold sea water. This part he was sure of; the priests at home always used salt water to clean their hands.

He came back into the tent. He lifted Dreamer's tunic up over her breasts, and shifted around until he was kneeling on the woman's shoulders, pinning her. 'You hold her ankles.'

'We need more people. You always have a whole pack of helpers.'

'We'll have to make do.' Sweat was running into his eyes. He took his big, familiar blade in his right hand.

'This is about Sabet,' Heni said abruptly.

Kirike halted, his knife poised. 'What about Sabet?'

'You couldn't save her. The priest couldn't; nobody could. We're here on the wrong side of the ocean because of Sabet. Now you do *this* because of Sabet. Even if you save this woman it won't help Sabet, or your baby. And if you kill her—'

'Shut up!' He wiped the sweat off his brow with the back of his hand. 'Just hold her.'

Heni grunted, but held the woman's ankles.

Kirike muttered a prayer to his Other, the clever pine marten. He hefted his blade again, and, trying to be as sure and confident as if he were butchering a seal, he pushed his blade into her flesh, just above the pubic hair, and rapidly made a slit up to her navel. He knew it had to be deep enough to sever the skin, muscle and womb wall, yet he must not harm the baby.

Amniotic fluid spilled, its stink strong, and Dreamer stirred in her drugged sleep. Where the bleeding was heaviest Heni touched the spot with a glowing ember, held between two splinters of seal bone.

'Now the baby,' Kirike said. 'Let's be quick.'

Heni put down the ember, hooked his fingers into the wound, and pulled the stomach walls apart. Kirike quickly widened the cut in the womb and dug out the child. He cupped it in his hand, a greasy creature with shut, swollen eyes that seemed barely human. With a swipe of Etxelur flint he cut the cord and, keeping one hand inside the abdominal wall so it wouldn't spring back, handed the baby to Heni.

Heni cradled the child, tied off its cord with a bit of twine, and wrapped it in skin cleansed in sea water. Now they were in the midst of the operation they worked together quickly and well, as Kirike had known they would.

But Kirike's job was not over; even if the baby survived the mother was yet to be saved. In his mind's eye he imagined what the priests had done, how they had worked to save Sabet. He had to fix the womb. Reaching in he scooped out clots, and felt for the placenta. It was extraordinary to look down and see his own bloody hand thrust into the belly of this woman, who he had never met a month ago, whose very language he couldn't speak.

He removed the placenta and dumped it in a bowl, but a loop of intestine escaped through the wound. 'Help me . . .' Heni, holding the child, reached over with one hand and pushed the

141

pink-grey worm back into the hole. Kirike kept pressing the womb, which he knew had to be held firmly as it contracted. Had he compressed it enough? He had no idea.

Dreamer stirred again.

'We have to turn her over to drain her. Hold the wound . . .'

Heni put the baby down and grabbed hold of Dreamer's flesh at either end of the wound, by her navel and her crotch. He kept hold as Kirike pushed the woman over on her side, and the fluid in her abdominal cavity drained out. Then they rolled her back.

'Now the pins . . .' These were splinters of bone that he pushed into the flesh to either side of the wound. He looped thread around each pair of pins, and pulled them tight. Thus the wound was closed, one stitch at a time. Heni held the ends of the wound firmly until the stitching was done. Then Heni smeared a poultice over the wound, made of herbs given them by Jurgi the priest.

When it was done Kirike gently lifted Dreamer up at the shoulders, and she moaned again. Heni got a bandage of sealskin under her lower back, and pulled it around her body.

Kirike thrust his head out of the shelter. He tipped the placenta out of the bowl into the sea, and let his hands trail in the water until they were clean. Then he stopped, breathing in, relishing the air's freshness after the stink of blood. He was shuddering, but not from the cold, though it was a clear starlit night. He started weeping, whether for Dreamer, the baby, Sabet, himself, even Heni, he didn't know. He touched his face and felt the tears frosting.

And he saw pale rings of light in the water, two of them, concentric around the boat.

He reached down and dangled his fingers. The disturbed water glowed, purple, orange, yellow and grey-white. He knew that if he looked closely enough he would see the myriad living things in every droplet, burning up their little lives for the sake of this gentle light. Looking away from the boat he saw sleek, pale bodies swimming around and around the boat, stirring up the water and making it glow in the inner ring. And a fin, more ominous, circled in the outer ring.

Sharks would be drawn to Dreamer's blood, the placenta, even to the scent of it from the woman and baby inside the boat. But the dolphins in the inner ring were circling the boat, keeping the sharks away. He muttered a silent prayer, thanking the dolphins.

When he ducked back inside, Dreamer was already conscious, her eyes huge, and she held the scrap of baby to her breast.

Heni was grinning as if he had fathered it himself. 'I told you we could do it!'

23

The Year of the Great Sea: Summer Solstice.

A sound like a stampede, or like thunder, came rolling across the ocean from the north.

In her house Ana looked up, distracted from her work on the paint. Lightning had been sleeping on one of Zesi's old skins. He opened his eyes and lifted his ears. It was probably nothing, probably just a storm, just weather. Ana murmured to soothe the dog. Lightning closed his eyes, soon asleep again.

Ana tried to concentrate on what she was doing. Sitting cross-legged on the bare floor, she had lumps of red and yellow ochre, brought by a trader from mines far away in Gaira. She ground these lumps against a sandstone block, making piles of powder that she collected on the scapula of a deer. She also had charcoal powder set aside, and a pot of grease from deer fat, and another of pig's urine. She mixed these ingredients together in different proportions to make paints in shades of red, orange, yellow, that she ladled carefully into the hollows of bird bones. On the day of the midsummer Giving the priest would use these to mark faces and bodies, and to stain the tattoos of the hunters and racers and swimmers and wrestlers.

It was slow and careful work, and she had to get on with it. The solstice, only days away, wouldn't wait for her.

It was also quite a responsibility. In years past she'd helped her mother prepare the paint, and before that her grandmother, Mama Sunta, but now the job was hers alone. It was delicate work, you could easily waste a whole batch of the precious

144

ochre, and getting the colours just right was important for the priest's ceremonies.

Thunder, though. Odd. Distracted, she put down the ochre lumps.

She was alone in the house, and had the door flap shut against draughts, though bright midsummer daylight seeped around its loosely fixed seams. The house was tidy, orderly. Neither of the Pretani boys had come back from the disastrous summer camp, Gall having run off after the murder of the snailhead, and Shade having headed home. Ana and Zesi had thrown out their abandoned gear, their skins and their weapons and their piss-pots, and they had practically taken the house apart to get rid of the boys' male stink. Yet the house wasn't the way it had been before, in the old days before their mother had died and their father disappeared. It had become a lifeless place, where the tension between the sisters crackled . . .

Summer storms were unusual. Earlier the day had been bright and clear, the sky the colour of eggshells. Not a stormy day at all.

She heard a commotion outside, raised voices. Glad of the excuse, she stood up. Lightning lifted his head. 'You stay,' she said. 'Good boy.'

She pushed her way out of the house. As she emerged, blinking in the bright noon light, she saw people streaming over the bank of dunes towards the Seven Houses. Nobody was smiling.

Arga dashed up to her. 'Ana, I came to tell you!'

'What is it – a storm?'

'No, silly. It's Shade. He's back! The Pretani are back!'

And Ana understood the grim expressions on the faces of the adults. She hurried after the crowd.

Here they came – she counted – a dozen Pretani, clambering over the dunes. All male as far as she could see, all big men, they wore heavy brown cloaks and headdresses and thick fur boots; they must be hot on this summer day. Some of them were beating drums, wooden bowls over which fine hide was stretched, their leather-topped sticks making a cacophonous, threatening noise. But that wasn't the thunder she had heard earlier, she was sure.

'Moon and sun,' muttered Zesi, who came to stand beside Ana. 'That's Shade.' She pointed at one of the men in the lead.

'You can tell from this distance? Well, I suppose you'd know. You saw more of him than me—'

'Oh, shut up.'

'And the big man with him—'

'His father, I guess. The Root. The big man of the Pretani.'

Now Ana looked more closely, she saw how the Root looked more like Gall than his younger son, the same stocky build, the same blunt face. 'Better keep Lightning tied up, then. We don't want to scare them to death.'

Zesi almost smiled. It had been a long time since either of them had laughed at the other's jokes.

'What's the Root doing here? He hasn't attended a Giving for years.' So long ago Ana could not remember it; he had always sent brothers, sons, hunters.

'Well, it might be to do with that business about Gall,' Zesi said, sarcastic. She was tense, distracted; she pushed loose red hair from her eyes. 'Did you hear that thunder?'

'Yes.'

'But not a cloud on the horizon. Strange storms. The Pretani arriving. It's an ominous day.'

The Pretani reached the houses. To a gesture from the Root the drumming stopped abruptly, and the hunters stood still as tree trunks.

The people of Etxelur, in a loose knot, stood facing them, the wide-eyed children restless. The Root didn't even look at them. His headdress was the almost intact head of a huge bull, lacking only its lower jaw, with twisting horns and black stones pressed into its eye sockets. The moment stretched. Arga giggled nervously. The Pretani's sudden silence and stillness was frightening, Ana thought. As it was meant to be.

From the beach floated the sounds of laughter, of people

146

working, the calls of gulls. Evidently the Pretani weren't going to speak first.

Zesi stepped forward. 'Shade. It is good to see you—'

The Root spoke, his voice loud, used to command. In his own language he snapped, 'Speak to me, not him. And use the heroes' tongue. You know how to speak, don't you, woman?'

'She does.' Jurgi, the priest, came up now, panting; he must have run from the beach. 'As do I.' He bowed. 'You are welcome, Root. It is many years since you graced the Giving in person—'

The Root sniffed the sea air, pawing at the sandy ground like a bull. 'It's only tradition that brings us back at all, priest. You know that. Tradition that dates back to the days when Etxelur was great, and everybody came here, from across Albia and Gaira as well as all Northland. A thread of tradition that's fraying and close to breaking altogether, if you ask me. But this year, after I sent my sons into your country, I find one boy has gone rogue, and the other addled. All because of trouble with women, I hear – if you can call these scrawny bitches women at all.'

Ana grabbed Zesi's arm; she felt her sister's muscles bunch.

Jurgi spoke quickly. 'Whatever the reason, we're honoured you're here. Please.' He gestured at the Seven Houses. 'If you would like to rest, to eat or drink—'

'If I need a shit I won't be asking your permission, priest.'

Jurgi said smoothly, 'Then come see what we're working on.' He led them away from the houses. 'You understand the Giving will be held on Flint Island as usual, on the north shore, facing the sea. But we're busy preparing all over Etxelur. Josu, show us what you're doing.'

The stoneworker, squatting over his hearth in the lee of the dunes, had been concentrating on preparing his flints. Now, startled as the Pretani approached, he tried to get up, and he almost fell over, betrayed by his damaged leg. 'Sun and moon—'

'It's all right,' the priest said. 'Your flints. Can you tell us what you're doing? Use the heroes' tongue.'

Josu stumbled over his words. He showed the Pretani how he

worked. In the centre of the hearth, with charcoal burning sullenly, he had dug out a sand bath. Here he placed lumps of flint, the high-quality stuff mined from Flint Island. Heat, if applied correctly, could change the quality of the stone and make it easier to shape. But you had to keep the heating slow and gradual, and at a temperature that Josu continually checked by sprinkling water on his sand baths. Too rapid a heat shock, for instance if you just threw a lump of flint onto a fire, and it would shatter uselessly . . .

The Root glared at Josu without speaking, and moved on.

Further along a group of women had gathered the bones of a mature male deer, a big animal, specially hunted for the purpose. The skeleton had been roughly reassembled on the sandy ground, and the women were carefully working the bones. Jurgi, smiling at the women, picked up a flute made of a shin bone, a rattle made of a hip socket containing beach pebbles, a bull roarer carved from a bit of scapula, a rasper from a chipped rib. 'You see, we like to turn the whole animal into music, even little drums and rattles for the children. Then at the solstice when we march to the Giving place we bring the spirit of the animal with us, and—'

The Root spat. 'Cripples with lumps of flint. Whistles for children. Is this how the men of Etxelur spend their time, priest? No wonder you let your women chop your balls off.'

The priest tried to intervene again, but Zesi wouldn't stay silent this time. 'We live differently to you, Root,' she said in passable Pretani – a skill she had probably picked up, Ana thought with an inward twist of pain, during the spring days she had spent, secretly, with Shade.

The Root said, with a kind of dangerous calm, 'In Albia, no woman would dare speak to me at all – let alone this way.'

'None but my mother,' Shade said dryly.

'Silence, boy.' The Root leered at Zesi. 'What else can you do with your tongue, little girl? Maybe that's what drove my boys wild.'

Zesi's face twisted into a snarl.

148

This time it was the priest who pulled her back. 'You are our guests. We have food, drink – the fruits of the sea, which—'

'Fish, you mean. You all stink of fish.' Root put his hands on his hips and glared around. 'What a pitiful display this is. Etxelur is dead, or all but. Twitching like a calf after its brains have been stove in. What kind of Giving will this be anyhow?' He glared at Zesi again. 'I heard your father is dead.'

'Not dead. Missing.'

'Since the autumn equinox – that's what I heard. *Dead* – that's what you call a man missing so long. But he was the Giver. Who will Give this year? His eldest son – that's the custom, isn't it, priest? Oh, but wait. He had no sons! How typical of a ball-less Etxelur hunter of little fish that he couldn't even father a son.'

Jurgi said, 'Zesi will Give, as the senior woman of Kirike's house. It's unusual but not without precedent—'

'A woman, Giving!' The Root bellowed laughter, and his men dutifully joined in, though Shade looked away. 'That I've got to see. And what of the wildwood hunt? It's the Giver, or his son, who stands for Etxelur on that too. Who will lead this year?' He reached out to chuck Zesi under the chin. 'You, tongue girl?'

She flinched, but snapped back, 'Yes.'

The priest murmured, 'Zesi, think about this—'

'Yes, I will go on the wildwood hunt. And when I bring down a bull with bigger balls than yours, Root, you will apologise for your insults.'

The Root laughed again. 'Then bring on the autumn! That I have to see.' He turned to his men.

In her own tongue Ana murmured, 'Zesi, oh Zesi – what have you done?'

'I can hunt as well as any man,' Zesi shot back.

'That's true,' the priest said. 'But it's not the hunting that's the danger. It's the Pretani . . .'

'I will fulfil my promise.'

'*Whale!*'

24

The cry had come from a boy standing on the crest of the dunes that stood over the Seven Houses. He waved and pointed east, towards the mouth of the bay.

The Etxelur folk forgot about their visitors and ran that way, scrambling over the dunes.

The Root glanced at Shade and his hunters, and began to stride that way too. The priest walked with them, at times half-trotting to keep up with their long paces, and Zesi and Ana followed.

They soon crossed the dunes and clambered down to the beach, and walked towards the mouth of the bay, opposite Flint Island. The Pretani looked extraordinary as they marched along the strand, Ana thought, their hoof-like feet kicking up brown-yellow sand that clung to their furs and their bare, sweating legs. They were out of place, like aurochs driven along a beach.

And at the neck of the bay she saw the whale, huge and glistening, stranded on the stretch of tidal marsh land opposite the island. It must have lost its way in the open ocean and swum into the bay – or it might have been driven that way by Etxelur fisherfolk.

The whale still lived; its big tail fluke quivered, and its skin glistened wet. But its life was effectively over. Its own weight would crush it, if it wasn't finished off by spears and knives.

The people ran towards it, shouting their pleasure and excitement. Etxelur folk went whaling, but it was a dangerous venture to chase down such huge, powerful animals in skin boats with bone harpoons. To have such a beast delivered to their own shore without risking any lives was a gift of the little mother of the sea. Soon the process of turning the whale into a mountain of meat, oil, and bones would begin.

But even before she got there Ana heard shouting voices, and saw raised fists and shaken spears.

'Snailheads,' Zesi murmured. 'That's all we need.'

A group of the strangers were confronting the gathering Etxelur folk. The snailheads, here for the Giving, were led by Knuckle, the man Ana had met at the summer camp, who faced Jaku, uncle of Ana and Zesi. These two were screaming in each other's faces. Etxelur folk and snailheads, gathered round, were joining in, backing their champions and yelling insults. All this was played out beneath the huge, sad eye of the dying whale.

The priest tried to get between the arguing men. 'What's this about?'

The snailhead, Knuckle, roared in his broken traders' tongue, 'Our find! Ours! Our fish!'

Jaku laughed. 'It's a whale, you fool. A whale, not a fish. Don't you have whales where you come from? Maybe you don't. Why don't you snailheads just go home?'

The Root boomed laughter. 'Like day-old calves butting heads.'

Knuckle stared at him, and switched to the traders' tongue. 'Pretani?' And he saw Shade behind his father. '*You*.' He marched towards Shade. The man's extraordinary elongated skull, painted today with green spirals, had veins that throbbed at each temple. 'You! Brother of the man who killed *my* brother. I told you at the camp – stay out of my sight.'

The Root growled, 'You don't tell a Pretani what to do.'

'I see your ugly face. Father of killer?'

Root glared at the priest. 'What did he say? Tell me, priest.'

Jurgi, exasperated and alarmed, twisted his hands together. 'He said – it doesn't matter what he said—'

But then the arguments began again, everybody shouting, Jaku, Knuckle, the Root, Zesi, their followers waving fists and spears and knives, and the priest crying out for order, a three-way fight conducted in four languages, if you counted the traders' tongue.

Ana pulled out of the angry mass, dismayed. She looked up at the whale's huge eye. She was so close to it she could smell the sea on it, see the barnacles that peppered its flesh. The eye rolled, and she thought it looked down on her.

And somebody was clapping, above the fighting. Clap, clap, clap, steady as a heartbeat.

'The priest's right,' came a voice in the traders' tongue. 'Who said what, it doesn't matter. You're all so busy squabbling you forget what's important – the whale, whose life is being given up for you.'

The clapping was having a quieting effect; the squabbling groups shut up and turned to see. The voice was coming from above her – *on top of the whale*.

'And besides,' came the voice, 'if a whale is *driven* ashore, as this one was, the ownership goes to the one who did the driving. Isn't that the custom, priest? Sorry we've been away so long. But you have to admit we brought home a decent present for the Giving.'

Ana stepped back until she could see two men standing on top of the whale, one taller, the other heavier, the latter apparently winded by the effort of climbing up there. They were silhouetted against the sky, but she knew who they were immediately.

She couldn't move. She could barely think.

Zesi's shriek broke the silence. 'Father!' She ran forward and pressed her hands against the whale's damp flank.

Kirike knelt and reached down to Zesi; the whale was so big that, reaching up on her tiptoes, she could only just touch his fingers. He looked around until he saw Ana, and smiled at her.

Somebody started applauding, one of the Etxelur folk. One by one others joined in. The rest, the snailheads and the Pretani, just stared, bemused.

The priest was shaking his head. 'Trust Kirike and Heni to make such a show of coming home. But it's the will of the little mothers that they should show up on the very day the Root and his boys arrive . . .'

Ana still couldn't move. None of this seemed real.

A woman approached her, walking around the head of the whale. She was tall, with rich dark hair tied back in a knot. She wore skins that were stained by salt water, and she carried a baby, a lump no more than weeks old. She looked tired, but oddly resilient. 'You must be Zesi, or—'

'Ana.'

'Your father told me all about you.' Her language was the Etxelur tongue, spoken slowly but clearly enough. The woman staggered, and tucked the baby closer to her chest, and smiled. 'Forgive me. We have been at sea for moons.'

'Months.'

'Months. Yes . . . I have forgotten the land, how to stand. I am Ice Dreamer. I hope we will be friends.'

A dog yapped. It was Lightning, racing across the sand, come to greet his long-lost master.

25

Ana lay back in the crook of her father's arm. He was drinking a nettle tea she had made him. Lightning lay on Kirike's other side, contentedly curled up against his leg.

They were in their home. The afternoon had grown ferociously hot. There was plenty going on outside – she could hear the shouts of the people beginning the long process of butchering the whale, and even from here she could smell the sharp stink of blood and blubber and brine – but she was grateful for some time in the shade. And after so long in his boat, Kirike said, so was he.

He didn't *smell* like her father, not yet. There was too much of the sea on him. And she thought he had lost weight, grown greyer – grown old in the nine months he had been away. Grown that bit stranger. But she didn't care. It was *him*, solid and alive, as if back from the dead; she had him back, and there was nowhere else she wanted to be but here with him.

But the stranger was here too, the woman he had brought back with her baby. She was sitting with the priest, talking quietly. Even her name was odd: *Ice Dreamer*.

They were trying to work out where she had come from, how far away was the land where Kirike had picked her up. They had lifted the mats from the floor, and the priest scrawled a map in the dirt, showing the familiar countries, Albia, Gaira, and Northland between, and a vaguer sketch of what lay to the west, mostly picked up from traders' tales: a warm sea to the south, a cold, icebound ocean to the north, and beyond a greater ocean to the west a vast continent. Dreamer spoke of her land, which was evidently a big, complicated place of lakes and forests and ice. But she was even vaguer than the priest, for as a child she had grown up far from any sea, believing she lived on an endless plain – just land, going on for ever. She hadn't even known the ocean existed.

Neither recognised what the other drew, and there seemed no way of connecting them up, save for a dim impression of Kirike and Heni's westward journey, hopping between rocky islands and ice floes, and then a similar step-by-step journey back.

'It is as if we inhabit different worlds,' the priest said, doodling with his stick. 'Ours to the east, yours to the west. Connected only by an accidental journey that might never be made again . . .'

Dreamer was sitting cross-legged with her baby on her lap. Out of her heavy skins, she wore a light tunic over her heavy breasts. Her face was well defined, the bones of her cheeks high, her brow proud, her nose thin and straight. She was beautiful, Ana thought, watching her. Strange, beautiful.

Dreamer shifted to see what Jurgi was sketching now. He had drawn three concentric circles, a line piercing to the centre. Unthinking, he'd drawn it over Etxelur in his map. Dreamer asked, 'What is this? I see that sign everywhere here, on your houses, carved into the rocks. Even on people's faces. I have seen it in my own country.'

'You have?'

'We saw it carved in the rocks,' Kirike called over. 'Over the beach where we picked her up.'

'The sign is very old,' the priest said. 'It means many things. For one thing, we use it to remember the better world of the past.'

Kirike grunted. 'When Etxelur was strong, and did not have to take insults from a bull-man like the Root.'

'But I think it means other things too,' Jurgi said. 'Circles come back to where they started. As the moon and sun cycle in the sky, as the seasons give way one to another, always

155

returning.' He glanced at Dreamer's baby. 'As a baby girl is born, who grows to be a woman, and gives birth in turn.'

'Maybe he has drawn sharks and dolphins swimming around a boat,' Kirike said.

Ice Dreamer flashed him a smile, bright in the dark.

Ana didn't know what they meant. They shared memories, experiences she didn't. She felt an odd, unworthy pang. Resentment. Jealousy. Ugly emotions she didn't like to recognise in herself.

Ice Dreamer said to Jurgi, 'Much separates us. Your language is like none I ever heard.'

'That isn't so much,' said the priest. 'The traders who cross the Continent by the valleys of the great rivers say that everywhere languages are spoken that are as different from mine as mine is from yours.'

'But she did not speak the traders' tongue, even,' Kirike said.

'Even so, Ice Dreamer, much more unites us than divides us. You are human. Two arms, two legs—'

'Half a belly, or at least that's how it feels.'

'I can tell you,' Kirike said now, 'she's the same inside as we are. If not, she wouldn't be here now.'

The priest said, 'Nothing here seems so very strange to you, does it? Nothing about the way we live.'

'No. We too have houses. Spears. Fires, hearths. Only the small things are different.'

'But what of the greater things – the greatest of all?'

'You mean the gods.'

'The stories of the past, of those who made the world, and destroyed it,' said the priest. They looked at each other, suddenly curious.

As they spoke of ice giants and wolves in the sky, Kirike hugged Ana closer and kissed the top of her head. 'I'm sorry I missed your blood tide.'

'It was fine. Mama Sunta was there, and the priest, and Zesi . . . They helped me. But my Other is an owl.'

'So Jurgi told me. Your Other can represent many things,' he said gently. 'I'm sure the priest has told you that. And everything has its place. The night needs the owl as a summer's day needs the swallow.'

'Am I the night, then? Am I death?'

'No. But you're a much more serious girl than the one I left behind, and I'm sorry about that. And I'm sorry about your sister too.' He looked towards the open flap of the tent, as if hoping Zesi would suddenly appear, or fearing it. 'She's hardly spoken a word to me since I came back.'

'I love you,' Ana said. 'I missed you. She loves you. But she's angry.'

'Why? Because I went away?'

Ana said carefully, not wanting to be disloyal, 'She *liked* having all the responsibility. As Giver, as senior woman of the house . . . Even though she complained about it all the time. What people say isn't always what they mean, is it?'

'No, child, it isn't.'

'Did you know she told the Root she would take the wildwood challenge?'

'No.' His muscles hardened, his grip on her tightening. 'I won't allow *that*. I'd rather go myself. Those Pretani animals don't go into their wildwood to play, but to earn their killing scars.'

She snuggled in closer. 'You'd better tell her that yourself.'

The priest and Ice Dreamer seemed to have finished telling each other their stories.

'Different stories, but the same elements,' the priest said. 'The birth of the world in ice and fire, the coming of death . . .' He massaged his temples. 'I think these stories are not lies. I think our first mother was real, and your Sky Wolf was real. It is a consolation of humanity that we aren't born with the memories of ten thousand generations of misery. Each new mind is as bright as a celandine in spring, and as empty of thought. But the bad thing is we forget the past – what to do when the rainstorm comes, how the world was made. This is why we need grandmothers, and priests. To remember for us.'

'Yes. My people believe the world was different, before. Better. Then it was ruined, by ice and cold. Now lesser people own the world, and we are the last of those who went before. In fact I may be the last of all – or my baby is.' The baby woke up coughing, and cried. Dreamer held her on her lap and looked down at her, concerned. 'Oh, child, what's wrong?' She murmured something in her own unknown tongue.

Kirike took his arm from around his daughter's shoulders, and crossed to the woman and huddled with her over the baby, his back to Ana. Lightning followed him, curious, wagging his tail. Ana was left alone.

26

Novu could *hear* Etxelur long before he saw it. It was the drumming that carried furthest inland, and occasional snatches of song.

Loga led his party down a broadening river valley towards a marshy estuary. It was a bright, clear morning, the sun still low in the east. Novu was laden with trade goods, as was Loga, and indeed so were his two wives and their children. The ground was thick with green bracken that clawed at their legs and towered over the smaller children, and it was hard going.

But on this warm midsummer day the world was dense with life, birds singing vigorously, the birch trees heavy with leaves, flowers like foxgloves and irises clustering in open spaces, dragonflies humming over open water. All of this was still alien to Novu, who didn't even have names for many of the living things he came across in this strange, damp, green, western country. But he was impressed with the abundance of life. This place made Jericho with its fields of grain look barren.

Now Loga led his party up an animal track over a softly eroded ridge, and the view opened up to the north, and Novu saw Etxelur at last.

Trails ran down from this ridge to a bank of grassy dunes that fringed a beach of yellow sand. Seven houses, squat and purposeful, a vivid green, stood behind the dunes, and smoke threads rose into the still air. The beach was at the outlet of a bay, much of which was fringed by flat, marshy land where water glimmered, blue-green. To the north the bay was closed by a causeway that led to an island, a lump of sandstone fringed by beaches of shingle and sand. And beyond that lay only the sea, stretching to the horizon, flat and perfect. There were more houses everywhere, on the beaches and the dunes and in the marshes, houses that were cones and half-balls, all of them the brown of reeds or the green of seaweed. You had to look closely to see them; aside from the rising smoke, they looked natural, like something washed up by the sea, not human at all.

Novu took a breath of fresh, salty air. A place more unlike Jericho, its harsh landscape and walls of brick and stone, was hard to imagine. Yet he sensed this was a good place. And he heard that drumming again.

Loga was looking at him suspiciously.

'What?'

'Smiling. You. Why?'

'I don't know.' He held out his arms. 'Beautiful day. Beautiful place. People happy; I can hear them. And I'm young and fit and unusually good-looking.' He did a few steps of a hopping dance, which made the younger wife giggle as she cradled her infant. 'Why not smile?'

'Suit yourself,' Loga grunted. 'We go that way.' He pointed west. 'They're all on the island, the far side. We cut around the bay and take that causeway. Sea rises up soon. Walk quick or we swim,' he snapped at the women and children, and strode off down a fresh trail.

They trudged on, their faces drawn. They had been walking since dawn. Novu, feeling benevolent, reached down and lifted the pack off the back of the youngest walker, a six-year-old boy. He grinned his thanks and went running ahead, chasing butter- flies. Loga made no comment.

'So,' Novu asked, 'why the celebration?'

'Solstice.' Loga pointed at the rising sun. 'All people celebrate midsummer, different ways. Here, the Giving feast. Big event for all people around, people of the coast, of the land. People happy. Good trade.' He grinned, dreaming of profit.

'You're all heart, my friend.'

'What?'

'Never mind.'

It wasn't long before they had rounded the marshy land at the end of the bay, and then walked out along the causeway, a remarkable strip of land that cut the sea in two. The world was flat here, a panorama of mud flats and the brutal plain of the sea, fringed by lumpy sand dunes and the bulk of Flint Island. But the island was still so far away that the mist washed out its colours to a blue-grey, so that it looked unreal, a marking on a wall, not solid at all. The sea, at this time of the tide, was far away from their feet, and the causeway was a trail that led across a broad stretch of mud flats. Grass grew here, long, tough stuff. But you could tell the sea had been here recently. The grass was beaten down, there were standing pools of brackish water, and there was a tide line above the path they were following, marked by a litter of broken shells and seaweed tangles. This was an odd, eerie place, suspended between two worlds – a place where grass grew, yet which was daily covered over by the sea.

A crowd of curlews dipped and swooped overhead, making their odd chuckling cry.

After the causeway, they rounded a last sandstone bluff and came to a long, broad beach facing north, fringed by a line of dunes. The beach was thronged with people, slim figures busy everywhere, silhouetted against the brilliant light reflecting off the sea. He heard laughing, shouting, singing, the shrieks of the children splashing in the clean blue sea – many, many children, swarming around the adults. There must be hundreds of people here, he thought, not as many as in Jericho, but a larger gathering than any he had encountered since leaving home. Smoke rose up from scores of fires, and cooking smells reached Novu, even here at the western end of the beach, meat and salty fish.

Loga led his party along the beach, to a patch of dry sand between the shoulders of two dunes. 'This will do. Shelter from the wind if it picks up.' He glanced around. 'Bit far from centre, the middens. Better to be closer, for passing trade. Arrive too late.' He glared at one of the children. 'If that one not sick, we'd have gained a day.' But he shrugged.

The women settled wearily to the sand.

Novu dropped his pack. 'I'll go take a look around.'

Loga grunted, indifferent, unfolding his skin packs.

Novu walked along the beach. After a while he slipped off his boots, slung them over his shoulder, and walked on the fringe of the sea where the sand was wet. His feet, hardened by months of steady walking, enjoyed the crisp coolness of the water, the softness of the sand.

There were many different communities here, he soon saw, gathered on this bright beach. Folk evidently from the estuaries had their flat-bottomed skin boats drawn up on the beach, and wooden trays of eels and strange-looking crustaceans set out on the sand. Ocean fishers had bigger, deeper boats and racks of fish, with some spectacular catches on display; one huge cod looked longer than Novu was tall. A group of goat herders had a dozen animals penned up inside a wicker fence, reinforced by posts thrust into the sand. Another group who evidently hailed from the forests inland had set up a pole, a tree trunk stripped of branches and bark and carved along its length with distorted faces, images of gods perhaps.

The people themselves were all different too. The men with the god-pole wore trousers cut away to leave their crotches exposed, and Novu, wincing, saw that their dangling cocks had been sliced and stitched and tattooed. He saw heads shaven bald, or with hair raised in sticky spikes, and skin adorned with tattoos in black, red and even green, and distortions of noses and ear lobes and necks and even heads stretched like great tubers. Another group of estuary folk wore skulls heaped upon their heads like hats. All these groups spoke in their own languages, all of them sounding different from anything even Novu the hardened traveller had heard before.

But this was a day of sharing, evidently, and he heard people chatting in the traders' argot as they gave each other fuel for the fires and swapped food, a bit of fish for a slice of meat. And the

162

children who played in the surf and in the rocky pools, many of them naked, seemed entirely unaware of their differences as they ran and swam and chased and shouted and played with their barking dogs, big skulls, dangling ear lobes, tattooed buttocks and all.

He reached what seemed to be the central part of the beach. Here, before the dunes to his right, he saw odd, curving formations – almost like walls, almost like something from Jericho. Close to he could see they were middens, banks of shells and other waste, but carefully shaped. And before them stood a wooden structure, a kind of stage of wood planks set on piles driven into the sand, with a curve that roughly followed the crescent shapes of the middens. Poles stood around the stage, and trophies dangled in the air: the skin of a bear, the toothsome jaw of some huge fish, and flags of hide bearing a symbol: concentric circles cut by a dark radius. Nobody was on the stage for now, but maybe this would be the focus of the 'Giving' that Loga had mentioned – whatever that meant.

He stood in the middle of the beach, alone, surrounded by groups, families. He felt oddly excluded, out of place. He wondered if he should go back to Loga and his family. But he didn't really belong there either.

He noticed a woman sitting alone, save for a baby wriggling on a skin on the sand beside her. Bare-legged, sitting up straight, she was tall, striking, with black hair pulled back from a fine-boned face, and a slightly darker complexion than those around her. She had a pile of stones, big rough-cut flint blades, and she was working on one, holding it over a leather apron on her lap and pressing its face with a bone tool. Bits of flint were scattered on the sand before her. Concentrating on her work, alone with her baby, she seemed utterly unaware of the clamour around her.

Drums pounded suddenly, making Novu jump. And then came a roar. He turned and saw a deer running along the beach, a huge one, its fur bright brown in the sunlight, its head ducking, antlers like tree branches splayed. To Novu's astonishment, children were running *towards* the animal, clapping and smiling, and he heard music, the piping of flutes and whistles, clatters and rasps.

But as the beast approached he saw it wasn't a deer at all, but a skin stretched over a frame of bone and wood. A bull of a man ran at the front, brandishing the great head on a pole, while under the skin children in ornate clothing played whistles and shook rattles, all of them carved from white bones. Behind the deer came more men whirling bits of shaped bone on ropes in the air; it was these that made the rhythmic roaring sound.

The deer hurried past, trailed by excited children, and continued up the beach.

Somebody spoke to him. He turned. The striking woman on the beach had been joined by a girl, who knelt beside her – red-haired, younger, slimmer, with a rather serious expression. She wore a tunic that was cut open at the waist to reveal a belly marked with a tattoo of concentric circles, like the sign on the flags, and a smaller mark on her hip in the shape of an owl.

The flint-making woman was smiling at him.

He hadn't understood their words. 'I'm sorry,' he said in the traders' tongue.

The girl said, 'I just asked if you were all right. The music deer made you jump.'

'It was a shock.'

The older woman swept a bit of sand smooth with her forearm. 'Please,' she said, her accent different from the girl's.

He sat beside her.

'The deer runs at every Giving,' the girl said. 'It is the start of the day, in a way. You never saw the deer before? This is your first time here?'

'Oh, yes. And I've come a long way to be here.' He sipped from his water skin, and offered it to the women, who shook their heads. 'My name is Novu.'

'Ana.'

'Ice Dreamer.'

These names were strange to Novu, but he was used to that. 'Ana. You live here?'

'Yes. Etxelur is my home. My father is the Giver today—'

'I meant to ask you about that,' said the woman, Ice Dreamer. 'He got Zesi to agree in the end?'

'Not without a fight. And in return he had to agree to let her go on the wildwood hunt with the Pretani, and he wasn't happy about *that*.'

'I can imagine.'

Ana looked at Novu. 'Zesi is my sister.'

'Ah. And what exactly is this Giving?'

'Everybody comes together and gives everything they bring,' Ana said. 'My father organises it. We have plenty to give ourselves, oils and meat from a whale, the produce of the sea—'

'We have a similar custom in my country,' Ice Dreamer said. 'Every summer we would come together and share. Those who had gone short in the winter are helped by the generosity of their neighbours.'

'Knowing that next year it might be their turn to give.'

'That's the idea. So why are you here? To Give?'

'No,' Novu said. 'I came with a trader. He hopes to do business. I travel with him, but I don't trade.'

'Then what do you do?'

'I make bricks.' He used a Jericho word; there was no word in the traders' tongue.

Ana frowned. 'What is a—'

How do you describe a brick? 'A block.' He mimed with his hands. 'Made of clay and straw. Like a stone.'

Ana pointed. 'There are stones lying around all over the place.'

'Not like my bricks.'

'What do you do with them?'

'Build houses.'

That made her laugh. 'We make houses out of wood and seaweed.' She pushed a wisp of her red-gold hair out of her

165

eyes, her freckled face scrunched up against the sun. 'Is this place different from where you come from?'

'It couldn't be more different.'

'Do you like it, though?'

Novu glanced around, at the sea, the beach, the children, the laughing people. 'Yes,' he said. 'It would be good to stay here for a time. Though I've no idea what I'd do here.'

'Make *bricks*,' Ice Dreamer said, and she laughed too.

A man's voice could be heard shouting, before the platform.

Ana jumped up. 'The races! I'll talk to you later, Ice Dreamer. And you—'

'Novu.'

'Yes.' She stared at him for one heartbeat longer, then ran off.

Dreamer picked up her baby, sitting her on her lap.

Novu touched an unfinished blade. It was bigger than any spear point he'd ever seen, longer than his outstretched hand when he laid it on his palm. The shape of a leaf, it had two worked faces, a fine edge, and peculiar fluting channels down at the thicker end.

'I haven't been here long either,' Ice Dreamer said now. 'Ana's a good kid. Reserved, mixed up, but good-hearted.'

'I never saw a blade like this before.'

'It is the way my people, the True People, always made them.' She pointed. 'You see, you use pressure from the bone tools to work either side of the blank, shaping the edge. And then the fluting, which is used to attach the blade more firmly to its shaft – you knock out a thin section of flint to achieve that.'

'It's bigger than any blade I've seen.'

'It is meant to bring down bigger animals than you have seen, I imagine. Bigger even than the music deer. I have made these before, but under instruction . . . My craft is poor. But I will improve with practice.'

He blurted, 'Could I have one of these?'

She seemed surprised. He continually had to remind himself that people generally didn't want *things*, not outside Jericho. But she said, 'Of course. Come back when I've finished one.'

He nodded. 'Thank you . . . Where is your country?'

'To the west of here.' She pointed at the sea. 'Further west than you can imagine. And yours?'

'Further east than *you* can imagine.'

'We are both far from home, then.'

'We are.'

She asked, 'Why did you come here?'

'It was more a case of leaving home. And you?'

'That's a long story.'

'I have time,' he said.

'And so do I. Here. Hold the baby, while I try to finish this blade . . .'

The baby was warm in his lap, heavy, and he thought she smiled at him.

27

The dozen runners jostled behind the line scratched by the Giver in the sand.

Shade, braced to run, looked along an empty stretch of beach lined by cheering children. It looked an awfully long way to the prize at the far end, a big convoluted shell full of rattling stones that hung from a pole. Only one man could grab that shell; only one man could win the race. The day was hot, the sun high, and the dry sand was soft under his feet and would be tiring to run on – which, of course, was the idea. After a morning of sports he was already exhausted. The sun had got to him too; his skin, used to the shelter of the forest, was red raw across his back and belly and thighs.

And Knuckle, a snailhead with a grudge, was right alongside him, itching for the race to start.

Zesi stood watching beside her father, the Giver. Arga held her hand, the little girl holding her own trophies of shells and beads that she had won in the children's deep-diving contests; she looked excited and happy. Zesi was brave enough to smile at Shade. He dared not smile back.

Now his father came up behind him. Even in the bright sunlight the Root wore his finery of bull skin and skull. Shade could smell smoke on him, rich, tangy fumes. The Root had spent much of the day in the dreaming house, as the Etxelur folk called it, where the leaders smoked pipes full of dried weed, and burned strange logs, and breathed the vapours from seeds cast on hot stones – all prepared by the Etxelur priest, who wore a crown of poppies today – plants brought here from far away, for they did not grow in Etxelur – and a huge axe of creamy, beautiful flint was suspended from a rope around his neck.

The Root leaned over his son. 'We lost the fishing challenges.'

'We are hunters,' Shade hissed. 'Not fishers.'

'Yes, but we lost the spear-throwing as well.' His speech was slightly slurred. 'We couldn't begin to compete in the dolphin riding. The Giver himself won most of the swimming races.'

'Is that my fault?'

'I won't go away a loser,' the Root said softly, sinister. 'If Gall were here he'd win his challenges one way or another.'

'But he's not here, is he?'

'No. All I've got is you. And if you're any son of mine, you won't – lose – this – race.' He straightened up and backed away.

Knuckle, standing beside Shade, growled, 'I follow your cow language.' He was sweating hard, that extraordinary long skull coated in sand, and his tongue when he showed it had a huge stone plug sticking through it, obscuring his speech.

'Leave me alone, snailhead.'

'I will leave you alone in a heartbeat, when race runs. But make it interesting. If you beat me I have reward for you. See our priest, down there by the shell? Today we make our boys into men, into truth-tellers. If you beat me we make you one of us.' He ruffled Shade's hair. 'Don't worry, not touch your pretty skull. An honour – for a man. Are you a man, little boy?'

'Do your talking in the race, Knuckle.'

'Oh, I will . . .'

Kirike pulled a bull roarer around his head, once, twice, three times. Lightning jumped around his feet, excited as the rest. The watching people hushed.

Shade lined up with the others, as the runners jostled and pushed. He had the feeling it would be more of a long fight than a true race.

Kirike released the bull roarer. The bit of bone sailed in the air. The crowd yelled. Drums sounded like thunder.

Shade lurched forward, fighting for space between strong, pressing bodies.

169

But before he had made three strides he got a punch between the shoulder blades that laid him out flat on the ground. Heavy feet trampled over his back, and his face was pressed in the sand.

As soon as they were clear he pushed himself to his feet and ran. Most of the runners were already far ahead of him, and people were pointing, children laughing at him. He wasn't the worst off; two others had fallen and lay without moving.

And Knuckle looked back, grinning. It was too much to bear.

Shade ignored the rest and threw himself after the snailhead. When he got close enough he lunged headlong, arms out-stretched, not caring how his sunburned skin scraped over the hot sand, and with one reaching hand clipped the snailhead's heel. Knuckle fell. This time Shade was first up. He ran over Knuckle, stepping on the snailhead's swollen skull for good measure, and hurtled after the rest.

The watching people screamed and shook their fists, willing on their favourites.

An Etxelur boy, skinny as rope, was first, to collect the winner's shell.

But Shade had beaten the snailhead. Surrounded by the runners' families, the Root stood with his arms folded. Shade knew he wasn't about to be praised for failing to win, but he had fought off the challenge of the snailhead, and Shade could see a kind of grim satisfaction in his father's face under the bull's black muzzle.

Knuckle grabbed his lower arm, sweating, panting, evidently winded from his fall. 'Well done, boy. You fought dirtier than me.'

'I did, didn't I?' Shade tried to shake his arm free.

But Knuckle was strong. 'I made promise. Come on – priest over there.'

The snailhead priest was a skinny man who looked extra-ordinarily old, with a tube-like head grotesque even by snail-head standards. He grinned and waggled his tongue at Shade; it contained a plug of stone so wide he couldn't close his mouth around it.

Knuckle said, 'I told you – honour you. Today you become a truth-talker, one of us. Oh, don't look for your father. I spoke to him. He knows. Doesn't mind a little pain for you.'

Shade saw it. 'You're going to make a hole in my tongue, aren't you?'

'Clever boy. Here.' He held out a narrow flint blade, very sharp, blood-stained, and folded Shade's fingers around it. 'When priest working, squeeze hard.'

'I'll cut my palm to shreds.'

'True. But you forget other agonies . . .'

Now the priest stepped forward. Because of his own tongue plug he could barely speak, but his mime was clear enough. He had a bone needle that he would push up through Shade's tongue. That would be followed by a length of aurochs horn, narrow-tipped but quickly widening. And then would come the stone plug, as wide as Shade's thumb. The priest beckoned with one hand, holding the needle with the other, while Knuckle shoved him forward.

But a snailhead woman ran up. It was Eyelid. She had her baby on her hip, but she was pointing. 'There.' And she gabbled snailhead speech so fast Shade couldn't follow.

Knuckle screamed in anger. He immediately let go of Shade and went running.

Shade turned to see. A group of snailhead men had hold of a struggling figure. The Root and his Pretani hunters were running over too.

The man the snailheads held was Shade's brother, Gall.

For the second time that day, Shade ran after Knuckle.

At the centre of a mob, Knuckle faced Gall. Both were held back by their countrymen, snailheads and Pretani. Others were running up, even children, intoxicated by excitement, eager to see the day's latest spectacle. Kirike the Giver came running up too, pulling people away; his daughters followed, Zesi with an anguished expression on her face.

171

The Root forced his way through, brushing lesser men aside. Shade ran after his father.

Gall was filthy, ragged. He must have been living wild for months, since the incident at the summer camp. But tracks ran down his muddy, sand-coated face, as if he had been weeping. Knuckle, the muscles in his neck distended, was screaming abuse in his face, in his own language. As he strode up, the Root roared back in the Pretani tongue.

'Enough,' Kirike cried, trying to force his way through. 'Enough! Speak in the traders' tongue, all of you. What has been happening here while I've been away? Who is this man?'

'My son,' the Root rumbled.

'I saw you were here,' Gall said, his voice thick. 'Father – I have not been far from here. I hunted. I lived as a man – but alone. And when I saw you—'

'When you saw me, what?' the Root said, silencing him. 'Did you expect me to fix the mess you have made for yourself? Did you expect me to take you home like a lost calf? What sort of a man expects that?'

Kirike asked again, 'What has happened here? Knuckle, what do you want?'

Knuckle pushed his face at Gall. 'I want to know why this man killed my brother, and then ran away.'

'Is this true?'

The Root glared at his son. 'Well?'

'Yes! Yes, I killed Gut! I can hardly deny it – all saw the spear thrown – it was a good kill, father, clean. Look at my brow. I fixed my own kill-tattoo.' There were two lines cut into his forehead now, Shade saw, one more ragged than the other, and half-healed.

But the Root showed no pleasure. 'A man does not kill for no reason. Why? What had this snailhead done to you?'

'Nothing,' Gall admitted.

'Nothing? Nothing?' Knuckle was screaming now. 'Then why kill him?'

As if goaded, Gall yelled, 'Because I could not kill my own brother!'

There was a shocked silence. Shade felt his own face burn. Zesi covered her eyes.

Kirike asked quick, incisive questions, and the truth came out. Gall had raged at the developing love between Zesi and Shade. Unable to cope with the consequences of striking down his brother, he had taken out his anger on a snailhead whose only crime had been to flirt briefly with Zesi.

The Root glared at his sons. 'Let him go.' He nodded to his hunters. 'And you, Shade, come here. Stand before your brother. Let us speak the truth. When I sent you here I knew of Kirike's two daughters. I promised the elder, Zesi, to Gall as a bride . . .'

'You might have spoken to me first,' Zesi snapped. 'What am I, a piece of meat to be traded by strangers?'

The priest held her arm, his ornamental axe gleaming on his chest.

The Root said to Shade, 'Yet you took the woman for yourself.'

Shade looked at Zesi, despairing. 'It wasn't like that—'

The Root said levelly, 'You dishonoured your brother, and yourself. You dishonoured me. And you, Gall, in your rage and your cowardice – you should have faced your brother – you took a stranger's life without purpose, and fled from the consequences. You too have dishonoured me.'

He took his sons' upper arms and held them both before him, face to face. Shade was shocked by the hatred in Gall's face – and yet this was a man who had destroyed himself, effectively, rather than take his brother's life. Gall's one act of fraternal loyalty, the only one Shade could remember in his life, even if it had come accompanied by a killing.

The Root pronounced, 'Hear me now, all of you, you Pretani and you lesser folk. There is bad blood between my sons. That blood must be let. Otherwise it will fester. From now on I will

173

have only one son. Only one of you will walk away from this place. Which one is up to you.'

Shade said, 'You can't—'

Gall growled, 'He can.'

The Root said, 'You others, you snailheads. You stand here and see me lose a son. Whichever of them survives, will you accept that as vengeance for your loss?'

The snailheads looked at Knuckle, who nodded, curtly.

'Then let it be done—'

And Gall's hands were immediately at Shade's throat, massive, unbelievably powerful, crushing his windpipe. Gall, taller, pressed down; Shade fought to stay standing.

The surrounding people, shocked, stood back. Zesi cried out and might have run forward, but her father and sister held her back.

But Shade still had the snailhead knife in his hand – the toy knife meant to get him through the pain of the tongue stud. He worked it in his grip, pushing out the blade.

Gall, grunting with exertion, said through clenched teeth, 'Brother, I should have finished you off that day at the camp. I should have strangled you at birth—'

And Shade drove the knife into his brother's belly, under his tunic, straight into the flesh and through muscle walls, guts.

Gall grunted like a speared ox. Still he stood, though foam flecked his mouth and his eyes bulged. And still he crushed Shade's throat. Shade, unable to breathe, saw him as if at the end of a holloway, long and deep and dark.

And so Shade braced himself, and pushed the blade upwards under Gall's ribs and into his heart. Gall shuddered and groaned, and hot blood gushed over Shade's hands, arms, stomach. At last those gripping fingers released their hold.

Gall fell forward on to Shade. He was heavy, and Shade, weakened, bloody, could barely hold him. But he lowered his brother to the ground, gently, and knelt over him.

The Root glared down at them, expressionless. Then he turned and walked away.

A wider ring of people stood, shocked, their mouths wide with horror. Ana had her arms around Zesi, who could not look at Shade.

Kirike came forward. 'Come,' he said. 'We'll clean you up – we'll take care of your brother, we'll talk to your priest—'

There was a rumble, like thunder, or an immense drum. It came from out to sea. People turned to the north, to the ocean, distracted, even Kirike, even Shade.

And a single wave, almost stately, anomalously tall, came washing from the sea to break high up the beach.

TWO

28

All across the northern hemisphere tremendous masses were on the move, as ice melted and water flowed. Under this pressure the seabeds suffered their own spasms of compression and release. Huge subsurface salt deposits, relics of previous eras of drying, shifted and cracked – weak points in the rocky substructure, their failure causing uplift and fracturing on the surface.

Far to the north of Etxelur the seabed was particularly unstable. As the ice had receded over Scandinavia, rivers swollen by meltwater had eroded away whole landscapes and deposited the debris in the shallow ocean – the ruins of mountains and valleys dumped in fans and scree slopes and undersea dunes. This gigantic spill was never in equilibrium; it had been deposited too quickly for that.

Huge volumes of mud slid and settled in the deep dark. Strange weather systems gathered over the restless seabed, ocean storms whose rumbling thunder could be heard far away.

Given enough time, a more significant adjustment was inevitable.

29

It was a half-month after the midsummer Giving that the party for the wildwood hunt gathered outside Zesi's house.

When Zesi emerged, her tied-up pack in her hands, the Pretani were already there, ready to leave. The dozen hunters, bristling with spears, were laden with sacks of salted meat and the fruit of the sea. The food was a gift from Etxelur, from Kirike. The most precious gift of all was a small sack of herbs, unguents and seeds, prepared by the priest, a souvenir of the dreaming house, sophisticated beyond anything the Pretani could produce. On a late summer morning that was already hot, the Root stood outside the house, arms folded, massive in his skins, silent and unmoving as an oak tree. The Root would lead the walk. The Pretani would have it no other way. Kirike stood with him, talking quietly.

Shade stood by his father, face blank, eyes downcast. He wouldn't look at Zesi.

And now Jurgi the priest walked up to the party, pack on his back. Zesi felt her temper burn.

Zesi, the chosen challenger from Etxelur, was allowed one travelling companion. Her father had brusquely rejected her selection of various hard-bodied, hot-headed young men. To her horror and amazement he chose Jurgi – a priest, who had gone through none of the challenges and rites of manhood, who hunted only for exercise, who had never had a woman.

'Yet he is the one,' Kirike had said, stern and unmoving.

'It's supposed to be my choice!'

His blue eyes were bright with anger. 'You're lucky I'm

allowing you to go at all. You have no control. It is said that in my absence it was as if the community was being led by a child. And by lying with the Pretani boy you brought shame on us all, and caused anger and death to be brought into the heart of the Giving – death at the midsummer solstice. You know I'm not one for omens. Pray that the little mothers are more forgiving than I am.'

'But Jurgi is scarcely a man at all!'

'He's a better human being than you'll ever be. I trust him to keep you safe, and from doing more harm.' And he had walked away, refusing to discuss it further.

Zesi had seethed. She knew better than to argue when she was beaten. But now that old anger and humiliation returned.

Jurgi wore a simple cloth tunic, leggings and boots of softened deerskin, and as well as his pack he carried a hide cloak, warm and waterproof, tied over one shoulder. He wore none of his priest's finery, his face was scrubbed clean save for the circle-and-line tattoo on his cheek, and the thick greasy blue dye in his hair had been washed out leaving it a natural brown. He looked normal until he grinned at her, showing his wooden teeth.

'Just don't shame me, priest.'

'I'll do my very best.'

A few more of the folk of Etxelur were gathering now, to see off the party. Ana came out of the house and took Zesi's hands. 'I wish you weren't doing this.'

Zesi glanced over at Shade. 'And I wish things were different. I wish Gall still breathed, disgusting fool that he was.'

'It was all the fault of the Root's scheming. We shouldn't let it come between us.'

Zesi looked hard at her sister, for the first time in a long age. Ana had always just *been* here, in the background of her life, not objectionable, never very interesting. But now she was growing into a woman. She was thinner, paler than Zesi – less beautiful, Zesi knew. But she was more serious, more dependable than Zesi was, probably. A better person. And in the middle of this

181

mess, a better friend than Zesi deserved. Zesi hugged her, impulsively. 'I'm sorry.'

Ana, hesitant, hugged her back. 'What for?'

'I don't know. For all I've done, and for all the horrible things I'll do in the future, that will hurt you one way or another. For that's what I'm like, you know.'

'Well, that's true,' Ana said dryly, making Zesi laugh. 'But we'll always be sisters. No matter what we do we can't wipe that away.'

'I wish I had your wisdom.'

'And I wish I had your eyebrows. Now go, and keep safe.'

Arga came running up, followed by a bouncing Lightning. Arga was crying. 'I slept late! I nearly missed you!' She grabbed Zesi's waist, and Lightning jumped up at them. 'If you'd gone before I could say goodbye—'

'It's only a couple of months.' But Arga looked up, her round face streaked with tears, and Zesi saw that two months was a long time in such a young life. 'I'll be back before the summer is done.' Gently she pushed Arga away. 'I'll teach you dolphin riding.'

'Ha! Or I'll teach you, more like . . .'

The Root rumbled in his own tongue, 'Are we done? It would be good to get past those sand dunes yonder before the sun goes down . . .'

So they set off, the Root and his son leading the hunters, and Zesi and the priest following. The Etxelur folk waved and clapped, and for a while Arga and an excited Lightning ran alongside the little column.

Zesi glanced back at Ana and her father. It struck Zesi that Kirike hadn't spoken to her all morning, hadn't embraced or kissed her – hadn't said goodbye. Even now he didn't so much as wave.

She turned and walked up towards the dunes.

They marched steadily south.

The coastal plain gave way to rolling hills, and for the first few days they followed faintly defined trails through banks of heather and bracken. The high moorland was thick with billows of gorse, prickly green and yellow, and with broom, a subtly gentler shade. The thorn bushes bore white blossom, and butter-cups with big heavy bright yellow heads dotted the grasslands. Ground-nesting birds rose at their approach, piping their indignation.

Once, on a ridge, Jurgi pointed out vast herds far away, cattle or deer, like the shadows of clouds on the earth. The priest said, 'The Pretani are ferocious hunters, but if there were a hundred times a hundred more of them they could never empty the world of game.'

As they walked, Zesi was aware of Shade all the time – *all* the time – as if he was the centre of the world, and the brightest thing in it. And in the night, when he lay just paces away from her, she ached for him deep in her belly. But she dared not speak to him, even come close to him. If he was drawn to her in the same way she saw no sign of it. Perhaps the murder of his brother, all because of her, had burned out whatever he felt for her.

The Pretani, men of the forest, were uncomfortable in open country, and they eyed the world around them suspiciously. Each night when they made camp it always had to be under trees, even if they stopped at some copse long before the sun was down, and wasted travelling time.

It was only when they rounded the vast salt marshes at the eastern neck of the Moon Sea, and walked west into a landscape coated more thickly with forest, that the Pretani started to look happier. Still, this wasn't like the oak wildwood of their home; here birch dominated a more open forest, with groves of juniper and alder and rowan and cherry. Occasional pines grew tall, with lichen clinging thickly to their branches. Zesi knew that forest like this cloaked much of the southern reaches of North-land, all the way to the south coast where the snailheads came from. The going was easy, the forest open enough to let in

183

plenty of light, and the Root led them confidently through an undergrowth of fern and bracken and vivid moss carpets.

That first evening in the forest, when they camped in comforting gloom under the trees, Zesi sat with the priest, preparing a meal of salted meat with mushrooms fried on a hot rock in the fire. The Pretani had picked the mushrooms for them, knowing what was safe to eat here and what was not. The scent of the burning birch logs was strong and resinous, and the flames licked bright orange.

Zesi heard the drumming of a woodpecker, loud and regular.

Jurgi got up, took a stick, and hammered on a tree trunk. The woodpecker stopped drumming and came fluttering into sight in the high branches of the tree, a big bird, black and white with a splash of red on its underbelly. 'It drums to attract the females. Thinks I'm a rival.' Jurgi dropped the stick and waved his fingers. 'Fly away, little man. I'm no threat. Unlike these Pretani.' He sat with Zesi again.

'It occurs to me,' she said, 'that I don't know any of their names. The Pretani, aside from Shade and the Root. I know everybody's name in Etxelur.'

'They run things differently in Albia. The Root and his sons matter more than anybody else, save maybe their priests. What they say goes. Everybody else just has to obey—'

'Like a child.'

'No, not that. You may guide a child's behaviour, but you expect her to grow into an adult who will make her own decisions. No, the other Pretani are like dogs, like Lightning. Who must always do as they're told, all their lives. I know it's odd but it's the way they are. And they're not unique. You should talk to Novu.'

'Who? Oh, the rock maker.'

'*Brick* maker.' He used Novu's own word. 'I think it's similar where he comes from.'

'Why would anybody want to live like that?'

'Because it works. The Pretani seem to control a lot of their

184

country. And it suits the top men. Look how big the Root's belly is.'

That made her laugh.

She watched Jurgi as he sat at ease, bare to the waist, cross-legged, picking bits of meat and mushroom from the hot rock. She thought back to how she had looked at Ana as she had set off from Etxelur – as if she had never seen her sister before. It occurred to her that she rarely *looked* at people. She was too busy blundering through life, in pursuit of something or other. People were a means for her to achieve her goals, or they got in the way. 'You're doing well,' she said now. 'On the walk, I mean.'

He grinned. 'Thanks. I'm enjoying learning how to hunt from the masters. The range of signs they look for, the animals' scent, piss, scut, saliva, signs of feeding, broken twigs . . . Even a bent blade of grass tells a story. And they don't just track the animals, they seem to try to guess how it *thinks*, where it will go, the decisions it will make. Remarkable. No wonder the Pretani eat so well.'

'I thought you'd turn back in a day, or I'd be carrying your pack after two.'

He shrugged. 'I'm a priest. Priests don't have to do a lot of walking, or carrying. But I was a boy before I became a priest. I won a lot of the kids' challenges at the Giving feasts – this was when you were small, I guess you wouldn't remember. Once I was chosen I gave all that up. People don't want to find themselves being beaten in some race by a priest – or, worse, to beat him. It complicates relationships.'

'How were you chosen?'

'Old Petru touched my shoulder one day. You remember him, the priest before me? He told me he saw I was more interested in people than in hunting or fishing.'

'In people? Not in the spirits?'

'Petru said the way to hear the spirits is to listen to other people. I think he was right. And listening is the point of having a priest in the first place.'

'Is it?'

'Oh, yes.' He studied her coolly. 'Even when no words are spoken, there is always something to listen to.'

That confused her, and she went on the offensive. 'I still don't understand why my father was so keen for you to come with me.'

He glanced over at the Pretani. 'A man of Etxelur beside you when you sleep will make you seem less available to our hosts.'

'I don't need some man to fight for me.'

'I understand that. As does your father. But he doesn't want you fighting at all. There has been enough fighting. That's why he chose me. I am a man, but not a man who fights. Now, are you going to eat the rest of that mushroom or not?'

She took some more mushroom, but the flesh was heavy, tasteless. Suddenly it made her nauseous. She left the rest to him.

The nausea didn't go away. That night she slept badly, her stomach churning.

And in the morning, in the dawn light before most of the Pretani woke to begin their ritual of comparing overnight erections and noisy pissing, she found her belly convulsing. She staggered to the root of a tree and threw up, expelling half-chewed lumps of fungus. Jurgi rubbed her back until the vomiting was over, then gave her a wooden cup of water. He wasn't perturbed; oddly he seemed to have been expecting this.

It had probably been the mushrooms.

30

The Root, following well-defined tracks, led them south until they broke out of the woodland and reached a coastal strip just north of an immense estuary. This was the mouth of a river pouring from the south-west, such an immense flow that the sea was discoloured by fresh water far from the shore. The Pretani called this the Great River.

Zesi knew where she was, roughly. All of Northland was like a great neck connecting Gaira and the eastern lands to the peninsula of Albia to the west. Just here that neck was close to its narrowest; only a few days' walk south of here was another mighty estuary, fringed, so she had heard, with cliffs of dazzling white rock – the homeland of the snailheads.

They walked on, skirting the mud flats of the river mouth, disturbing flocks of birds. On the salt marsh sea lavender grew, attracting buzzing bees, and redshank and curlews fed busily. In the distance Zesi often saw threads of smoke rising, and flat-bottomed boats sliding over the glimmering waters: folk of the marshes living off prawns and crabs and eels and birds' eggs, as such folk did everywhere. She felt a flicker of curiosity. Would these isolated folk speak the same kind of language as the Pretani, or Northland folk, or another sort of tongue entirely? But the Pretani marched on without stopping, and she never found out.

Now they followed trails that ran south and west, parallel with the river and pushing deep into the heart of Albia. Willow grew by the water's edge, and where the river widened into a flood plain trees grew sparsely, mostly hazel and alder.

But it was on the higher land away from the flood plain that the true forest started to take hold, dominated by oak and lime, with groves of hazel in their green shade. Some of the oaks grew huge, much larger than any tree Zesi had seen before, with massive wide trunks that towered up to dense tangles of branches. You had an overwhelming impression of age, of weight, of stern solidity. Zesi could see why the Pretani's imaginative lives were so dominated by such trees.

But she found the country difficult, claustrophobic. Away from the scraps of higher ground the great trees grew so thickly they formed a canopy that excluded the light, and at the oaks' feet little grew save ferns and mushrooms amid a litter of dead, crisp-crunching leaves. Sometimes she would hear the rain hiss on the leaves far above, but barely a drop would reach the ground. The most attractive places were, oddly, places of death. When one of the great trees fell, perhaps struck by lightning, it could bring down its neighbours and open up a stretch of the canopy. In the brief gift of sunlight plants and saplings grew feverishly around the wreck, competing to reach the canopy before it sealed over again.

It was always quiet here in the gloom, with the birdsong restricted to the canopy far above. She rarely saw animals or their signs – deer and wild boar, perhaps a squirrel scurrying in the higher branches, badger setts, mouse holes around tree roots. But the Pretani hunters were usually successful when they went on a raid.

And the nights were strange, the forest full of the cries of birds and animals she didn't recognise. Sometimes in the dark she heard shuffling, twigs cracking and leaves rustling. There were bears in these woods; the Pretani told her all about the size of their claws.

The Pretani were at home here. In the forest shade, with their dark fur cloaks and massive frames, they were like figures carved of oak wood themselves. As they walked they looked out for the hives of wood ants, huge brown mounds that could be as tall as a person. The Pretani would shove their arms into these and bring out handfuls of big wriggling insects that they popped into their mouths and ate like berries.

Jurgi said the hives reminded him of Novu's rapt descriptions of Jericho.

On their third day in the forest, with the sluggish river a few hundred paces away, they came to a particularly gnarled tree, obviously very old. It was not tall, but its branches were a tangle, its flank scarred by the stumps of fallen limbs. Its bark was cracked and punctured, and the trunk was pocked by deep holes.

The Pretani seemed to recognise the tree. The hunters dumped their packs by the roots and dispersed to empty their bladders, set up lean-tos. The Root slapped the tree's bark, and walked around it as if checking it was healthy.

Zesi murmured, 'He treats that tree like an old friend.'

'The very old trees are special,' Jurgi said. 'The priests come to them for certain types of plants and fungi and insects that flourish nowhere else. And then there's the very age of the thing. Look at it, bent like an old man – a witness to generation after generation. These Pretani aren't altogether without sensitivity.' He sighed, and began to unfold his and Zesi's packs.

Zesi walked off into the forest, looking for wood for the fire. She came to a younger oak with a broken, dangling branch. It would come away with a hard tug, she decided, and would make a good mass to be dragged back to camp.

She thought she heard something overhead, a rustle in the leaves. She glanced up but saw nothing but shadows.

She got her hands over the branch and shoved it down. Its joint with the tree creaked.

'No.' It was Shade. He came walking from the camp. 'The branch isn't dead.'

'It's broken.' She knew that the Pretani, obsessed with the spirit of the oak, would only use its wood on their fires if it was already fallen. 'See? It's nearly come away from the trunk.'

'Yes, and it may fall soon, but for now it's still alive.' He

189

pointed at green leaves at the end of the branch. 'If you bring that back to camp—'

'The Root will shove it down my throat.'

'Something like that.' They stood there, on either side of the dying branch, facing each other. It was the first time they had been alone since leaving Etxelur – the first time, in fact, since the day of the Giving, the day of Gall's death.

He turned away.

'Wait.' She grabbed his arm, the bare flesh below his elbow. The feel of his skin was vivid, a shock, like a sudden spray of cold sea water here in the dense heart of the forest.

He didn't look back, but he didn't pull away.

'Please. It can't be wrong for us to talk.'

'But what we did was wrong.' He shrugged. 'You were for Gall. It would have united our house with yours. That's the way my father plans. He thinks of long times ahead, of his children and his grandchildren and how they will fare in the future. He thinks like a tree that will not die. We are young; we think with our bodies. You were not for *me*.'

'Oh, yes, I was,' she said hotly.

'No.' He turned. 'Maybe it all drove me crazy, a shy forest animal. The way the light is in Etxelur. The sea, the huge sky. You. I forgot that I am Pretani.' Gently, he pulled his arm away. 'You'll see when you know us more. We aren't as like beasts as you think.' He touched the damaged oak, laying his hand on its bark reverently. 'The tree is the centre of our world. We are named for its parts. It feeds and sustains us and holds up the sky. We believe that somewhere a mighty tree connects the deepest dark of the earth with the highest reach of the sky, where branch and root reach around and tangle up with each other, so that all is one.'

She wished his hand lay on her as it lay on the trunk of the oak. 'You sound like a priest.'

He smiled. 'Wait until you see our priest! He lives in a tree, I mean *in* it, in a chamber carved into the trunk . . .' There was another rustle high in the trees. He glanced up, frowning.

She didn't want this fragile intimacy to end. 'I wish we could run away. Just go.'

He stared at her. 'Are you serious?'

'Why not? We don't need people. My father spent nearly a year on a boat, just him and Heni. We are young, healthy. We can hunt and build houses for ourselves. Let's get away from here, find a land of strangers, trade with them. Anything is better than this – to be close to you but not able to touch you.'

He shook his head, grinning. 'But we have responsibilities. And—'

'Look out!'

Strong palms slammed into her back, and she was thrown face down in the leaf mulch. She heard a creak of wood, a sharp crack. Something heavy smashed into the earth beside her.

Winded, she raised herself up on her elbows.

Jurgi the priest was on his back, unmoving. A rotten, lichen-choked branch lay across his belly, and there was an ugly gash on his forehead.

'Priest? Priest!' Shade knelt down and inspected Jurgi, feeling at his neck for a pulse. Then he took Jurgi in his arms and stood, lifting him, groaning as he took the priest's weight. He glanced back at Zesi. 'Are you all right?'

She stood up. She was winded, and her palms were bruised from breaking her fall, and there were leaves in her hair. 'I'm fine. What happened?'

Shade kicked the fallen branch. 'He knocked you out of the way of this. Saved your life, possibly. Come on, let's get him back to the camp.'

One of the Pretani hunters, a man called Alder, turned out to have an instinct for medicine. Jurgi was put on his back on a bed of leaves. Alder checked his breathing, dug his fingers into Jurgi's mouth to be sure there was no danger he would swallow his tongue, and dribbled sips of water into the priest's mouth.

Then he went to work on the wound. He had a roll of treatments, pastes and dried herbs, not unlike the priest's own

191

medicine bag. He cleaned out the wound with water and a bit of skin soaked in some clear liquid that made Jurgi, still unconscious, start and moan.

'The wound is deep but clean,' Alder said to Zesi. 'I do not believe it needs leeches. My treatment has stopped the bleeding. If it starts again we will use embers from the fire to staunch it. I do not believe it needs sewing up. I will leave the wound open. That is our custom, so the spirit of the air can caress it. Tomorrow I will bandage it with an oak-leaf compress. His head will be sore—'

'You're right about that,' murmured Jurgi. Waking, wincing, he stirred on his pallet.

'Lie still,' ordered the Pretani. 'I will make nettle tea. That will ease the ache. But *lie still*. That is the best treatment.'

'Thank you.'

When Alder went off for the tea, Zesi held Jurgi's hand. 'I didn't know he knew medicine,' she said. 'That Pretani.'

Jurgi grunted. 'Nor did I. But I knew a man like the Root wouldn't travel far without a medicine man. I— Ow!'

'Don't move, you idiot.' She squeezed his hand. 'Shade said that falling branch would have crushed my skull if you hadn't shoved me aside.'

Lying back, he squinted up at the trees, the canopy darkening as the light faded. 'I'll tell you the oddest thing. I thought I saw something move up there, above you. Climbing in the trees. A big animal . . . It pushed the branch and made it fall. I *think*. It might have been shadows. I've never seen anything like it.'

'You saved my life.'

'Then I'm doing what your father asked me to do, for both of you.'

She stared at him, puzzling out his meaning. '"Both of you . . ."' Her hand flew to her belly.

He tried to smile. 'You didn't know, did you? Or maybe you did, deep down.'

She didn't want to follow him down this path. 'There's nothing to know.'

192

'Of course there is. The women knew, back in Etxelur. Ana suspected, I think. Even Arga. And Ice Dreamer, who's just had a baby of her own. Think about it. When was your last bleeding?'

'I was never regular. I never count the days—'

'Think about your sickness in the mornings! How many of the Pretani's wretched trees have you marked with your vomit? You just didn't want to know, because it gets in the way of your goals.'

'Shut up,' she snarled. And then she squeezed the hand of the man who'd probably saved her life, and, it seemed, her baby's. 'Sorry. You're right. You know me too well. But – my father let me come on the wildwood challenge, even knowing I was pregnant?'

'Could he have stopped you?'

She touched her stomach again, through the layers of deerskin. 'It is Shade's, you know. It can only be his.'

The priest said softly, 'You don't have to tell him. We can complete the challenge and get out of here, get back to Etxelur, before the baby shows. And . . .'

'What?'

'I have treatments. If you want to lose the baby – it is best when it is small. It is not pleasant, but not painful. We could say you are ill, infectious. Go into the forest for a day—'

'No. Not yet.' She glanced over at Shade, who was talking quietly to his father. 'I need time to think this through.'

The priest lay back, his eyes closing. She could see purple gathering around the wound on his forehead, an almighty bruise coming.

The Pretani medicine man came across with a bowl of nettle tea. He glanced down at Jurgi, closed the priest's mouth with one finger under the jaw, and walked away. Zesi grabbed the bowl herself and sipped the tea, relishing the way its heat stung her tongue.

193

31

A month after his midsummer arrival at Etxelur, Novu was building his home.

It was far from complete, but, only a short walk from the Seven Houses, already it was like nothing else in Etxelur. Within a boundary stone wall, two low boxy houses stood so close together they touched. Their walls were a weave of sapling wood plastered with mud, and their roofs were planks set horizontally and heaped with rough thatch. The ground around the entrance was trampled, and little grew here save for a cluster of tree mallows, their pink flowers a bright contrast to the paleness of the bare sandy soil.

Ana sat on the ground near the low, dark doorway, waiting for Novu to emerge. It was like the mouth of some ground-dwelling animal's burrow. She could hear him moving around inside.

Somewhere a curlew called. It was a bright summer morning, the sky a washed-out pale blue that spoke of the intense heat that was to come later in the day. She wasn't sure why she was here. Something about this stranger from the east fascinated her.

At last Novu came crawling out of the hole in the house wall. He was naked save for a scrap of cloth around his loins, his skin greasy, his hair tied back, and he smelled of oily smoke from his lamps. He carried a bowl full of his night soil. As he got to his feet, he seemed embarrassed to see Ana sitting there. 'What do you want? I mean – sorry. Good morning. Let me get rid of this.'

He walked up and over a low dune's shallow slope, and dumped the waste on the far side.

'You're a late riser.'

He grinned as he walked back. 'Or you're an early one. Have you been sitting there long? I don't get much light in there.'

'That's obvious. It's so weird that you bury yourself in the dark.'

'But it reminds me of home.' He lifted his head to the sun, closing his eyes, and sniffed the salty air. 'Although I do admit it's nice to smell something other than myself.' His words were heavily accented, but his language was mostly Etxelur now, mixed with the word-rich jabber of the traders' tongue.

He was good-looking, she thought, in his own dark way, strong-featured with the nostrils of that big shapely nose flaring as he drank in the air. When he had arrived here, after months of walking with the traders who had owned him as a slave, he had been scrawny, underfed, his muscles small and hard, like walnuts. Now he was filling out, and his bare skin had tanned a rich brown in the summer sun. But he would always be small compared to Etxelur men. Small in height, more lightly muscled, prone to flab, and with those oddly worn teeth.

He was watching her calmly. 'See something you like?'

Embarrassed, she looked away. 'No.'

'So what are you doing here? You are a curious one, aren't you?'

'I suppose. I never met anybody like you before.'

'I should think not. I came a very long way. You want to come in and take a look around?'

That was why she was here, but she looked into the dark hole dubiously.

'Come on. You'll have to crawl, mind, the door's a bit low . . .' He got down on his hands and knees and wriggled inside, disappearing like a huge bank vole vanishing into its hole.

195

She got to her knees and followed him. She could feel her back scraping the door frame.

Inside, she found herself in a space high enough for her to sit up but not to stand. Stone lamps filled with what smelled like whale oil burned smokily. The floor was flat, much of it paved with slabs of sandstone from the beach that must have been hard work to haul in here. A hearth was set in the centre of the floor, a circle of heavy stones, but there was no sign of fire.

The walls were flat and smooth; she could see the marks of his hands where he'd pressed and stroked the damp mud before it dried. Alcoves had been dug into the walls, and were heaped with objects. A second door had been cut into the wall, leading to an even darker space.

Novu was sitting on a pallet set against one wall. 'Take your time. Let your eyes open to the dark. See what I've done.' He pointed up. 'I'm cutting a chimney. See the hole in the roof? When I break through I'll clog it with thatch to keep the rain out. It's been so warm I haven't needed the fire yet.' He wrapped his arms around his bare torso. 'I know your winter is going to be colder than I'm used to. But I'll be warm enough in here, with the fire.'

'Where does that door go?'

'The other room. There will be more rooms eventually.'

Rooms. A Jericho word that didn't have a precise match in Etxelur. Here, houses weren't divided up into *rooms.* 'Is this how people live in Jericho?'

'Not quite. I've seen places like it. This is the best I can do for now, until I start making bricks. When I make bricks I will build a better house. I will build many houses, all made of bricks, all jammed together.' He grinned. 'I will have many children and grandchildren, and we will live in houses as they do in Jericho.'

'What's in the holes in the wall?'

'My stuff, and my treasures.' He moved around the room, showing her heaps of garments, tools, fire-making gear, dried food, water sacks. His 'treasures' were stones, high-quality flint

196

and bits of obsidian, some of them shaped into tools. He laid these things out on the floor.

She picked up an obsidian flake, finely worked, light, smooth, glinting in the lamp light. 'This is beautiful.'

'A gift from Loga. You know, the trader I came here with. Not as significant as the gift of my freedom. A reward for all the work I did helping him get himself and his wives across the Continent to this place. It comes from a lode quite near my home.'

She fingered other pieces of flint, richly textured, pale brown. 'These look like Etxelur flint, from the island.'

'I worked for these pieces too. Just as I worked for the obsidian.' He sounded defensive.

'I'm not denying it.'

'For instance I help your father with his catches, when he comes in from the sea.'

'Are you going to make tools?'

He picked up a flint core and hefted it in his hand, feeling its weight. 'Oh, this stuff's too good for tools.'

'So why do you want it?'

He frowned, thinking it over. 'Because it's real. More real than us. Nothing lasts in this world, does it? Your clothes wear out. Your houses rot and fall down. Plants and animals wither. People grow old and die. Only the stone remains.' He held up the flint. 'Stone, that doesn't die when we die.'

She looked at the stone, at the earnest boy with the strange accent, trying to understand. 'Stone doesn't die because it is already dead. People die, but . . .' She thought of the clumps of mallow outside this very house. 'Every spring, the world begins again. Why do you people live like this? All heaped up like rats. Pawing over bits of stone.'

'Ana, in Jericho, there are single *houses* where more people live than in the whole of Etxelur.' He gestured. 'This is a huge country, and a rich one. But there's nobody here! And your dwellings, those huts made of wood and seaweed – sometimes, if I look at them, and I look away, I barely see them at all. Just lumps on the ground.' He held out his hand like a knife, the palm vertical. 'In my country there is none of this blurring into the green. In Jericho, there is nothing but people. And pigs and chickens, obviously. And goats. But still, the point remains. Jericho is a totally human place. Carved out of the world, separate from it. I have to live like this – live my way. I learned that in all those long months walking with Loga, and the other who held me before him. I need to live with walls between me and the green – walls that will last. Otherwise I would go insane, I think.'

'Some say you already are insane.'

'That doesn't surprise me. So why are you hiding away in this hole with me?' His insightful gaze made her uncomfortable. 'How's Knuckle?'

She turned away. 'I don't care about Knuckle.'

'That snailhead cares about you. That's the gossip, anyhow.'

All this was true. But Knuckle was too old for her, too strange, too complicated. She didn't want to discuss this with Novu. 'Who gossips with *you*?'

'Arga. Ice Dreamer, though she knows even less about what goes on than me. That business with the Pretani was bruising for you, wasn't it? I remember how it all blew up on the very day I arrived, at the Giving. One brother killing the other, who had killed a snailhead in turn . . . I barely knew what was going on.'

'It was my sister's row.'

'Yes. But you were caught up in it, weren't you? Maybe you feel nobody notices you, that you get brushed aside. Is this why you come to me?' He grinned, clever, probing. 'Coming here is an escape from home, isn't it? Why, Ice Dreamer spoke to me the other day, and she said—'

'Zesi. Knuckle. Ice Dreamer.' She rolled onto her knees, and brushed away his laid-out stones with her arms. 'I came to see you in your stupid house, with your stupid stuff. Not to talk about this.'

'I'm sorry.' He held up his hands. 'I talk too much. It's got me in trouble before. You should ask my father. Please, you can come talk to me any time—'

But she was already squeezing out through the doorway, it seemed narrower and tighter than when she'd gone in, and she emerged with relief into the open air. She plucked one of the mallows, pressed it to her nose, and walked away towards the dunes.

32

Dreamer's sobs broke into her troubled dreams. She woke to find her eyes wet, her throat sore.

Kirike sat over her, a shadow in the dark. 'It's all right . . .' She couldn't see his face, but she sensed his presence, his calm mass. And she could smell him, the salt-sea smell he never quite shook off. He was speaking comforting words in her own tongue, the tongue of the True People.

She sat up, clutching her hide cover to her body. There was only a little light from the dying fire in the hearth, and from the deep blue of a pre-dawn sky that leaked through the open door flap. She replied in the Etxelur tongue. 'Did I wake you?'

A snort from the dark, a slim shape moving in the shadows. Ana, fetching water from the skins. 'You were screaming in your dreams. *Again*. Yes, you woke us. It's a wonder Dolphin isn't crying too.'

Dreamer turned and looked for her baby. Dolphin Gift lay on a tiny pallet a pace away from her, under a lamp that burned smokily. Dolphin slept peacefully, one little hand with fingers like buds showing outside her wrap of soft, woven cloth. This was the wisdom of the women of Etxelur, that you didn't lie with your newborn for fear of rolling over on top of her, and that the lamp, burning some mixture of oils, was good for an infant's breathing. 'She's fine. It's not long since she fed; she'll sleep a while yet.'

Kirike murmured, 'That little mite was born at sea and slept through ocean storms. She's had to learn to be a good sleeper in her short life.'

'But you're not at sea now.' Ana came over and sat cross-legged beside them.

Ana's face, shadowed, was youthfully smooth, yet somehow pinched, Dreamer always thought. As if the spirit inside was old before her time. But here she was with wooden cups of water, which she handed to Kirike and Dreamer. Complicated the girl might be, resentful and wary, but she had a good heart.

'No,' Dreamer said. 'But I dreamed I was at the coast, watching the tide.' She had never seen the ocean before she had stumbled to that distant shore, with Moon Reacher already dead in her arms. She had never seen the tide, never imagined that a body of water as big as the world could rise and fall, rise and fall. 'I dreamed they were all there. Moon Reacher and Mammoth Talker and Stone Shaper, and all the others I knew before, my mother and sisters and the priests. All on the shore. Then the tide came in and covered them over. When the tide went out the beach was empty. When I die – if Dolphin were to die – there would be nothing left. Not even the memory. All of them deader than the dead. "The world is dead and we are already dead; this is the afterlife, of which even the priest knew nothing. Even our totems are dead . . ."'

'Enough,' Kirike said sharply. 'You're safe now. With us. You're not going to die. And nor is Dolphin Gift.' He leaned over and smiled at the baby.

Abruptly Ana stood, unravelling her legs in a single graceful movement, and pushed out of the house through the door flap. She left her cup of water standing on the floor.

Dreamer cursed in her own tongue. 'I'm sorry.'

'You've nothing to be sorry for,' Kirike said grimly. 'That child needs to learn to think about the feelings of other people.'

'Oh, Kirike, be fair. She was trying, she brought me water. And she's not a child. She's of an age to take a man, to have children of her own.'

'I know. There are younger mothers in Etxelur.'

'I see that snailhead boy is paying her attention.'

'Knuckle? Well, she could do worse. They're a strange lot, and they've come to live a bit too close for my liking. But maybe it would be a good alliance, the two of them. Smooth the friction.' He glanced around. 'There's room in this house for Knuckle, and a baby or two. We'd have to have a conversation about the business of binding the babies' skulls.'

'But is that what Ana wants? I know what an intrusion I am in her life. She lost her mother. Then she lost *you*. And now, even when her father comes home, he brings *me*. A brand new family to replace the old.'

'Dolphin's not my child. You're not my woman.'

She took his hand, the palm scarred by the cuts of fishing lines. 'That may not be how it looks to Ana.'

He stared into her eyes. 'And how does it look to you?'

She didn't reply.

He hesitated, then pulled away. 'Try to sleep a bit more.' He walked back to his own pallet.

33

Led by the Root and Shade as usual, with Zesi and Jurgi bringing up the rear, the hunting party rounded a bend of the Great River of Albia. The forest stood all around them, tall trees growing right down to the water's edge.

And there, lying in the water, was a canoe – a tremendous log, dug out and shaped, by far the largest canoe Zesi had ever seen.

Men stood on the riverbank by the canoe, or sat around a big smoking fire. They wore tattoos in the Pretani style. More men laboured in the canoe, polishing its surfaces, bailing out water. When they spotted the Root the men by the fire leaped to their feet and started jumping, waving, shouting. The Root's hunters waved back.

'So,' the priest murmured to Zesi, 'after all these days of walking, we have arrived. Evidently the Root will ride the rest of the way home in this mighty craft. I wonder how long these men have waited here for their leader to return.'

'That canoe,' Zesi mumbled.

'What about it?'

'Priest, it is *huge*.' The men inside the canoe were dwarfed by the craft. And she saw now that the big central hull was flanked by outriders, four of them, fixed to the main hull with beams and ropes, there to keep the boat stable in the water. Each of the riders alone was larger than any canoe in Etxelur. She tried to imagine the labour involved in felling this immense tree, in shaping it as a canoe – the fires must have been banked day and night – and then somehow hauling it to the water.

The priest said dryly, 'It had to be a big boat, Zesi. With men like the Root, even a simple canoe must be bigger than anybody else's in the whole world. If you have power, you must flaunt it to impress.'

'Well, I am impressed.'

The Root brushed by the fawning men by the fire and went straight to the boat, where they walked along one of the out-rider beams and settled into a place near the prow. The bailing men cringed and kept out of his way.

Shade followed, and then Zesi and the priest. The boat was so massive it barely shifted in the water under their weight, almost as stable as if they walked on dry land. Zesi saw that the boat's hollowed-out interior was finely worked, smoothed and greased from one end to the other, and the hull itself had been shaped to give the canoe a sharp prow and stern. Zesi had to sit among the Pretani hunters, on shallow log benches. Alder the medicine man, friendlier than the rest, made room for her.

A few of the men who had been by the fire jumped in now, to much jabbering in the Pretani tongue, and those who had been bailing took their places and pushed paddles into the water.

The canoe glided away from the bank. After a few strokes one of the rowers began to sing, a doleful but rhythmic chant, and the others joined in. It seemed to help them maintain the pace of the heavy paddling. The river here was broad, sluggish, calm, but they were heading upstream, against the current, and the paddlers were soon working hard, and sweat gleamed on grimy torsos.

Out on the river the heat was intense, the air humid. The water looked thick, almost oily, and was dense with life, with tiny fish that clustered around the boat and green fronds that waved under the water, and the fat pads of lilies by the shore. Insects swarmed over the surface, clouds of them that caught the sunlight, but they did not trouble Zesi. Sometimes Zesi thought she saw movement in the trees, in the solid canopy like a roof to either side of the river. Fleeting, elusive motion tracking the canoe, a blur of shadows, a glint of sharp eyes. She saw the Pretani mutter and point, and she thought she heard them say, '*Leafy Boys.*'

They turned a bend and startled a group of young deer that had come to the water. The animals, light-boned and big-eyed, watched the boat for a heartbeat, and then bounded away into the forest's shade, almost silent, their muscles working with a springy suppleness, their white tails bobbing.

'The men who paddle,' the priest said to Alder in the heroes' tongue. 'They are not like the others . . .' They lacked the Pretani's characteristic arrays of facial kill scars and tree tattoos, though some had other sorts of designs on their bodies. One man had his whole ears slit in two from the lobes upward, with the two halves bound by some kind of thread. They all looked skinny, dirty, subdued, and some bore injuries, including stripe marks on their backs.

Alder smiled. 'They are slaves.' The priest had to translate for Zesi; there was no such word in the Etxelur language.

'Why would a man be kept as a slave?'

'He doesn't get the choice,' the priest said. 'Like Novu, remember? As a slave you work or you die.'

'In fact,' murmured Alder, 'you work and then you die.'

Zesi asked, 'But why would you keep a slave, then?'

The priest said, 'With his slaves the Root can gather more food, to feed more hunters, who go out and capture more slaves. It is how he extends his power. And without slaves I doubt if he could have made this boat, for instance.'

Zesi looked at the paddlers with horror – and yet with interest. How would it be to command such men, to have such power? To be able to treat another human being as if he was another limb . . . But her father's face swam into her mind, and she imagined what he would say if she voiced such ideas.

'It is not our way to own slaves,' she said firmly.

'Let us hope it will never become our way to be enslaved . . . Look – a settlement.'

You could see it through a screen of willows at the water's edge, a clearing cut into the forest, or perhaps burned, with houses roofed with leafy thatch. As the slaves' singing wafted across the still air, children came running down to the water's edge and shouted and jumped, waving.

The water front had been cleared, and a jetty had been set up in the water, a platform of logs set on piles driven into the river mud. The boat pulled into the bank. A couple of the Root's men jumped out and tied up the boat, while others came hurrying from the settlement beyond, typical Pretani, shouting and waving.

Again the Root did not pause. As soon as the boat was fixed he stood and stalked off, and walked right through the settlement. Shade, Zesi, the priest and the rest had to scramble out of the boat and follow him.

Zesi glanced back at the paddling slaves in the boat, who were doubled over, panting, exhausted. Yet a Pretani was already shouting at them, gesturing, and they picked up their paddles to make the journey back.

They hurried through the settlement in the wake of the Root. Among the houses Zesi glimpsed the usual mob of children, dogs, food pits, hearths, people preparing food or working at stone blades and spear shafts and bits of clothing. In this place, most of the workers were women.

Zesi met the eye of one girl, baby at her breast, who laboured over a huge wooden bowl of stew at a fire. She seemed very young – younger than Ana – and, pale and blonde, she looked nothing like the Pretani. Whereas women 'owned' Etxelur, men owned Albia; if you married a Pretani man you were expected to come live in such a settlement as this, live his way. Dull, languid, drenched with sweat, the girl barely seemed aware of Zesi's presence. Zesi had to hurry on.

Once across the clearing they cut into the forest, following a wide track kept clear of new growth; Zesi could see where saplings and bracken had been hacked back, and to either side oaks towered. The trail ran straight, and the Root led confidently.

Soon the way opened out into another, much larger clearing.

206

This roughly circular space was dominated by a single oak at the centre, wide and tangled, ancient even by the standards of this forested peninsula. Around the oak a ring of posts had been set up, each a tree trunk massive in itself, cleaned of bark, planed and cut so that the posts were all but identical. And outside the ring of posts there was a circle of trees, all of them oaks, some quite young, none as massive as the big specimen at the centre. It was obvious they had been deliberately planted, or perhaps moved. There were only a handful of houses, massive and old-looking, their hide covers stained black by smoke.

Aside from the track they had followed, Zesi glimpsed more ways cut into the forest, leading off from this place. Maybe this was how the Pretani lived – inside the forest itself, in these clearings cut and burned into the tree cover, linked by their wide, straight ways. And if the Root lived here perhaps the network was centred on this huge, impressive site.

The Pretani men dumped their packs and stripped off sweat-soaked tunics. More men, and a number of women and children, came out of the houses to greet them. The women did not seem so deferential here. One of them walked up to the Root himself and immediately started to harangue him.

Shade saw Zesi staring, and he grinned. 'My mother. And his number one wife. He has several, as is the custom for the Root. But she is the one who counts, the one he has to listen to—'

There was a cry, unearthly and agonising. Zesi saw the branches of that big central tree rustle, and out leapt a figure, a man, green as the tree itself. He dropped to the ground on all fours, capered over to the Root, and performed an odd dance, more animal than human. Then the green stranger sniffed the air, and ran straight over to Jurgi.

Zesi felt for her blade.

'Don't be alarmed,' Jurgi murmured. 'I've heard of this. This is their priest – he lives in their most sacred tree. It's rare for him to come down to the ground at all.'

The Pretani priest stood tall. Zesi saw that he was no more than a boy, slim, naked under a kind of net cloak of green leaves, though his skin itself was dyed a livid green. Young he may have been but he evidently recognised Jurgi as one of his own sort. He jabbered a lengthy speech in Pretani. Jurgi replied with a few words, backed up by phrases in the traders' tongue. Then the priest scurried away and clambered up his tree, lithe as a cat.

'What did he say?' Zesi asked.

'It was a welcome, of a sort,' Jurgi said.

'What sort?'

'If we keep quiet and obey all the rules, we might live long enough to be dishonoured by defeat in the wildwood hunt. That sort.'

Shade approached them. 'Look – you can use the house over there. There'll be a feast tonight, to welcome home my father. It would be best to stay out of the way.'

Zesi snorted. 'Not much of a way to treat a guest.'

The priest touched her arm to hush her. 'Look over there.' He gestured towards the Root and his wife, who was, Zesi saw now, pointing at her and Jurgi.

'They're arguing about us,' she said.

Shade said with a tired smile, 'About you, Zesi, I'm afraid. About all that happened at the Giving. For my father the issue is settled. Not for my mother, who rejects the honour of men. You being here is – provocative.'

Zesi said angrily, 'If that woman wants some kind of showdown—'

'No,' said both Shade and Jurgi, together. 'Please,' said Shade. 'Just stay out of the way. Look – don't come out of your house tonight. During the feast. You may not like what you'd see.'

Zesi did not enjoy being hidden out of sight. But she stomped off to the house.

The house itself was massively built, laden thick with leaves sandwiched between two hide layers, and it was cool inside. There was a hearth, unlit, a couple of hide pallets stuffed with leaves, and bowls of water.

It had been a long journey. After a wash to rinse the grime off her limbs and a soak of her feet, and a piss into a pit at the rear of the house, with relief Zesi lay down on one of the pallets. It crackled softly, smelling of autumn and wood smoke, and she fell into a deep sleep.

She didn't wake until evening, with the scent of cooked meat in her nostrils.

She sat up, suddenly hungry. The house was dark. By the light of a lamp of oil burning in a stone bowl, the priest was unwrapping a parcel of meat covered with leaves. He sat by the hearth but the fire still wasn't lit; the night was too warm.

She could hear chanting outside, laughter, running footsteps, a kind of singing.

She came to join Jurgi. 'They're having their feast.' She found her blade, grabbed a bit of meat and sawed at it.

'Yes. Making quite a row at times. This is the Pretani in the wild, I guess. And I think the Root is using his Etxelur gift, the herbs and unguents and seeds. I'm glad he didn't ask me to administer it for him—'

A scream cut through the night like a blade, making them both jump.

Zesi hurried to the door flap.

The priest called after her, 'Zesi – no – you heard what Shade said.'

'I'm just going to peek.' She loosened the flap's ties, making a crack so she could see out.

Fires blazed all around the grove, making a light bright as day. People danced, frenzied, men and women alike, even older children, in the flickering shadows of the ring of poles. There were no drums, no flutes, as there would have been in Etxelur; the only music came from the people's ragged song. The Root and his green-clad priest stood before the great old tree at the heart of the clearing.

And a man was suspended from the holy tree, his arms outspread, his wrists tied by lengths of rope to the branches.

209

Zesi could see how he shifted his weight, agonised, struggling to breathe, his face a grimace in the firelight.

It was Shade.

Jurgi's hand was on her shoulder; otherwise she might have lunged forward. 'Stay,' he whispered. 'This is their way. This is Shade's way. Come back inside.'

But she shook him off and stayed to see more.

The Root stood on a log before his son. He held up a blade and swiped it across Shade's forehead, creating a vivid red gash. She understood. This would be the kill tattoo, a memory of Shade's brother that he would carry for ever.

The blood ran in a sheet over Shade's forehead and into his eyes. Suspended, he thrashed, but made no sound.

34

They were woken before dawn by Alder the medicine man, who came to their house, his finger held to his lips. *Hush.*

Zesi rolled off her pallet and pulled on a tunic. She glanced over at the priest. 'The hunt?'

'Evidently.'

She quickly emptied her bladder, and grabbed a blade and a spear. While she waited for the priest she tested her weapon one last time, feeling its balance, stressing the attachment of the point to the shaft with resin and dried rope. She had made the spear herself, with her father's help, and used and repaired it many times. It was short enough to be used as a stabbing spear, long and well balanced enough to throw if need be.

Zesi felt her heart beat harder as she faced the unknown challenges of the day, of a hunt in a terrain she didn't know, surrounded by men who longed for her to fail. Bring it, she thought. I am ready.

They stepped out of the hut. In the dying light of last night's fire she saw half a dozen Pretani waiting for them, hunters, the green-clad priest, gathered around the Root and Shade. The Pretani carried spears and light packs, and they all had their faces and arms dyed dark green. The new scar on Shade's forehead, crudely stitched and stained black, was livid.

As soon as Zesi and the priest emerged, the Root set off without a word. The others followed, and Zesi and the priest had no choice but to jog after them.

At first the Root led them along one of the wide ways that led from the ceremonial centre, but he soon cut off onto a track

211

which, if it existed at all, only the Pretani could see, and they pushed into the deeper forest.

The dawn sky was visible only in glimpses through the endless canopy, and the trees grew dense, their massive root systems sprawling, always ready to trip a careless foot. The Pretani moved silently, all but invisible in the homogenous gloom of the forest in their brown tunics and green and black faces, and Zesi had to concentrate hard to keep them in sight at all. She saw no animals – no deer, no boar, no sign of cattle. Evidently they knew to keep out of the way of Pretani hunters.

The light was brighter when the Root at last called a halt, at the base of yet another massive tree. Jurgi was breathing hard, but the Pretani didn't look as if they had worked at all. Some of them glanced up at the canopy, wary, narrow-eyed.

The Root beckoned to the priest and Zesi. 'So,' he whispered. 'What do you imagine we are hunting?'

Zesi said immediately, 'Aurochs.' The wild cattle, a huge and ferocious prey, had always been the target of the wildwood challenge.

'Not today,' the Root said.

Jurgi frowned. 'The hunt is a custom. A way of binding our two peoples. And we always hunt aurochs. It is central to the meaning. Your own priest should advise you that to defy tradition is to court problems.'

But Zesi glanced at the Root's priest, hunched over, grinning, showing green-dyed teeth. 'He won't help you, Jurgi. Look at him. He does what the Root tells him, not the other way round. If not aurochs, what are we to hunt?'

The Root glanced upwards. 'Leafy Boys.'

Jurgi looked up, squinting. 'And what are *Leafy Boys*? There is no Etxelur word—'

'Of course not. Not all knowledge resides in salty Etxelur heads. It will be a new challenge for you, Zesi, daughter of Kirike.' He pointed to the tree behind her. 'Here's how we will organise it. Each of us will climb a tree. You, Zesi, take this one. Priest, yours is over there—'

212

'I've never climbed a tree,' Jurgi moaned.

The Root sneered. 'Then you can thank me for a new experience. If you see a Leafy Boy up there—'

'What do they look like?' Zesi asked.

'You'll know when you see them. If you find one, drive it out along a branch. In distress they call to each other, bring each other out of the foliage. And they leap from tree to tree – flit between the branches like birds. It's a marvellous sight. We'll soon see where they're congregating, which tree. Then we'll close in. Got that?'

It sounded simple enough to Zesi – just entirely unfamiliar.

The Root stalked away, and his hunters dispersed. Zesi saw Shade looking at her. He had an expression of confusion on his face, faint concern. But he trotted after his father. The priest, with an uneasy frown, jogged over to the tree that had been picked out for him.

Zesi was left alone with her tree. She was distracted by all those looks of disquiet. Something wasn't right here. But she was in the hands of the Pretani. There was nothing for it but to climb.

She had spare rope around her waist. She took this now, tied either end to her spear, and slung the spear over her back, leaving her hands free.

Then she walked up to the tree, stepped on its roots, and stroked its bark, which was sagging and wrinkled. It really was a very old tree. 'Forgive me,' she whispered to it. She looked for her first foothold, and found it in a bulge in the bark – some infestation, perhaps. She stepped up, fingers probing at cracks in the bark. The lower branches weren't much more than her own height off the ground. When she had hold of the lowest she was able to pull herself up. From here the next branch, oddly bent back on itself, was only just above her.

On she climbed, up through the branches, arms and legs working, her back soon aching, the breath coming short, her palms scraped by the bark. When she glanced down, the tree trunk seemed to narrow to its roots, far below in the litter of the forest floor.

If her Other had been a squirrel this might have been enjoyable. She took a deep breath and climbed on.

Something moved, above her.

She stopped dead, peering up. A shadow shifted in the dense canopy, something massive, silent save for the faintest rustle of the leaves.

Her spear was useless, for there was no room to wield it here among the branches; she might have been better to leave it on the ground. But she had her blade, which she took from a fold in her tunic and tucked into her mouth, leaving her hands free. If she climbed higher, got a bit closer – she remembered the Root's instructions about chasing her Leafy Boy to the end of a branch—

She saw the stone out of the corner of her eye, flying up from the ground, a whirling blade. She flinched back, but it caught her on the back of her shin, just above the ankle. Blood flowed, hot, and she cried out, her voice loud in the stillness of the forest.

Her injured leg slipped, slick with blood. She lost her grip and fell, landing heavily on her back on a thick branch. She would have fallen further if she hadn't grabbed onto branchlets with both hands. The branch creaked and swayed, and her leg ached, but she held on.

It was deliberate! Someone had thrown the blade, and injured her, deliberately. Maybe even tried to kill her.

She tried to sit up, moving one hand at a time. If she could bandage her shin with a bit of tunic it would hold until she got down to the ground and the priest could treat it properly. Even so climbing would be difficult, with one weakened foot, and she had dropped her blade in the fall. She searched for her spare.

And it came down on her from above, a heavy, meaty tangle of thrashing limbs and muscles and *teeth*, a row of white teeth before her face.

She fell back on her branch, clutching with one hand, and got the other hand around the beast's throat. She pushed back the face, those teeth. The creature thrashed and twisted and pummelled her with feet and fists and knees. It was so close in the green gloom she could barely make out what it was. A boy! It was a boy, with a scrawny torso and stick-like arms on which muscles bulged, skin stained green with leaf fragments, hair long and filthy, and a bright emptiness in the eyes. He might have been eight, nine, ten years old; he was strong, and wild.

She lost her grip. She fell backwards and crashed through one branch, two, before slamming down on another, winded, still high above the ground.

She backed up against the trunk of the tree, scrambling to find her blade.

But she was too slow. The boy swung down, grabbing onto whippy branchlets with a clean instinct, and he was on her again. All she could do was cling to him, trying to push him away, kicking feebly with her one good foot.

And now there were more of them, a second, a third, a fourth, heavy, lithe shapes crashing down through the foliage and joining the pile on top of her. She couldn't move, she could barely breathe, as the squirming bodies pinned her and fists and feet slammed into her face, her sides, her belly. She couldn't even see their faces. She thought of the baby lying helpless inside her.

Now she felt small hands dragging at her tunic, pawing between her thighs, and something pressed against her bare stomach – a penis, hard. All this was wordless, the boys silent save for grunts and snarls.

Something heavy slammed into the pile of boys, with a sound like chopping meat. One of them gurgled and fell away, and she felt the weight lift. It had been a spear; she could see the shaft. The other boys screamed and spat. Another spear flew, missing the boys.

With a final volley of blows and punches they scattered and spread. She could hear them go, crashing through the branches with no regard for the noise they made.

She was a mass of pain. She tried to hang onto the branch under her, but it was slick with blood.

She fell again. Another branch slammed into her back, stunning her, and she dropped towards a distant, leaf-strewn ground.

35

The priest woke her.

She had been dreaming of falling. She grabbed at his arm, the pallet under her body.

'It's all right.' Jurgi's face was over her in the gloom of the Pretani house, his hands on her shoulders, reassuring. 'You're safe. You're down.' His smile was dimly lit by firelight.

She remembered the tree, the boys. 'My leg—'

'A gash. I cleaned it, stitched it.'

Her hand flew to her stomach.

'Your baby's fine too,' he murmured. 'I heard its heart beat. He, or she, is going to be a tough fighter.'

'How . . .' Her throat was dry as dust.

'Drink this.' He lifted a wooden bowl to her lips and let her take swallows of tepid, strongly flavoured water. 'Willow bark tea. From Alder. Kills the pain.'

'What pain?' She tried to lift her head off the pallet; a pain like a thunderclap echoed through her skull. '*Ow.*'

'The Root was worried about the damage your head might have done to his tree on the way down. Look, another few days and you'll be fine. But I had to wake you now.'

'Why?'

'Because Shade asked me to. He wants you to see what's going to happen tonight.'

'And what's that?'

'He's challenged his father.'

'Over me?'

He smiled, but it was a bleak expression. 'Yes, over you.

Wherever you go, trouble follows . . . Come on. If you can stand I'll get you outside.'

She managed to sit up, and the priest threw a cloak around her shoulders and helped her to her feet. Her leg ached deeply, evidently it had been a bad cut, but with the priest's help she could hobble. It felt as if her head had been cracked like an egg.

'So,' she said. 'The Leafy Boys. Those things that got me.'

He pulled open the door flap and helped her through. 'They *are* boys – human, though they don't look it.'

Outside the air was fresh, cooler than it had been. Puddles stood on the ground of the clearing, and the sacred posts gleamed, wet. It had been raining, then; the weather had turned while she'd been unconscious. She couldn't see anybody else.

Jurgi helped her to a log, and she sat, gratefully. He said, 'I believe it was a Leafy Boy that threw down the branch at you, that time. Remember?'

'When you saved me.'

'And almost got killed myself.' The priest glanced up at the night-black forest canopy. 'They live in the trees. The canopy is so solid, the Pretani believe, that you could climb a tree and cross this country from north to south, east to west, without ever touching the ground. And there's food up there, the fruit of the trees, the squirrels and the birds to hunt. And to drink, water that pools in the big leaves and hollows in the trunks. It's a place to live, if a strange one.'

'How do they get up there? The boys.'

'Nobody knows how it started. Maybe a bunch of kids got lost somehow, or they were outcasts . . . They go naked. They lost the knowledge of speech. They're more animal than human, I think. It's a harsh life up there – one slip and you fall. Shade says they rarely breed.'

She grunted. 'A gang of them tried to breed with me.'

'Oh, they rape. They rut with each other like dogs. But even if one of them becomes pregnant, how could they handle the birth, look after a baby? It's thought they keep up their numbers by stealing children from the ground, kids old enough to cling to a branch but too young even to remember their own names – toddlers of two or three.'

'And the Pretani hunt them. What do they do, eat them?'

'No, they have taboos about that. They display their skulls in their houses. I've seen them. And trade the little finger bones with other folk to make necklaces.'

'I could have been killed.'

'You'd have been fine if you hadn't been hit by that stone. Once you were injured the Leafy Boys were on you in a heart-beat. It was the stone that caused it. Or rather, he who threw the stone. For it was deliberate.'

She remembered the stone's flight. 'Yes. Yes, it was. Who?'

'It was their priest. He hasn't been seen since – I suspect he won't be back until we're safely gone. It was a trap, you see – a trap for you. To get you isolated in a tree, in the Leafy Boys' domain, and then to draw them to you. Ingenious in a way. And, with luck, it could be made to look like an accident. But their priest was seen.'

'Who by?'

'Me.' He grinned fiercely. 'I did promise your father I wouldn't let you come to any harm. From the beginning of that hunt, something didn't feel right. I spoke to Alder. He took my tree and I took his, which was close enough to yours for me to see. And another saw too, another who stayed close to you.'

'Shade?'

He nodded.

She said, 'That runt of a priest wouldn't do anything without the Root's say-so.'

'Exactly. Which is what tonight's drama is all about. Look, it's starting . . .'

As they watched from their log the Pretani emerged from their houses, the Root first, then his son Shade, and then the hunters. The Root and Shade were both naked, but each carried a single blade in his right hand. There was still no sign of the priest, Zesi noticed.

Last of all to emerge was the Root's wife. Aside from Zesi she was the only woman here. She stood and watched as the men walked through the ring of posts towards the sacred tree. It occurred to Zesi that she didn't even know the mother's name. And yet Zesi sensed she was the most important person here.

Shade and the Root faced each other. The hunters stood around them, reflecting the circle of the silent, watchful posts. Zesi thought it was like the stand-off between Gall and Shade.

'I speak first,' the Root said. 'It is the custom.' He spoke in his coarse Pretani tongue, and Zesi struggled to follow.

'Then speak,' Shade said, his tone dripping with contempt.

'Why are we here, son?'

'Because I challenged you, father.'

'Why did you challenge me?'

'Because you tried to kill Zesi of Etxelur. Tried in a way that lacked honour.'

'The Leafy Boys attacked her.'

'They were drawn by her wound. The cast stone caused the wound.'

'I did not cast the stone.'

'The priest is your creature. It is as if you cast the stone yourself. You shame yourself if you deny it.'

The Root shrugged. 'I do not deny it. Why do you care if the Etxelur woman lives or dies?'

'Because I lay with her. Because she carries my baby.'

The hunters gasped. Zesi saw the mother cast her a look of pure hatred.

'And why,' Shade asked now, 'do you want to see Zesi dead?'

'The same reason.' It was the mother who answered, her voice shrill. She pointed at Zesi. 'Because she carries your baby!'

The Root rumbled, 'Be silent!'

But she would not. 'I regret the day I told you to find brides for the boys in Etxelur! One son dead already. The seed of the other wasted in the belly of an Etxelur woman. Now she has Shade's baby. She is *here*, stirring up trouble. Shade will leave me and go to her. It's as clear as night follows day—'

'I challenge you,' Shade said to his father, 'because you are less than a man. You tried to kill a woman. You tried to kill my child, your own unborn grandchild. Your clumsy meddling in our lives . . . You compound mistake after mistake. You have destroyed your family, and you keep destroying it, even to the next generation. And you did all this because of her,' and he pointed to his mother. 'I challenge you because I cannot challenge her.'

Jurgi murmured to Zesi, 'He either loves you as no man loved a woman before. Or he's gone insane. Or both . . .'

Alder stepped forward. 'The priest is not here. I will say his words. The challenge has been issued. Yet neither need die. Agree a price. A finger from each man, an eye. Make your blows, your cuts. Then turn your backs and walk away.'

The Root shook his huge head. 'It has gone too far. Blood has already been spilled. It must end here.'

Shade said, 'And I—'

The Root moved with blinding speed. He grabbed his son's hand, the hand holding the blade – and he drove it deep into his own belly. The Root groaned, and his eyes rolled. Yet he held onto Shade's shoulder with his other hand, dropping his own knife.

Shade, his arm already soaked in blood, was shocked. He tried to step back. 'Father—'

The Root wouldn't let him go. He gasped, 'I will not live to see two sons die. Now, son. As it was with your brother. You did it well for him. I saw you. Up and to the heart.' Father and son were locked in a ghastly, struggling embrace. 'The heart! The heart!'

Weeping, Shade braced, obeyed his father, and thrust deep.

The mother screamed and fell to the ground. The hunters rushed forward towards their leader.

The priest put his arm around Zesi. 'Into the house. Come, quickly.'

*

221

The following morning Alder, grim-faced, summoned Zesi and the priest from their house. They were to watch the last of it.

Zesi saw that a pit had been dug into the ground, in a gap in the outer circle of young trees. An oak sapling lay on the ground, neatly uprooted; dirt still clung to its roots. Shade stood over the pit, naked, his father's blood still staining his belly and legs. His men stood behind him.

Nobody else was here; the women and children and slaves stayed in their houses as the men pursued their drama of blood and death.

Shade raised a hand to beckon Zesi forward.

With the priest, she came to the edge of the pit. The Root's heavy corpse lay in the pit, on his back. He was naked, un-adorned, with pink-grey guts spilling from the huge, ragged wound in his belly. He looked as if he had been thrown in there, without ceremony.

Shade glared at Zesi, his eyes bright, his face unreadable. That new wound over his forehead seemed to be seeping blood – and she wondered if it would soon be joined by a second kill scar. There was little left of the Shade she had known, the boy who had come to Etxelur just months ago.

'I wanted you to see this,' he said to Zesi. He spoke in the Etxelur tongue, his accent thick. 'To see what you have done. Because of you my brother is dead, my father is dead – *both dead at my own hand* – and my mother is gone, off into the forest, insane with her grief.' He glanced down at the corpse. 'We did this to ourselves. But we broke ourselves on *you*, Zesi, like a dog dashing out its brains against a tree. When this is done, go from here. Go to your home.'

She said hotly, hand on belly, 'I carry your baby.'

'Pray to your little mothers that you never see my face again.'

Then he bent, picked up the young tree, and rammed it upside down into his father's pit, branches in the ground, the roots in the air, a grotesque mockery of life.

36

Off the Scandinavian shore, deep under the sea, huge mounds of silt were in motion. The undersea landslip would not be a large event, on a planetary scale. Only a volume the size of a small country, a mass of mud entirely submerged, sliding deeper into the abyss.

But an equivalent volume of water, pushed aside by the silt, would have to find somewhere to go.

37

Ana led the way along the track across the Flint Island marsh, with Novu following, Dreamer with her baby in a sling on her back, and then Arga. Arga, at least, was singing the ancient song of the trail, which she was trying to learn. Nobody else seemed happy.

The track felt solid underfoot to Ana. But then, earlier in the year, she herself had helped set down a new layer of logs on this very track, cut and shaped, to press down on the old. Sometimes she wondered how long this had been going on, how many generations had worn away while the rows of logs, one on top of the other, had been pushed down ever deeper into the soft mud, the soaked and rotten wood of the lowest at last dissolving away.

The four of them had crossed the causeway and come to this marsh on the north side of the island to show Novu and Dreamer a new place, a new kind of landscape for them, and maybe to trap some birds or an otter or two. It had been her father's idea, a way for them all to get to know each other better, his daughter and the two newcomers. So Kirike had pronounced, before he had got into his boat and paddled away over the horizon with Heni, once again leaving Ana to work it all out.

The sourness wasn't just to do with this pack of strangers and misfits, Ana thought. Everything felt wrong this late summer afternoon. It was too hot, the air dank and clammy and full of midges, the sun too bright and reflecting off the standing water. There was something odd in the air, a kind of tension. It was a day when she didn't feel comfortable in her own skin.

But dragonflies hovered over the water, and on patches of

dryer land butterflies flickered between purple sedge and pale pink-white cuckoo flowers. The birds were beautiful too. They disturbed a reed bunting, the white collar around its black head bright as it flapped off indignantly. And a flock of lapwings took to the air, flying so tight and close it seemed impossible they didn't collide with each other.

Novu was startled by the lapwings. As usual these days he carried a big skin pack on his back; Ana had no idea what he was carrying in it, but its weight made him sweat. 'Those things were *close*.'

'Lapwings rarely attack people,' Ana said dryly.

He glanced to either side of the path, which cut across sodden ground. 'The water looks deep just here.'

'So it is. The path is safe.'

'How do you know to walk here?'

Arga piped up, 'Because this is where the logs are!'

Novu grinned, good-natured enough. 'Yes, yes. What I mean is, how did your grandmothers know where to put the logs in the first place?'

'The song tells you where,' Arga said, and she sang, ' "Over the water bridge, and by the smiling ridge, walk to the afternoon sun, until you come—" '

'Which came first, the trail or the song?'

'The trail,' Ana said.

'The song,' Arga said.

'Maybe a bit of both,' Dreamer murmured. 'It is the same in my country. The land is overlaid by the lore and tradition of the past. And over and through this landscape of memory move the living.'

'But it's all so strange. *There's nothing here.* At home we build walls. Marker stones!' He stood on the causeway, in the middle of the marsh, and held up his arms. 'In Jericho, at any moment, you know exactly where you are.'

'Well, you're not in Jericho now,' Arga said. And she ran at Novu and shoved him in the back.

He flailed comically, then went into the water head first. He came up coughing, reeds clinging to his body, a sticky slime hanging like drool from his face. The water wasn't quite knee deep, but, pulled back by his heavy pack, he was having trouble standing in the soft mud.

Laughing, Ana and Dreamer knelt down and pulled him out, landing him on his belly on the log path. He managed to stand. He had his foot stuck in an eel wicker basket. Panting, dripping, he said, 'Thanks a lot, Arga.'

'At least it shut you up,' Ana said. She began to wrestle the basket off his foot. 'This is one of Jaku's. He'll be furious.'

They got the wrecked trap off him, threw it back in the water, and continued on.

At the edge of the marsh the land rose up into a line of dunes before the beach, the marsh green giving way to yellow-brown sand. Here Ana stopped, shucked off the pack she was carrying and dumped it on the ground. 'We'll get ourselves set up here, it's dry enough. Then we'll see what we can catch in the marsh.'

Dreamer said, 'Arga, will you help me down with the baby? She's due a feed.'

Arga happily lifted the baby out of its sling on Dreamer's back. She unfolded its wrap while Dreamer found a dry place to sit, and dug out fresh dry moss to pack around the baby to absorb its soil.

Novu, still dripping wet, dumped his pack on the ground beside Dreamer and walked a little further up the dune slope.

Ana followed him. The sand was soft and gave easily, but there was a better grip from the clumps of dune grass, long, tough, deep-rooted.

They reached the crest of the dune. This was the north coast of Flint Island, where the great crescent-shaped middens faced out to sea. To the north, beyond the scattered rocks where seals lay languid in the heat, there was nothing but the sea lying still and flat.

'You have slime in your hair,' Ana said. She scraped it away with the side of her hand.

'Thanks . . . Incredible.'

'What is?'

He waved a hand. 'The sea. All that emptiness. I walked for month after month to get here. If Jericho is the centre of the world, here I am at its very edge.'

She frowned. 'The edge of the world? But the sea is full of life. Fish and dolphins and whales. Look, you can see the seals.' She pointed. 'I think that's my father, fishing.'

'Your eyes are better than mine.'

'To me, this is the centre. The shore, Etxelur, the sea, the whole of Northland, the estuaries, the beaches, the tidal pools, and the fringes of forest where we hunt. If you go too far south there's nothing but forest, choking the land. *That's* the edge.'

'I see an edge. You see a centre. Can a world have two centres?'

'I don't know . . . Ask the priest.' She felt snappy, irritable, her head somehow stuffy. 'Can't you ever just talk about normal things?'

But he didn't reply. He seemed distracted, his eyes squinting against the brilliant sunlight, his lips pursed in a frown. 'Listen.'

There was a sound like thunder, rolling in off the sea, as if from a storm very far away.

And Dreamer called up from the base of the dune, 'Ana? I think you'd better come down and see this.' She had opened Novu's pack.

Novu stared, horrified, then ran down the dune.

In the boat, the sound of thunder made Heni sit up. Kirike had thought he was asleep.

The boat rocked at Heni's sudden movement. But it was already full of a healthy catch of salmon and, bottom-heavy, settled back on a smooth sea.

Heni fixed his hat on his head and looked around. 'You heard that?'

'If it was a storm it was far away . . .'

They both sat silently, listening, the only sounds their

227

breathing, the lap of the big, slow waves, the gentle creaking of the laden boat, the net ropes scraping against the boat's hull.

The two men had paddled off to the north-east of Flint Island, out over the deep sea. From here much of the mainland was out of sight, only the island itself visible in the misty air. Kirike liked to be distant, so far out that the land was reduced to a kind of dream, and the world shrank down to his boat and the steady work of the fishing, and the companionship of Heni, the most enduring relationship in his life.

But was there to be a storm? The weather today was hard to read. The air was hot and, out on the breast of the sea, promised to get a lot hotter. The sky was free of cloud but there was a washed-out mistiness about it. The day felt odd to Kirike. Tetchy. Skittish.

Heni asked, 'Can you have thunder without a storm?'

'Maybe it's a big storm very far away.'

'Maybe. But do you remember the day of the Giving?' On that day too there had been a rumble out of a cloudless sky, and a big, strange wave. Men whose life depended on listening to the moods of sea and air couldn't help but remember something like that. 'Something's going on. Maybe the little mother of the ocean fell out of bed.'

Kirike laughed. 'Twice in a month?'

Heni sighed. 'So do you want to go back?'

Kirike glanced at the catch, the big, heavy fish that lay glistening in the bilge. 'Nobody would blame us if we did. We've enough already.' The salmon were early this year. The autumn was the best time to catch them, when they came swimming in from the ocean, funnelling into the big river estuaries on their way to their spawning grounds upstream. All you had to do was lower a net into the river, and let the fish swim in. It was much too early for the peak catches now, but this late summer day had been fruitful enough: there were times when the little mothers were kind to their hard-working children. But still . . . 'Do *you* want to go back?'

Heni lay back in the boat's prow, his broad-brimmed leather

hat tipped forward to keep the sun off his face, and chewed on a bit of wood. 'Seems a waste of the sunshine. Thought I saw some dolphins playing further out. We could try driving a few ashore.'

'Sounds like hard work.'

Heni squinted up at the sky. 'Or we could just lie here and soak up the heat. Maybe we deserve it. We had enough months freezing our arses off when we got lost in the winter. I sometimes feel like my bones never thawed out.' And as if to prove the point he coughed, a deep, racking heave that twisted his body. He had to hold onto his hat to keep it from falling off.

It was a winter cough, a cough that should have dried out by now but had clung to his lungs all summer. Kirike had a deep guilty fear that this was one legacy of their unlikely jaunt across the ocean that Heni was never going to be free of.

Heni said, 'You'll have to face Ana's nagging when we get back.'

'That's not fair . . . She's not happy.' He thought back over conversations with Ice Dreamer. 'Since her mother died, her whole world has fallen apart. That's what her nagging is about. Just anxiety. I think in her head she longs to put everything back the way it was.'

'But you never can. And then there's Ice Dreamer and her kid. Living in your own house! That can't be easy for Ana.'

Kirike turned away. 'She's nothing to be jealous about.'

'So you haven't tupped Dreamer yet.'

'Little mothers help me, but you're coarse sometimes.'

Heni laughed, but it broke up into another cough. 'Oh, come on. She's a shapely one now she's over her pregnancy, and a bit of life to her too. And she's suckling, isn't she?' He winked. 'So she can't get pregnant again.'

'It's not like that . . . It's less than a year since Sabet.'

'Ah.' Heni nodded. 'I know. I'll tell you what I think. I never saw two people closer than you and Sabet. You fit together like a bone in its socket. And then you lost her. Give yourself time.

229

Dreamer's a smart woman. She'll wait, if she wants you. *I* needed the time.'

Heni hardly ever spoke of his own past. 'You're thinking of Meli.'

'It was different for me when she went. The boys, the ones who had lived past childhood, were grown, off with their wives and their own kids. I was free. And once I was over the loss I found the world was full of willing widows.'

That was always true. Men often died younger than women, as they pursued more dangerous occupations like forest hunting and deep-sea fishing – but women died too. So there were always widows and widowers, often with broods of growing children. In Etxelur men and women took only one spouse at a time, unlike the Pretani, say. First marriages were always delicately arranged and negotiated, to build ties between communities. But after that the rules were relaxed.

'Willing widows, and you tried them all out,' Kirike said.

'And across the ocean too,' Heni said, and he yawned hugely. 'I hope all those hairy girls with their flat faces and strange eyes remember my name to tell their good-looking children . . . *Oh.*'

The whole boat was lifted up into the air.

Kirike, startled, gripped the boat's frame. The surge was smooth, but powerful and relentless, and completely unexpected on such a smooth sea.

And then it passed. The boat slid down the face of the water and came to rest, bobbing slightly, creaking.

They stared at each other. It had been a wave, a single huge muscle of water that had lifted them as if in the palm of a huge hand. They could see it passing on towards the shore, a glistening hump.

'By the first mother's left tit,' Heni said, 'I never felt anything like that in my life.'

Kirike shook his head; he felt too hot, his thinking fuzzy. Two strange things in one day. 'Do you think it had something to do with that thunder we heard?'

'Maybe.'

The wave receded. Diminished by distance it looked harmless – soon it was hard even to make out. But Kirike knew from experience that it would grow when it approached the land, the water heaping up on itself. 'That is a *big* wave,' he said.

'And it will break when it gets to the shore.'

'Yes.'

They stared at each other for a heartbeat. Then they hauled up their nets and reached for their paddles.

38

Ana hurried back down the dune, followed by Novu.

Something spilled from Novu's pack, glinting.

'It's my fault,' Arga blurted. 'I was trying to help. I was opening the packs. Look, I opened yours, Ana! I was just trying to get to the food and the embers and stuff, and the water bags. I didn't mean anything.'

Novu, panting, his arms folded around his body, had a complex expression on his face; his eyes flickered, as if he were a trapped animal looking for escape. 'You should have asked.'

'It's just a pack.'

'It's *mine*.'

'I didn't know he had all that stuff in there!'

Ana frowned, baffled. 'What stuff?'

Dreamer gestured. 'Take a look.'

Ana leaned down. The crudely sewn deerskin sack was stuffed with stones: flints, mostly, but a few shining gleams of obsidian, spilling out onto the sand. She tipped the sack up so the rest fell out.

Novu darted forward. 'Hey! Careful. You'll damage the pieces.'

Ana looked at him, and began to sort through the stones. Some of them were unworked lumps of flint, even complete nodules, and some finished tools. 'I wish Josu was here; he would know this stuff. But I can see this is good quality.' She picked up an axe-head, finely worked. 'And I think I recognise this. I used it once; I borrowed it to cut wood, and I remember leaving that chip in the blade . . . I think it is Jaku's.'

Arga nodded. 'Yes, that's my dad's.'

'All of this is mine,' Novu said with a touch of desperation. 'I worked for it all! You saw my house, Ana. The pieces on the shelves. This is what I do. I work for stones.'

'No one could work this hard,' Dreamer said dryly.

Ana rummaged through the rest of the pieces. It was quite a collection. There were knives and spearheads, and many intricately carved blades, no larger than a fingernail, that could be stuck in bone shafts to make scrapers and awls. Most looked fresh to her, as if they had yet to be used.

And she found one big axe blade made of a sheet of beautiful, milky brown flint shaped to a perfect symmetry. You could barely see the marks of the hammer, so fine had the knapper's work been.

Dreamer gasped. 'That's beautiful.'

'Yes, it is. And it belongs to Jurgi. The priest. He wears it on special occasions, like weddings and the Giving. This is old, and very precious.' She looked up at Novu. 'There is nothing you could do that would make Jurgi give you this blade. Why, it's not his to give. The priests have held it for generations, passing it from one to the next. And you *took* it, and hid it in your house, your pack? Why are you carrying it now? Were you afraid somebody would find it?'

Novu started pacing, muttering in his own language. When he spoke aloud he lapsed into a mix of the Etxelur language and the traders' tongue. 'It's not like that. You don't understand.'

Dreamer looked stern, but oddly weary. 'What is there to understand? You're a *thief*, Novu.' She used a traders'-tongue word. There was no precise matching word in Etxelur.

Ana was slowly working it out. 'You must have gone into houses when the people were out, and just taken things. Flints, tools. Whatever you liked. You even went into the priest's house, and went through his bags, the sacred, ancient stuff.'

'It was easy,' he said lightly. 'The man's gone wandering off in the forest, hasn't he? There's nobody *in* his house.'

Ana could see emotions chasing across his face. He liked to be

233

cheeky, to be daring, elusive, unpredictable – although he had hinted that it was those qualities that had caused him to be thrown out of his home by his father in the first place. He was trying to laugh this off.

But then, before their three serious faces, something seemed to snap. He sat down suddenly, his legs folded up, his elbows on his knees, his head hanging.

Exchanging glances, the others sat more slowly, facing him.

'All right. Yes. I took the stuff. Even though I know what you've all done for me.' He lifted his head. 'You, Ice Dreamer. You spoke to me when I first showed up here.'

Arga put in, 'And I showed you how to set hare traps.'

'You did,' he replied solemnly. He turned to Ana. 'And you, Ana . . .'

Ana couldn't face him. She burned with a kind of embarrassment. How could she have been so stupid as to waste her time on this man?

'Please, Ana. Look at me.'

'I owe you nothing.'

'No.' Beaten, he dropped his head again. 'All right. Let me just tell you why I did this. I didn't do it to hurt you, any of you. I did it because I had to. This is what we do, in Jericho! We have stuff. We collect it and keep it, we buy it and sell it. And if you don't have stuff you have no power, you have nothing, you *are* nothing. Oh, by the blood of the bull gods, I have turned into my father! I despised him for this . . .' He looked at Ana and spoke with a blunter edge to his voice. 'Look, you have been kind to me. But I think you adopted me – like raising a lost puppy. That was what *you* needed. But I'm more than that. I'm a man of Jericho.'

'You could have told me how you felt,' Ana said.

'Would you have listened? Could you have understood? Well, maybe you could. You're better than me; that's obvious.' He straightened up. 'So what now? Shall we go back? Maybe we should wait for your father to get back from his fishing . . . I'll

234

leave tonight. I'll find somewhere. I learned how to live away from people, when I was walking with the traders.'

Dreamer glanced at Ana. Arga looked hugely distressed.

Neither wanted Novu to go, Ana saw. And she realised that if she fixed this mess, here and now, she could persuade her father to accept her solution later. 'Take the stones back,' she said impulsively.

'What?'

'Give them back to whoever you stole them from. And don't sneak around doing it when they're out. Do it to their faces. Apologise.'

He rubbed his chin doubtfully. 'One or two will kick my arse. Your uncle Jaku for instance.'

'You'll deserve it. And when Jurgi gets home, tell *him* what you did. He'll probably kick your arse too. And never do this again.'

'I swear I won't.' He looked at her uncertainly. 'It might not be enough. They might throw me out anyway.'

'I'll have to speak to my father. I can tell him I'll watch you until you've got through this madness, and you can be trusted.'

He regarded her. 'You're so angry. Why are you helping me?'

'I don't know,' she said hotly. 'Maybe it's because I'll look less stupid this way.'

He laughed. 'Well, that's a good enough reason. I'll owe you everything, Ana. My whole life, maybe.'

Dreamer said sternly, 'Just remember that.'

Ana glanced at her cousin. 'Arga? Do you want to say anything?'

But Arga was frowning. 'Can you hear that?'

'What?'

The girl stood up, looking around at the open ground. 'Rumbling. Like aurochs running. Or thunder.'

Dreamer said, 'I hear it. Coming from the sea, I think.'

Gulls flew overhead, a sudden low flurry of them erupting from behind the dunes, cawing loudly, heading inland.

Dreamer murmured, 'Unusual weather makes me nervous. We say it is the anger of the gods.'

Ana said, 'If we climb these dunes we can see. Come on, Arga.'

Young and fit, Arga led the way, scurrying up the dune slope. Ana followed. Novu hastily packed away his stones, and Dreamer picked up her baby.

39

Lightning the dog spotted the wave before Josu did. But then, Josu was always engrossed in his work.

On sunny, windless days when the tide was low, like today, Josu liked to work on the beach. And so he had come down from his house before noon, with his work pack and blanket and a water pouch and a bit of dried meat. It was difficult for him to walk on the soft sand, but he had worked out ways to get everything carried safely to where he needed it.

He had found a patch of clean sand and spread out his hide blanket. He settled down with his boots off, with his good leg folded and his bad leg out straight. He smoothed his thick cowhide apron over his legs, to avoid cuts from flying shards of stone.

Then he had unwrapped his pack and set his tools out to one side, mostly of reindeer bone, good and hard, tools some of which he'd owned since he was a boy learning the skill, and his raw materials to the other side, his cores and fresh nodules, and broken tools that people had passed to him. Flint was valuable stuff, and you could almost always reuse even the most damaged tool, maybe turning it into smaller blades for fitting into a bone handle.

Then he had got down to work. He always liked to start on something big, to get his fingers working and his eye in. Today he picked a new nodule, knocked off some bits of chalk with an old hammer, and then turned it over in his hands, studying its strengths and its flaws. Soon he'd spotted a likely point for a striking platform. He chipped this carefully with a reindeer-bone chisel. Then he set the core between his legs, steadied it with his left hand, and struck it carefully with his right. The first blow wasn't quite right, and he produced only a shard of flint. But the second and the third were better, each blow releasing a flint flake like a roughed-out blade, and each time leaving a new section of striking platform for him to aim at.

He always aimed his blows down and away from his face, to avoid the danger of flint shards flying into his eyes, for he had seen the damage that could do; his hands bore the scars of tiny stabbings and scrapes, but he could live with that.

Gradually the flint nodule was whittled down to a core, the pile of roughs beside him grew, and the golden sand before his legs was covered with flint shards. He knew that when he stood up he would leave the pattern of his legs on the sand, outlined by the bits of flint. He always took care to sweep sand over such mess, to avoid the children cutting their feet on it.

While he was working, others had drifted down to the beach. Fisherfolk laid out nets to dry, or pushed out boats to follow Kirike and Heni. Rute and Jaku came down to set up drying racks for Kirike's anticipated catch. They nodded cheerfully to Josu. Their daughter Arga wasn't with them today. But they had Kirike's dog, Lightning. He was a yappy thing who came straight over to Josu, tail wagging vigorously, and he grabbed a corner of Josu's apron and began tugging it. He'd have had the whole lot in the sand if Josu hadn't held on. 'Get away, you daft dog! You always do this. Get away with you!'

Jaku whistled, and threw a brown tube of seaweed into the sea. Lightning immediately let go of the apron and bounded off after the weed, barking shrilly, splashing into the water.

Josu was left in peace; he resumed his work with relief.

Despite such disturbances he felt content with his life, especially on such a day as this. He'd lived out his whole life in Etxelur, had rarely travelled much more than a day's walk from this very spot, and he wouldn't want to be anywhere else. Oh, he was aware that some of his stock had gone missing recently – some of the better flint cores too, fresh from the lode on Flint

Island. He wasn't bothered. People had always played tricks on him, especially children. They mocked the way he walked. They'd pinch his tools, or call him names, or push him and run away faster than he could catch them. But children usually grew out of it. And if it got too bad, he could always turn to Kirike or Heni or Rute who would soon get to the bottom of it, and all would be right again, until the next time.

He'd been lucky to be born here. There were people like the Pretani who would have drowned a crippled little boy at birth. He was thirty years old now, there were few older than him in all Etxelur, his work was treasured, and he had no complaints. Nothing troubled him. Not even the fact that he'd never found a wife, had no children . . .

There was a deep roaring sound, a rumble.

Josu looked around, confused, faintly alarmed. The sky was cloudless. Gulls cawed noisily. He looked up to see the birds flying overhead, not wheeling and squabbling as they usually did, but heading inland, fleeing the sea. And Lightning was barking shrilly, not in play. The dog, his fur glistening wet, stood on the sand looking out to sea.

A few paces away from Josu, Jaku straightened up from the fish rack he'd been tying together. 'What's wrong with that dog?'

Rute shielded her eyes against the sun. 'Look out there.' She pointed out to sea.

Josu looked that way. The sea looked flat, calm – just as usual, save for a single dark line drawn across it, like a charcoal scribble. A wave, steadily approaching the shore. It didn't seem so remarkable. Then Josu saw a figure before it, frantically swimming towards the shore, perhaps a child. The wave towered over the swimmer, and calmly engulfed her.

Jaku murmured, 'By the little mothers' blessing—'

It seemed unreal to Josu, a scene from a dream.

Rute pulled apart the fish rack. 'We'd best get off the beach. Lightning! Here, boy!'

'It won't come this far up,' Jaku said.

239

'I'm not going to wait to find out. Oh, help me with the rack, you idiot, don't just stand there. And whistle for the dog.' She glanced over at the toolmaker. 'You too, Josu. I think it would be safer.'

'Yes.' Josu looked again at the sea. The wave was growing taller yet, as if water was piling up on water, standing on its own shoulders, the faster surface layers overtaking the lower that were dragged back by contact with the land. 'I wouldn't want to lose my tools.'

But Rute was not listening. She was already moving away, picking on Jaku, calling for Lightning.

Belatedly, Josu started to move. He wrapped up his tools and his cores, and the new flakes in their separate skins. Then he bundled his packets and his water skins and his apron in the hide blanket. He was rushing, and was making a mess of his packing.

The dog was still barking, close by. He could hear people shouting. All around him children were running, away from the sea.

And the wave climbed up the beach. It wasn't like a wave but a slab of water, as if the whole sea had risen up. He could taste the spray.

Josu stood hastily, his bare feet scattering flint shards. He didn't have his boots on, but there was no time. He began to run, holding his bundle before him. But he went down, his withered leg betraying him, and he spilled his goods over the sand. He scrambled to pick them up, his tools, the packet of cores.

The water fell on him, a huge weight that smashed down on his back and pushed him down into the sand. For a heartbeat he could feel his bundle under his body. But then he was driven forward, scraping over the sand, and he lost it all.

He was turned on his back. He could see the light, far above, the sun's disc fragmented by the surface of the water, like a shattered flint nodule. But the water was turbulent, full of mud and seaweed. He coughed, gasped, and the water forced its way

240

into his mouth, his throat. The pain was huge, like a great fist slamming into the core of his being.

So it was over, so suddenly. He felt a stab of regret about all the flint pieces he hadn't been able to finish.

The pain soon receded, a tide going out.

Ana and the others watched from the dune crest.

It wasn't like a tide. It was a single great wave; she could see its arc right across the bay, breaking on the beach and then running on, past the usual high water line, higher than any tide, even pushing into the long grass that fringed the dunes. People who had already fled from the beach had to run further inland.

Arga, silent, slipped her hand into Ana's.

Novu was staring like the rest. 'I never saw an ocean before I left Jericho. I don't know anything about oceans. Is this what oceans do?'

'I never saw anything like this,' Ana murmured. 'Or heard of it.'

'Strange events,' murmured Dreamer. 'Things nobody ever saw before, or since. This was how our world ended.'

'Shut up,' Ana hissed, holding tight to Arga.

Novu pointed. 'Look. I think it's going down.'

As rapidly as it had risen the sea level was dropping, as if draining through a hole in the world. The water ran back down the beach towards the ocean, or it pooled in hollows in the sand and the rock banks, creating smooth ponds bright in the sun.

People tentatively emerged from the dunes. They showed each other marvels – seaweed heaps high on the dunes, a dolphin stranded and gasping.

Arga tugged Ana's hand. 'Do you think it's over?'

'No,' Dreamer said. 'Look. It's still going out. *Too far . . .*'

The strange tide kept drawing back, far beyond the usual low water mark, and Ana saw a plain of glistening sand emerge, and strange rock formations she was sure she'd never seen before. All over the exposed floor there was movement, silvery wriggling.

241

People started walking, then running, down the beach towards the new strand.

'Look!' Arga said, excited now, pointing. 'Fish! There's fish everywhere! We can just go and take it. Come on.' She tugged Ana's hand.

Dreamer said, 'No. This is very wrong. We should stay—'

'What's *that*?' Novu, shielding his eyes, was pointing out to sea.

And now Ana saw what the retreating sea had exposed, far from the usual shore: an earthwork of raised ridges, circular, their flanks draped with the deep green of seaweed. Water glimmered in the ditches between the circles.

'It's like something from a priest's story,' Arga said. 'Is it real?'

Ana said, 'Let's go see. Come on!' Hand in hand they ran down the dune.

Dreamer called, 'No! Come back! Something is wrong – oh, please come back!'

But Ana only ran faster. Soon she and Arga were running on sticky mud that only moments ago had been sea floor.

40

Ice Dreamer, running with Novu, struggled to keep up with Ana and Arga. She was burdened with her baby, a precious warm bundle sleeping in her sling, and she had yet to recover her full strength from her hard winter. Novu was slow too. His pack of stones, a self-imposed burden, was heavy on his back, and he was tiring quickly. The wet clinging mud of this exposed seabed, pulling at every footstep, wasn't helping.

The sun's light poured down from a misty washed-out sky.

'Everything is wrong,' Dreamer said in her own tongue.

'What? Oh, this heat! It's like being baked. And this sand, sticky as snot.'

'It's going to be just as difficult to run back.'

He frowned. 'Do you think we'll have to?'

'I don't know. But then, I don't know why the sea has suddenly gone away.'

The girls were mercifully slowing, distracted by wonders.

Water poured off rock formations that were thick with life. Exotic plant-like creatures, brightly coloured, withered as they dried – sponges and sea serpents, the girls said. A fish dangled from a rock, clinging to it with its mouth. Crabs stirred, their flat bodies pale orange and pink, burdened by huge claws. Even the sea-bottom mud was dense with living things, mussels and cockles, the casts of worms, and strange fish that clung to the mud with flattened bodies and both eyes on one side of their heads. Everything was draped with seaweed, dark vivid green, that steamed and gave off a rich salty stink. It was difficult to walk without stepping on something squirming for life, or dead already.

Dreamer stared down at extraordinary animals with no heads but five pointed limbs, stirring in the mud at her feet. Dreamer had never seen such beasts in her life. 'The gods were at play when they made these.'

'It's so strange,' Arga said. 'It's as if it all fell down from the sky.'

'In a way it did,' Ana said. 'We're walking on the sea bottom. The fish swim in the water as birds fly in the air.'

'And if the air went away,' Dreamer said grimly, 'we too would be lying in the dirt, gasping for breath like these fish.'

Ana glanced at Arga. 'Dreamer, you're frightening her.'

'Good! Then listen—'

'Tell it to my father.' Ana twisted away and ran off after Arga, further from the shore.

There was no choice but to go on after them. 'Come,' Novu said grimly to Dreamer. 'Look, take my arm.'

They continued their plod across the clinging sand, following the girls.

And the inverted world got stranger yet. They came to the wreck of a boat, a huge one, much bigger than Kirike's, or any Dreamer had seen in this place. Little survived but its wooden frame, blackened, and rotted, with barnacles clinging thickly. The remains of a reindeer-bone harpoon was still attached to a loop by a strip of rotted hide. Ana and Arga stared as they hurried past, at wooden ribs like the skeleton of some vast animal.

Then they came to a stand of trees, bare of leaves and with their roots exposed, standing drunkenly in the mud. They were big heavy oaks, perhaps centuries old when they died. They stood beside what looked like a river valley, a broad stripe in the muddy landscape, populated now only by remnant puddles of sea water. Dreamer saw neat heaps of wreckage, posts and pits and what looked like sewn skins. They might easily once have been houses, just like those Ana and her family lived in now.

Giddy with the heat, Dreamer shook her head and tried to think. Did sea creatures build houses? Did oaks grow under-water? Surely not. She remembered Kirike's talk of the precious lode of flint, creamy and flawless, lost under the risen waters of the bay south of Flint Island. Maybe, then, today was not the first time the sea had behaved strangely. Maybe before, perhaps long ago, it had risen up and covered over these trees, these houses, like that precious flint lode.

Ana and Arga were slowing again.

Ana said, 'It's still far away. The earthwork, the curving ridges. They must be bigger than we thought, and further away.'

'Good,' Dreamer snapped as she came up, panting. 'At last you're talking sense.'

'If the sea hasn't come back by tomorrow, we'll come out again and explore properly.'

Arga looked doubtful. Sea-bottom mud coated her lower legs, brown-black and clinging. 'But it might not be here tomorrow. After all, it wasn't here yesterday,' she said reasonably.

Ana pointed. They were close to a dune-like feature, a ripple of sand on the wet seabed. 'Look – let's climb up here. We'll be able to see, even if we can't reach it today.'

'All right.' Arga sounded relieved. Maybe under all the brav-ery she too had been scared by the strangeness of the day. She ran over to the dune and immediately began to climb, getting down on all fours to scramble up the muddy slope.

Ana followed her, and then Novu and Dreamer, more cau-tiously. If crossing the plain had been hard, this was twice as difficult, for the mud was slick and sticky. By the time they reached the crest they had all fallen more than once, and were smeared with black mud down their fronts.

From the dune's narrow crest, panting hard, Dreamer could see the sweep of the sea-bottom plain. The true shore was far behind them, frighteningly far, blurred by mist, with those big arcs of the holy middens standing proud. All over the exposed seabed people worked, hauling away fish and crustaceans and seaweed. Children were playing, splashing and rolling in the

245

mud, using huge dead silvery fish to play-fight. All this on a plain that had been deep under the sea this morning.

Ana and Arga were peering further north. And in this day of strangeness and wonder, a new marvel revealed itself to Dreamer.

The earthwork ridges were sweeping circular arcs that curved away from her view – cupped one inside another, like the rings in a tree trunk. She tried to count them – one, two, were there three? She was not high enough to see clearly. Water glinted, pooled in the ditches between the ridges. Though the walls were streaked with mud and draped with seaweed and fish corpses, they were too regular to be natural, no work of wind or rain or ice.

All of this Dreamer saw from afar, through a blurring curtain of heat haze that made it seem unreal, a vision in a dream.

'It's like your town,' Ana said to Novu. 'It's like Jericho. The way you talked about it.'

'It's as big as Jericho,' he murmured. 'But people live in Jericho. They live in houses – not houses like yours . . . I don't see where people would live here.'

'I can see one house,' Arga said. 'I think so, anyway. See at the middle of the big rings, there's a sort of hill? And there's something near the top of the hill. A kind of white box, like a big skull.'

Dreamer strained to see. 'Your eyes are sharper than mine, Arga—'

Ana said, 'That's North Island! The hill in the middle. I recognise it – I was taken there for my blood tide, when the sea lowers and reveals it . . . I never knew all this lay hidden by the water.'

Dreamer was feeling giddy with the heat and the exertion, and with the extraordinary sights around her. 'You're missing it,' she mumbled.

Ana turned to her. 'Dreamer? Are you all right?'

'You're missing the most obvious thing. Look!' She pointed to the shore of Flint Island, beyond the exposed sea plain. 'Look

246

at the middens, where you celebrate the Giving, where you buried your own grandmother at midwinter. Your most sacred sites. Now look at these circles in the mud. What do you see?'

Ana turned her head from one to the other. 'The middens, their shapes – they match the curves of the shining walls. Like ripples on a pond.'

'Yes,' Arga said, excited. 'All with the same centre where you threw your stone.'

'And that's not all.' Dreamer grabbed Ana's tunic and lifted it, exposing her belly. And there, above the cloth she wore over her loins, was Ana's blood-tide tattoo. Dreamer traced it with a trembling finger. 'Can you see? Three circles, cut to their common centre by this tail. You have this symbol scrawled over your bodies, your tools and weapons, your clothes, your houses. And look!' She gestured at the earthwork. 'Three circles . . .'

Arga and Ana jabbered to each other in their own rapid tongue, barely comprehensible to Dreamer. 'The Door to the Mothers' House! This is it! She must be right.'

There was a dull roar in Dreamer's ears. The heat, the exhaustion were draining her. She clung to Novu's arm, determined not to faint.

Novu looked out to sea. 'Can you hear something?'

'Only the blood pounding in my head.'

'Something else. A rumbling.'

The girls jumped, excited. Dreamer, growing dizzier, was losing her ability to translate the girls' words, and their prattle blurred in her mind as they repeated their name for the earthwork, over and over. 'The Door to the Mothers' House. Door, mothers, house . . . *Ate, l'ami, nt'etxe . . . Att-lann-tiss . . .*'

There was a scream, from far away. Shouting voices.

Novu pointed north. 'What's *that*?'

Dreamer peered, and saw a band of blue-black, flecked with white, racing over the exposed mud. The sea, returning.

Ana cried, 'Run!'

*

The four of them scrambled down the dune slope, slithering, half-sliding to the bottom. But Arga landed awkwardly on her ankle, and cried out.

Down on the plain, Dreamer, gasping for breath, couldn't run. She couldn't even lift her feet out of the mud. 'I can't – I can't—'

'You have to.' Novu held her arm, urging her on.

'Let me take the baby,' Ana said. Dreamer felt hands working at the sling on her back. 'I can carry her, and run faster than you.'

Dreamer made an instant decision. 'Go, then.'

Ana held the baby in one arm, and grabbed Arga's hand with her free hand. 'Come on, Arga!' She began to run to the shore, but Arga limped badly, crying out.

Novu said, 'You too, Dreamer. Come *on*.' He pulled at Dreamer, his arm around her shoulders.

They began hobbling towards a shore that seemed a terribly long way away. Ahead she saw people fleeing, abandoning the fish they had gathered, running from the advancing sea.

Novu, trying to support her, tripped and fell heavily in the mud. They had gone only a few paces. He rose, filthy, cursing loudly in his own tongue. And he shucked the bag of stones off his back and dropped it in the mud. 'There will be other treasures.' He leaned over, got his shoulder under Dreamer's belly and hoisted her up, holding her legs.

Her head and upper body flopped over his back. It was shocking, suddenly to be carried like a child.

He began running. His back was drenched with sweat where it had been under the pack. His strides jarred and winded her.

She strained to lift her head. That wall of returning ocean looked terribly close. She looked for Ana – and there she was, cradling the baby, and trying to drag Arga. But the younger girl was crying and stumbling, her ankle obviously damaged. No matter how hard Ana pulled her hand, Arga could run no faster than a hobble.

Ana seemed to be calling to Dreamer, but her voice was drowned by the water's gathering roar. Then Ana stood still, panting hard. She looked at the baby in her arms, and the limping, weeping Arga. It might only have been a heartbeat. It seemed an eternity to the watching Dreamer.

And then Ana ran, with the baby, abandoning Arga. The girl in the mud screamed in terror. But Ana ran on, fast and sure over the mud, cradling the baby in her arms. Dreamer whimpered her relief.

But now the water was close. The new wave was a wall flecked with foam and laden with debris – with *whole trees*, drowned and ancient and now ripped out of the earth. The very ground shook under the water's tremendous tread.

She closed her eyes and tucked her head against Novu's sweating back.

41

The second wave had upended the boat.

Kirike swam up into sunlight. He coughed, spewing water from deep in his throat. After too long underwater his limbs were shaking, his chest aching, his heart hammering. His head was full of fear, for himself, for his daughters and his family, even for Heni.

But, exhausted, for now he could do nothing but roll onto his back, floating in the water, the hot sunlight beating on his face.

Something touched his hand. It was a frond of seaweed. The sea was silty and full of debris, the weed and plants that usually clung to the rocks of the seabed. And a cod floated on its side, a big one, apparently perfect, stone dead.

'Grab hold.'

The familiar voice came from behind his head. He glanced back, shielding his eyes. He saw a hand, strong, streaked with blood, reaching out to him. Heni's. He took it.

He was hauled backwards out of the water and landed on his back in the boat, like a huge fish, lying in water that pooled in the bilge. He sat up. He had lost his boots, he realised, a strange detail. But the boat was intact, though it rode deep in the water.

Heni was working, lashing their nets and harpoons to the boat's frame with lengths of line. He was as soaked as Kirike, he had lost his battered old hat, and blood spilled from a deep cut on his arm. 'Nice swim? Well, there's work to be done.'

'What work?'

'A bit of bailing might help.'

Kirike found a wooden bowl and started scooping out the

water. He was ferociously thirsty, his mouth and throat burning from the salt water, but their water skins had vanished.

He glanced around. There was no sign of land. 'We've gone further out to sea.'

'Good thing too. The further out we are, the safer we are.'

'From what?'

'From the next wave.' He glanced at Kirike. 'There's been two so far. Why not a third?'

'Right.' Kirike bailed harder. 'So we paddle south until we hit the coast—'

'North,' Heni said bluntly. 'I told you. The further out we are, the safer we are.'

'We're going to have to talk about that.'

'Maybe. For now, bail.'

So Kirike bailed, throwing water over the side of the listing boat, into a sea littered by the corpses of fish, lethally shocked by the passage of the huge wave.

The huge wave crashed down right on top of Arga, knocking all the air out of her lungs.

Suddenly she was tumbling in dark water, and her head was full of a deep roaring noise. She let the sea take her. She knew she couldn't fight the water, which rushed and churned, not like any sea she'd swum in before.

And she knew not to breathe in. She could hold her breath as long as anybody. She had won the deep-diving at the Giving. If she had beaten everybody that day she could beat this strange sea now. It was just the sea. She had swum in the sea since before she could remember.

She tried not to think about Dreamer and Novu and Ana, who had run off leaving her behind when the wave came. Ana had had to take the baby. It wasn't her fault. She'd had no choice. Arga thought of the sunlight, her parents Jaku and Rute who would be snug in their house, safe from the raging sea.

At last the water calmed. She settled to the bottom, onto a

251

layer of rocks. There wasn't much light. The water was full of sand and broken seaweed fronds, and bits of fish net and smashed wood. A shoe floated by her face, small, sewn from a bit of doe skin for a very young child.

And a man drifted past her, eyes wide, mouth open, bubbles streaming from the nostrils.

Now the panic came, the struggle for air.

The current turned. It felt as if a huge invisible hand grabbed her. She knew all about currents in the ocean and their dangers. But she'd never felt an undertow like this. She was dragged backwards, scraping painfully over the rocks, dragged further away from land, and her mother.

When the second wave hit, smashing into her back with a thunderous roar, Ana kept running. She had the baby in her arms, and she couldn't afford to fall over. It was futile to fight the huge strength of the wave, but she could run with it, struggling to stay upright in its grasp, feet paddling at the sand and rocks, the baby clutched to her chest.

All over the beach people ran, or fell and thrashed in the water. Some got tangled up in the fishing nets that were still draped over the beach. They would die if they could not free themselves. She knew all these people. She knew their names. She couldn't help them. All she could do was try to keep the baby out of the water.

And the wave drove past her and on up the beach, higher than any tide, pounding into the bank of dunes that fringed the beach, causing landslips like huge bites. To her left she saw the middens where only months ago she had buried her grandmother. The sea swept over their smooth curving faces as if the ancient structures were no more than ripples in the sand. Still the sea drove on, pushing even beyond the dunes and into the grassy meadow beyond. Before the rushing water, laden with detritus, houses folded like toys.

Ana saw one woman swept off her feet and driven headlong into a stout alder trunk. She bent backwards like a twig. It was

252

another image that Ana knew she would never forget, if she survived this day.

But the water's strength was fading, at last. She could feel the surge weaken.

She stood still, panting as the water drained around her legs. She had come fifty, a hundred paces beyond the old shoreline, but she was still standing in waist-deep water, from which protruded trees and the leaning remains of fishermen's huts. Above her head gulls wheeled and cried. Her arms aching, her legs battered and sore, soaked and gasping for breath, she longed to fly up with the gulls and be safe. She wondered how the world looked from up there.

'Ana! Ana!'

She saw Novu waving, from a bank of alder not twenty paces ahead of her. He was clinging to a tree. Ice Dreamer was beside him, slumped against the trunk. It was very strange to see trees in full leaf sticking out of sea water.

Clutching Dolphin, Ana splashed that way. She almost fell, tripping over a tangle hidden under the water. 'Dreamer, here, I have Dolphin, I saved her . . .'

Dreamer, her hair a soaked tangle, lifted her head. Blood ran from a cut on her brow. She seemed barely conscious. But she smiled, reaching for the baby.

Novu took Ana's arm. 'Listen. Grab a branch, or a trunk. Help me hold onto Dreamer.'

'Have you seen Arga? I had to leave her—'

'Ana!' He all but yelled in her face, his eyes so wide she could see white all around, his mouth gaping open, blood and snot running from his nose. '*Listen to me.* It isn't over. When this wave goes back it will pull just as hard out to sea, and will try to take us with it. So grab a branch!' He helped her hastily. 'Like this. Get behind the trunk and hook your arm over.' He wrapped his own arm around her, and held onto Dreamer with the other arm, and braced himself against the tree trunk. 'Here it comes. Get ready . . .' The tug grew smoothly, pulling at her feet and legs, almost seductively. She heard people

253

scream, and the water roared once more. 'Hang on!' Novu yelled, the spray splashing over his back. 'We can get through this. Just hang on!'

42

'I tell you that we want to go out into the open sea, as far as we can. When the next wave comes, the deeper the better.'

'And I'm telling you we're going home. I've got family, Heni. Daughters. A niece—'

'Oh, and I can't see straight because my sons are grown and gone, is that what you're saying?'

'I didn't mean that—'

'You're not thinking, man. If we go back now, if we're in shallow water when the next wave comes, we'll be killed.'

'How do you know there will be another wave? I never heard of anything like this. Nor have you.'

'Look. I'll do you a deal. Just help me paddle out to the deeper water and wait a bit. If no wave comes, fine, we'll do it your way.'

'I'm not waiting at all.' Kirike looked for a paddle.

But Heni held both paddles in his hands. He sat in the stern of the boat, on the hearth board, looking back calmly at Kirike.

Kirike stood, and the boat rocked. 'Give me a paddle.'

'I'd sooner break them and chuck them over the side. You know I'd do it.'

'And you know what my family means to me.'

'Enough that you paddled across an ocean rather than be with them?'

'Why, you—' Kirike stood over him and pulled back his fist.

Heni didn't flinch. 'I'm just telling you the truth, man. I know you love your daughters. But when it comes to your family you just run, one way or another. So let me do the thinking.'

Kirike dropped his arm. 'I can't fight you. I don't even want to. You'd probably win anyhow, you always were stronger. Sorry, my friend.'

And, without letting himself think about it, he slid over the side of the boat and back into the sea. The turbulent water embraced him again, horribly familiar.

When he surfaced for his first breath, he glimpsed Heni standing in the boat, waving at him. 'Come back, you idiot! You'll kill yourself!'

He turned away, dipping his head in the water, and concentrated on his strokes.

He had always been a good swimmer, long in the arms, with big feet to kick at the water, and a good muscular trunk. He had swum out further than this as a boy, he was sure of it. But now he was no longer a boy, and he had already endured one immersion today. His body felt bruised and sore, and his lungs were strained. And what if Heni was right, what if another wave did come? Well, if it did, he would just ride it home.

None of it mattered, his doubts, his weariness, the treachery of the sea. His decision was made, he was committed. He tried to clear his mind of everything but the smooth clean motion of the strokes. His whole was life reduced to this moment, the swim ahead of him, the next stroke.

Don't panic, he told himself. Just don't panic.

Don't panic.

Arga lay on her back, in the sea water. The sky was bright, and the sun was still high, she saw, amazed. Hardly any time had passed since she had been on the shore with Ana and the others. And now she was here in the middle of the ocean.

People had died. They must have. She had seen dead bodies in the water. People had died, people she knew, just in that little bit of time.

But she hadn't died. When the current had relented, she had at last been able to swim up to the surface of the water, scrambling like an otter up into the air and the light, and she had taken a breath to beat all the breaths she would ever take, *alive*.

She knew she was safe in the water. You could float in the sea water without taking a stroke. Uncle Kirike had taught her that, and he was the best swimmer she had ever seen. Just lie back and relax and let your body float.

And *don't panic*. That was the most important thing of all, Kirike had always said. It was as if the sea could smell your panic, and would use it to pull you down if you started thrashing around and screaming.

But she'd never swum out of sight of the land before. To get home she needed to go south, but the sun was still too high in the sky for her to be sure of which way that was. What if she swam the wrong way, and wore herself out without reaching the shore? Or what if another of those big waves came and broke over her?

Unsure what to do, she did nothing.

The ankle she'd twisted still ached. It eased slightly if she twisted her foot in circles this way and that. She concentrated on the small pain of her ankle, and by doing so was able to ignore the fact that if she died, her aching ankle would die with her.

She saw a shadow, out of the corner of her eye.

She twisted to see, lost her balance in the water, and splashed and got a mouthful of brine before she steadied herself, treading water. What had she seen? Was it the shore, a boat, another wave?

It was a tree branch, complete with green leaves, sticking up in the air out of the sea.

She took a couple of strokes to get closer. She found, not just a branch, but a *tree*, a whole tree, an alder, with branches and roots to which muddy soil still clung, floating in the sea. It was one of the strangest sights she had ever seen.

She swam closer and grabbed a branch, and started to pull herself out of the water. A bird, some kind of finch, flew away with a flutter of wings. She hoped it would find somewhere else to settle. The climb was hard going, for the tree rolled as she hauled her weight into it. But soon she had pulled herself out and sat, dripping, on top of the branches, near the point where they were anchored to the trunk. The roots at the other end of the trunk were like gaunt fingers.

She imagined the strength that had plucked this whole tree from the ground, as she would pull up a blade of grass.

She shook out her hair and ran her fingers through it, pulling out bits of seaweed. In the sun's heat her thin tunic soon dried on her body. Her ankle was showing a livid purple bruise. She was ferociously thirsty. She gathered green leaves and crushed them in her mouth. The sap moistened her tongue.

What would she do when the sun went down? How long should she stay before trying to swim to shore? She had lots of questions, but her fuzzy head offered no answers.

Sleep rose up, overwhelming, like another great wave. Lodged in the branches, she lay down so her head was on the trunk, cushioned from the bark by her hands.

She barely stirred when the next wave came, and lifted the floating tree high in the air.

Kirike was closer to the shore when the third wave came. He swam, making his steady crawling strokes, ignoring the fatigue, trying not to track the time.

And he saw the wave coming. Suddenly it towered over him, a cliff of water, its face flecked with debris, and the air was filled with a rushing, stormy noise. He stopped, just for a heartbeat, looking up, unbelieving.

Then he swam. He made his strokes desperately now, working the water with his feet and arms. In the last moment, in the shade of the wave, he took a final gulp of air.

The wave slammed down and he was immersed, surrounded by rubbish, dead fish, seaweed, silt, bits of floating wood. He fought to stay upright, to kick towards the surface. But then a current grabbed him, incredibly strong, and he and the fish went plummeting down into the darker deep, incredibly fast and far. The water squeezed his chest and he lost his air, his last precious lungful bubbling before his face.

He slammed into the floor of the ocean. His leg twisted in mud and his head smashed against a rock. Through churned-up silt he saw his own blood, deep crimson red, clouding the water. He fought on, but his leg was a mass of pain when he tried to kick.

Now another current picked him up and hurled him away like a leaf in a breeze. Still he struggled.

But he had to breathe. The water forced its way into his throat and lungs, an agonising intrusion, and he convulsed.

It wasn't death that he feared but the thought of all he had left undone. He had to get to the shore, to Ana.

But the darkness closed around him. Still struggling, he sank into the welcoming mud.

43

When Ana, Novu and Dreamer staggered to Arga's parents' house, Rute and Jaku were both inside. Lightning had followed them back from the beach, and when the three of them came in he jumped up at Ana, tail wagging in pleasure.

Jaku was stunned to see them. Their presence pushed back the nameless fears in his head, just a little.

But Rute continued preparing a fire in the hearth. She barely looked up. Since they had watched the sea take Josu, Jaku didn't know what was going on in his wife's mind.

Now Jaku took in the state of the three of them, Ice Dreamer draped over Novu, Ana clutching Dreamer's baby. They were panting, soaked, battered, all of them smeared with blood and sea-bottom mud. Novu was all but naked, as if the clothes had been ripped off his back.

And his daughter was missing. Somehow he hadn't seen it immediately. 'Where's Arga? Wasn't she with you? You were going down to the sea—'

'We got caught by the second wave,' Ana said. 'We hung on . . .'

Novu insisted, 'We have to go on. All of us. Get to the high ground. As high as possible above the next wave.'

'What next wave? *Where's Arga?*' Jaku faced Ana. He wanted to shake her, but she held the baby close.

'I'm sorry,' Ana said, desolate. 'She hurt her leg. I had the baby. I couldn't carry Arga too—'

Rute, still working the fire as if this was a normal day, just a friendly visit, actually smiled. 'Arga's a strong swimmer. She'll be all right in the sea.'

Ana said, 'Rute. Aunt – you have to come with us. It might not be safe here.'

'No, no, I've got this fire to build. Arga's going to be cold and wet when she gets in. And hungry, mark my words. She takes a lot of feeding, that girl!' She kept heaping up peat blocks, and she inspected a bowl of broth hanging on a rope from a house post.

Jaku touched Ana's arm. 'She's been this way since the beach. At first she was all right – she reacted quicker than I did. But then the first wave came and took poor Josu, just like that. Since then she's been like this.'

'You have to come,' Novu said grimly. 'If the next wave is bigger than the second, as the second was bigger than the first—'

Jaku looked back at his wife, despairing, his head full of a formless anxiety over Arga. 'It's no use. Even if I tried to drag her we'd be too slow. We're going to have to take our chances here. Who knows? Maybe there won't be another wave.'

Ana's eyes brimmed. 'Oh, Jaku—'

'Go.' Go, he thought, before I begin to hate you for abandoning my daughter. 'Take her, Novu.'

Novu nodded curtly. Still supporting Dreamer, he took firm hold of Ana's arm and dragged her out of the house.

Lightning followed, wagging his tail, but then looked back at Jaku, obviously confused. Jaku made a sweeping gesture after Ana. 'Go with Ana, you stupid dog! Ana, call him.'

'Lightning! Come on, boy!' Lightning, thinking he was going to play, ran after her, yapping.

Jaku went back to his wife, who was continuing to build her fire. He knelt beside her. 'You're doing a good job.'

She smiled. 'You know me. The most important skill in the world, Mama Sunta used to say, knowing how to make a good fire. Could you pass me more kindling? There's a new heap in the corner.'

So they worked in silence. Jaku deliberately thought of

261

nothing else but the fire, the fine art of layering the fuel over the kindling so there were plenty of gaps for the air to flow through. At length it was time for Jaku to unwrap the ember from last night. He placed it reverently in the middle of the fire. Rute took some bits of dried moss and dropped them on the ember, blowing on them as they started to smoke.

But then she sat back and looked at the floor. 'Oh. That will make a mess of things.'

Cold, muddy sea water was seeping over the floor. It was coming in from the door, which faced north like all the houses in Etxelur, a steady flow that soon became a gush. They stood up, suddenly ankle-deep in cold sea water.

There was a roaring, like some huge gruff animal approaching, and the sky seemed to darken.

Jaku held his wife and hugged her close. 'It would have been a good fire,' he murmured.

'Yes. Shame it's going to waste.'

The ground shook. He felt his heart expand with a huge love, for his wife, his daughter, for this place where he'd lived such a happy life. He longed for Arga, but it was better that she wasn't here – that there was a chance she was alive somewhere else. 'You know, Rute—'

The third wave was like a slap from a giant, smashing the house and ending their lives in an instant.

Ana, Novu and Dreamer reached the summit of Flint Island's single low hill, which had long ago been cut open to reveal its precious flint lode. They flung themselves down, exhausted.

Ana handed Dreamer her baby. Dreamer hugged Dolphin close, murmuring, 'Thank you, thank you,' in her own tongue and Ana's, over and over.

More people came struggling up the hill, children, adults carrying infants, some burdened with bags of tools or clothes. Ana knew everybody by name. Nobody spoke, for there was little to say.

Only Lightning was full of energy. He ran around, sniffing the

262

baby's wrap and tugging at the adults' tunics, wagging his tail in his demands to play. Eventually he saw a pair of pine martens, driven to this high ground as the people had been, and ran off, barking.

There was an interval when the sea looked calm, as if it had returned to normal, settling back to its usual tide line. Then Ana saw the third wave. Rushing in from the horizon, it was a wall of grey water that would have towered even over its predecessors.

The beach, littered with corpses and struggling people still tangled in the fishing nets, was covered over, erased.

Then the wave broke over the dunes, and the great curving middens, already eroded, were broken open. Ana saw the pale glint of exposed bone, the work of uncounted generations undone in an eye blink. The water pushed through the dune line and into the lower land beyond, pooling across meadows, tearing whole trees out by their roots, crushing houses. It did not stop until it poured into the calmer waters of the bay behind the island, and had covered all of Etxelur.

44

The sky was huge. Arga had never seen so many stars. But her mother had always said that with the stars the more you looked the more you saw, and it was true.

She tried not to think of her mother, however. If she did, she remembered how far away she was from home. After all, if she lifted her head and looked around, she could see nothing but stars all the way down to a pitch-black horizon. No line of fires, no sign of the shore.

She thought she slept a bit.

When she woke, she found her unconscious body had snuggled down to find a more comfortable position, enfolded by the tree. Lying here like this, even her sprained ankle didn't hurt any more, and she seemed to forget how hungry she was, how thirsty. The tree didn't even roll that much as it rose up over the waves, which were gentler now. It was as if the tree was embracing her, holding her safe. Well, it was as far from home as she was, its very roots ripped out of the ground.

The tree was all that was real. The only sound she heard outside her own head was the soft lapping of the water against the branches and trunk. Maybe she ought to be afraid of the huge expanse of sea beyond, but she couldn't see it, couldn't hear it.

She slept again.

The next time she woke she saw light. A pink-grey sheen was seeping into one side of the sky, reflecting from flat layers of cloud. The other way, to the west, the stars still shone, though more palely. Above her head the sky was a deep blue dome, with only the brightest stars left visible. She felt a vast reluctance to be dragged into the day, from the safety of the dreamlike night.

And she heard something, a small splashing, a creak like a branch in the wind.

She sat up, making the tree rock, and looked east. She saw a shape silhouetted against the light, cutting through the water, and for an instant she thought it was a shark. Then she made out the clean profile of a boat, and the shadow of a man, alone, working two paddles. Smooth slow ripples spread from the prow.

She waved, and tried to call. 'Hello?' But her throat was sore and dry, her voice no more than a whisper, dwarfed by the sea. 'Hello! Hello! I'm here!'

45

Through the night they huddled on top of the hill, Ana, Dreamer and Novu, with Dreamer's baby cupped between their bodies. Other refugees crowded the slopes.

In the starlit dark, Ana slept only fitfully. All night Lightning cuddled up against Ana's back, his head tucked in against her tunic, with occasional twitches, snuffles and yipped barks as he chased pine martens in his sleep. Once the baby stirred, hungry, and mewled; Dreamer held her close and fed her, murmuring soft words in her own transoceanic language.

Ana longed to be the one cuddling in, to be sleeping between her mother and her father as she used to when she was very small. But that wasn't going to happen, not ever again.

They began to stir not long after dawn. Oddly Ana had just fallen into her deepest slumber, and she had trouble waking up.

Novu walked away and stepped behind a rock to make water; she could hear him groan from stiffness and bruises. Dreamer sat cross-legged, rocking her baby and murmuring to her, for a brief moment lost in the bond between them, but when Ana sat up Dreamer smiled warmly at her. Ana understood. Without Ana, Dreamer's baby might not even be alive to see this morning. But with that thought came the memory of how she had been forced to abandon Arga.

Ana moved over to a broken heap of rocks, took off her loin wrap, and squatted to piss. The hill's small summit, the flint lode, the sandstone tufted with grass and sparse heather, looked deceptively normal. After all, even the great third wave had not climbed as high as this. All around her people were moving, children and adults waking, and picking their way down the slopes.

Lightning came sniffing at Ana's bare rump, wagging his tail, and she pushed him back. 'Oh, get away, you silly dog . . .' The dog roamed around, marking stones and patches of turf with sprinkles of urine, and he licked at the light dew on the blades of grass.

'He's thirsty,' Novu observed, hitching his trousers. 'Well, so am I. There's no spring up here, is there? We've no food either.'

'We'll find water easily enough when we climb down,' Dreamer said.

Ana asked, 'Is it safe to go down?'

'The sea's gone back,' Novu said, pointing north. 'It looks normal to me. Lapping away as it always has. It's what it's done to the land that's going to be interesting. Are you ready? There's no point staying here.'

'Help me with the baby,' Dreamer said.

With Novu's help Dreamer fixed Dolphin in her sling on her back. Ana pulled on her boots.

Then the three of them stood together, looking at each other. Ana flexed her arms and legs, spreading her hands; she was stiff, sore, but everything worked. 'We're all whole, at least. No broken limbs, no cracked heads.'

Novu was bare to the waist, his tunic ripped apart. Like the others he was covered in minor cuts, and bruises that were beginning to yellow. He said, 'Today's going to be difficult. Just remember – one footstep at a time. I learned that on the road. That's how to get through the tough times.'

A bubble of fear and resentment burst inside Ana. 'Brave words from the thief who hides away in a hole in the ground.'

Novu flinched.

Dreamer said, 'That was yesterday, Ana. Today the world is different, and we are different people in it. I have a feeling we're going to need each other.'

This was very adult, but Ana didn't much want to be an adult right now. 'Enough talking. Let's go.' She turned away, ignoring the others.

The dog ran around and barked, mouth open, tail wagging; he thought it was time for a walk.

She led the way down the path they had climbed in such haste yesterday, with Lightning running at her heels. It was a well-worn track that led down from the flint lodes, a track she had walked many times.

It was a calm morning. She heard gulls calling somewhere, the distant sigh of breaking waves. Everything felt normal. That dismal flight yesterday was like something from a nightmare, not connected to the mundane reality of the morning at all.

Then, on the hill's lower slope, she first came to the pale sand. She stepped forward onto it cautiously. White, full of stones and shells, it crunched under her feet.

From this ragged edge onwards the sand covered the ground like a layer of snow.

'Look at this.' Novu walked to a stand of trees, alder and lime. Most of the trees still stood, though one had been knocked flat, its trunk snapped. Novu kicked at the trees' roots. 'There's no soil . . .' Ana saw that the surviving trees were rooted to a reef of gravel. Only scraps of peat and topsoil and grass clung to the roots. 'I never saw anything like it,' Novu said. 'It looks as if the trees grew out of the gravel bank.'

'The waves,' Dreamer said slowly. 'If they sucked people out to sea, so they sucked away the earth itself.'

The dog was digging at the roots of one of the larger of the surviving trees. He pushed his small face forward and lapped. Ana remembered there had been a spring here where she had sometimes drunk herself. But Lightning backed off, staring at the water as if puzzled.

Novu bent down, cupped some of the water in his hand and sipped it. 'Salty. Like the sea.'

'It can't be,' Ana said. 'There's a spring here. Springs are fresh water.'

268

He shrugged and backed away. 'Check for yourself. There's nothing for us here.'

'Let's go on,' Ana said.

She led them towards the beach. This was the way they had walked yesterday morning, but now everything had changed. Water stood in pools, briny and lifeless. Even the path they followed, trodden by generations of feet, had vanished under the strange all-covering layer of pale new sand.

The beach itself was littered with debris, with great banks of seaweed and driftwood, even whole trees, and sheets of turf, the skin of the land ripped off and dumped here. All the works of people had vanished, the drying racks for the fish, the boats. There was no sign of the fishing nets and tangled-up bodies. Maybe they had been swept to sea, or deposited somewhere else. But there was a reef at the high water mark of other sorts of corpses: fat seals, glistening fish, and many, many birds, their fragile wings broken and twisted.

A few people were here, looking dazed, poking among the beach's litter. The dog nosed around seaweed heaps, curious. There was a gathering stink of rot, and scavenger birds circled. Novu climbed over the sea wrack, and Ana wondered spitefully if he was searching for his bag of stolen stones.

Dreamer pointed. 'The dunes have gone – or they're changed, at least.' So they had; the neat line of dunes, bound together by marram grass, had been broken and smashed, and sand lay heaped up in disorderly piles. 'And the middens.'

Novu said, 'It's as if those who made your world – the little mothers? – returned to smash up what they built.'

That swelling of fearful anger threatened to rise up again in Ana. 'Whatever caused this was nothing to do with the mothers.'

Dreamer touched her shoulder, trying to soothe her. 'I'm sure you're right. Your father told me of your gods, in those long days and nights in the boat. The mothers built the world; perhaps now they will return to help you build again.'

'Come on,' Novu said, clearly shaken by Ana's flare of anger, growing uneasy. 'We need to get back to the mainland. That's where we'll find food and water, and people, and we can start sorting out this mess. Do you think the tide is low enough for us to cross the causeway?' And he led the way west along the shore.

Dreamer followed, then Ana, and then the dog, frisky, anxious, his tongue lolling from his thirst.

46

It was approaching low tide. The causeway should have been crossable, a strip of muddy ground gleaming above the surface of the sea. But the causeway too had been wrecked by the waves, erased as a child might tread over a line drawn in the sand.

So they walked further along the island's beach until they found a boat, stranded high above the normal water line. Just stretched skin over a wooden frame, it was light enough for the three of them to carry down to the water. There were no paddles or bailing buckets.

They crossed close to the line of the causeway, where the water was shallowest, and launched the boat. They had to paddle with their hands, while water gradually seeped in through the skin seams. Lightning jumped onto Ana's lap to escape the bilge water, whining, the fur on his legs drenched. The crossing became a grim race between their slow passage and the boat's sinking.

Once on land they walked around the curve of Etxelur Bay, skirting the boggy tidal flats. Even here there was damage, the ancient wooden walkways broken and submerged, the dipping willow trees uprooted, and that blanket of pale mud and sand lying over everything. Ana saw no sign of the birds that normally inhabited the marshes, the buntings and lapwings and curlews. They had either fled inland or were dead. The only birds that moved here today were gulls, pecking curiously at the churned-up mud.

Suddenly Novu ran forward, clapping his hands. 'Get away!

Get away, you monsters!' Gulls flapped into the air before him, big heavy birds, grey and white and black, squawking in protest.

Ana was startled. 'What is it? What's wrong?'

'They were working on his face. His eyes.'

The corpse lay twisted, half-buried in the mud and the pale new sand. One hand stuck up in the air, fingers clenched. The mouth was open, and a bloody fluid leaked from the eye sockets. Lightning ran forward, curious, but Novu held him back by the scruff.

Ana felt Dreamer take her hand. 'Do you know who this is?'

'I think so,' Ana said slowly. The face was muddy and squashed up. 'I think this is Lene. Used to play with Arga, though she's a few years older. A her, not a him, Novu. There are words we say for the dead. And the body – there's no midden to place the bones.'

Dreamer murmured, 'We'll have time enough for that. Come, child. Let's see all of it first.'

So Ana let herself be led on around the bay, towards the Seven Houses.

They started to see more bodies. They found more people drowned in mud, hands and questing faces thrust up into the air, adults and children blanketed by the white sea-bottom sand. Ana did not have the stomach to dig out their faces to see who they were. A child had been thrown against a rock wall, her head crushed like a hazelnut shell. A man's face had been scraped away entirely, leaving eyes that gleamed like oysters in bloody bone.

'People are fragile,' Ana said.

'All life is fragile,' murmured Dreamer. Her baby on her back, she held Ana's hand firmly.

They were approaching Ana's own house now. The dog could smell home, and he bounded forward, tail wagging, barking.

Novu came to walk on Ana's other side, offering silent support. 'I envy the dog,' Novu said. 'He lives in the present.'

Ana said, 'I don't envy him what he's soon to find.'

The Seven Houses had been flattened, as if kicked over and

272

stamped down, and then covered by a dumped layer of the pale sea-bottom sand. A few broken support posts stuck out of the mud blanket, scraps of ripped seaweed thatch. The big communal open-air hearth was barely visible, a scatter of stones and scorched earth under the sand. Ana could see from the pattern of the mud flow that the water had come from the east, forcing its way from the sea up the narrow estuary of the river they called the Little Mother's Milk.

Dreamer pointed. 'That was your house, wasn't it?'

'Yes. There should have been nobody home . . .' She found what looked like the door flap. She shook it clear of the clinging white sand, and pulled it back. The ground beneath was wet and smelled of salt. Her heart hammered. She knew it was unlikely, but she had half-hoped, half-feared, to find some trace of her father.

Dreamer found something of her own: one of the big spear points she had worked so hard to complete. It was still attached to its short, stout pole to make a stabbing spear. Dreamer hefted this now, brushing pale mud from it, staring at it as if she'd never seen it before.

'Ana – Ana! Oh, it is you, thank the mothers . . .'

They all spun around. A man came running towards Ana from the direction of the houses that had stood further west along the coast. He was barefoot, and the left side of his face was a mass of bruises. Ana knew him. A little younger than her father, he had fished with Kirike many times.

She ran to meet him, and embraced him. 'Matu!'

'Thank the mothers,' Matu said again, panting, speaking too quickly. 'We thought we were the only ones left!'

Dreamer asked, 'Who is "we"?'

Matu pointed. 'My wife, the boys. We all survived. They're back that way, poking around the ruins of our house. My grandfather built that house. Nothing left, nothing . . . We clung onto a tree while the first waves surged. I nearly lost my grip on the youngest.' He blanched as he spoke, terrified even by the memory. 'Then we climbed the tree, and hung on when the big wave hit. It was morning before we dared climb down! We went home but the houses were smashed, and there was nobody else here, and we thought we were the last.' He grinned, a big beaming smile that split his grubby, bruised face. 'And now here you are! I shouldn't have lost my faith in the mothers.'

'You're not injured?'

'None of us are, not badly.'

Dreamer shrugged. 'That is the whim of the great sea, it seems. You die or you live; there is no in-between.'

Matu asked Ana, 'So what should we do first?'

Ana frowned. 'Why are you asking me?'

He seemed taken aback. 'Well, the children are hungry – we are all thirsty – there are the dead to think about.' He glanced at the sky. 'The weather has been kind. Perhaps the little goddess of the sea thinks she is in our debt, after what she allowed to happen yesterday. But that won't last. We have to think of shelter.' He looked at her expectantly.

She could think of nothing to say to him.

'Look!' Novu turned and pointed south, inland. 'I could swear that's a boat! But – a boat coming over the land?'

It was indeed a boat, carried overland by a party of men. The boat was more or less intact, though its skin was torn in places. The men were snailheads, Ana saw, and they were led by Knuckle, who jogged at the head of the party. It was a very strange sight, even on this strangest of days.

The party reached the Seven Houses. The men were all panting, sweating hard. Knuckle, naked save for a loincloth, wiped his brow and grinned at them. He said to Ana in the traders' tongue, 'We heard the wave. We found people running away from it. We hurried this way, towards your coast, and we found this boat – up a tree! Very far from the sea. Something has happened to the world.' He mimed with his hands. 'Very big. Very strange.'

'Yes,' Ana said. 'Big and strange.'

'We thought you would need this.' He gestured, and she saw

274

now that the boat was not empty; it contained sacks of food, fruit and dried meat and hazelnuts. One of Knuckle's men reached into the boat for a sack of water, which he splashed over his hot face and into his mouth.

'Thank you,' Ana said. She couldn't think what else to say. This generosity would save lives.

Matu reached. 'Oh, please – the water.' He switched to the traders' tongue. 'I apologise. Water. May I give some to my children?'

Knuckle frowned. Then he reached into the boat and threw a skin to Matu. 'We brought water for us to drink, while we ran. Not for you. What about your springs, your lakes?'

Dreamer said, 'Salt in them. Perhaps the big waves poisoned the ground. We've had nothing to drink.'

Knuckle's eyes widened. 'We will help you. Tell us what you need, what to do.'

And Matu turned to her again, expectantly, clutching his water bag.

Ana shrank in on herself. 'You're asking me? I don't know. If my father was here, or my sister—'

'But they're not,' Dreamer murmured. 'You are the Giver's daughter. Who else are these people to look to? Yesterday you saved my baby's life, you made a decision, at what might yet be a terrible cost. And earlier, it seems so long ago now, you made the decision to spare Novu for his theft, you showed wisdom. You can do this, Ana.'

Still Ana shrank back until she felt she could shrink no further, unable to feel, able only to react. *The woman broken on the tree. Arga's cry, when Ana let go of her hand. Her father, lost again.* They were all looking at her, Matu exhausted and desperate, the snailheads.

'The basics, then,' she said slowly, in the traders' tongue so all could understand. 'Water first. Without that the living will die. Knuckle, leave the food here. Send half of your men back with the boat, to where the water is fresh. Have them bring as much as they can. They can carry it in the boat. The rest of them –

Matu, go to your family first, and then lead Knuckle and the rest. Find the living. Everybody who has been spared, bring them here. Knuckle, we need shelter for the coming nights. Anything will do. Use the ruins of these houses to make lean-tos.'

Knuckle and Matu nodded.

Novu asked, 'And us?'

'And we three will consider the dead. Everybody knows the dead and the living cannot mix. That way lies disease. Our way is to lay out the bodies on the platforms and let the birds and the worms clean them, then we put the bones in the middens. We have many more bodies than the platforms could have held, even if they were not wrecked by the sea. For now we will place the bodies on the ruins of the middens, with the bones of our ancestors. When the birds and worms are done, we will build the middens over them. And Etxelur will continue.'

Matu said, 'Oh, it will continue all right. Thank you, Ana. I'll take this water to my family.' He hurried off, and Knuckle followed. Some of the snailhead men emptied out the boat, and set off back inland.

Dreamer patted her shoulder. 'Well done,' she whispered. She tucked the stabbing spear inside the straps of the sling that held her baby. 'Let's start.'

The tide was coming in by the time they had made the crossing back to Flint Island and reached its north shore. More debris was washing up, Ana saw, more tree branches and roots and lumps of sod, and darker, unmoving shapes on the sand.

She climbed up onto the broken-open midden. She glanced around at the ancestors' bones, exposed and scattered by a wave which had shown as little compassion for the dead as for the living.

She heard shouts from the beach. Novu was jumping in his excitement and pointing out to sea. Close by, Lightning was exploring another limp body.

It was a boat, Ana saw, still far out, being paddled by two figures too remote to make out. That could be her father – but his hadn't been the only boat out yesterday.

She slid down the midden's broken flank, and hurried down the beach. She refused to get excited, not until the boat had made it to shore.

And, closer by, she saw what Lightning was so interested in. It was a human body, washed up from the sea, limp and unrecognisable. The dog barked in his excitement, wagging his tail.

The boat landed. Novu helped one of its occupants pull it up the beach. The other occupant, smaller, slim, jumped out and came running towards her, hobbling on a damaged leg.

And as Ana neared that broken body she saw the red, tightly curled hair, the strong arms splayed in death, and she knew who this must be. She felt as if she died too in that moment, her human part withering away, leaving only a hard black core.

She was barely aware of it when Arga, stinking of salt, her skin burned by the sun, hurled herself into her arms. 'It's all right,' Arga said, burying her face in Ana's chest. 'You had to save the baby . . . It's all right . . .' Heni stood grimly behind her.

Lightning was whining, licking the dead man's salt-crusted face, trying to make his master wake up, as he always had before.

THREE

47

The third and greatest wave was the last.

The waters had scoured west across the coastal plains of northern Albia, and to the east across Gaira, flooding wetland and ancient forests. The coast of Northland was actually the last to be washed over by the tremendous ripple. It pushed its way into the river estuaries and swept over the lowlands, probing for a way across the rich plains to the valley of the snailheads to the south, thus forcing a passage that would cut Northland in two, and unite northern and southern oceans. That triumph was denied it.

Exposing a landscape that was devastated but intact, the water retreated.

For now.

48

The Year of the Great Sea: Autumn Equinox.

It was a huge relief to Zesi when she and the priest at last emerged from the forest cover.

It was around noon. She and Jurgi faced an open landscape of low hills studded with stands of trees, through which snaked the shining trail of a wide, sluggish river – a river that would head northward, just as they would, until it and they reached the sea. The sky was a deep, clear blue, cleansed by recent rains, and fat white clouds drifted. An autumn sky, she thought.

And as they walked into the sunlight Jurgi turned around, raised a grimy face to the sun, and, walking backwards, began to sing a song in praise of the little mother of the sky.

'I wish you wouldn't,' Zesi grumbled.

'And you're a misery.' A cloud of midges hummed around his head; distracted, he swatted at them. 'What a relief it is to break out of that awful dense clinging forest with those mad Pretani. Like being in a great green belly.' He breathed in deep and spread his arms, and for a moment she feared he was going to sing again. 'The sky and the sea – the greatest gifts of the first mother. Just to stand here – you can feel your mind expanding, filling the world.'

She grumbled, 'When I look at that sky all I see is a threat of rain. When I look at the land I see the distance we still have to travel before we get home. And when we get home I will see only the work that has to be done before the winter comes, all the things that my father won't have got around to sorting out yet.'

'You are a leader,' he said. 'And that's a good thing. We need leaders. Nothing would get done otherwise. But leaders need calm too. You can share some of your energy with me. And I will share my calm with you.'

'We'll see,' she said, noncommittal. There was a bite in the wind from the north, a breeze that sent ripples scudding across the long grass. 'Look how low the sun is, even though it's noon. The year is late. It took us much longer to work our way back out of the forest than it took to go the other way.'

'Are you surprised? Those trails they follow are narrower than a stoat's back passage. Shade and his boys probably hoped we would never make it out at all.'

'I told you, if I never hear that name again, I'll be happy.'

Jurgi grunted. 'And now that he's buried his father and brother, dead at his own hands, Shade probably feels the same way about you. Anyway, come on.' He turned around and strode off north, his pack on his back. 'We'll eat up a bit more distance before we have to make camp for the night.'

She followed his lead, hitching her own pack on her back, settling her stabbing spear in the straps, and marching on.

The priest seemed to have thrived on the adventure. He had become stronger, healthier in every way since joining her on this summer jaunt. She had to admit he had been a good companion during this long summer of walking.

But what had she taken away from her journey? Her understanding of the world had expanded hugely. She now knew the country of the Pretani; she no longer thought of the Pretani as mere savages but had glimpsed their culture, their background. Maybe you had to leave home to learn about the world – even to learn about home itself.

But these were lessons she had learned at what felt like great cost.

She hadn't wielded the blades that had been plunged into the bellies of the dead men. She hadn't created Pretani society with all its peculiar tensions and challenges. But if she had never existed, the Root and Gall would probably still be alive, and Shade would still be the bright, curious, loving boy she had met, instead of the bitter thing he had become in the course of a single summer. She'd made a mess of her time in Etxelur too, in her father's absence. What was it about her that caused her to trail death and unhappiness wherever she went? It was the darkness in herself she'd had to confront this summer that disturbed her most, more than all the horrors she had seen in Albia.

And then, of course, there was the baby.

It was her first child. She had no idea how it was supposed to feel, growing inside her. She could have asked Jurgi. In Etxelur tradition medical lore was scattered in everybody's heads, which was how her father had been competent enough to deliver Ice Dreamer's baby in a boat out on the ocean – but the priest, above all, guarded and supervised that lore. But pride kept her silent. *She* was the experienced hunter, she was in control while they were away from home. She did draw comfort from the priest's silence on the matter. She had the feeling that if there had been something to be worried about he would have spoken out.

This priest had a way of guiding you without opening his mouth at all. Curse the man!

But despite everything she was, at last, going home. Keeping up with the priest, she walked briskly, swinging her arms, concentrating on the simple pleasure of not having to pick her way along some cramped, confusing trail in the enclosure of the woods, and relishing the raspberries and blackberries they plucked as they marched.

Suddenly Jurgi stopped dead. He breathed in deeply. 'Why – I'm sure I can smell salt.'

She sniffed suspiciously. She could smell it too. They shouldn't be smelling the ocean this far south. Something was wrong.

They didn't speak further, and walked on.

They sheltered that night in a copse of trees, dominated by an old oak. But when they awoke in the morning that smell of salt in the air was stronger.

The scent gathered in the days that followed. And they started to notice changes in the land.

They came to a stand of trees, obviously dying, their roots waterlogged, their leaves limp. Zesi approached cautiously. Through her boots she felt the coldness of the damp ground around the tree roots. Only the alders seemed to be flourishing. One big oak that must have survived centuries was clearly suffering. There was no sign of life in the soggy undergrowth, no voles stirring. She found the mouth of a badger sett, stopped up with leaves and abandoned.

She touched the bark of the silent oak, then crouched down by its roots. A few acorns floated in a puddle, and she collected a handful absently. Then she dipped a finger in the water and tasted it.

'Salt?' the priest asked.

'Salt, yes. I think I remember this place. We are still at least a day from home, from the coast and the sea. How can salt water be poisoning these trees, this far inland?' She looked north, troubled; she sensed a great silence. 'Something has happened, priest.'

'Yes. Though I can't imagine what.'

It got worse the next day. They saw more dead trees, more standing puddles of water that always proved to be brackish. In one place the river opened out to a marsh, where at this time of year the wading birds should have been flocking, preparing for their flights to their winter homes, and the reeds turning from green to brilliant gold. But there were no birds, and the reeds were wilted and the willows bare. The place stank of salt and rot and death, and Zesi and Jurgi made a detour to avoid it.

Then they started to notice a strange covering over the land, a pale, whitish, sandy mud. It had clearly been there for some time, many days or even months, for it had been worked on by the rain and was washing away into rivulets and streams. But in places it stood thick, banked up like snow. Zesi bent to explore this strange stuff; it was gritty and full of stones and broken shells from the sea, and very salty on the tongue.

As they walked on the blanket of pale mud grew thicker, until it covered whole swathes of land. In places it included big blocks of peat, torn from the ground. Sometimes it obscured familiar features in the landscape, making tracks hard to spot. There were no raspberries to pluck now, nothing to eat, even fresh water rare.

But then they came to a place where somebody had taken a stick and scrawled in the mud, making the symbol of Etxelur, the three concentric rings and the radial slash. They both stood over this, oddly reluctant to go on.

'Hello! Hello!' A man stood by a copse, carrying a wicker basket. He was waving vigorously. His call had been in the Etxelur tongue. 'By moon and sun, I'm glad to see you, Zesi, Jurgi, we all will be!'

He was Matu, a friend of Zesi's father. They sat together, and shared dried meat and water.

His skin tunic was filthy, his legs were coated with the white dirt, and his basket was less than half full of acorns. He had been out since dawn, he said. They were half a day from home. 'But you have to come further south every day to find acorns, to find a tree that's not been poisoned by the Great Sea. I've never known an autumn like it. Well, none of us have. We're trying to get ready for the winter, we all are. But I sometimes wonder if I'm working off more fat than I'll get back from my share of the acorns. But what can you do?'

Ana and Jurgi glanced at each other. *The Great Sea?*

'Tell us what happened,' Jurgi said gently.

So Matu told his story. He mostly spoke to the priest. Jurgi seemed to have a knack of listening, of keeping the man's anxious gabble flowing. But neither of them knew what to make of Matu's account, of how the ocean had risen up and

286

smashed Etxelur, drenched the land with salt water and mud, and poisoned every stream and well.

This wasn't the Matu Zesi had known, this gaunt, anxious man with the hollow eyes, and gabbling speech. She'd never been much interested in him. He was a decade or so older than her, quiet, not particularly competent, short, squat, balding, with watery eyes. He was never a leader, never the sort of man who could challenge or excite Zesi. She supposed that without people like Matu no community like Etxelur could exist – there would be no stage for the more exciting exploits of people like herself. But now this uninteresting, unprepossessing man lived on where so many others had died.

And there was something crucial he wasn't telling them.

She broke into Matu's descriptions and grabbed his arm. 'My family,' she snapped. 'You say many are dead. What became of my family?'

Matu was frightened, she saw, intimidated by her. Yet he faced her, and spoke clearly.

And so she learned that she and Ana and Arga were alone now; Kirike was dead, and Arga's parents, her uncle and aunt.

She grabbed her pack and spear and stood up. 'Let's go home.'

49

They walked down the valley of the Little Mother's Milk, and at last came home to Etxelur.

Everything had changed. Much of the land was blanketed by the white muddy sand, which this close to the coast lay waist-deep in places. The old houses were gone, smashed and ruined, just as Matu had described. Even the sheltering dunes had been swept away, leaving heaps of sand and ragged clumps of marram grass.

All that Zesi recognised of her own home, the site of the Seven Houses, as they walked quietly up, was the basic shape of the land, its relation to the river valley to the east. Debris lay scattered on the ground – torn clothes, a necklace of pierced shells tied tight to suit a little girl's neck. There was only one structure here now, on the site of Zesi's own old house, a single pole thrust into the ground with a kind of lean-to of posts and kelp and skins heaped up around it.

And there was only one person here, a girl. She had her back to the newcomers. Dirty, sweating, she was working at a pit dug into the ground. She had a heap of gravel, and with her hands she shovelled this into the pit. Zesi recognised what she was doing. This was a winter store, designed to keep acorns safe from rot and rodents. You sealed the walls with wet clay, and laid down a layer of pebbles and chopped-up reeds, then poured in your acorns, then another layer of rock and reeds, then more acorns. When the acorns were dug out in the leanest times of the winter, they would have lost their bitterness. But Zesi could see the pit was all but empty – a third full, maybe a quarter.

'It's going to be a hard winter,' she murmured.

The girl spun around. It was Arga. Like Matu, she had lost so much weight she was barely recognisable. But a smile as wide as the moon spread across her face. 'Zesi! Oh, Zesi!' She got up and hurled herself at her cousin. Zesi felt the girl's shuddering sobs. 'Zesi, Zesi – you've been gone so long.'

'Only a couple of months—'

'I thought you were dead!'

Zesi stroked her hair. 'Now why would you think that?'

'Because everybody else is. My mother and my father and Kirike and—' She stopped, and her hand flew to her mouth. 'You didn't know.'

'Matu told me. I knew. It's all right . . .' But despite her soothing Arga was crying again, desolately.

'Poor kid,' Matu murmured. 'She's lost so much. In fact, she's lucky to be alive, and that's a story in itself. But at least she's got you home now, Zesi – and Ana.'

'Where is Ana?'

Arga said, 'Out fishing, with Heni.'

Zesi gaped. 'Fishing? Timid little Ana, fishing?' And she laughed, something in the shock of the day and the absurdity of the idea forcing the bubble of humour out of her.

But Arga looked confused, Matu disapproving.

Matu said, 'Yes, she's out on the ocean, fishing. Things aren't as they were when you went away, Zesi. We've all had to do things we weren't used to – things we find difficult, or even that scare us to death. We do them anyhow, to stay alive.'

'I'm sorry. I'm just – this is hard for me.'

He relented. 'I know. This is the day you learned your father died. Well.' He glanced at the sky, where the lowering sun was covered by a thin skim of fast-moving cloud. 'Weather's turning, and it's getting late. The boats will probably be coming in soon. Why don't you go and meet them?'

'Oh, yes,' Arga said, eager now. She tugged at Zesi's hand. 'We'll go to the island. Ana will be so glad to see you, it's been so long . . . Come on.'

Zesi slipped off her pack and her spear, and the priest added his pack to the pile. As they followed Arga and Matu she said to Jurgi, 'You know, I expected to be the centre of attention. Home from our adventures in Albia.' She patted her stomach. 'With news of my own. Instead—'

'I know. Whatever happened here, these folk have lived through something we'll probably never understand. But these are still our people, Zesi. And we are theirs. Just hang onto that.'

Arga and Matu led them around the bay towards the causeway to Flint Island.

Nature was following its course, Zesi saw. The grey seals, plump after the summer's riches, were arriving for their breeding season on the offshore rocks. They always returned to the same places, as if coming home.

But the seals were an exception, life going on amid the destruction. The beaches and marshes and tidal flats all showed signs of the ruin that the Great Sea had wrought: the dunes smashed, houses flattened, even the mud churned up and studded with dead trees and whole clumps of peaty earth. That awful layer of pale sand and mud lay over everything, thick with stones and smashed shells. There was a stink of death, and of rotting fish.

Everybody looked thin, hollow-eyed, over-worked. They seemed pleased to see Zesi and the priest back. But they were few, terribly few. Not many of these survivors seemed to be seriously injured, but there were few young, few old, and many families with gaps, a husband or wife missing, a child or two. She couldn't have imagined a greater contrast to the happy crowds of the day of the Giving.

They came to the causeway to Flint Island. People were working out on the line of the causeway itself, doing some kind of repair work with timbers and baskets of gravel; boats stood in the shallow water alongside, laden with supplies. Arga called Novu's name, and at the middle of the causeway the man from

Jericho straightened up, waved, and came back along the causeway, picking his steps with care.

Arga said, 'The Great Sea made a mess of the causeway. Well, it made a mess of everything. You always have to ask Novu or one of the other builders to help you across, because it isn't finished yet. That's the rule.'

'Whose rule?'

'Ana's rule,' Novu said as he approached, his strange accent thick. He too had changed since Zesi saw him last, the softness of his dark skin gone, his muscles prominent under a loose tunic. He didn't look like a man of Etxelur, not quite, but he didn't look like the creature who had arrived here with the trader either. He held out muddy hands to Zesi. 'It's good to see you back. Ana will be glad to know you're here.'

'So you're building the causeway?' It was a strange thing for her to have to say; the people rarely 'built' anything more elaborate than a house.

'Ana asked me to take charge,' Novu said, with what appeared to be pride. 'We build things in Jericho. The Great Sea smashed the causeway, so I'm building it back. We're filling in the gaps with gravel embedded in mud, and then piling logs on the top until you get a surface that breaks the water at low tide.'

The priest asked, 'Where do you get the logs from?'

'There are plenty. The Great Sea did a lot of damage far inland. You get whole tree trunks swimming down the river. Or you get trees washed up from the ocean as driftwood.' He grinned at Arga and ruffled her hair. 'Like the one that saved Arga's life.'

Zesi raised an eyebrow at the priest. That was evidently a story worth hearing.

'Come on,' Novu said. 'I'll take you across. It's pretty secure at the centre line, but a lot narrower than you were used to. Just tread where I tread.'

So Zesi and the priest crossed the new causeway, treading in Novu's footsteps, followed by their excited, tearful retinue. It wasn't difficult, provided you knew where to put your feet.

Arga held Zesi's hand tightly, as if she might leave again.

From the causeway Zesi got a good view of the ocean to the north, for the first time since returning to Etxelur. Something in her heart lifted at its grey hugeness. But she heard the people muttering curses at the little mother of the ocean, which you would never have heard a few months ago. As if in response a storm was gathering far out to sea, and rain fell in sheets that swept across the water.

When they reached the island Novu and Matu led them along the northern beach. At least here the white sea-bottom mud had mostly washed away on the tide. But everything had changed here too – the line of dunes, even the very shape of the shallow bay. Was it really possible that all of this had happened in a single day, as Matu had described?

The priest murmured, 'Look at the middens.'

By now it was no surprise to discover that the holy middens, too, had been wrecked. A few people were working up there even now, using broad-bladed shovels to heap up the debris, and Zesi saw the gleam of bone, pale on the middens' upper surfaces.

'The dead?' Jurgi murmured.

'This is the best we can do,' Matu said. 'Ana said we should lie them out on the ruins of the holy middens, and then build up the middens around them.'

Jurgi nodded. 'That was wise.'

Zesi had never heard the word 'wise' used about her kid sister before. Of all the strangeness she had encountered today, in some ways that was the strangest of all.

She looked out to sea again. Many boats seemed to be out, but as that storm gathered the boats were coming in, and people were running down to meet them. 'Everybody's fishing.'

Matu said, 'You know how rich the autumn is. But everything's been mixed up by the Great Sea. The cod are coming inshore, and we're relying on them. The geese and the swans, they're around. But the salmon have failed to come up the rivers this year. The eels haven't come down either.' Just as the

292

salmon came to the land and swam upriver to spawn every autumn, so eels would swim downriver to their own breeding grounds far out to sea. A failure of these tides of life was serious for the people of the coast. 'Even inland the hunting is bad.' Autumn was a key time for hunting too, when the deer and the pigs and the wild cattle were fattest, ready for the winter, and their fur was in the best condition. 'Either dead already or they've fled south. There are some who say we should do the same—'

'Not me, by the little mother's hairy left tit.'

Zesi swung around at the gruff, familiar voice. It was Heni, striding towards her from his beached boat. He bore a big basket of shellfish he'd been using for bait.

'Oh, Heni—' She ran to him, and he dropped his basket and enfolded her. He was a squat man but powerful, and he smelled of fish and salt and sweat, of the sea. He was the nearest to her father she would ever see again. Yet even now the tears would not come.

Stroking her hair, he murmured, 'I was with him, you know. Kirike. On the day he died. We were out at sea. I was a coward. I wanted to paddle away from shore, where we would be safe. *He* wanted to come home, to be with his family. We fought. He jumped over the side and tried to swim in. I— There was nothing I could do to stop him. You know your father. We found his body. He's on the middens if you want to see him. I was a coward,' he said, desolate.

'You're alive,' the priest said grimly. 'You made the right choice. Kirike was a brave man, a very brave man. But sometimes it takes more courage to do nothing.'

Heni seemed to notice the priest for the first time. 'You! You poppy-squeezing faker.' To Zeni's amazement Heni raised a fist.

Matu immediately got between the two men, and Novu wrapped an arm across Heni's chest, pulling him away. 'No more,' Novu said, pointing at Arga, who was starting to cry. 'We've had enough upset without that.'

Heni made a visible effort to calm down. 'All right, I won't do anything stupid. But you, priest, you let us down. Where were you when the Great Sea came? Where were you when we tended the sick? Where were you when we gathered up the dead? Where were you when poor Ana tried to find words to say over the bodies, all those bodies, up on the holy middens? *Where were you?'*

'It's not his fault,' Zesi snapped. 'He didn't cause the Great Sea. He couldn't have stopped it—'

'It's all right, Zesi,' Jurgi said. 'He's right. I'm the priest. I wasn't here, at the one time in my whole life, probably, I was needed the most. He's right to blame me, for I wasn't here to help him blame the gods.' He glanced at the middens. 'And I wasn't here to spare Ana. I will always regret that.'

'Oh, I survived.'

Ana was walking up from the sea. Like the others she looked too thin to Zesi, her clothes filthy with fish blood and crusted with salt, her hair tied back from a sweat-streaked forehead. Her face was expressionless. 'Hello, Zesi.'

'Oh, Ana—' Zesi wrapped her sister in her arms. She felt Ana respond, putting her own arms behind Zesi's back, but stiffly. She stepped back and faced Ana, the two sisters dry-eyed. 'Come. Let's walk.'

They set off together along the beach.

'You survived Albia, then,' Ana said.

'Only just . . . It's not the time to tell you about that. One thing you should know, though.'

'What?'

'I'm pregnant.'

That made Ana stop. 'The father is Shade?'

'Yes.'

Ana shrugged, and walked on, slowly. 'I don't suppose we'll ever see Shade again, or the Root.'

'The Root's dead. It got complicated. Even *more* complicated.'

Ana said gravely, 'We need babies. We are few, now. Less than half left alive. There are snailheads here. They help. But we

294

will have to work hard to live, Zesi. Work for the rest of our lives.'

Unless, Zesi thought dismally, we leave this desperate, half-drowned place and go south to the rich lands beyond this layer of white death, beyond the reach of another Great Sea, lands she'd walked through only days ago. She took a breath. 'Heni told me about father.'

Ana nodded. 'We have his body. It's on the midden still. Even the gulls are few this autumn, and slow in their work.'

'I'll say goodbye to him—'

'Sometimes I think it's because of me.'

'What do you mean?'

'You remember that night, the night of my blood tide, in the midwinter? When the owl became my Other. Since then Sunta died and Gall and father, and Rute and Jaku and so many others—'

'No. Hush.'

'I am the owl. I am death.'

It was alarming to hear her say such things; she was only fifteen years old. Zesi stopped walking and hugged her again. 'You're my kid sister,' she said, trying to tease her gently. 'What makes you think you're so important, that the mothers should send down a Great Sea to batter us all?' But that seemed to be the wrong thing to say. 'Look, things are never going to be as they were. But I'm home now, and I'll look after you.'

Still Ana didn't respond. Zesi became aware that the others, following at a distance, were watching them, Novu and Matu and Arga and even Heni. No, they weren't watching *them*. They were watching Ana, waiting for her to speak.

Ana turned away from Zesi and glanced at the racing sky. 'The storm's coming,' she said. 'Let's get these boats above the tide line. Novu, you'd better see if the causeway is still safe to cross. If not we'll have to make shelter here . . .'

To Zesi's blank astonishment, the people hurried to follow Ana's orders.

50

They made it back across the causeway, but the storm closed in before dark.

Zesi was welcomed into the rough hut that had been built on the site of their old house, the house she had grown up in with Ana and their parents and grandparents. Now there were only Ana and Arga and Zesi. The house, such as it was, was cramped, and as the wind picked up it creaked noisily, and rainwater leaked through the makeshift roof. It wasn't cold, at least; there was no need to try to build a fire in the rough hearth.

After eating some dried fish Ana, clearly exhausted, curled up on a pallet, her face to the wall, having said little to Zesi.

Zesi had thought Arga at least might be more curious. In her head during the long walk home she had rehearsed the kind of stories she might tell Arga about Pretani – exciting anecdotes for a seven-year-old, rather than the full truth of death and vengeance and twisted honour. But to Zesi's disappointment all Arga wanted to do was play fingerbones, a complicated game where you moved knuckle bones and fancy shells around a board scraped in the dirt. Arga had lost her parents, and most of her playmates of her own age; this was all she wanted. So, by the light of a lamp of whale oil in a stone bowl, Zesi played one game after another, almost always getting beaten.

At least playing a kid's game was better than facing the dark thoughts swirling around in her own head. It was the end of a long day when she had discovered her home was smashed and her father dead, along with around half of all the people she had ever known. And yet she found her thoughts turning to Ana, and the way everybody had deferred to her, out on the beach. Even Heni! Zesi had always been the leader, the strong one, the bright exciting one who everybody applauded. Now she had come back from a near-lethal adventure – she had come back with a baby – and nobody wanted to know, and it was her skinny, dull kid sister who got all the attention and respect.

Was she jealous? Was she so mean, so shallow, that she was *jealous* of Ana, even on such a terrible night – the night she had learned they had lost their father? She didn't want to feel like this. She tried not to hate Ana for making her feel this way. Tried not to hate herself for these unwelcome emotions.

The door flap was pushed back, letting in the wind and a shower of raindrops. It was Matu. 'Ana, I'm sorry.' He didn't even look at Zesi.

Ana rolled on her back, instantly awake. 'What is it?'

'The Milk. The storm has caused a surge on the river. It's looking like it's going to flood again. Some of us are heading for the higher ground.'

'I'll come.' Ana rolled out of bed, pulled on boots and a skin cloak, and pushed out of the hut. Arga followed.

Zesi was left sitting by the abandoned game. She had been utterly ignored in the whole exchange. But water was soaking in under the bottom of the walls, and pooling on the floor, in the shallow dip of the hearth. She grabbed her cloak and pushed her way out of the shelter.

The storm was wild, the wind howling, and the rain came at you flat and hard. Zesi was soaked in an instant. The ground was pooled with water, and she could hear the rush of the river. It was still not yet dark, with light coming from the horizon, a deep twilight that rendered everything blue or black or grey.

Novu was here, holding onto Ice Dreamer who had her baby in a sling before her, and Heni, the priest, a number of others. Arga started crying over her acorn pit, which was brimming with water, ruined.

Zesi saw terror in the eyes of the survivors of the Great Sea, of which this storm must be a terrible reminder.

'We should go,' Matu shouted. He had his family clutched close to him, his sons, his wife. He pointed south. 'If we climb up into the hills, we'll get wet but—'

'No,' Ana said.

'What?'

'We won't run any more.' She glanced around, and Zesi saw a cold determination in that young, pinched face. 'Matu, make sure your children are safe. Dreamer, take your baby. Zesi, maybe you and Arga should go. The rest of you—'

'We can't defy the river,' the priest shouted.

'But we can,' she snapped back at him. 'You go if you want to, priest. The rest of you, help me.' And she got to her knees and began to scrape at the muddy ground, making a mound. 'Get the shovels. We can't stop the river flood. But we can rise up above it.'

The others stood frozen, for a single heartbeat.

Then Matu pushed his wife away. 'Go, take the boys. Hurry, hurry. I'll be fine . . .'

Novu ran off, and quickly returned with shovels, shoulder-blades of deer and cattle strapped to stout poles. Matu took a shovel, and so did the priest. Soon there were six, eight, ten of them, all digging as Zesi watched. Some of the shovels were meant for clearing snow in the winter, but they did a good enough job in the sticky mud.

Soon a mound began to rise up above the sodden ground. Still the storm lashed down, and now water surged from the broken banks of the river. Even as the water ponded around them the diggers pushed their blades into the mud and heaped it up.

There was something about the whole situation that Zesi couldn't bear – Ana's strange doggedness in the face of the danger of the rising river, the way the others followed her unflinchingly. *Even the priest*, she saw, even the priest, who was as new to this as she was.

She pushed her way through to Ana. 'This is mad. You'll get somebody drowned.'

Ana didn't look up. 'You weren't here when the Great Sea came. I was. Dig, or go. Look after Arga.'

Zesi hesitated, torn. Arga had gone with Matu's family. Soaked to the skin, her hair flattened against her skull, Zesi ran after her.

When she returned in the morning, coming down from the low hills to the south of the settlement, Zesi found a low dome of black, glistening earth, and a dozen diggers sitting exhausted on top of it. The river had subsided, but water pooled around the mound. The storm had long blown out, and the sun had broken through, and the diggers smiled up into its light, filthy and soaked but safely above the water.

If Ana saw Zesi coming, she showed no signs of it. 'This is the future,' she said gravely. She held her own shovel over her head like a hunter's spear. 'The future.'

51

The Year of the Great Sea: Winter Solstice.

Heni lifted the door flap and brought Arga into Ana's house, his arm around the girl's thin shoulders. Arga had been on a great adventure. Wrapped in a blanket of thick aurochs skin and with goose fat smeared on her bare arms, she looked as if she had been very, very cold; but she was beaming, that big moon smile.

Lightning, asleep by the fire, stirred and grumbled at the draught. When he saw Arga his tail gave a fluttering wag, and then he subsided into sleep once again.

Through the door flap Ana glimpsed the day, and was surprised to see how low the light was already. But it was only a few days from midwinter. She had sat in here all day with Zesi and Novu and Ice Dreamer and her baby, talking by the smoky light of the whale oil lamps, with others coming and going with bits of business. These deep-winter days without sunlight, brief and dim, felt like they were no days at all.

'Come sit with me, by the fire.' She made a space for Arga between herself and Ice Dreamer, and got a dry cloth and began to rub Arga's wet hair.

'And shut that flap, curse your bones, old man,' Zesi snapped. 'You're letting all the heat out.' Zesi, big with her child now, was grumpy, restless, frustrated by the way her pregnancy slowed her down, habitually ill-tempered.

'All right, all right.' Heni shuffled in, huge in the cramped house, and he shucked off his big fur jacket, wet and smelling of sea salt. 'Is that Kirike's fish stew?'

'Here.' Novu handed Heni a wooden bowl of the stew, which had been simmering for days, with extra fish, stock, roots, nuts, oil and spices steadily added until the flavour became deep and enriching. It had been Kirike's favourite winter dish; he had been able to keep a single pot going for days.

'Ah.' Heni raised the bowl and drank deeply of the stock, and he belched, rubbing his belly. 'That's going to get me warm through.' He glanced at the chunks of fish in his bowl. 'There were more bodies down on the beach.'

Ana asked. 'Anybody you recognised?'

'One was a snailhead, I think. You could only tell from the funny shape of the skull. Face chewed off. Other kinds of people I didn't know at all. One had a necklace of tiny skulls, otters maybe. Chucked it back in the sea.' Heni inspected a lump of cod. 'But we have to eat.'

Ana nodded. They had been through these arguments. The folk of Etxelur had become uncomfortable eating the fish which had so evidently been feeding on the bodies in the ocean. But they had lost all their summer store to the Great Sea, and the autumn hunts had been disastrous on the shattered, salt-poisoned land. This autumn and winter, it was only the sea that kept them alive – the murderous sea turned provider. 'We have to eat.' She deliberately scooped up a cup of the broth, gathering bits of fish, and took a mouthful, chewing deliberately, though she was not hungry. 'With respect.'

Heni put the cod in his mouth and chewed carefully. 'With respect.'

Zesi snorted. She tended to scorn such rituals.

'So,' Ice Dreamer said, and she hugged Arga. 'You've been diving again, down to the Door.'

'She has,' Heni said proudly. 'That little one can hold her breath, I counted it this time, a full hundred and fifty of my heartbeats. And I've got a big old heart that beats pretty slow, I can tell you. I've never seen anything like it, like you're half-dolphin, girl. I'm always relieved when she comes up for air, because I couldn't fetch her if she didn't.'

301

Arga smiled shyly. 'I like it. It's easy.'

'It's ridiculous that you sent her out diving today, Ana,' Zesi said. 'It's midwinter!'

Arga said, 'It's not that cold when you're in the water, even if it's snowing up in the air. And as long as you keep moving you're all right. Anyhow the goose fat keeps you warm.'

Zesi pressed, 'And if you got stuck? If you caught your foot?'

'I wouldn't catch my foot. I'm not a baby.'

Novu leaned forward, fascinated. 'Never mind all that. Tell us what you saw this time.'

Arga's smiled broadened. 'I went to the house on the hill, in the middle, North Island. I went inside!'

Since the day of the Great Sea, and despite the hardships they had suffered, Ana and the others hadn't been able to put aside the memories of what they had glimpsed when the sea had rolled back. She and Novu and Dreamer had talked endlessly of the circular banks they called the Door to the Mothers' House, for Ana believed it truly to be the drowned heart of old Etxelur. They had even made sketches with bits of charcoal on skin of what they had seen.

Zesi had mocked all this, as she mocked much of what Ana got up to with Dreamer and Novu, 'your cabal of strangers' as she called them. Ana ignored her, though this infuriated Zesi even more. For she knew, deep in her gut, that this was important, for herself, for Etxelur, for the future.

Of course the Door was submerged once more, as it had been for generations before that one strange day. It had begun to seem that those brief glimpses were all Ana would ever be allowed.

But then in the late autumn Arga, the best diver in Etxelur, had come up with the idea of swimming down to see if she could see any more. Once Ana and the rest were convinced she could do it they had leapt on the idea.

So Heni had started to take Arga out on his fishing trips. He had been wary at first, and she had scornfully refused his offer of tying her to a length of fishing line so she could be hauled up if she got into trouble. She kept insisting she wasn't a *baby*. But as Heni had watched her dive he soon grew confident in her abilities, and trusted to her own native sense to keep her out of trouble.

Her first dives had been scouting trips to establish just where the Door was. It wasn't difficult if you knew where to look. The central mound really was North Island, and from there you could sometimes see the rest, Heni said, huge shadows beneath the water, unnaturally perfect arcs.

And then Arga had begun to inspect the Door. She would make two, three, four dives a day, until Heni judged she was getting too tired. She only dived on good days, when the sea was calm and clear and she was able to see what she was exploring. As the winter had begun to close in there had been talk of stopping the dives. But Heni pointed out he was going to have to go out fishing every day anyhow, and Arga was keen to carry on. Ana suspected it was good for Arga, better than sitting around in a hut all winter brooding on how she had lost her parents.

And, gradually, they were coming to map the Door, the strange structures lost beneath the sea.

Surrounding the central island were three circular ridges, which Novu called 'walls', sharing a common centre, nested one inside the next. Between the ridges were ditches, dug deep and full of sea-bottom mud. Arga said she saw the wreck of a boat in one of the ditches – a *big* boat, bigger than anything Etxelur had, similar to the giant wreck that had been exposed on the day of the Great Sea. The ditches had evidently been dug big enough to allow such boats to pass. Arga had found a straight ditch cutting through this complex of rings to the centre. This was surely another passage for boats. This discovery thrilled Dreamer, for it was another similarity to the rings-and-tail tattoos worn throughout Etxelur.

The walls themselves were tall, taller than Etxelur's middens, several times an adult's height if you measured them from the bottom of the ditches. Once Arga had dived down to the outer-most wall. Under a layer of silt and seaweed and barnacles she had found a harder surface, too tough for her to pick apart with her hands. It was gloomy down there, but she said this surface gleamed in the murky light with bright colours, red and white and black, the colours of shells and stones embedded in some denser material.

In recent days Arga had been exploring the very centre of the complex.

'It's not an island, it's a mound, like the ones you build, Ana. You can tell by the shape. Somebody built it. And just under the very top of this mound is a house.' Every adult in the shelter was rapt as the girl spoke, her eyes bright with intelligence, the remnant of the goose fat on her cheeks and neck shining in the light of the oil lamps. 'But it's not a house like this one, wood and skin and seaweed. It's stones, carved into shapes and heaped up.'

'Like Jericho,' Novu murmured, 'or some of it.'

'There might have been a roof once, but it's open now, you can swim down inside and there is a heap of stone blocks on the floor. And on top of that—'

'Yes?' Novu asked.

'Bones.'

'Bones?'

'It was confusing. I'll tell you what I *think* I saw. I'll probably have to go back to be really sure. On the top was a woman.'

'A woman,' Ana said.

'Well, a person. There was nothing left but the bones, all the rest had been eaten by the fish. She's all sprawled out on top of a deer. I know a deer's bones! But this was a big deer, bigger than I ever saw.' She reached up with her hands, indicating height. 'Big antlers.'

Novu frowned. 'Loga told me traders' tales of how giant deer live up in the northern lands, the north of the Continent, where it is always cold. They are hunted for their huge antlers and their big bones, which make deep-throated flutes. They are never seen as far south as this.'

'Nevertheless,' Dreamer said, 'such animals exist?'

'Oh, yes.'

Arga went on, 'There was something under the deer too. I only saw it dimly, and the woman and her deer were in the way. It was skulls. Cattle skulls, bulls with horns. There were lots of them, all lined up together and heaped up in big layers. It was difficult to see. There was kelp everywhere, fronds waving in the sea, like a forest.'

Jurgi nodded. 'The bulls, then the deer, then the woman, all sitting on top of the stone heap.'

'That's what I saw. All in this stone house. That's all.' She sat back, and drank some more broth.

Ice Dreamer, suckling Dolphin Gift, gave Arga a playful pinch. 'You know how to spin out a story, don't you?'

'It's all true!'

'I know, I know. But you tell it well.'

Novu shook his head. 'What does it mean?'

'Think of how it would have looked,' Ana said. 'The mound was above the level of the ridges. From anywhere in the Door, if you were on the ridges or in a boat, you could look up and see the mound, and the house of stone, and the woman inside, riding her deer.'

'They must have been dead,' Novu said. 'The woman and her deer. Who would sit there all day until the roof fell in on them? Maybe she was stuffed. I heard of people doing that, keeping corpses by taking out the innards and filling them with sand and spices. The deer too.'

'Ugh,' Heni said.

'Stuffed and painted. What a sight it must have been! So, Arga, did you see—'

'Hush,' Dreamer said. One-handed, she gently took the broth bowl out of Arga's hands. The girl had fallen asleep, just like that, and was slumping on Ana's shoulder.

'She's worn out, poor thing,' Heni said. 'For all she's brave the cold does take it out of her, I think.'

'I told you,' said Zesi. 'You're risking her neck with these stunts. If her father was alive—'

'But he's not, so that's enough about that.'

Zesi poked at the fire and stirred the broth, her ill temper evident in her every movement. She hissed at Ana, 'We need to talk.'

Ana put her fingers to her lips, and mouthed, *Not now*. She sat with the sleeping Arga, letting the girl's head fall to her lap, rocking her gently.

52

When Arga was deeply asleep on a pallet beside the dog, Ana, needing air, pushed her way out of the house.

She waited just outside the house for a while, letting her eyes adapt to the dark. She was surprised by the deep cold outside. Since Heni had brought Arga home the weather had changed, the murky air and cloud cover clearing away. Now the sky was a blanket of stars, frost coated the ground, and a sliver of moon offered a little light. Her breath steamed before her mouth, catching the colourless moonlight, and she pulled her skin wrap tighter around her shoulders. She could really have done with a thicker layer, but she didn't want to go back into the house to face more of Zesi's glares.

A spiderweb stretched from the centre pole of the house down its flank; it was heavy with dew that had frozen in the cold snap, so that its threads were thick with ice crystals. But she could not see the spider that had built the web. Perhaps the cold had driven it away. Cold brought beauty and death in equal measures.

She walked away from the house, and climbed the bank of dunes just to the north. These had been wrecked by the Great Sea, and the going was harder than it had once been. But tonight there was a crust of frozen sand that crunched under her feet, making the way a little easier.

When she reached the ragged ridge of the dunes she walked west. A thousand moons reflected from the ripples of the bay, to her right, and she could see the hulking forms of boats, upturned on the beach above the high-water mark. In the very early days after the Great Sea people had been forced to sleep under their boats, for lack of any other shelter. Tonight, she knew, as on every calm night, a few boats would be out, for no fishing weather could be wasted this hard winter, day or night. Meanwhile, to her left the land lay sleeping under a fine blanket of frost. The new houses of the people were shapeless heaps, shadows in the dark. And she could see the mounds she had ordered to be built, rising up from the plain. For now they were just heaps of earth, but they would show their worth when the next flood came.

The more she walked, the more the world seemed to open up around her, the stillness of the sky and the land, the calmness of the sea. She concentrated on the soft crunch of the frosty grass and sand under her feet, and the different texture of the light at night, the moon shadows that made dips and gullies seem deeper, the lack of colour that changed her sense of distance. It was as if she was walking in a different world altogether, a world separated from the clutter of the day.

Something rustled in a patch of long grass.

She stood still. She made out a round, pale body, long ears, a single black eye looking warily at her. It was a snow hare, already in its winter coat. She felt unreasonably glad to see it, for the Great Sea had left the land depopulated of its animals, even its birds – even the owl, her own Other, whose hooting calls were rarely heard this winter. But the hare was a great survivor.

After an instant of sublime shared stillness, something startled the animal. It bounded away in a spray of loose sand and frost. She glimpsed it once more, zigzagging across a meadow, compact and strangely graceful.

'I'm glad it didn't find my trap.' The soft whisper came from Matu, bundled up in thick furs; he clambered awkwardly up the dune face. 'Wouldn't have enjoyed killing a snow hare.'

Ana was disappointed that she was no longer alone, but she smiled. 'You're out late.'

'Just checking the catch. Anyway it's not that late. Fishers know how to track the passage of the night by the stars.' He looked around the sky and pointed. 'See the Bear?' This was a distinctive pattern of seven stars that resembled a bear in a crouch. 'When his body is pointing *that* way, the night is still young, and morning's far away. That's how it is tonight. Of course tomorrow night the positions will be a little different, and the night after that, different again. We experienced fisherfolk know the sky's secrets.' He smiled, gently mocking himself, for she knew that, like her, he had never been out fishing before the Great Sea forced him to.

She said, 'Ice Dreamer comes from a land far from here. But her people, too, call those stars the Bear.'

'Do they?'

'So she says. Perhaps it really is a bear, thrown against the stars in some long-gone age.'

He squinted up at the stars. 'It doesn't really look much like a bear, does it? You could think it looks like something else, a dog or a deer, and call it that. Perhaps our people and Ice Dreamer's knew each other before. Maybe we were once the same people, who have separated, carrying the same stories over the world.'

'And maybe everybody talks too much about stupid things that don't matter.' This was Zesi's harsh voice. She came walking along the dune ridge, following her sister's footsteps.

Ana's heart sank. So much for her quiet walk in the night. 'What are you doing here?'

'Looking for you. I said we needed to talk. Besides, Arga woke and asked for you. Poor little kid depends on us now, you know.'

'I know.' Ana refused to be made to feel guilty. 'She knows I never go far—'

'No. You stand around out here and talk, talk, talk . . .' Zesi was wearing only a tunic, not even a coat, so her belly showed, prominent. The hairs on her bare arms were stiff with the cold. 'What are you talking about now – star patterns? People who wandered around in the deep past?'

309

Ana said, 'Ice Dreamer's legends are all of a different kind of past, where—'

Zesi put her hands over her ears. 'I don't – *care* – what that woman says. I've had enough of her. And Novu, that other stranger you spend all your time with. What a waste of time it all is! Stars and legends! Mounds of earth! Bones under the sea! The people should be fishing. Hunting. Gathering the last acorns and hazelnuts – oh, I've heard enough. Tonight has driven me to a decision. This is what I want to tell you. In the morning I will speak to the priest, and some of the others, and talk about what we must do to get through the winter – and who must lead.'

'You're going to challenge me?' Ana, astonished, laughed.

Matu was not a man who grew angry. But now he faced Zesi and said sternly, 'In those first days after the Great Sea, when those who survived envied the dead, Ana made us *want* to live, by not giving in, by keeping going. Perhaps others could have taken that first step. Her father if he had lived. Perhaps you, if you had been here, Zesi. But it was Ana. We remember that. And you should show her respect.'

Zesi snorted, the breath streaming from her nostrils. 'Respect? For her? Don't make me laugh.' And she turned on her heel and walked away, along the ridge of the dune.

Ana sighed. 'Come on, Matu. Let's get back in the warm.'

53

The next day dawned clear and frosty, and at noon there was just a hint of warmth in the sunlight.

'A promise of the spring to come,' Ice Dreamer said. 'Or a memory of the summer past.' She sat on a bundle of furs heaped up on the dunes over Ana's house, lifting her face to the light.

From here Ana, sitting with her, could see much of the bay, and the grey outline of Flint Island. Dreamer's baby sat up on her lap, gurgling and smiling. They gathered around Dreamer, Ana and Arga and Novu, sitting on the ground in the brief warmth of the sun. They worked as they talked; they had a heap of hazelnuts to shell.

Dreamer's face was strongly shadowed by the sun, and age showed in the lines around her eyes and mouth, and in the grey streaks in her tied-back hair. Yet she was still beautiful, Ana thought, strong and beautiful. No wonder her father hadn't been able to abandon this woman when he found her on that distant shore. Kirike's and Dreamer's was one story among many cut short by the Great Sea.

Dreamer said now, 'What a night we had. What an extraordinary thing you have found, under the sea, Arga. More than earth and bones – you have found the story of your people. A story of times long gone, when huge boats must have sailed through those great ditches, and must have – *must* have – sailed across the western ocean to bring your mark to my far country. A story lost for generations, and now found again.'

'Yes,' Ana said. 'And it's all thanks to you, Arga.'

Arga submitted to a hug, but she seemed to have had enough

praise, and soon wriggled free. 'The question is, what do we do now?'

'What do you mean?'

'The Mothers' Door is our treasure. So we can't leave here. Can we? We can never leave this place—'

Ana said slowly, 'You're right. We would forget. Living somewhere in the south or in Pretani, mixed up with the snailheads and all the others, we would forget the Door – forget who we are.'

Novu said gently, 'But when the ocean rises, if another Great Sea comes—'

'We will build more mounds,' Ana said. 'As we have since the night of the storm when Zesi returned. So high the sea can never cover them and drive us away.' Maybe this was why the little mothers had given her the determination to stay and dig that night. Maybe it had been the seed of something much greater in the future.

'Yes,' said Dreamer reasonably, 'mounds will save you from an occasional flood. But what if the sea doesn't retreat again?' She waved a hand at the bay to the north. 'How long could you survive, on the highest mound, sticking out of the ocean?'

'We'd swim a lot,' Arga said seriously, and she looked hurt when they laughed.

'Perhaps there is more we could do,' Novu said thoughtfully. 'My people once built a wall around Jericho, to keep out floods from the hills. Even here we built the causeway to the island after the Great Sea destroyed it. Perhaps there is more we could build.'

'Like what?' Ana asked.

'I don't know. I'll have to think about it.' He got to his feet and surveyed the coast. 'Shall we walk around the bay? The tide is low and the causeway should be passable. We might get some ideas.'

Ana and Arga stood up, eager.

Dreamer said, 'Before you go, don't forget about Zesi. She

312

spoke to the priest earlier. She said she would call her meeting about now. About who should lead, and what we should do.'

Somehow Ana had forgotten all about her sister. 'Oh, I haven't got time for that. Come on, Novu, Arga.'

So they set off, the three of them, talking and laughing in the sunshine.

They walked all the way out to Flint Island, around its eastern promontory to the south shore, then back to the causeway. They talked and planned and dreamed all the way around.

By the time they got back to the house the sun was dipping to the western horizon, and the day's brief warmth had long bled from the air. They were all hungry.

But Zesi, rubbing goose fat into her boots in a corner of the house, looked furious.

They found that Zesi had held her meeting – so Ana heard from Ice Dreamer, who had got the story from the priest. Even Jurgi had been there reluctantly. Only a few people had bothered to turn up, and fewer yet had stayed as Zesi started talking about Ana's flaws, and the mistakes she had been making.

The last to stay had been Lightning the dog, who only wanted Zesi to throw a stick for him. Everybody laughed at this. Zesi stalked away, seething.

But, Ana reminded herself, a few people *had* come to listen to what Zesi had to say. Ana could never take for granted the goodwill of the people.

And Zesi's challenge had lodged a seed of doubt in her own mind. What if Zesi was right? What if she *had* been driven mad by the horrors of the Great Sea? She was still only fifteen years old, after all. Sometimes she still had nightmares of the man with no face, her father's corpse washed up by the sea. Who was she to shape the future? What if this nascent scheme to save Etxelur from the sea was just a fever dream?

If she was mad, how could she ever know?

54

The First Year After the Great Sea: Late Winter.

Cheek, the snailhead toddler, ran ahead of Ana's group along the new causeway. Her mother Eyelid, walking behind Knuckle, watched Cheek cautiously, but didn't try to stop her. Lightning ran after the child, wagging his tail and barking.

The causeway, rebuilt, cut across the ocean to Flint Island, a smooth arc. The way was solid underfoot on an upper surface of wood, logs pressed into mud. Gentle waves lapped to either side. To the left lay the open sea, and to the right the bay, where a couple of boats worked this morning searching for eels. And on the bay's southern shore Ana could see new houses sitting on their flood-defying mounds of dark earth. Half a year after the Great Sea, Etxelur was recovering.

It was a bright winter day, not yet a month after the mid-winter solstice, and the weather was benign, the wind low, the sea calm, and the ocean water reflected a diffuse, cloudy sky: a world grey above, grey below, and bitterly cold, yet full of light. Ana offered up silent thanks to the little mothers for the weather, as she walked between the priest and Knuckle, with Novu stepping quietly behind them with the rest of the snailheads. Maybe the mildness of the day would soothe the snailheads' mood – and make them more amenable to giving Ana what she wanted of them today.

Little Cheek was a bundle of furs, with hide bandages wrapped around her growing snailhead skull. But she was wide-eyed, fascinated by the water that lapped so close to her

314

feet. Knuckle watched her indulgently. Eyelid was the wife of Knuckle's dead brother Gut; Cheek was his niece. Knuckle had grown closer to Eyelid, since Ana had rejected his tentative advances. Ana was glad for them.

Not that she knew them all that well; they were still very odd by Etxelur's standards. Walking now with Eyelid, she tried to think of something to say to her. But with the snailheads, as with the Pretani, the men decided everything of significance, while the women did the work – or anyhow that was how it seemed to Ana. Eyelid wouldn't even speak to the Etxelur folk save through Knuckle.

'Cheek can't remember the ocean,' Knuckle said now. 'She was last here at midsummer. Long ago for a three-year-old.'

'For all of us,' said the priest. 'Because of the Great Sea the world has changed since those days. But I don't suppose the little girl will remember that either.'

'No,' said the snailhead grimly, 'and she's lucky for that.'

Ana nodded. 'Well, it wouldn't have been possible to walk this way just a few months ago. It's taken a lot of hard work to restore the causeway.'

Jurgi glanced at her with approval; she was learning subtlety, and was steering the conversation the way she wanted it to go. It had even been her idea to bring the snailheads out to the causeway, the nearest they had to a demonstration of the dream they wanted the snailheads to share.

Knuckle said now, testing his tread on the logs under his feet, 'Better than I remember. I never trusted that muddy track.'

Novu stepped forward and said, 'The old causeway was a gift of the gods. What we did this time was to start again from the beginning. Of course the natural track was the starting point. We pushed rocks and gravel and brush into the mud. And then we laid logs over the top, pressing them down. Now the causeway's stronger than before and higher. And it's sturdier. You can feel that. It's already withstood a couple of winter storms. I don't know if it could survive another Great Sea.' He glanced out at the placid ocean. 'I'd like to find out.'

'Don't challenge the gods,' the priest murmured, 'lest they take you up on it.'

Knuckle asked Ana, 'So how is your sister? Produced her Pretani pup yet?'

'No. Well, not the last time I saw her.' Which was another gift from the gods, as far as Ana was concerned. Zesi, fuming, frustrated, continued to oppose all Ana's projects, and ranted at anybody who came within earshot about how their father wouldn't have run things this way. She would have been particularly difficult this morning, for she had been central to the mess that had led to the death of Gut, Knuckle's brother, at the hands of Gall the Pretani. But her long pregnancy was keeping her out of the way, and Ana was grateful to be able to get some work done.

They reached the island, and walked around its northern shore towards the holy middens, now half-rebuilt themselves. Cheek ran ahead along the sand, kicking at washed-up seaweed, and the dog ran after her.

Suddenly Ana saw oystercatchers, a pair of them flying low along the coast. They were big birds, black and white with distinctive orange beaks and a plaintive, repetitive cry. They were probably both males, this early in the year, preparing for their flight up the river valleys where they would stake out territory on a shingle bar, to build their ground nests. She felt her spirit expand, as if thawing out, at this latest sign of the turn of the season.

Knuckle watched the birds fly, his great head gleaming in the sun's watery light. 'We were coastal folk, like you, down in the south, before the sea drove us away. We live in the forest now. But the forest has its charms, even in the winter. You can see the squirrels run in the bare trees, and the nests of the rooks.'

The priest nodded. 'It is said a rook always comes back to her old nest.'

Knuckle grunted. 'Just as you have come back to yours – even though the ocean told you it didn't want you any more.'

316

Ana said, 'This is our home. Our ancestors' bones are piled deep in the middens.'

The snailhead raised a shaved eyebrow. 'That's your choice. So why have you asked us here? I think you want something,' he said bluntly.

'I suppose that must be obvious,' said the priest. 'But you're right. We have something to show you. Come. Just a little further.'

They walked away from the beach and cut south across the island, picking their way along a trail that led through sea-battered dunes, and then around the island's central hillock.

They soon broke through to Flint Island's south coast, where they had a clear view of the promontory just on the other side of the bay. On the narrow beach here logs had been heaped up, stripped of their bark. A couple of men were working on them, using heavy flint axes to sharpen one end of each log.

While child and dog ran off to play with another mound of seaweed, the adults shared skins of water, carried by the priest.

Knuckle looked around, sniffing the cold air. 'Never came here.'

'There's no reason why you should,' Novu said, stepping forward. 'Yet it's an important place.' He waved a hand. 'You can see we're at the mouth of the bay. The narrowest point, where Flint Island comes closest to the mainland. When the tide rises the water rushes through here to fill up the bay. When the tide goes out the current is just as strong the other way. The kids like to swim here.'

'Never much liked swimming myself. So what are those lads doing hacking away at logs?'

Novu took a deep breath, and Ana remembered how hesitant he had been when he had first described his grand scheme to her and the priest and Dreamer, in the confines of her house. It was all founded on Ana's determination, but it was Novu's vision, and now he had to describe it all over again.

'We want to build a dyke across the bay. Just here, between

317

this headland and that promontory, across the bay's neck at its narrowest.'

Knuckle frowned. Ana wondered if he was familiar with Novu's Jericho word 'dyke'. 'What? Another causeway?'

'No. Well, you could walk across it, it will be wide enough, but it's not just a causeway. It will be a kind of wall. Look around. Once this bay was dry land – that's what the Etxelur folk say. Their grandparents mined flint here. But then it became marshy, and then salty, and the grass and the trees died, and the houses had to be moved up to the beach. Now it often floods high beyond the beach, even at a normal high tide. And if you get an exceptional tide or a storm—'

'The sea has taken the land back. Just as in the south, our home under the cliffs of white rock. That's what the sea does.'

'Yes. But that's what we want to fight against. We'll build a dyke, right across the bay. It will rise up high above the water – above the high tide level. So then, you see, the ocean won't be able to break into the bay again. The bay itself will be like a lagoon, isolated from the sea.'

'No more flooding,' Knuckle said.

'No more flooding.'

'*If* you can build this dyke.' Knuckle stepped forward and peered at the sea, where it ran between headland and promontory. 'How? You built the causeway where the old one ran. There is no causeway here.'

'No. In fact the seabed is deeper here, because it's been scoured by the tides. That's why we need the logs, these sharpened stakes. You see, we'll drive them into the sea-bottom mud, in parallel rows—'

'You built dykes like this before?'

'No,' Novu said defiantly. He'd faced this question before. 'But my people have. I've seen it done.'

'Hmm. Seen a bird fly. Doesn't mean I can do it myself. Doesn't mean I should try.' He turned to Jurgi. 'You will defy your gods?'

The priest said, 'We fight the ocean, but not our gods. When the great cold retreated, our ancestors walked into this land behind the little mothers. While the mothers built the hills and river valleys and beaches, the people named each living and non-living thing, and gave each a story. We made the land hand in hand with the gods. There's no reason the gods will be unhappy if we build it again.'

Knuckle eyed him. 'You're a clever man, priest. I think you have a way of saying what needs to be said. And when will you start to build your wall?'

Novu gestured at the men sharpening the logs. 'You can see the work's already started. But the spring equinox will be the key time. The days of the low tide. That is when the seabed will be easiest to reach.' He walked to the sea's edge and sketched great arcs with his hands. 'We plan to work out from either side of the bay, and meet in the middle.'

Knuckle turned and looked around at them, Ana and Novu and the priest, and the two men desultorily hacking at the logs. Ana imagined what he saw: scrawny people in their ragged clothes, stick-thin already and with the hungriest part of the winter still to come, and yet here they were talking of expelling the sea itself. Knuckle said gently, 'Ana, Jurgi, you have done well to survive. But this wall across the sea is a dream. Look at you. You don't have the strength . . . Oh.'

Ana smiled.

'This is why you asked me to come here. You want us to help build the dyke?'

'There are more of you than us now. I don't know if we can do it alone. We'll try. But with your help—'

'We're half-starved ourselves.' He glanced at Cheek, who was tugging on a piece of seaweed with the dog. 'I see a busy year, full of the work of staying alive. That will be hard enough.'

'I know what I'm asking.'

'Do you?' His face grew harder. 'You Etxelur folk look down on us, for we are newcomers to your land. Why should we come here now, risk our own chances of life, just to help you?'

Jurgi said, 'But it isn't just about us. Think. The sea is rising.

319

We know that. Our grandmothers were driven back from the floor of this bay, just as you had to retreat north when the sea lapped higher against your white cliffs. We could give up. We could simply walk away from here, and go south – but *you're already there*. And as the sea rises more and more, as we head further south and others come pouring north—'

'All right!' Knuckle snapped.

Ana nodded. 'So will you help us?'

He looked around, at the channel into the bay. 'I don't know. Not for me to say, not alone. The elders will talk about it. That's all I can do.'

Novu said urgently, 'But you must make them see—'

Ana touched his arm, hushing him. She said to Knuckle gravely, 'Thank you. We can't ask any more of you. Look, you're our guests here. Let us feed you. If you'll come to our house—'

Knuckle glanced up at the sun. 'Yes. We need to eat. Which is the quickest way back? Eyelid, Cheek – this way!' And he marched off across the beach.

55

The First Year After the Great Sea: Spring Equinox.

Ana led her sister up the rough trail to the top of Flint Island's solitary hill.

It was a bright day, and though the breeze that blew off the sea had a bite in it, the sun was strong, for perhaps the first time this year, Ana thought, after what had seemed a long, cold winter – hot enough to make Ana sweat under the pack of water skins she carried on her back. Zesi was additionally laden with her new baby, just a couple of months old, a little boy she'd defiantly called Kirike, who she carried in a sling. Zesi kept up a tough pace, and if she felt any weakness from a winter of hunger and the aftermath of a long and difficult labour she seemed determined to show no sign of it. But Ana saw how pale she was, how hard she was breathing.

It struck Ana that Zesi didn't speak to her baby once during the climb – whereas Ice Dreamer talked to Dolphin Gift all the time, and she was already responding with gurgles and smiles.

Responding to the warmth, chaffinches were working the exposed ground, a gang of a dozen of them busily and expertly poking in the grass, their round pink bellies bright in the low sunlight. Mixed in with them were bramblings, so like the chaffinches save for the white flashes of their bellies, visible as they ducked and bobbed. The sisters startled the little birds, and they fluttered into the air, spiralling in pairs to the safety of the trees' lower branches.

They passed the flint lode, a dent in the hillside, but nobody was working today. A pool of stagnant rainwater lay in the bottom of the working, where Ana saw bright beads of frog-spawn, each with its telltale black dot, another promise of new life.

Then they reached the shallow summit of the hill, a place of sparse grass and rocky hollows where more rainwater pools glimmered. Here sat a tremendous stone that the people called the First Mother's Knuckle Bone, for they imagined it had been spat out by an ice giant when he consumed her huge body.

Zesi paused by Knuckle, the sleeping baby lifted by each heavy breath. 'So? Here we are. What do you want?'

Ana slipped off her pack and dug out a couple of water skins; she threw one to her sister, who caught it one-handed. 'Zesi, I need to talk to you about the dyke. Novu, the priest, the others are waiting to see you later. But I wanted us to speak first.'

'So why come up here? Why not speak in the house?'

Ana stepped to the edge of the summit, looking south. They stood over the mouth of the bay. Its enclosed expanse swept off to their right, while to the left was the open sea where the people's boats were scattered. Everywhere the sun reflected from the water. Ana pointed down at the mouth of the bay. 'There. *That* is what I brought you up here to see . . .'

The tide was rising, and you could see the water rushing to fill up the bay, small waves breaking against the rocks of the promontory on the far side. And you could also see two fine lines curving out from the land, one from the headland on the north side, one from the promontory to the south. A gap still lay between them, in fact there was more gap than line, but the intent was clear.

'Novu's folly,' Zesi said dismissively. 'I saw it before. From you standing on that mound of mud in the rain with a spade, all the way to this. And you brought me all the way up here just for this?'

'Down on the coast all you can see is the problems. From up here you can see the dyke, the whole thing, as Novu dreamed of it.'

Zesi grunted. ' "Dreamed" is right. But it isn't finished.'

'Well, no. The work is going slower than expected – the snailheads may yet help us, they haven't decided, we never have enough people—'

'I know you don't have enough people. Most of them have been out with me on the northern shores, hunting cockles at low tide. We can't eat a stranger's dreams. And we're already past the equinox. You said you hoped to be finished by now.'

'We did. It's going to be harder to work through the days of the higher tide, but it's not impossible. Novu says we can still finish it if—'

'If, if, if. Always "if" with that fool. Never "when".'

Ana sighed. 'This is what you've been saying all winter. Even though nobody supported you at the meeting when you challenged me. You've been going around attacking the dyke, attacking me. Putting people off, word by word.'

Zesi patted the baby on her chest. 'And I'm going to keep on saying it. Just be grateful I was stuck in the house for as long as I was, little sister, or that dyke wouldn't have been started at all.'

'Look, Zesi, I don't care about beating you. I don't even care if you beat me.'

'Well, that's good, because you will be beaten.'

'All I want is for the dyke to be finished.'

'It never will be. Get used to the idea. Are we done here? Then let's go find the other idiots, and get this over with.' She crumpled the empty water skin, threw it back at Ana, and began to stride down the trail that led to the mouth of the bay.

Novu was waiting for them at the bottom of the trail. Zesi walked straight past him, ignoring him, and headed to where Dreamer and the priest were waiting further on, at the abutment of the dyke itself.

Arga was here, working with a heavy scraper at the end of a thick log. When she saw Zesi coming she ran to her cousin. Zesi smiled and leaned down, so Arga could see the baby in his sling;

Arga made cooing noises, and tickled the baby's face. Her knees were grimy where she'd been kneeling to work.

Ana followed with Novu, more slowly. 'At least she behaves like a human being around Arga. But what's Arga doing here anyhow? She hasn't got the muscles for heavy woodworking.'

Novu shrugged, looking tired, unhappy. 'Look around. Nobody to collect more logs, nobody to work on those we have left. Things aren't going well.'

'Maybe Zesi really is getting to them.'

'Either that, or it's just the turning of the seasons. People have other things to do, in the spring.'

'Well, we must try to speak to Zesi. That's why I brought her here.'

They joined the priest. He waited with Dreamer, who had left her own child at home this morning; she stood tall in a simple smock, her rich dark hair tied back, her arms folded.

'So,' Zesi said, looking around at them all. 'You've got your whole gang here, little sister. Two outsiders, and a priest who's away with the spirits.'

Jurgi just laughed. 'Good morning to you too, Zesi.'

Dreamer stayed as ice cool as her name. 'Outsiders? Were we outsiders during those long nights in the house, Zesi?' When, as Ana knew too well, it had been the priest's medical expertise and Ice Dreamer's patient support that had got Zesi through her labour.

Zesi was too tough to be deflected by that. She sneered and turned away.

Novu said impatiently, 'Zesi, you've come all this way. Let me at least show you what we've built. Come, walk with me.' He led the way out onto the tongue of the dyke, which pushed out from the shore and out across the mouth of the bay. It was little more than a single pace wide, but it rose up above the water surface, offering firm footing.

The others followed, including a sceptical Zesi. Arga ran ahead of the others, skipping, confident.

Zesi at least seemed intrigued by the construction. 'So this is what happened to all those logs we cut.'

'Yes. Look – they have been driven into the seabed, sharpened end first. It wasn't as hard as it looks for the bed is very soft here, thick with mud. We build two parallel rows, as you can see. We jam them in as close together as possible, and caulk them with tallow, as you would caulk the seams of a boat. Then we drop rocks into the space between them, gravel and mud and sand and brushwood – anything we can carry, really – to force the water out. And that's the dyke, and it's waterproof, or as good as. Look.'

They had already reached the end of the dyke, as far as it had been built. Looking out Ana could see the other side, reaching towards her from the promontory on the south side of the bay mouth. At least people were working over there, hauling big bags of rubble out from the shore.

Zesi patted her baby absently as she looked around. 'The logs will rot in the water. The whole thing will just crumble and wash away.'

'But this is just a start,' Novu said eagerly. 'We can pile on more material, more rocks and mud, over the logs to seal them in. That way they won't rot at all, and even if they did it would make no difference. When the first dyke is established it will be easy to build on it in future years.' He reached up. 'It can go as high as you like, as we deal with freak tides – or with the sea rising.'

'So when will it be done, brickmaker? You said it would be complete by now. You are no more than – what – a third finished? ' She gestured at the heap of logs, abandoned on the shore. 'Where are your workers? Where, indeed, are your logs?'

Novu sighed. 'You know as well as I do. We made a good start. But in the spring there's hunting to be done, fishing, boats and nets to be repaired. Nobody's actually refused to carry on. But they're drifting away. We can't get everything done, *and* build the dyke – that's what people started saying to me.'

'And you've dragged me all the way to see this vain joke of yours because—'

'Because we want your backing,' the priest said simply. 'You know, Zesi, you fight for the respect you feel is your due. But you don't need to try so hard. You *are* respected. You are your father's daughter; you are a strong woman in your own right. People listen to what you say – and it's entirely negative about the dyke.

'I know it's a difficult year. It will be a long time before we have anything but difficult years. But we have to find a balance between the needs of the present and this plan for the future. For if we don't do this, sooner or later we will have to abandon this place, our ancestors' land, and become rootless, like the snailheads. We are a great people. Remember that, Zesi. We once built the Mothers' Door! And we forgot about it, nearly. We need to be a people who can do something more than just survive—'

'What we need is less talk from you,' Zesi said bluntly. 'If you thought you would sway me with this nonsense, this walk into the sea, you haven't. I'm going to keep on arguing against you until this foolish distraction is abandoned, and we get back to what's important in life. I'm going back.' She held out a hand. 'Arga. You come too. Enough of this.'

But Arga was staring south across the bay. She pointed. 'Look!'

Ana turned. There on the water, coming around the point of the bay, was a small fleet of boats. Even from here she could see that the people paddling them were snailheads. And behind them came what looked like a raft, wide, thick, huge. It was logs, a mass of them, strapped together and floating on the water.

'I don't believe it,' Dreamer said.

'I do,' Ana said, warm deep inside. 'It's taken a while for Knuckle to come through. But here are the snailheads, coming to help us.'

One of the snailheads was standing on his boat, waving and shouting.

Novu waved back. 'I can't hear what you're saying, if that's you, Knuckle. But I love you, even if you are an ugly lophead!' He grabbed Ana. 'You see what this means? With lumber, with more muscles, we'll get this first barrier finished in a heartbeat. And then—'

Ana had to laugh. 'Yes, Novu? And then? What dreams are you cooking up now?'

'Not dreams,' Zesi hissed. 'More madness.'

She was seething, Ana saw. But while Zesi might be able to talk around some of the Etxelur folk, she had no hold over Knuckle, who hated her so much he would never listen to her.

Novu said, 'Come on, let's help those snailheads get all that lovely wood ashore.' He ran back along the dyke to the beach, shouting instructions out to sea.

56

The First Year After the Great Sea: Summer Solstice.

Jurgi the priest, in his Giving finery of poppy crown on his head and new flint axe at his neck, waited for the snailhead party on the southern bank of the outflow of the Little Mother's Milk. He had brought food for the visitors, dried fish and hazelnuts, and sacks of drinks.

Kara, wife of Matu, had come with him to set up this small feast. Kara had laced her hair with flowers. She was still thin from the winter's deprivations, as they all were, but she looked welcoming and beautiful.

And here came Knuckle, leading a party of a dozen snail-heads down the valley of the Milk, with Eyelid, wife of his dead brother, at his side. They strode easily, smiling in the midsummer sunshine. The country was generous at this time of year, and they hadn't needed to carry much – bundles of spare clothes, a few tools, skins for overnight shelters. Eyelid's daughter Cheek was running around, weaving complicated patterns of her own around the adults' steady plod. She grew more active and confident every time Jurgi saw her.

Jurgi saw how easily Knuckle and Eyelid walked together, their arms brushing. The company of others was a subtle and consoling gift of the little mothers.

As they approached, the snailheads broke from their walk to fall on the refreshments Jurgi had brought. The children soon found the honeycombs.

Jurgi, smiling, came up to Knuckle with a skin sack.

'Blackcurrant juice,' he said in the traders' tongue. 'I remember how much you like it.'

'Good man.' He took the sack, removed the wooden stopper from the sewn neck, and poured the thick liquid into his throat. 'Honour to have the priest of Etxelur come to meet us.'

'The honour is mine. It's been a hard year – hard for everybody in Northland. But without you we would be much worse off.'

Knuckle nodded, his great misshapen head gleaming with beads of sweat, and he looked down at the children gorging on the chunks of honeycomb. 'In the end we knew you were right – and Ana, your young goddess. If you had been forced from the coast, it would have been our turn next. Time to take a stand.'

'Exactly. Look, your people are welcome to go on around the shore to the Giving feast. The stand has been set up by the middens as usual.' He glanced up at the sun. 'I think the games will have started by now. But come with me along the river valley, Knuckle. I want you to see what's become of your gift of logs and labour. I think you'll be impressed – and surprised.'

His chin smeared with fruit juice, Knuckle grinned, showing his studded tongue. He turned to Eyelid and his people, and they had a short, jabbered conversation in their own guttural language. The children were keen to get to the beaches, for swimming in the sea was a treat for these inlanders. The younger men and women wanted to take their chances in the contests, the running and throwing, and to see how the crop of Etxelur youngsters – those who had survived the Great Sea – had blossomed in the last year. But Eyelid decided she and Cheek would walk with the men.

So, led by Jurgi, the four of them set off up the valley of the Little Mothers' Milk, heading roughly west.

Away from the estuary the valley soon narrowed, the languid water passing between walls of sandstone. The trail they followed was sometimes hard to make out, so high was the bracken around them. The flowers' colours were bright in the midsummer light, and fat bees hummed in clouds of pollen.

'World full of life,' Knuckle said. 'Less than a year since whole place smashed by the Great Sea.'

'But some have not returned. Otters, for instance.' On impulse the priest bent down, rooted at the base of the bracken, and came up with a handful of soil. It was speckled with white. 'And the sea-bottom mud is still here as a reminder. In time it will be hidden, but it will always be visible to anybody who cares to dig down into the ground. Like the extra thickness of a healed bone.'

Knuckle grunted. 'You are thoughtful. Glad I'm not a priest, having to think. Happy to live in the now.' The path dipped closer to the water, where the air was thick and hot. 'How far is this mystery of yours?'

The priest grinned. 'Just a little further . . .'

The valley opened out here and the river broadened, becoming shallower as it ran over its bed of gravel and mud. On the south bank, where they walked, a broad grassy plain stretched away, studded with tall bright thistles and churned up by the hooves of the cattle that came here to drink. To the north the land rose up into the low hills that divided this valley from the bay.

The priest pointed to the north bank, where a rivulet descended between two green hummocks towards the river. 'See that?'

'A stream. So what?'

'It wasn't there this time last year. We need to cross the river. There's a ford just further down.'

They walked on to a place where the river was wide and very shallow. Following the priest's lead, the snailhead slipped off his boots and walked out across the river's gravelly bed. Knuckle enjoyed the walk in the water, childlike, as he hopped from one stone to the next. He slipped once, and laughed as he recovered, splashing water over the priest.

Cheek was delighted by the water, and gurgled as she splashed with her mother.

Soon they were all on the north bank. The rivulet, descending from the slope, emptied into an area of marshy land.

The snailhead spread his hands. 'We came all this way to see this?'

'Taste it.'

Knuckle grunted. 'Thirsty anyhow.' He took a healthy scoop of water in his cupped hand, tipped it into his mouth, and immediately spat it out. He looked at the priest, astonished. 'Salt!' The snailhead looked up at the innocent hillside. 'Salt, like the sea!'

'Salt. But it wasn't this way before. Come on. You might want to put your boots back on. We have to climb.'

Cheek and Eyelid decided not to follow. They stayed playing in the stream, while Knuckle climbed after the priest.

They followed the rivulet's little valley, cut into natural folds in the landscape, up the side of the hill. It wasn't steep, but the priest had to take big strides over the long grass. He walked close to the rivulet, and he could smell the salt of its water, growing stronger as they climbed further.

They were both breathing hard by the time they had reached the summit of the hillock. From here, looking north over the shoulders of rounded hills, they could see the complicated geography of Etxelur, the bay, Flint Island, and the sea beyond. A soft breeze blew from the sea.

'Nice view,' Knuckle said, panting.

'Yes. But I brought you here to see this.' Jurgi pointed at a pond that nestled on the hillock's broad summit.

You could immediately see that the reservoir was artificial. *Reservoir*: another of Novu's words from Jericho that had become part of the Etxelur tongue. Several paces across, it had been a natural feature, a pond gathered in a dip, but it had been deepened and made neatly circular, and lined with stones and clay and mud to make it waterproof. In a confident flourish two rings of earth had been dug up around its perimeter to make a crude approximation of the three-ring symbol of Etxelur.

And the reservoir was brimming with water – even though, as

the priest indicated to the snailhead, water flowed out of the pond through a breach in the wall to feed the rivulet.

Knuckle tasted the pond water. 'More salt,' he said without surprise.

'It mixes with the natural runoff. I can't imagine it will do much harm to the wildlife of the Milk, its flow is so tiny compared to the river's grander flow. And ultimately, of course, it will be washed all the way to the estuary and out to sea.'

'Fine. But how does salt water get up here in the first place?'

'Come and see.'

The priest led him over the summit to the hill's north face. From here more ponds were easily visible, one, two, three of them, cut in a row down the side of the hill that led to the marshy shore of the bay. Each of these ponds was as neat and circular as the first; each of them had been made by deepening and sealing a natural feature. There were people working between the second and third ponds, two rough lines of them.

The snailhead nodded. 'I begin to see. The saltwater comes from the sea—'

'No. *From the bay*. Behind the dyke.' Jurgi pointed to the curve of the dyke, which was now complete and swept across the mouth of the bay at its narrowest point, shutting out the wider sea. 'That's important.'

'So the water is lifted up to these ponds. One after another, until it runs out on the far side of this hill to the river—'

'And then out to sea.'

The snailhead shook his head. 'How is it lifted?'

The priest grinned. 'A good practical question. I'll show you.' He led the way down the hill a little way, until he came to a length of rope to which a kind of sled had been fixed. The sled, made of sewn, caulked skin sitting on wooden runners, was big, several paces long. The rope was fixed to one end of the sled, and trailed on down the hill from the other end, to the next sled. 'We had our boat-builders' help; they made the sleds the same way they make their craft, from wooden frames over which skin is stretched and then caulked . . .' He lifted up the sled; large as

332

it was, it was light when empty. 'See these rails? Just like a sled you drag over the snow. It glides easily over the ground, even when full.'

'Full of what? Water?'

'That's the idea.'

'I feel dull-witted,' said the snailhead. 'Following your path one step at a time. You fill this sled with sea water. And you drag it with this rope, all the way up the hill from the bay—'

'No. Only from the next reservoir down. And there's more than one sled. See, there is a whole set of them, connected in a loop by the rope.'

The snailhead squinted to see. 'Like a necklace. A necklace of sleds.'

'That's it, exactly. There is a necklace between each pair of the ponds, the first to the second, the second to the third, all the way up from the bay. Come on, I'll show you.'

Climbing down the hillside towards the bay, shallow on this side, was a lot easier than climbing up the other.

They came to where the people were working, between the second and third ponds. Most of them stood in a line, facing downhill, hauling on a rope. As they pulled, they dragged laden sleds up from the lower pond towards the higher. Others worked at the ponds, dunking each sled to fill it at the lower pond, or tipping it out into the upper pond. A few people guided the return of the empty sleds from upper to lower, making sure the descending line didn't snag the ascending. Arga was busy with this today; when she saw the priest she waved.

The dragging was heavy work, and the people who hauled, men and women side by side, sang an antique song about the moon's treachery – gloomy but rhythmic, a steady beat that helped them work together. Some of them were snailheads, the priest noted, and that was lucky; he hadn't thought to make sure Knuckle's countrymen were here today to impress him, but the mothers in their beneficent midsummer mood had smiled on him anyhow.

'You see the idea,' the priest said to Knuckle. 'It's a lot easier to raise the water in stages than all at once. We have teams; we take turns. Ana works out who should work when. We all pitch in, all of us who are able.'

'Do you? It seems a dismal labour. People always want to make sure their families don't go hungry first. How do you get people to work if they don't want to?'

'Ana has her ways,' the priest said. Which was true.

The way they had to work on these big projects was new to the people of Etxelur. In the old days, if you wanted to build a house, you would have just done it yourself, with the help of your sisters and brothers and their spouses and children and your friends. If you wanted to fish, you just built a boat and went fishing. And so on. None of it needed much coordination, or permission, or compulsion – unlike these complicated new tasks. Ana had had to develop a harder side, using her own strange authority to face down grown men and women, to shame them to do their share. And when that didn't work she had developed a new system of what she called gatherings, bringing everybody in Etxelur together to confront the unwilling one. Most people would rather just put in the work than face that. But Knuckle was right to guess that not everybody was happy.

One way or the other, however, the work was getting done.

'We've been working on this since the spring,' Jurgi said. 'We started filling up the lower ponds even before we'd dug out the upper.'

The snailhead sat on the grass. 'Just watching them work makes me feel tired. All right. Ponds, sleds – all very clever. Now the real question. *Why?* Why haul water all the way up a hill, only to let it run away again?'

The priest sat beside him. From here the expanse of the bay was opened up, with the bulk of Flint Island beyond. 'Look at the bay. Look at the shore. Remember how it was last time you saw it.'

All around the shore the waterline was lower than it had been, exposing swathes of mud and sand, littered with drying

334

weed, laced by human footprints and worked by wading birds. Children were playing on mud flats all the way to the water's edge, picking shells and mussels from the sand. Their voices rose up to the watching men like the cries of distant gulls.

With their steady labour, the people had already removed a significant fraction of the water in the bay.

'You see? With the dyke and the built-up causeway we turned the bay from an open stretch of the sea into a sealed bowl. And we've been emptying that bowl, one sled after another. Now those children are playing in mud that just months ago was at the bottom of the sea.'

The snailhead frowned. 'It is hard to believe.'

'And look in the centre of the bay,' the priest said, pointing. 'Can you see – it's just breaking the water—'

'Like an island.'

'Yes. That is Etxelur's flint lode. Once the finest flint anybody knew about, finer even than what we mine from the island. Lost to the rising sea for generations.'

'But no more.'

'But no more. Soon we will be able to walk out from the shore, all the way out, and mine it as our ancestors did.'

'You are not just keeping the sea out. You are taking your land back.'

'Yes.'

'It is mad.'

'Probably.'

'It is magnificent.'

'Certainly. And it's all because of you snailheads, and your logs, and the work you contributed—'

There was a scream, from the other side of the hill, behind them.

Knuckle turned immediately. 'Cheek?' He ran back up the grassy slope.

The priest scrambled to his feet, and laboured to follow through the long grass. As he reached the summit, he stared in disbelief.

Zesi stood over the highest reservoir. She had an axe in her hand. She was breathing hard, and, turned away, was looking down the southern hillside.

The reservoir, which had been brimming, was drained.

Knuckle ran forward, past her, and on down the hill. 'Eyelid! Cheek!'

Jurgi climbed the last few paces to stand beside Zesi, and he began to understand. She had taken her axe, a heavy thing with a flint blade, to the lip of the reservoir, where it drained into the rivulet. And when she had breached the reservoir all its water was released at once. A mass of water had surged down the rivulet and pooled at the hill's base. He could see how the force of the water had displaced the rocks of the river bed.

And blood was splashed over those rocks.

'I did it because of Ana,' Zesi said, breathless, looking shocked at her own handiwork. 'Because nobody would listen. I did it for everybody in Etxelur—'

Eyelid was in the river, soaked with water and blood, pulling at the rocks, calling Cheek's name over and over. Knuckle ran on down the hillside to her.

The priest was appalled. 'By the mothers' tears, Zesi, what have you done?'

57

The next morning Ana sent word that she was calling a gathering.

By noon, all of Etxelur had come together on the beach before the Giving platform. The snailheads were here too.

Jurgi, slipping through the silent crowd, made sure he stood close to Knuckle. The snailhead was white with anger and hatred – just as he had been almost exactly a year ago, when he had lost his brother.

On the stage itself stood Ana and Zesi. Ana had her arms folded. Zesi, standing alone, wore the same skin tunic she had yesterday; she looked as if she hadn't washed, hadn't eaten, hadn't slept.

Everybody was utterly silent. In the background was a wash of noise, from the lapping sea, the gulls crying.

When Ana decided everybody was assembled she began. 'We are here because of what my sister has done—'

'I did it for you,' Zesi blurted. She turned to the people. 'For all of you. I wanted to show you how fragile this thing you're building is. How much danger you're putting yourselves in. How much effort you are wasting—'

'Shut up,' Ana said softly.

Zesi immediately complied, trembling. Jurgi felt a twinge of fear at Ana's power, her authority even over her rivalry-ridden older sister.

Ana said, 'Today we consider what was done. Not why. The why doesn't matter. Let Knuckle and Eyelid come forward.'

But Eyelid, weeping, stayed with her family.

Knuckle strode forward. He spoke to Ana, his Etxelur language crude and thickly accented. 'Last year, brother died, because of this woman. This year, niece dies. Because of this woman.' Muscles bunched in his neck, and his hands were clenched into fists so tight that blood trickled from palms pierced by his fingernails. 'Punish her your way, but punish her so she never forgets what she did. Never forget my niece.'

Ana walked up to Zesi.

Zesi cowered. 'I didn't mean it! Can't you see? I meant to protect you. I never meant to harm anybody! Do you think I intended for this to happen? Oh, you fools, listen to me . . .'

But she fell silent before Ana's cold gaze.

When Ana spoke it was softly, yet the priest was sure everybody present could hear. 'Zesi, my sister, you are dead to us. Dead as the child whose life you took. Dead to those of Etxelur. Dead to all our allies. Dead to the snailheads.' There was a growl of agreement from Knuckle's people. 'We will not feed you, we will not look at you, we will not speak to you, for you are one with the dead. Go from this place; you do not exist here.'

As she uttered these words the priest watched Ana's face. It was hard and cold as stone, ancient and implacable. It was the owl's unblinking stare, the priest thought suddenly, the stare of her deathly Other. Ana was barely sixteen years old.

Zesi looked shocked. But then a spark of her old defiance returned. 'Fine. I'll go. I'll go back to Albia. I'll take my son. Kirike is the son of the Root. He has a place there, and will win one for me. The moon take you to its ice heart, Ana . . .' But Ana did not react, and a new horror broke over Zesi's face. '*My son*. Where is Kirike?'

'He is of Etxelur,' Ana said. 'You are as dead to him as to me. Don't try to find him. Go. I can no longer see you.' She turned away.

As one, the crowd before the platform broke up and moved away, murmuring quietly. Knuckle had his arm around Eyelid, who was weeping steadily.

Nobody was looking at Zesi, as if the curse Ana had laid on her had made her truly invisible. She pursued Ana as she walked off the stage. 'Ana! You can't do this! My baby – give me back my baby!'

Her agonised pleas filled the priest with darkness and dread, and he wondered what consequences would flow from this moment.

FOUR

58

The years passed, and the world followed its ancient cycles, seasons succeeding each other like intakes of breath.

For Northland, there was no repeat of the calamity of the Great Sea – not yet anyhow. But the ocean rose steadily, fuelled by melting ice and the very expansion of its own water mass in a warming clime. It bit away relentlessly at the surviving land and there were surges when it was assisted by storms or landslips. Before the sea's advance anything living on the land had to retreat, if it could, or die. Humans too, their lives brief compared to the sea's long contemplations, had to make way for the water.

That, at least, was how it used to be. Now the northern coast of Northland was acquiring a kind of crust, of works that defied the sea's advances.

And the humans who lived there, though as always they grew and aged and died to be replaced by new generations, weren't going anywhere.

59

The Fifteenth Year After the Great Sea: Late Spring.

Qili, following the northern shore of Northland, walked steadily west, as he had done for many days.

The sea was a blue-grey expanse to his right, stretching to the northern horizon, and he saw fishing boats working far out, grey outlines against the sky. On the wrack-strewn beach gulls and wading birds worked, squabbling noisily. The day was warm, less than two months short of midsummer, one of the hottest days of the year so far, and the sun was high in a clear sky. Qili had his boots on a bit of rope slung around his neck, and he walked in the damp sand that bordered the sea. The cool wavelets that broke over his feet eased the ache of callused soles, but did nothing to relieve the weight of the pack on his back, grubby and stained after his long walk from home at the mouth of the World River, far to the east.

He rounded a headland of gravel that spilled from the feet of eroding dunes, and the view to the west opened up. And he saw Etxelur, birthplace of his grandfather Heni, for the first time in his life.

It was just as his father's visitor from Etxelur had described. There was Flint Island lying just offshore, and there the bay cupped by the island's bulk and the gentle hills of the mainland. With land and sea mixed together, an estuary-dweller like Qili could see at a glance how desirable it was as a place to live.

But there, cutting across the sea, stretched between island and mainland, was a line, dead straight and bone white. It was clearly unnatural, sharp and straight in a world of curves and randomness.

All along the Northland coastline he had glimpsed similar works, walls to keep the water out, channels to let it run away, many of the works fresh cut from the earth. Everywhere people were working the land to keep it from the clutches of the sea. A part of him quailed at the thought of this reshaping of the world. Yet, standing here before the great dyke, he felt a spark of wonder. He was seventeen years old.

A pair of birds flew over his head, casting sweeping shadows. Their outspread wings had a clear white stripe along their brown surfaces, and behind sharp bills they had bright red necks; their call was a low-pitched 'whee-t'. He watched, entranced.

'Phalaropes. We call them phalaropes.' The words were in the traders' tongue.

Two women were approaching him, coming from the west. They were bare-footed, dressed in simple dyed-cloth tunics that left their arms and legs bare. The older woman, perhaps in her early twenties, had a serious face and blonde hair tied back behind her head. The younger, perhaps younger than Qili, was more exotic, her hair thick and jet-black, her features strong, her skin a rich brown. Her tunic was open at the waist, and he saw a marking on her belly: three concentric circles and a single radial stab, disappearing into the wrap around her loins. She was taller than he was. He'd never seen anyone quite like her. She was undoubtedly beautiful, but intimidating.

As they reached him they stood apart, and he saw that both had bone-handled stone blades hanging on loops from their leather belts. If he had been meaning to attack them, he could not have reached both with a single movement. That was a reasonable precaution, strangers were often unfriendly, but he had no such intention. And he couldn't take his eyes off the weapons' blades, shaped from a rich, creamy, pale brown flint. Back home only the big men and the priests would wear such things. Was Etxelur really as rich as they said?

The women were watching him, waiting to see what he

would do. He smiled and spread his hands, showing they were empty.

The older woman asked, 'You speak the traders' tongue?'

'Not well.' He glanced up. '*Phalaropes*. We call them red-cheeks. They are early this year. Often not seen before . . .' He stumbled on the word.

'Midsummer? No. My name is Arga. This is Dolphin Gift.'

'I am Qili. I come from a land east of here, at the mouth of the World River. You are from Etxelur.'

'How could you tell?'

'Well, I can see it,' he said, gesturing to the island. 'Just as has been described. And I recognised the marking on your stomach,' he said to the younger woman. Dolphin scowled at him. He said, 'It was the same marking as on the cheek of our visitor.'

'What visitor?'

'His name was Matu son of Matu. He said he was from Etxelur. And he said he was searching for sons of Heni of Etxelur.'

'I see he found you.' Arga smiled, and her face was transformed, a smile as wide as the moon.

'I am Heni's grandson, not his son. I never met Heni.'

'But you have come to celebrate his death and life.'

Dolphin Gift said, 'That's a long way, just to see the end of some old man you never knew.' Despite her looks, when she spoke she had just the same accent as Arga.

'My father is too ill to travel. He is quite old – thirty-three.'

Arga nodded. 'We think Heni was fifty! He said he stopped counting once he passed forty, and there is nobody left alive who can remember his birth.'

'I come for my father, who remembers Heni with affection – even though he rarely saw him.'

'That was Heni for you,' Arga said. 'Always out on his boat.'

'And I come for myself, for I am curious to see Etxelur. Everybody knows about Etxelur. The traders come here from across Northland, across Albia and the Continent, to bring their goods to you in exchange for your flint – so I have heard, anyhow. But I never met anybody from Etxelur before Matu son of Matu came in his fishing boat to our estuary.'

'Well, here you are,' Arga said. 'I'm glad we happened to meet you. Anyone of Etxelur would have made a grandson of Heni welcome. Walk with us.'

'I'll carry your pack.' Dolphin held out her arm.

He didn't need his pack carrying, but something in her manner didn't encourage argument. He slipped off the pack, and she picked it up with one hand.

They began to walk towards Etxelur, along the beach. The women kept to either side of him, just out of his reach, showing residual caution.

Arga said, 'When poor Heni died we sent Matu out in his boat off to the east, while his brother went west, hoping to find Heni's sons. For we didn't want to lay Heni in the midden without family present.'

'You honour Heni, to do so much.'

'Heni helped Dolphin's mother give birth to her, out in a boat rolling around in the middle of the western ocean. And he saved my life when I was swept out by the Great Sea.'

This took some translation. 'We call the big wave the Gods' Shout.'

'Without Heni I wouldn't be standing here now, I wouldn't have loved my husband, I wouldn't have had my two children.'

Qili frowned, puzzling out a sentence that was long and convoluted in the traders' tongue, which, rich with words but with crude grammar, was better suited to simple exchanges. 'Your husband?'

'Died, some years ago.'

Dolphin said morbidly, 'Killed trying to deal with a failure of one of the dykes.'

'*Dykes*. Matu explained that word. I am curious about the dykes.' But they said nothing more, for now. He glanced at Dolphin, who walked with her head hung low, staring at the shallow craters her feet left in the soft moist sand. 'I am curious

347

about you too,' he said at length. 'You don't seem happy to have found me.'

Dolphin glanced at Arga, who looked away. 'Oh, it's nothing to do with you. It's about Arga and my mother. Ice Dreamer, she's called – you'll meet her.'

'*Ice Dreamer*.' This was a name like none he had ever heard.

'She's not from here. My mother thinks I don't keep the right company.'

'She's talking about a boy,' Arga said.

'A man,' Dolphin snapped. 'We aren't children, Arga. My mother has Arga supervise me when *she* can't, to make sure we don't start humping on the beach—'

'Don't be ridiculous, Dolphin.'

'You're the one being ridiculous. Everybody else my age has got babies. You had a baby when you were thirteen.'

Qili said, 'I have two children myself. They're boys aged one and two.'

Dolphin wasn't listening. She snapped at Arga, 'Kirike and I are getting old waiting, while you fools keep us apart!'

'You've no need to wait,' Arga said. 'Just find somebody else.'

'You see,' Dolphin said to Qili. 'She takes my mother's side. She always does.'

'I just want to avoid upset,' Arga said. 'And I agree with your mother that if you and Kirike were together there would be nothing but upset.'

Qili frowned. 'Why?'

'Because of the past,' Dolphin said bitterly. 'Long story. All to do with who Kirike's mother and father were. The past! All because of the stupid things our parents once did. Sorry. You walked a long way to arrive in the middle of an argument.'

Qili shrugged. 'We have arguments at home. At least here they are different arguments.'

Arga asked, 'So what do you argue about?'

He hesitated, and decided to be honest. 'Mostly about whether to trade with Etxelur.'

'Really?'

'Some people find you scary.'

Arga considered that, then nodded. 'Sometimes I find us scary. Well, you can make your own mind up, because we're nearly there.'

60

They approached the mouth of the bay. He could see the wall between island and mainland clearly now, a white, smooth-surfaced barrier against which the waves lapped.

'Come,' Arga said, 'I'll show you where we live.'

She led him up a sandy slope and behind a row of dunes. The dunes had evidently been battered by the Gods' Shout; they were misshapen and the marram grass was not yet fully regrown. He had seen such sights all the way along the North-land coast. Behind the dunes, visible beyond low hills, was a grassy plain that extended off to the south.

And, tucked in just behind the dunes, a row of low hillocks stood, round and neat, perhaps twice as tall as he was, their slopes covered with grass. *They were not natural*, he saw immediately, with a jolt of shock, they were too regular for that. Houses stood on top of these mounds, heaps of kelp thatch over frameworks of stout logs. A low wall stood around each house, gleaming white.

Arga saw him staring, and smiled. 'Everybody reacts the same, the first time. Come and see.'

Steps had been cut into the side of the nearest mound. Arga climbed these effortlessly. Qili followed, the grass cool under his bare feet. In turn Dolphin Gift followed him, still carrying his pack.

'This is where you live,' Qili said to Arga.

She nodded. 'The house I share with Ana herself.' The door flap was a leather sheet with the characteristic symbol of Etxelur etched into it, the three rings and the radial tongue. 'We started building these mounds right after the Great Sea. Even before the dykes. It was Ana's own idea. Up here, the worst floods can't get us – even if the dykes were to fail, which they won't.'

He bent to inspect the wall. It ran right around the house, sealing it in, yet it was low enough for him simply to step over. 'Does this keep out the water too?'

'No. It's just for show.' She showed him what the wall was made of – square-edged blocks, stuck together somehow and coloured white – and he learned words that were new to him, and new to Etxelur too, he found, brought here by a man from far away: *brick, mortar, plaster*. 'To make the bricks we haul clay from the valley floor on wooden sleds. It is mixed with straw and cut into blocks and left to dry in the sun. To make the plaster we burn limestone in hot pits until it disintegrates into powder. This we mix with water and pour it over the walls, shaping it with our hands. It dries to give this smooth white cover. Well. I think Ana is at the flint lode in the Bay Land this afternoon. Would you like to rest now?'

He shook his head. 'I'd be better to wash off the travel dirt with a swim, but that can wait. I'm keen to see Ana – and the rest of Etxelur.'

'Good. Come on. Leave your pack.' Arga began to make her way down the mound's slope.

'And you can leave me behind too,' Dolphin said. 'I've got things to do.'

'You'll stay with me,' Arga said with a mild authority, 'until we've found your mother.'

With a snarl of disgust, Dolphin followed Arga and Qili back down the path.

Arga led Qili through the collection of mounds, each topped by houses and scraps of wall, and rows of sun-drying bricks on the ground. The people they met, pursuing their daily lives, seemed friendly enough to Qili, and when they learned he was a grandson of Heni they made him welcome. The children ran everywhere – there were always children, wherever you went – and they smiled or pulled faces at the newcomer. Everyone

351

seemed fluent in the traders' tongue, even the children, but their language was sprinkled with many unfamiliar words.

They climbed the dunes and paused at the summit. From here, looking north, Qili could see a strip of beach, beyond which lay a grassy plain studded with sparse trees – a gentle bowl shape, rising towards the sides, and its floor rippled with low hills, like dunes. This bowl of grass and trees and ditches was sheltered by the hills to the south, the bulk of Flint Island to the north – and to the east and to the north-west by two walls, both shining with plaster, that stood proud above the land.

'The dykes of Etxelur,' he said. They looked much more impressive than when he had seen the dyke from the ocean side, covered up by the sea.

'Exactly,' Arga said. 'And if you listen closely you'll hear the sea breaking against their outer walls. Walk with me.'

They walked down the dune, crossed a strip of sandy beach to mud flats, and then they came to the plain. The ground was soft, the soil rich, and criss-crossed by narrow channels.

'This is Etxelur Bay,' Arga said. 'Or it was. Now we call it the Bay Land. When I was born this place was at the bottom of the sea.'

This had been described to him by Matu son of Matu. Seeing it was quite different. He gaped, unable to believe.

'When the ground was first exposed it was muddy, salty. Well, you'd expect that. Once we cleared away the seaweed, the first things to grow were plants from the salt marshes. But in time the rain cleared the salt away, and we helped it by breaking up the soil, and the grass started to take. Then the trees, willow and alder at first – well, you can see that. I suppose they are better able to stand whatever salt is left in the soil than others. One day there will be birch and oaks here, growing where we stand.'

Qili found it hard to understand what he was seeing. 'Grass and flowers and trees,' he said. He looked down, peering through the long, sparse grass. 'Soil. But under it, in the earth—'

Arga knelt down, pulled aside the grass and dug her hand into

352

the ground. She pulled up rich black crumbling earth, but when she broke it up in her fingers Qili saw it contained fragments of sea shells. She grinned at his wonder. 'Come on, I'll take you to meet Ana. Wait until you see the flint lode.'

They walked forward, past willow trees and over gentle dune-like slopes.

'Don't mind her,' Dolphin murmured to Qili. 'She's like this with every visitor we get. She has to show off. Maybe it's because she was there when it was first getting built.' She yawned elaborately. 'Believe me, if you grew up with it, it doesn't seem so special. You get used to it.'

But as they neared the northern dyke's land side the wall loomed high over Qili's head, perhaps three times his height, smooth and strong, excluding the sea itself. Qili, cowering in its shadow, wondered how anybody could possibly *get used* to living in a place like this.

61

When Qili emerged from Arga's house the next day, the weather was if anything even brighter, even more cheerful. He heard a melodic, bubbling cry, and looked up to see a pair of curlews flapping overhead in their usual leisurely way, with their pale bellies and distinctive curved beaks, perhaps on their way to the marshy ground to the west.

Too beautiful a day for a funeral, he thought. But already people were emerging from the houses on the mounds and making their way towards the coast.

Arga and Dolphin Gift followed Qili out of the house. They wore simple smocks and cloaks, their hair had been plaited into tight coils, and their cheeks were marked with the ubiquitous rings-and-slash symbol, painted on with a mixture of ochre and goose fat. The house belonged to Ana, he had come to understand, as the senior woman in her family. But last night Arga and Dolphin had stayed with Qili, and Arga's children had stayed with a friend to make room for him. Meanwhile Ana, and Dolphin's mother, Ice Dreamer, had visited Etxelur's priest to discuss the ceremony for Heni.

They walked together down the mound's steep slope, and set off once more towards the beach. They joined a sparse crowd that converged at the abutment of the dyke that spanned the mouth of the bay, running north to Flint Island. Dolphin anxiously scanned the crowd, evidently looking for somebody.

Close to, Qili was able to see the detail of the dyke's construction. Rows of fat wooden piles contained a core of rock and sand and mud. Further out into the water this foundation was

354

buried under rock, with a facing of mud bricks coated with white plaster. On its dry side the dyke was a wall three times the height of a person, brilliant white, smooth-faced – but on the other side the sea lapped not far below its edge. Arcing across the bay mouth, unnatural and intimidating, the dyke oddly made Qili think of death; pale as bone, it divided the living world in two.

And he was going to have to walk across it, he realised now. The people were funnelling towards the abutment and starting to stream onto the path across the top. Children ran ahead, shouting, chased by barking dogs.

As they walked forward Arga said to Qili, 'We always use the dyke on occasions like this, to get to the island. Saves getting your feet muddy on the Bay Land. Of course before the dyke was built you had to walk all the way around the bay . . .'

Qili found it hard to listen, as he followed her steady pace.

Soon he was out on the dyke itself, with a drop down to the Bay Land to his left, and the sea lapping not far below the lip of the wall to his right. It was an extraordinary experience, a little like walking a cliff edge, or as if the whole world was unbalanced and tilting over, and he had an odd fear of falling. Once a child jostled him, rushing past; Qili, stumbling, was glad of Arga's supporting hand.

'Kirike! Kirike!' Suddenly Dolphin was jumping and waving.

A man a few paces further along stopped and turned, waved back, and pushed back through the sparse line. When he met Dolphin they embraced. He was tall, strong-looking, darker than most of the Etxelur folk, many of whom were pale and red-haired or blond.

Arga tutted loudly. 'I suppose I was never going to keep them apart today.' She said in a lower, gossipy tone, 'Kirike is Ana's nephew. But he's half Pretani. And it wasn't a happy chain of events that led to his birth. Ana's sister – his mother – was called Zesi. Not here. Dead, probably. A long story – you don't want to know.' Arga sighed. 'But, look at them. I don't know if Ice Dreamer is doing the right thing in keeping them apart. Nothing

Dolphin does now with Kirike is going to change the past, all the feuding and the blood that was spilled. And look at the boy! As handsome as an aurochs bull and about as smart – I'll swear he's more Pretani than Etxelur. But what a piece of meat he is. Why, if I were a few years younger . . .' She had a dreamy look on her face.

Qili was embarrassed by this display of elderly lust. Arga must have been twenty-one, twenty-two at least.

To Qili's relief they stepped out on the dry land of the island. They walked around the shore to the north beach, where two great middens, each curved like the crescent moon, stood on the dry ground above the tide mark. The one closest to the sea was smoothly faced and intact, but the other was damaged, eroded and breached, with shells and stones and mud spilled on the sand.

'This is our holiest site,' Arga murmured to Qili as she led him through the throng. 'Where your grandfather will be interred. But you can see that the Great Sea didn't spare the holy middens, even. We kept one as the Sea left it, to remember. The young complain sometimes, for they can't see the point of all the hard work we do. But *this* is the point, our most sacred place smashed to pieces, and there was nothing we could do about it.'

Qili faced the sea, which stretched untamed to the horizon, and breathed deeply of the salty air. He saw a group of eiders gathered to nest on a heap of offshore rocks that protruded above the receding tide. They were picking at molluscs with their beaks, or resting in the sun, preening and sleeping. Qili had always rather admired eiders. They liked exposed places, and braved the rough seas around the rocky shores, places they didn't have to share with anybody else.

He was glad to be at the shore. He welcomed the openness and the lack of enclosure compared to the strange artificial bowl of the Bay Land. It felt more like home. But even here people were rearranging the world; two more dykes, both incomplete, pushed out to sea from the land, with heaps of logs and stones at their abutments.

He was brought to Ana and her closest companions, who stood before the middens. He'd met them all yesterday at the flint lode. Ice Dreamer was here, an older, greying, more elegant version of her vivacious daughter Dolphin, and Novu, the peculiar, dark, squat man from the Continent, and the priest, Jurgi, bare save for a strip of leather around his loins, his tattoos bright, his hair dyed blue, and his wooden teeth gleaming in his mouth. Today he had the upper jaw of a wolf dangling on a thread around his neck. Novu and Jurgi stood close together, Qili saw, their arms brushing, their fingers loosely cupped. They were old, Novu in his thirties, Jurgi even older in his forties.

Ana herself was a short, compact woman, her red hair shot through with grey, her rather expressionless face lined, her eyes close and calculating. A woman shut in on herself, Qili thought, and yet the centre of this little group.

Qili was struck again by how *old* all these people were. Qili knew only a few people of this great age back home, and they were elders who kept out of the way of the young folk. Here this cabal of ancients seemed to control everything about Etxelur. And they were evidently obsessed by the Great Sea, an event most people alive now couldn't even remember.

The reason he was here was at Ana's feet: a set of bones, fragmented but assembled roughly into a skeleton, respectfully laid out on a deerskin.

Arga led him forward, and he bowed to Ana. He stared down at these mute remains of a man he had never known. 'My grandfather.'

Ana nodded. 'I am glad you have come. Heni was much loved here.' She spoke the traders' tongue fluently. 'He was a close friend of my father, before the Great Sea took him. Like an uncle to me.'

'From what I hear he saved many lives.'

Jurgi the priest said, 'You can do nothing more valuable with your own life than that. Qili, do you want some time alone with

357

your grandfather? Do your people have any appropriate customs?'

Ana snorted. 'Well, you might have asked him that yesterday when there was time to prepare.'

'It's fine,' Qili said. 'He was one of you. I honour him in my heart.'

Ice Dreamer asked Arga, 'What about my daughter? What's she up to?'

'Guess who she's with,' Arga said reluctantly.

Dreamer shot an angry glance at her. 'I asked you to keep them apart.'

'What do you expect me to do, hobble them?'

Ana said sharply, 'Oh, leave it for today. How I hate funerals! Everybody forced to come together whether they love or loathe each other, all the tensions coming out.' She turned on the priest and Novu. 'And you two can stop fiddling with each other as well. You've got a job to do, priest; keep your mind on that.'

Novu and Jurgi moved apart, so their arms were no longer touching. Novu just grinned at Ana's attack, but Jurgi looked offended. 'I'll do my job as I always do it, as the mothers know very well.'

'Well, I hope the mothers turn away from the sight of you two licking each other's ball sacks in the dark. Company and con-solation is one thing, but you push your luck, priest.' Qili was amazed by her bluntness.

Her mind evidently moving on, she looked out at the sea, the incomplete dykes. 'I'd like to get people pushing on with the new dykes before the Giving. Do you think I can use Heni's death as an argument? After all it was him who used to take Arga out to swim around the Mothers' Door, and here we are trying to take the Door back from the sea.'

The priest frowned. 'Maybe we can be more subtle. The low tide is coming. Tell them of the moon, who has taken Heni; when the sea is low, and the moon distracted, we can steal something back from her . . .'

They held this conversation, evidently unthinking, in the traders' tongue.

Arga drew Qili aside. 'You mustn't be offended. They don't mean any disrespect to Heni. It's just the way Ana is. She always works on several things at once.' She flexed her fingers. 'Like a spider pulling on many threads. She uses occasions like this to bring the people together, to remind them who they are. And she pushes the work she wants done next – like the big dykes she's building out to sea. But at the same time she is sincere about what she said about your grandfather. I know her; I'm sure of that.'

Qili nodded. But he felt constrained by these people, this old woman with her manipulation and her scheming, as if he was caught up in her web. He longed for the day to be over, for an excuse to get away, to the simplicity of life in the World River estuary.

It was time to begin the ceremony. The priest pulled out his wooden teeth, spat on his wolf jaw, and shoved it into his mouth. Then, with a sigh, fangs protruding grotesquely, he began the short climb up the side of the midden.

62

In the heart of Pretani's endless forest, three big old oak trees stood tall around a clearing where hazel grew thick.

A young doe stepped out of the trees' shade, wary in the light. Me watched from his vantage above.

Clearings of this size were rare in the forest, mostly made by the grounders with their fire. Open spaces meant danger. Yet the doe was drawn to the hazels' lush leaves.

Me could *smell* her, smell the musky richness of her coat and the tang of her dung. His mouth watered at the thought of the red meat that lay under that fine coat. He hefted his weapon, a bit of branch broken off to leave a sharp point.

Shadows moved in the branches of other oak trees, one, two, Old and Mother. Two more Leafy Boys. The doe would not smell them, they had left no trace of their presence on the ground, for they had come this way through the canopy, moving from tree to tree.

The doe bent a slim neck and nibbled silently at a hazel.

A single leaf crackled.

The doe looked back over her shoulder. Her soft brown coat, her stillness, made her blend into the background, as if she was nothing but a pattern of light and shade herself.

It had been Old, in his tree. Me saw Mother cast a savage glare at him. Me barely breathed. He felt his heart beat heavy and slow in his chest.

After an unmeasured time the doe relaxed, subtly, and bent her head to her meal again.

Mother clenched her fist and pumped it down.

Me let go of the branches and dropped. He saw the others fall too, like pale, heavy fruit.

Me hit the ground on a bed of dead leaves and bracken. His legs flexed, absorbing the fall. Suddenly he was dazzled, in full unshaded sunlight, but he was ready.

But Old fell clumsily, landed heavily on his right arm, and cried out. The doe whirled. Me and Mother immediately began to move in. But Old was still down. The doe saw the gap and was through in a single bound.

Me glimpsed the doe only once more, her white tail disappearing into the forest shadows. It was already over.

Mother fell on Old. She yelled as she pummelled him with her fists. Old tried to defend himself, raising his left arm, but his right was bent awkwardly, and he screamed as he fell back on it.

Me shoved Mother back. He recoiled from the deep, savage anger that burned in her eyes. Nobody got as angry as Mother. But he faced her down. She snarled at him, teeth bared.

Then she leapt, slim, naked, strong, caught the lower branches of the nearest tree, and squirmed up out of sight. Me followed, climbing easily away from the dangers of the forest floor and the clearing. He glanced back once to see Old struggling to rise, his right arm dangling, like a grounder infant newly snatched from its mother, trying to stand.

Mother, still angry, led them on a relentless journey, jumping and swinging from tree to tree. Even Me had trouble keeping up. Old, he could see, with his bad arm, soon fell behind. But Me wasn't about to lose Mother and the protection of her company, and he chased her doggedly.

As the sun rolled across the sky and the shadows lengthened, they didn't see anybody else, no other Leafies.

Leafy Boys had no home. It wasn't a good idea for too many of them to gather in one place at one time. They were scattered through the forest, not organised, collecting in little hunting bands that formed and split up spontaneously. There was always a rush of noisy squabbling as people formed up. This wasn't the best group Me had ever been in. People were wary of Old because of his age, and of Mother for her savagery and anger. Now Me looked forward to finding others and going off with somebody else. That wasn't going to happen today, however.

As the shadows lengthened, Mother slowed at last.

She stopped at a particular tree, a big fat old oak. Me knew this tree, as he knew many of the forest's best trees. With strong branches and thick foliage it was a good place to hide, and there was a spring at the bottom where you could drink.

He and Mother clambered down. It was only the second time he'd touched the ground in many days. They lapped at the spring. Mother found some mushrooms growing from a broken root. That would fill their bellies, but on a day when they had found no meat they would go hungry tonight. Me could tell Mother was still angry, in the hard, jerky way she broke up the mushrooms.

They were already clambering back up into the branches when Old turned up, moving stiffly and cautiously. Me looked down on him as he splashed water into his mouth with his good hand, and picked at what was left of the mushrooms. Mother snarled softly and spat a bit of mushroom at him, but she did not drive him away.

The three sat in the tree's branches, silent. The sun dropped, and its light shone through the leaves, showing their fine veins and filling the canopy with a green light that dappled on the tree bark. Me held out his hand. Tiny discs formed on his palm, where the sun's light peeked through the leaves. In the back of his head curiosity stirred. How did the discs get there? But the light faded, and soon there were no more discs on his hand, no more shadows.

Moving slowly, the three of them piled up dead leaves at the root of a fat branch, and lay down together, wriggling, trying to get comfortable. Mother was in the middle of the three. She was the strongest and so took the safest place, shielded by the bodies of the others.

As Me lay down, his belly to her back, her hard buttocks

pushed into his groin and he felt his penis grow long. But he was hungry and would not have wished to rut, even if it had been someone other than Mother, who rutted with nobody. He turned away and relieved his hardness with a few strong tugs.

Then he closed his eyes, his back pressed against Mother's, and tried to sleep, ignoring the hunger that gnawed at his stomach.

The Leafy Boys lived almost silently. They hunted, fought, pissed, shit, rutted, slept, and died, but they didn't talk.

And they had no names for themselves. Me thought of himself as just that: Me, the centre of the world-forest. 'Old' had earned his label in Me's head because he was a little older than the others. Few survived beyond two, three, four years after your body learned to rut; you grew too heavy, too stiff for the work of climbing, and you fell, or you were done in by the grounders. Old knew this. You could see the fear in his eyes when he woke in the morning.

As for 'Mother', she had once got a baby growing in her belly.

The Leafy Boys didn't keep babies. They kept their numbers up by snatching grounder children. No Leafy girl had ever survived getting a baby in her belly – none but Mother. As the pregnancy developed she had hunted as hard as anybody else, until her belly was too big for her to move, and she had begun to starve because nobody would help her.

In the end, when the bloody water had gushed from between her legs, the others had driven her off with fists and sticks. Her clumsiness, her stink and her blood traces would make it impossible for them to hunt. Even the grounders might be able to smell her. So she had gone off alone, clambering through the canopy clumsily, her pain obvious. Me thought she would fall, and that would be that, and he would never see her again.

Some days later she came back, with her belly slack but empty. Again the others tried to drive Mother away, for she smelled strange, and had a bleakness in her eyes that scared everybody. But she had fought for her place. One had died, opposing her.

Since then Mother had hunted and fought as hard and skil-fully as ever. But she would let no boy rut with her.

A few days after her return, Me, fascinated by this new, savage Mother, had followed the trail of drying blood she had left through the canopy. The little body he had found lodged in the crook of a branch had already been discovered by the birds, and it had no eyes, no tongue, and its tiny fingers had been pecked off. A kind of vine seemed to come out of its stomach, attaching it to a bloody mass. Ever since then he often thought of the child eyeless in a tree. In the silence of his head, she was for ever Mother.

In the night's deepest dark the wind picked up. Me woke from an uneasy sleep. He heard a soft moan. It was Old, groaning for the pain of his damaged arm. Thick summer leaves rustled, and a branch creaked as it swayed, a deep, solemn sound.

A memory drifted into Me's head. He was small and light and wrapped in furs, and he was held by a woman who smiled at him. He often fell asleep thinking of the woman's smile, for then the cold didn't seem so bad.

He woke with a start.

The light was grey, the air still cool, and a fine dew lay on his cheek. It was not yet dawn. He felt Mother's slim body behind him, heavy with sleep.

Yet something was wrong.

He sat up sharply. Mother stirred, resentfully waking. Old, curled up on himself, stayed unmoving, his bad arm cradled to his belly.

Me looked around, and listened to the rustle of the wind in the trees, and sniffed the air – and he smelled smoke. He looked downwind, to the north. A glow broke through the canopy, red like a sunrise. They had been unlucky. If it had been upwind they would have been wakened earlier. Already the fire was close, and the glow spread to left and right, as far as he could see.

Instantly Mother moved, abandoning the nest. She scurried

along a branch and jumped to the next tree, moving south away from the approaching fire.

But Old still lay sleeping. Me hesitated for one agonising heartbeat. Then he kicked Old in the small of the back. Old, flustered and frightened, limbs flailing, winced at the pain of his damaged arm.

Then Me turned and fled, after Mother, not looking back for Old.

He barely looked ahead, beyond the next branch, the next tree. He had no need to, for the canopy went on for ever and there was always another tree to escape to. All that mattered was the next branch, the only danger losing a foothold or a grip.

Fires weren't that uncommon. They were started by storms, by lightning strikes. In spring or early summer especially when dead ferns and bracken and leaves carpeted the undergrowth, a fire could spread quickly. But there had been no storm, he realised vaguely. And this was midsummer, not spring.

He thought he was outrunning the fire. The smell of smoke, and a faint sound of crackling and popping, receded behind him. Yet unease remained. Something was wrong.

The net was slung between two giant oaks. He barely saw it before he went flying into it, and his whole body was tangled up as if in thick ivy.

He fell from the tree and plummeted hard against the ground, landing all wrong. Winded, tangled up, he tried to stand.

Hands grabbed him and pulled him down. Huge dark shapes loomed around him. He remembered another time when he was grabbed, taken away from a smiling face, hands stealing him up into the green. Now he was pulled down to the earth.

He heard a scream. Mother.

Then a heavy foot slammed into the pit of his stomach, and he folded over the pain.

63

Shade stood silent before the wooden post.

The sun shone down into the clearing, midsummer light pouring from another flawless sky, and all the posts in the great circle cast long, precise shadows across the clearing. But this post was the southernmost in the ring, and cast its shadow a little further than the others, and that was the one he watched.

All around the clearing the forest crowded dense and dark, and the canopy was a billowing green cloud high above. Birds sang, and a busy squirrel briefly distracted him. Women and children moved quietly around the forest fringe, gathering fungi and berries. He heard the grunts and shouts of the men as Bark put them through their training – wrestling today, it sounded like, fighting with bare hands. Shade vaguely hoped that there would be no serious accidents today, that nobody would die. Not long after becoming the Root on the death of his father he had ruled that no man could earn a killing scar from the murder of another Pretani – unless it was an unavoidable issue of honour, just as Shade's own brother and father had died. That had cut down markedly on the number of deaths, but they still happened, whether as genuine accidents or as petty grudge attacks.

Such thoughts rattled through his head like birds darting across the sunlit clearing. But he did not allow them to distract him from his purpose.

He was intent on watching the shadow of the southernmost post, as he did every day around this time, when the sun was out and the shadow visible. Every so often he marked the shadow, driving a slim wooden stake in the ground. As a result of his labours the earth before him, cleared of leaves and ferns and other debris, had a whole series of pegs in parallel curving lines, showing how he had marked the shifting of the shadow on previous days. Shade, aged thirty, was capable of great concentration.

It was time to place another peg. He stepped forward and thrust a wood sliver into the ground.

'You ought to get somebody to do that for you,' came a heavy, breathless voice.

'I have to be sure it's done right, Bark.'

Bark approached, panting hard, swigging water from a skin. Naked save for a sweat-soaked groin pouch, his body was like a slab of oak itself, covered with knotted muscles on his upper arms and thighs, the belly under the thick mat of hair on his chest. A little over twenty, about ten years younger than Shade himself, he was a second cousin, and Shade trusted nobody else as he trusted Bark.

'So how was the training?'

'Not bad. The wrestling went well. Only one broken finger, the priest will look at it when he's worked his latest dose of poppy juice out of his blood. The spear-chucking was a disaster. You know what fourteen-year-olds are like. More muscle than brains. Nearly got one through my own foot.'

Shade laughed. 'They'll learn.' He threw Bark another water sack.

Bark took a deep, thirsty draught, and looked down dubiously at the patterns of sticks. 'Tell me again why you're doing this?'

'Because I want to mark the moment of midsummer. To make the Giving that bit more special.' Shade's Giving ceremony was an amalgam of older Pretani traditions with what he'd seen at Etxelur. There was plenty of competition, plenty of feasting and sex and raucous behaviour – and lots of giving, the difference being that those who feared the Pretani gave to them, rather than the other way around.

'And these shadows you're chasing are going to help, are they?'

'Yes,' Shade said, a little impatiently. 'Look. Each day the post shadow, cast by the sun as it shifts in the sky, marks out a curve. Like this. It dips closest to the post at noon. But each day that curve moves too, because the sun climbs that bit higher as it gets to midsummer. I'm trying to find the one unique point where the shadow reaches at noon on midsummer day. I started last year, but we had too much cloud. This year I'm doing better. Next year I'll try again to check the result—'

'Year after year after year. Why?'

Shade snapped, 'So that I can put something here. A stone. A bear skull, maybe. And then, for ever, we'll know when it's noon at midsummer because we'll see the post's shadow hit the skull. You see? I explained it to you before.'

'You know me. Head like a leaky water skin.' He shook the empty skin to make the point and threw it back to Shade. 'In one hole and out the other. Anyhow the turning of the seasons is up to the gods. You should get the priest to do this.'

'I tried,' Shade said. 'All he wants is more poppy juice.' Shade often wished he had the ear of a decent, sober, sensible, intelligent priest. He remembered Etxelur, and the partnership of Kirike and the wise priest Jurgi.

Bark pointed, faintly mocking. 'Time for another peg.'

In fact he was overdue. Shade hastened to mark the shadow.

'Or one of the women. They could do this. The gods know you've got enough wives . . .'

That was true enough. There were always lots of widows among the Pretani, and as the Root Shade had had his pick. But all his children had died young, save one, Acorn, a little girl on whom he doted when his hunters weren't watching.

'And you should come training with us. You should hear what some of these boy-men say about you behind your back. Some of them are itching to challenge you.'

'There's always some hothead ready to gamble his life.'

'If enough of them have a go, one of them will win that

gamble in the end. Look, I'm serious. You need to keep in condition. Standing around watching shadows won't do that for you. And it wouldn't do you any harm to take down one of the boy-men some time. Just to show the rest you're still top.'

It was wise advice, of its kind. 'I'll think about it.'

Bark blew his nose noisily into his fingers and wiped his hands on his loin pouch. 'Right, I'm off for a shit, a swim in the river and some food, not necessarily in that order—'

Somebody screamed. A child, by the edge of the clearing.

The two men exchanged a glance, and ran.

Children came boiling out of the forest like ants from a kicked-over nest. One girl had a basket of fruit, but the others had abandoned whatever they had been collecting. Their mothers ran across the clearing towards them, and some of the men.

Shade saw his own daughter. He ran over and grabbed her. 'Acorn! What is it?' The girl, eight years old and still child-slim, was shaking, her eyes wide. She was so scared she couldn't speak. He knelt before her. 'Calm down, child. You're safe now. Tell me what happened. Was it a bear? A cat?'

'No – no – it came down out of the trees, it just dropped on us—'

'*What* came down?'

But now there were more screams from the forest. The mothers with their children scattered, and the men, shouting to each other, tried to form a line before the trees.

Acorn turned and pointed at a stout ash tree. '*That* came down!' she yelled. 'That!'

There was something clambering in the branches, Shade saw, some animal, big, agile.

It leapt down into the clearing, teeth bared, fingers outstretched. It was a boy, maybe twelve years old, naked, his skin covered in green smears – a Leafy Boy. The men faced the Leafy, but they stayed out of reach of his swinging paws.

Something was wrong. No Leafy Boy had attacked the people

so openly before. And, Shade saw now, the Leafy had a rope tied around his neck, leading back to the forest.

Now another Leafy Boy came flying out of a treetop, landing in a roll that took him into a group of men, knocking them down. He got up snarling – no, this one was a female, a she, with small hard breasts, but as muscular as the first. But she, too, had a rope around her neck.

She leapt onto one of the fallen men. He scrabbled to get away. She grabbed his own club and rammed it in his open mouth so hard that teeth cracked and bone splintered. The man, pinned on the ground, shuddered and gurgled, and blood gushed out of his ruined mouth.

There was a moment of shocked stillness.

Then Bark yelled, 'Rush them!' He went in first. He jumped on the boy, and the Leafy bit and scratched.

More of the men moved in on the girl, who still straddled her shuddering, dying victim. She seemed if anything more formidable, and fought with a reckless inhuman ferocity.

Shade himself pushed Acorn away and raced forward, reaching for the blade at his waist.

But then the rope at the girl's neck was yanked backwards. She clutched at her throat, but she was dragged off the downed man and, struggling and kicking, was pulled back across the grassy floor of the clearing.

The other Leafy was subdued now, his face bloodied, three men sitting on his arms, chest and legs.

'Don't kill him,' Shade snapped. He strode forward past the boy, following the way the girl had been dragged.

At the edge of the clearing a group of adults – people, not Leafies, clad in dirty skins – dragged the girl into the green shade, threw a net over her and bundled her up with rope. Still she kicked and fought.

Shade faced the strangers, his blade in his hand. 'Who are you?' he called in Pretani, and then he switched to the traders' tongue. 'Show yourselves, if you want to live.'

One of the group stepped forward into the daylight. It was a

370

woman, her body square and strong, her breasts flat under her tunic, her red hair tied back and shot with grey. Her face was familiar, and yet was laid over by a mask of scars. Lines around the eyes and mouth told of bitterness. He had the impression she smiled rarely.

Yet she smiled as she faced him. She spoke the Etxelur tongue. 'Hello, Shade. Do you remember me? You kicked me out of here, but that was long ago. And things have changed, haven't they?'

'What do you want?'

'To talk.'

It was Zesi.

64

They sat in Shade's house.

Shade had called for his priest to sit with them, feeling the need for spiritual support in this confrontation, but Resin, poppy-addled and terrified, was barely conscious. Bark, meanwhile, refused to go further than a couple of paces from the Root's side with strangers in the clearing. He sat just outside the house's door flap where he could watch Zesi and her grimy followers, who sat around the open-air hearth, sharing a deer haunch.

The two Leafies lay huddled together on the ground, pinned under a net weighted down with logs.

In the house, Zesi told Shade what had become of her in the fifteen years since the summer of the Great Sea, when she had left Albia after the death of the Root.

'So we got rid of you from here. And then Ana threw you out of Etxelur.'

'More than that,' Zesi said, every word dripping with bitterness. 'I am dead in Etxelur. What you see is a sack of bones walking around. And I nearly did die too, in those first days alone. But you know me. I was always a fighter.'

She grinned, cold, somehow more savage even than the Leafy child-woman she had unleashed on the Pretani. He wondered how he could ever have imagined he loved her. 'So you came back.'

'I had no real intention, no plan. Nowhere to go – I knew I wouldn't be welcome here. Yet I came this way. Perhaps drawn by your memory.' She didn't look at him when she said this. 'Or perhaps it was the forest. You can hide in a forest. Hole up. You can't do that in Northland, all those open spaces.'

'So you hid away.'

'Not well enough. They soon found me.' She nodded at the band who had accompanied her, most of them men, some women, all of them grimy and tough-looking. 'Them or their predecessors. Many of that first lot are long dead now.'

'Bandits,' said Shade. This was a traders'-tongue word. Bandits, rootless folk who preyed on others, were a plague, especially in the forests where they could hide in the shadows. 'I can imagine how they treated you. A woman alone—'

'You should imagine how I treated them. Before they learned to leave me alone one man had to die, choked to death on his own severed cock.'

He was careful not to react. 'So you survived. And you came to lead them.'

'Not just this lot. There are many bandit groups. The forest swarms with them. You know that.'

'I suppose it doesn't surprise me. You always were a leader. And now you have the Leafy Boys under your sway, I see.'

She grinned. 'Did you like my stunt? I'm sorry one of your people got killed – it shouldn't have gone that far.'

'Death always did follow you around, Zesi.'

'It made the point, though, about how vicious they can be. Imagine a swarm of them falling on your houses! They would chew your eyes out before you had time to shout the alarm.'

'And you control them.'

'Just those we capture. We smoke them out with fires. They have no language; they can't be trained. And they'll only eat red meat – never cooked. Some of the men think they're not human at all.'

'They steal our infants,' Shade said sadly. 'They are human enough.'

'Hey, you.' She threw a boar rib at Bark, who snarled back at her. 'The female over there is a gift, for you and your men, if you can handle her. Some of my men say it's worth the cost in bites and scratches. We kept her fresh for you. If you spoil her it doesn't matter, there are always more to trap. Go ahead. Enjoy.'

Bark wasn't about to leave Shade alone. But he beckoned over one of his men and spoke quietly.

Soon a group of the men, with the bandits' help, were cautiously separating the male and female Leafies. They hauled the squirming female over to the edge of the clearing, away from the women and children. Then they bent over her, half a dozen of them, like a pack of dogs shoving their muzzles into the open belly of a deer, Shade thought with disgust.

Zesi watched him, her face a mask of wrinkles and scars. 'Look at us,' she said. 'We've changed so much. I can't even count the kill scars on your brow.'

He grunted. 'Haven't aged well, have we?'

'You've survived here, Shade. But you've achieved nothing. You've just held onto what your father had.'

'Wait until the Giving,' he said angrily. 'See how many come to kneel at my feet.'

'Oh, they fear you. But they'd be rid of you if they could.'

'And you've achieved so much more, have you?'

She shrugged. 'Once I was a woman alone. Now I command the bandits, and the Leafy Boys. Think how much damage I could do with that.

'And think what we could do together, your hunters with my killers! We could take all of Albia and its patchwork tribes.' She gestured at the clearing. 'You could build your circles of wood up and down the length of the peninsula. From north to south, east to west, all would know your name, and all would bow to you.' She eyed him. 'You would be safe. You and your children. None would dare to challenge you.'

He felt uncomfortably that she knew him too well. He was not like his father and never had been. He craved safety and security for his family, his people, more than he desired war or loot, or to control others. But aggression seemed to be the only way to achieve that. 'Is that what you've come to propose, Zesi, a war? And what would you get out of it? What do you want?'

'Only one thing. Etxelur. If all of Albia is to bow to you, Etxelur will bow to me.'

'Etxelur has changed. It is rich now. Everybody knows that. Its flint is the best you'll find anywhere, and is prized.'

'You can have the flint – have it all. All I want is my sister's head under my heel.' She leaned forward and grabbed his hand. The unexpected touch sent a jolt through him; his body remembered her, even if his mind refused to accept her. 'And there's more. There's something else *you* want in Etxelur, Shade, even if you don't know it. Something we made together.'

He drew back from her touch, his head swimming. The priest murmured in his stupefied sleep. Shade asked with dread, 'And what is that?'

'Your son. *Our son*. Your only son, in fact – yes? I know how important sons are to you Pretani. You and I could never have built a life together. But maybe, together, we can build a world—'

There was another raw, guttural cry, shouting.

Shade said to Zesi, 'Everywhere you go, must you be accompanied by screams of pain and fear?' He pushed out of his house.

The Leafy female had got away. One man lay on the ground, his tunic hitched up around his waist, a wooden stake protruding from his thigh. Another Leafy lay dead on the ground – a third, another boy, his neck snapped.

'Incredible,' Bark said as Shade came up. 'Six men around her. This fellow about to stick his cock in her, it seems. Then this Leafy Boy comes charging out of the forest. Stabs the fellow with a stake, and drags the girl away. The lads caught him, and they did for him as you can see, but the girl escaped. Look at the state of him.' Bark lifted up the boy's right arm, which was clearly broken. 'A busted arm, and he still beat off six Pretani!'

'Just as I told you,' Zesi murmured in Shade's ear. 'All this wildness, all this strength. Imagine if we can control it,

375

together. It will be a Great Sea of violence. Do you want to hear my plan?'

Deeply uneasy, he asked, 'How does it start?'

'With stone.'

65

The Sixteenth Year After the Great Sea: Summer Solstice.

'Then it's agreed,' said Novu to the elders of the Bone People. Sitting on the dusty deck of the raft, in the shade of a cloth canopy, he showed them the basket in front of him. 'You get forty nodules of the best Etxelur flint. In return, you send forty of your strongest young people to labour on our dykes next year.' He spoke fast, fluent traders' tongue, and he smiled, keen to close the deal.

Ana sat beside him, raised above the rest on a heap of skins, themselves valuable commodities. 'They should be healthy, mind,' Ana warned. 'The people you send. Good workers. No ill, no lame, nobody too young or too old . . .'

Dolphin, watching, thought that if Novu's face was open and trustworthy, a natural trader's, Ana's face, in the shade of the awning, was stern, hard to read.

The leaders of the Bone People, in a line before Novu, Ana and Jurgi, stared back. They were greedy for the flint; they could barely keep their eyes off the creamy, pale brown stone. Yet they were wary of the transaction Novu was trying to conduct.

It got even worse when Novu produced his counting tokens, little clay figurines with circles on their bellies.

Dolphin was sitting with Kirike and others of Etxelur's senior families on this borrowed raft in the background of the talks. They had no real part to play in these discussions. They were just here to add some weight to the Etxelur party. It was midsummer day, and they were in the estuary of the World River.

Even in the canopy's shade it was intensely hot and humid, out here on the breast of the river. Midges hummed in the air. Occasionally, as a wave rolled down the languid water, the floor lifted and the wooden structure groaned like a great, relaxed sigh.

The Bone People elders were all men, for that was the way of these people from far inland, far up the river valley. They went naked, with their penises painted bright red with ochre, and each man wore a cap made of the upper skull of an honoured ancestor, and had a finger-bone from another grandparent shoved through the fleshy part of his nose. Their priest was just a boy, aged about fourteen. He had a whole tower of skulls on his head, threaded together through holes drilled in their crowns. He looked baffled, still a child, out of place in this meeting of adults.

Dolphin, distracted, saw a dragonfly that had somehow got under the awning, flitting about, confused. One of the Bone People snatched it neatly out of the air in his fist, inspected it, then crushed it and popped it into his mouth.

Kirike plucked her elbow. 'I'm bored,' he whispered.

'Me too . . .'

'There's some old man over there watching us.'

Dolphin peered past the Bone People into the gloom, and she saw a man in heavy furs, dark, strong-looking, with scars striped across his forehead, like a Pretani. He was maybe thirty. There were a few people from other groups here, though the meeting was dominated by Etxelur folk and Bone People. When he saw Dolphin looking at him the stranger smiled; she looked away.

Kirike said, 'Let's get out of here.'

'Wait until they're not watching.'

Kirike was restless, but sat still, as Novu continued his patient setting out of the counting tokens.

The Bone People were intrigued by the trading, but they were disturbed too, faintly troubled. And well might they be, for so were many of the Etxelur folk. Too many traditions were being defied. All Dolphin's life the midsummer Giving, presided over

378

by Ana, had been the most significant event of the year, as well as the most fun. People came to it from all across Northland. Some trade had always gone on – indeed traders like the one who had brought Novu himself to Etxelur could travel all the way across the Continent to such fairs, carrying their precious bits of iron and gold and obsidian and carved bone. But the point of the event wasn't the trade; the point was the Giving, the sharing.

That was how it used to be, anyhow.

The trouble was, Etxelur's huge projects, the dykes and drainage schemes, were always hungry for labour. But people still had to spend most of their time gathering food and building houses and making clothes and chasing children – the business of staying alive. And in Etxelur, it had soon become apparent, there just weren't enough people to fulfil Novu's grand schemes.

So Etxelur had started to buy labour from its neighbours.

Its treasure was the flint mined from Flint Island, and from the lode freshly exposed in the Bay Land. A rough exchange had soon been established: one nodule of high-quality flint in return for the labour of one healthy youngster for a summer. Many of these transactions were conducted at the Givings, and gradually the nature of the ceremony had changed, as Novu and the priest, watched over by a hawk-eyed Ana, spent much of their time conducting elaborate negotiations.

And now, this year, Ana had decreed a new departure. It was a year since Heni's death, and Qili's journey all the way from the estuary last year had given her the idea. *This* year, Etxelur's Giving wouldn't even be held in Etxelur at all. Instead, much of the population had made the long walk along the north coast of Northland to the World River estuary, and here Ana had built her Giving platform and set up a dreamers' house and organised the games, and Novu set out his trade goods. For, Ana argued, the estuary was the richest single site in all of Northland – and rich with people whose labour she could buy.

The heart had gone out of the Giving, complained old folk like

379

Arga. It was as if the rebuilding of Etxelur had become a madness that was eating all their lives, and turning them away from the wisdom of the mothers. Some had gone to the priest, asking him to speak to Ana, but Jurgi had always been an ally of Ana. Ana and her core team didn't seem to care.

And so here they were, on midsummer day, far from home, doing business.

Novu's tokens, made of soft clay, were crudely shaped into human figures, each with a shapeless blob for a head, and limbs divided from the body by grooves. And each had a pattern of circles and bars inscribed into its belly.

Novu, as he always did, went through the meaning of the tokens to make sure the Bone People elders understood. 'This man has a single circle on his belly. That means one worker, for one summer.' He held up a finger. 'This little man has two circles, that's two workers. Three, four, five. Now look.' The next figure had a radial bar cutting to the centre of one small circle. 'The bar stands for five, for one hand.' He held up his open right hand to demonstrate. 'And the circle is one more. Six.' He held up his left forefinger. 'And this next one, a bar with two circles, means seven. And eight, and nine . . .' This system was continued up to the most complex inscription, of four bars and five circles, which stood for twenty-five.

The boy-priest picked up one of the little men. His skull-tower cap wobbled. The boy made the clay man walk up and down on his stumpy legs, humming a kind of tune. Novu waited patiently until the boy had finished playing, and restored the token to its place in the row before him.

Despite her restlessness to be away, Dolphin always enjoyed watching Novu go through this strange procedure, the cleverness of the little tokens. It had come about because of too many disputes about who had agreed to what, how many nodules had been promised for how many young workers or sacks of lime or boats laden with fish – disputes that were either the product of bad faith, or of deals done in the dreamers' house where nobody could remember whether they'd agreed to

380

anything at all. One or two such lapses you could live with, but the building of Etxelur required a lot of planning, and a better way was needed.

Using tokens to record a deal was an idea Novu remembered from his home in Jericho, and what he had heard of practices among neighbouring peoples. He and Jurgi had worked out this system between them, basing it on the ancient concentric-circles symbol of Etxelur. Thus, as Novu produced two tokens to record the deal for forty workers – one little man with a four-bar, five-ring 'twenty-five' symbol, and another with a two-bar, five-ring 'fifteen' – he was giving the Bone People a reminder not just of the deal but of the spirit of Etxelur itself.

'Look, I will keep copies of the same tokens myself.' He held them up. 'Now we mark them so we know they record the truth.' He spat on his thumb, and pressed it into the soft clay of the heads of each of the four tokens, depressing the right side. Then he gave the tokens to one of the elders who, with prompting from Novu, did the same, pressing his thumb down on the left side of each shapeless face.

When this was done, the elder held up the little men he had been given, curious and, Dolphin thought, afraid, as if it was a new kind of magic. So he should be, she sometimes thought. The tokens were just bits of clay, yet they remembered conversations and deals more reliably than any human memory. What was that if not magic?

Ana and the others relaxed a little before moving on to their next business, which was a deal for a load of dried, salted eel. Ana drank juice from a sack, and spoke to the priest. Some of the Bone People got up and stretched their stiff legs, pacing on the raft's wooden floor.

Dolphin touched Kirike's shoulder. 'Now's our chance.'

He grinned and nodded. 'Just keep your head down.'

So they crawled away from the murmuring adults, making for the open side of the awning, and emerged into bright sunlight. Dazzled, Dolphin had to shield her eyes and look around to orient herself. The gangway to the next raft was a bridge of stout logs bound up with rope and lashed in place.

She grabbed Kirike's hand, and they skipped away, laughing.

66

Dolphin and Kirike felt welcome here on the World River. They were allowed to walk where they liked, stepping from raft to raft, and people smiled as they passed, and children ran after them. They were even offered bits of food. The Etxelur Giving was still a time of generosity and friendship. Meanwhile the contests were continuing, as spears were thrown and hapless target animals run through, and races were fought out on land and in the river.

The rafts were too many to count, tethered to each other and to the western bank of the river. Far bigger than mere boats, or the petty platforms Etxelur folk built in the marshes to go eel-hunting, the rafts were stout structures of planks strapped to huge stripped tree trunks. Some of them were very old, as you could see by the weathering of the planks and the support beams. And people lived here, in houses of wooden frames and brush and skin set up on the back of the rafts. Fires burned, built on stone hearths, fires burning on the river.

The river itself was so wide here that you couldn't see its eastern bank – it was a river with a horizon, like an ocean. Further downstream the river spread out into a tremendous delta, its water running between huge marshy islands where even more crowds of people lived.

This was why this place was such a valuable resource for Ana and Novu, why they had come here. All these people, all these communities stretching inland as far as anybody had travelled, all connected to each other by the river – and all available as a source of labour to be mined like Etxelur's own flint lode.

And yet even here there were signs of the long, slow battle being waged between sea and land. The river folk spoke of islands far out in the delta once occupied by their grandparents and now abandoned, drowned by the rising ocean. And in patches along the forest-clad bank, even after sixteen years, you could still see heaps of the pale salty sea-bottom mud that had been hurled far inland by the mindless energies of the Great Sea – the Gods' Shout.

They arrived at a raft where cages of wicker, weighted with stones, were suspended over the raft's side, just below the surface of the water. Inside each cage was a body. Bone showed through fish-chewed flesh, pale in the sunlight that dappled through the water. Even when they died, the people of the river were dominated by its tremendous presence; whereas in Etxelur you were laid out to be cleansed by sky, here it was left to the sharp teeth of the waters to strip your bones.

'I'll tell you what I heard today,' Kirike said. 'There are people here who spend their whole lives on the rafts – they never set foot on the dry land, not once in their lives.'

'I heard that too,' came a voice.

It was the dark man they had glimpsed watching them during Ana's meeting. He walked confidently across a gangway, carrying a bulky pack. Dolphin saw that Qili, Heni's grandson, was following him, looking faintly embarrassed. The stranger was smiling. Dolphin didn't smile back.

The man kept talking as he approached, in a fluent, lightly accented Etxelur tongue. 'In fact, to be a priest you have to be one of the water-dwellers, you can never be sullied by contact with the ground, for they believe that all their gods live in the river and that the land is dead. There have been a few scandals in the past when some roguish priest was found to be slipping ashore for his own purposes – you know what those fellows are like! And they had a crisis after the Great Sea when all their rafts got smashed, and those who survived had to clamber out on the shore.'

Kirike was interested. 'Ah. And that's why their priest back there is only fourteen or so.'

'Yes. The very first boy born safely on the rafts after the Great Sea, and he immediately got that tower of skulls stuck on his unfortunate head. This is a place where a single footprint in the mud can stop you being as a priest! But I suppose we all must look strange, from the outside.'

'And you look like a Pretani,' Dolphin said. 'Yet you speak the Etxelur tongue like a native.'

He just laughed. Tall, solid, heavy, the muscles prominent on his bare arms and legs, his face all but concealed by a thick black beard and two prominent kill scars, he looked out of place among the paler, more delicate river folk. 'Well, not quite a native, though you're kind to say so. But which of us is native anyhow? I know about you, Dolphin Gift, whose every drop of blood, like your mother's, comes from across the western ocean. I've travelled all over Albia and Northland and even into Gaira, and I never heard of anybody like that. What an extraordinary thing.' He turned to Kirike with interest. 'And you, Kirike. Black hair, solid build. Look at us, we're like brothers! I'm told you're half Pretani, and it shows.'

Kirike frowned. 'How do you know so much about us?'

He shrugged. 'Here we are at the mouth of the World River, yet everything revolves around faraway Etxelur. Everybody knows you, the names of Ana and her closest people. But you don't know my name – I apologise. I am Hollow.' He held out his two hands in the Pretani way of greeting.

Dolphin folded her arms and turned to Qili. 'Who is this character?'

Qili was clearly embarrassed. 'He came to the estuary and found me,' he said in his halting Etxelur tongue. 'That's all I know. He knew I went to Etxelur last year, and he asked questions about you—'

'I only asked Qili to introduce us,' Hollow said. 'No harm done, surely.'

'You were watching us,' Dolphin said accusingly. 'You followed us here.'

Kirike protested, 'Dolphin—'

'Everybody knows that whenever Pretani are around there's
trouble.'

'That may have been true in the past. But must the bad feeling
last for ever?' He glanced at Kirike. 'I'm not here for trouble. I'm
here to trade. Pretani folk always came to Etxelur Givings, in the
old days, and Etxelur folk came on our wildwood hunts.'

'Those days are gone,' Dolphin snapped.

Kirike, more circumspect, asked, 'So what do you have to
trade?'

'Ah. I thought you would never ask.' Hollow slipped off his
pack, crouched down and unfolded a parcel of skin to expose a
straight-edged block of stone: yellow-brown, carefully worked.
Hollow stroked its surface. 'Good Pretani sandstone. See how
finely grained it is? Easily worked.' He rapped it with his
knuckle. 'Yet heavy and hard-wearing. Look, you don't have to
know anything about stone to see its quality. If you have the
best flints in the world in Etxelur, we Pretani surely have the
best stone. If we can make a trade the bulk of it will be brought
to Etxelur by boat, down the rivers and along the coast—'

Dolphin shook her head. 'Why would we want stone?'

'For your walls. Your dykes, your channels cut in the ground.
Ask your genius from the east – Novu. Ask him about Jericho,
where they face their great walls with stone, not bricks or mud.
When he sees this stone he will hunger for it, believe me.'

'So why are you showing us?'

He stood up. 'Because it's as you said. There is bad blood
between Etxelur folk and Pretani. Those who make the decisions in Etxelur, especially Ana herself, won't have anything to
do with Pretani.'

'So that's it,' Dolphin said. 'Well, I won't help you get to Ana.
As far as I'm concerned you can shove this stupid stone up your
hairy Pretani arse.'

He was unperturbed. 'That's disappointing.' He looked at

Kirike again. 'I did know your father. It would be good to speak of him.'

Kirike blushed. To Dolphin's disgust, she saw that this blatant appeal to blood ties, from a man who looked so much like him, was swaying Kirike, who had grown up knowing neither of his parents. Kirike said to Dolphin, 'He's right about Novu. He often talks about stone buildings in Jericho. And the bad blood between Etxelur and Pretani can't last for ever. I can't see what harm it would do, Dolphin. Just to get Ana and Novu to look.'

Dolphin glared at him. 'Are you mad? Pretani aren't traders. They are killers who take what they want. You – Hollow – you've come here, you've learned our language, you've found out our names – all for a few boatloads of stone? What is it you really want?'

His vaguely good-humoured expression didn't falter, though she thought there was a greater lividity to the kill scars on his forehead. He murmured, too softly for the others to hear, 'Even if there was some grand scheme, I wouldn't tell you about it, would I? Remember, girl – you're an outsider. Foreign blood, like your mother.' He bent to pick up his stone block. 'Kirike – maybe we could talk about when I could meet Ana?'

Dolphin stormed away, crossing the rafts, making for the dry land. She didn't bother to check if Kirike was following her.

Qili hurried after her. 'I'm sorry. He seemed harmless enough – and anyhow I couldn't get rid of him. I didn't mean to cause any trouble . . .'

But Dolphin was in no mood to listen.

67

'What do you mean, we should be having more children?' Arga was indignant, almost shouting. 'Since when did you become a little mother, Ana?'

'Maybe we should calm down,' said Jurgi, glancing uneasily at the door flap of the stuffy raftborne house.

Ana just glared at Arga, apparently unmoved by her outburst.

It was dark in this house despite the brightness of the day, and they had lit some of the whale oil lamps they had brought from Etxelur; their smoky glow underlit Ana's face, making her look even older than she was, severe.

It was the day before the Etxelur water council. This was another invention of Ana's, a meeting she held every quarter around the time of the equinoxes and solstices, as a way of ensuring all the complicated activities in Etxelur were fitting together properly. They might have come all the way to the World River estuary but Ana wasn't going to let the chance of a council go by. And as she customarily did, Ana had summoned Jurgi, Novu, Ice Dreamer and Arga in advance of the council to see if they could guess the concerns that might be brought up, and to practise their answers. They'd all done this before, and the arguments were typical.

But Jurgi was far from comfortable. They were guests in a house loaned them by estuary folk, on a raft that rode the body of the World River. This wasn't Ana's house, from which people kept a respectful distance; anybody might be listening to their arguments. He said now, 'Let's keep our voices down at least.'

Novu was sweating heavily, his face slick, irritable. 'Maybe we should just go and sit out in the open and have done with it. Anything's better than this stuffiness.'

Ana grunted unsympathetically. 'I thought you and the priest enjoyed making each other sweat in the dark.'

Novu snapped back, 'And I am getting sick of the way you speak to us.'

Ice Dreamer smiled. 'I suspect she's just jealous of the consolation you two have found together. She is alone, more alone than any of the rest of us.'

'And you're alone too,' Ana shot back, 'since my father spoiled your plan to crawl into his bed by getting himself killed.'

'Shut up,' Arga said. 'Shut *up*. I can't stand your bickering.' She glared at them, one after another. 'Didn't you hear what Ana just said? She wants us to have more babies. Jurgi, you're still the priest. Can't you tell her why that's so wrong?'

'Yes, tell me, Jurgi.'

He bit back a sharp response. 'Arga has a point. It may be different in Jericho. But all across Northland, and even in Albia and Gaira, I never heard of any people who didn't space out their children.'

'This is the wisdom of the little mothers,' Arga protested. 'You can't have too many children, not too soon, not close together. It's always been this way. For when the flood comes, or the famine, and you have to run—'

Ice Dreamer said, 'It is the same in my country.'

Ana said dismissively, 'Yes, yes. *You can only carry one child, the others must be able to run – or die.* But times are different now. We of Etxelur don't have to run anywhere. And in the meantime we lost half our number to the Great Sea, and we haven't recovered yet, nor will we for a generation or two at this rate. We need more people, more than ever before—'

Arga snapped, 'More people to build your dykes and reservoirs!'

'Exactly.' Ana waved a hand. 'Look where we are! We have come all this way just to beg the loan of a few lumps of muscle from the river folk. Imagine if every woman in Etxelur had a child, and then another, and another. In fifteen more years we'd have a strong cohort of workers. We could do our own work, fulfil our own dreams—'

'*Your* dreams,' murmured Arga.

'And we wouldn't have to use up our precious flint persuading somebody else to do it for us.'

'They may not accept it,' said the priest uneasily. 'The people. They've followed you this far, Ana, but—'

'If you back me up they'll swallow it,' she said, sounding uninterested. 'Just say it's the will of the mothers. That always works.'

Jurgi felt a spark of anger at her casual insults. 'Take care, Ana. I am still a priest, *your* priest, and you should listen to what I say. You don't see all. You don't hear all. They come to me sometimes. They complain to me. Argue about whether the mothers *really* want us to do this, or that. I try to persuade them it's so. I'm not sure if I always succeed.'

Ana became thoughtful. 'So, even after all these years of us working together, they still come to you without telling me?'

The priest stiffened. 'The people's relationship with the little mothers has existed as long as the world. Long before you or I were ever born.'

'But the fact is there are still two centres in Etxelur. Two sources of decision-making. Or at least that's how the people see it, evidently.' She stared at him. 'I think I'm going to have to do something about that.'

He felt vaguely alarmed, having no idea what she might mean.

Arga was still angry at Ana. 'I'm telling you the people won't stand for it, this business of the babies. If the priest tells them they must, they'll challenge him. That's what I think.'

'She may be right,' said Ice Dreamer languidly.

Ana thought it over, and nodded. 'All right. Maybe it's too early to bring it up at this council. We'll leave it until the autumn equinox, and give ourselves time to work out how to argue for it. But argue it we will, for I'm convinced this is the only way forward for Etxelur . . . Until next time. Now, Novu, what's this rubbish I hear about stone from Albia?'

'It's far from rubbish,' Novu said. He shifted stiffly, and from the pile of goods beside him he produced a heavy block of stone, wrapped in skin. Unwrapped, it seemed to glow in the soft, diffuse light of the lamps. 'Look at this stuff. Now, Ana, yes, it's Pretani, and I know we have had our problems with them. But Kirike brought me this, and he thinks they are sincere, they really do just want to trade. I think we have to consider it. Just think what we could do with this – our dykes covered in this fine stone rather than my clumsy mud bricks and plaster!'

Arga said, 'Once again your dreams expand. Think how many more babies we will have to conceive to build everything out of stone!'

But Ana wasn't listening. She leaned forward and ran her hand over the stone's smoothly worked surface.

68

Me was prodded awake in the usual way, by a wooden spear shaft in the small of the back.

He sat up. He had barely slept. He was stiff from lying on the dew-soaked grass with the others. The tether was tight around his neck.

Above him the branches of a big spreading oak obscured the grey light of morning. But he was under the tree and not in it, for the grounders would not let the Leafy Boys climb. And this isolated tree stood in a clearing. It was agony for any Leafy Boy to be trapped down on open ground. Even when he started to move and got the stiffness out, the dread would linger.

The grounder who had prodded him walked around, kicking or poking the other Leafies. Then he paused by the side of the tree, propped his spear up against the trunk, and opened his hide trousers. Me saw his thick piss spray in the air, bouncing off the trunk, the golden droplets oddly beautiful where they caught the light. Then the grounder walked off to where his fellows had spent the night, gathered around their fire.

The other Leafies stirred, a dozen small forms emerging from heaps of dead leaves. They were all naked, filthy, miserable, and they all had tethers tied tight around their necks, fixed to a single stake in the ground. One girl moved stiffly, and Me saw from the bruises on her thighs and small breasts that the grounders had come for her in the night. He had a vague memory of a disturbance, a rustling of leaves, a scream muffled by a hand over a mouth. He had just lain still, thankful that it was not him.

Another grounder came over with a hide sack and dumped out a pile of offal, twisting grey guts. Before the grounder had turned his back the Leafies fell on it. The offal was tough and tasteless and the stomach contents were acrid, but the Leafies fought and snarled over it like pigs, their small backsides in the air, their faces red with blood. Me used his weight and strength to shove little ones aside. He was not shy; if you didn't fight you went hungry. Sometimes the grounders let their dogs go for the food, so you had to fight them off as well.

Me saw one small boy pushed out of the feeding group. This hungry little boy had been losing the fight for food for days, and was starting to look pale, scrawny. He pawed at his tether. The grounders wet the knot by pissing on it before tightening it, and when it dried out the rope contracted, making it impossible to pick apart even with a Leafy's small clever fingers. If they saw the boy trying the grounders would knock out his teeth; he would live, but he'd starve.

When the food was gone, the Leafies got as far from each other as they could, and began to perform their pisses and shits. Me, squatting, was ferociously thirsty, but the grounders never brought water. The Leafies would have to find what they could for themselves in the course of the day. Some days, in fact, they were left tethered where they had been during the night and not moved at all, and Me would finish the day enraged by thirst.

But today, it seemed, was not going to be one of those days.

The grounders were already moving. One of them kicked dirt over the fire. The others lifted their hide cloaks over their shoulders, and picked up their spears, and tucked knives into their skins. They started shouting, laughing, throwing punches at each other. Me, with a shudder of dread, recognised their mood. It was going to be another day of running and fighting and killing, and the grounders were getting themselves ready.

One of the grounders came over to the Leafies. He slashed through their tethers, wrapped the ropes around his wrist, and snarled at the children until they moved.

The grounders formed up and set off across the clearing at a heavy jog. The Leafies, driven ahead, ran in the horror of the open air. If one of them stumbled the reward was a kick or a prod with a stabbing spear.

But as Me ran, as always, the cold of the night worked out of his bones and muscles, his legs pumping, the breath sliding into his lungs. Me was young and healthy. He would have enjoyed the run, if not for the sheer terror of the openness, and the uncertainty of what was to come.

Before the sun was much higher in the sky they came to a landscape that was even stranger to the Leafy Boys, a place where water glimmered everywhere, in streams and ponds choked with reeds, and shallow islands rose up, and there was scarcely a scrap of forest.

The grounders charged on, making for the bits of high ground, driving the Leafies on through mud and marsh and shallow open water. Soon Me's bare legs were soaked, and clinging mud dragged at his feet. Huge flocks of birds rose up and flapped away, cawing their disapproval, and the air was full of noise and sprayed water. All the Leafies were terrified. But when he got the chance Me scooped up water, shook out the living things that swam in it, and sucked it down his dry throat.

One boy went down in a flooded gully, gurgling in terror. Me saw it was the little boy who hadn't been able to fight for the food. The grounder holding the tethers had to stop and drag the boy's scrawny body out of the murk, yelling with anger and impatience. But after a few paces the boy fell again. The handler hauled him up once more and shook him.

The boy spewed water from his mouth. He reached out to the grounder, like a baby reaching for its mother.

The handler thrust the boy into the water, driving down his neck with his strong outstretched arm. One of the other grounders called over. The handler shouted back, laughing, keeping his arm in place. When he raised his arm again the boy dangled, his tongue sticking out of his mouth, his lips blue. The grounder dropped him in the water, cut the tether with a slice of his knife, and turned to run on.

Me and the others had no choice but to follow. He knew he would never think of the boy again.

They approached one of the larger islands. There were grounders living here. Me could see houses, squat cones plastered with dried reeds, with smoke seeping out. A bigger fire burned in an open hearth, and there were stands where fish and eels were drying. Boats clustered, broad, flat-bottomed, some dragged up onto the dry land, some on the water where men pushed them to and fro with long poles. There were grounders everywhere, adults working in the water or loading eel on the racks or just lazing around, and children, many naked, their skinny legs muddy.

This was the target, then. The grounders and Leafies ran on without breaking stride.

A woman with a basket of fish saw them first. She just stared, for a long heartbeat. Then, yelling warnings, she dropped her basket and plunged into the water to grab one of the children.

More adults came out of the houses. Some of the men ran to a stack of weapons, like spears but with hooked points, perhaps meant for catching fish. One man, on a raft floating on the water, poled desperately to get away from the island.

All of this was too late, for the grounders were almost on them.

They let the Leafies go in first. Me scrambled up a shallow muddy beach. Children ran screaming, but Me charged through a pack of them, using his fists to slam them aside.

Soon Me and the others were in among the houses. Adults turned to face them, armed with spears and clubs. The girl who had been used during the night was close to Me, and she seemed filled with rage. She leapt at a man who was swinging a club. Me joined her, going for the man's legs as her lithe body wrapped around his neck. The man got in one blow with his club that winded Me, but then the girl's teeth were in his throat.

And now the grounders were on the island, roaring and laughing as they swung their weapons. Me saw one island boy armed with a spear, facing a grounder. The grounder stumbled, and the boy had a moment of advantage. But he hesitated. With a swing of the blunt end of his spear the grounder smashed the boy's skull.

Now dogs came running through the houses, snarling and snapping, to take on the Leafies. Me got hold of a dead man's club and swung it at the animals.

The air was filled with screams and cries, with the crunch of bone and the howling of the dogs, and the stink of blood.

69

Shade waded to the island, with Hollow and Bark at his side, their feet and legs caked in mud.

The fighting was done. The adults were dead or subdued, the survivors bound together near the ruin of their big outdoor hearth. Shade could hear that his men were still busy with some of the women. The small children had all been killed or driven off. Some of the men were still walking around the island, throwing little carcasses into the muck, and using the poles the islanders had used to push their flat-bottomed boats to shove the surviving kids back into the water, ignoring their cries and pleas.

The Leafy Boys, those who lived, had been fixed with their tethers, and had been thrown the carcasses of dogs to eat. It was extraordinary to see the naked creatures rip the skin of the animals with their teeth. The islanders cowered from them.

Shade inspected one of the islanders' sturdy houses. He stepped inside its reed cover and let his eyes adjust to the dark. The big support beams were stained black with smoke and, in the middle of this marsh, had somehow been kept as dry as old bones. The posts were of oak, the right wood for the task, and must have been hauled to this soggy place from far away. He wondered how they kept the ground drained to stop the beams rotting. There was stuff on the floor, clothes, half-prepared food, a necklace of fish bones, a toy animal made of straw that looked as if it had been much played with. The people who lived here not been long gone, but were never coming back.

He went to the fire, picked out an ember glowing red hot, cupped it in a bit of hide and brought it to a wall. He knelt down and teased out dry straw from the wall, set the ember down, and began to breathe on it delicately.

'Generations old,' he whispered to the house. 'Parents and grandparents and great-grandparents. This very morning a family woke here, thinking it was just another day.' The straw had caught; flames licked, and he stepped back. 'And now it's over.'

'And that pleases you.'

He turned.

Zesi stood by the door flap, silhouetted against the daylight. 'The ability to destroy, on a whim. To kill, or not to kill. The most fundamental power of all. And you don't even have to lift a finger to wield it. Feels good, doesn't it?'

And it did, though Shade sometimes felt uneasy to admit it. What did that say about him, about the state of his own spirit? Not for the first time he wished he had a decent priest to talk this over with. Maybe he ought to do something about getting Resin off the poppy.

Smoke was already gathering in the house, so Shade followed Zesi outside, where Bark waited. Then he watched with thoughtful interest as the fire ate up the reed cover of the house, leaving only a skeleton of posts, lit up by the flames. Then the oak, too, began to burn.

He was aware of the captive islanders sitting in their loops of rope, watching apathetically.

He turned, looking around at the island, the shining water that spread around this place, the drifting boats, the banks of gravel and mud. This soggy place, in the north of Albia, was rich and populous, comparatively, and peaceful. Now its human story was over. But some of the birds were coming back, to swim on the water and to plunge for food. The birds always came back, he had observed, as soon as the human fuss was over – and the other birds, the buzzards that enjoyed human flesh, and had, he suspected, learned to follow the Pretani around.

'What a disgusting place,' Bark said, wrinkling his fleshy nose. 'Water. Mud. Watery mud and muddy water. Fish and eels, and not a dry scrap of land or a decent tree anywhere.'

'Much of Northland is like this,' Zesi murmured.

'Well, there you are. The fight went well.'

'I could see that,' Shade said.

'The Leafy Boys did their job. I sometimes wonder if they're worth all the trouble. But they cost nothing to feed and they deliver a mighty shock, especially in those first few moments of the attack.'

Shade eyed the captives. Healthy adults and older children were the prize, the point of these raids. Workers and hunters. There seemed pathetically few of them as a reward for all the destruction and lost life. 'Let's get on with the breaking. Pick out the biggest man. You know the routine.'

Bark grumbled as he went over to the captives, 'Since I worked it out, yes, I know the routine. You.' He made the chosen man stand, bound his hands tighter, and brought him before Shade.

The man was tall, strong-looking, maybe twenty, twenty-one. He was bare to the waist, and had a tattoo of the kind these people seemed to favour, an eel wrapped around his thigh. He looked at Zesi and Shade with a spark of defiance.

Zesi brought over heaps of purloined hide. She set these on the ground, and she and Shade sat, sharing a water skin.

'Kneel.' Bark repeated the word in the traders' tongue. When the man did not comply Bark slammed his spear shaft into the back of the man's knees, forcing him into a kneel, grunting with pain.

The islander lifted his head, and said something in his own tongue.

'Speak traders' tongue,' Shade snapped back. 'Everybody speaks the traders' tongue.'

'Why?' the man said thickly. 'Why have you done this? Why have you killed our children?'

'Well, the children are no use to us,' Shade said, almost kindly. 'What is your name?'

The man considered. 'True. True, son of True.'

Shade gestured at the island, the burning house. 'And what do you call yourselves?'

'We are the People of the Great Eel.'

Zesi laughed. 'That's new.'

'We have lived here since the beginning of time, when the gods of water and land and sky fought the Great Eel at the Centre of the Earth—'

'Save it for your priest, if he lives,' Shade said. 'Well, you don't live here any more. And you are no longer the People of the Great Eel. You have no name, save a name I may choose to give you. We, by the way, are the Pretani, and I am Shade. Now we will take you far from here – some of you, those who choose to live; those who defy us we will kill, and throw their bodies to the water, so that the Great Eel may feast one last time.'

Zesi burst out laughing.

True looked at her as if he couldn't believe what he was seeing. Shade thought he knew how he felt. True said, 'You will take us far from here – what then?'

'You will cut stone. And then you will carry the stone, or drag it, to another place even further away.'

True looked bewildered. His face was very expressive for a big man, Shade thought absently. 'Stone? Like flint?'

'No. Sandstone. And not for tools. Big blocks of it.'

'The other thing you might do for us is fight,' Zesi said.

'Fight who?'

Shade said, 'We don't know yet. Others, like you. You will fight, so that others may be taken. And they in turn will cut stone, or fight. Some of the men who attacked you today were once as you are, captured. This is how we proceed. How we grow.'

True shook his head. 'You are mad. What is all this for?'

'That does not concern you.'

400

'How long must we do this, this cutting of the stone and fighting?'

Zesi sighed. 'There was me thinking you were clever. You'll do this for ever. Or until you die, at any rate.'

'My children.' He glanced over his shoulder. 'If they survive in the reeds—'

Shade said, again not unkindly, 'They are probably dead. And even if not, you will never see them again. But you're young. You may have more children.'

'And what will become of them?'

'They will cut stone.'

True looked still more bewildered, more shocked than fearful or angry. Shade had seen this reaction before. He simply didn't understand what he was hearing.

Zesi leaned forward. 'Let me teach you a new word. *Slave*. This is what you are. You are a slave. You will die a slave. And in future your children will be born slaves, and will die slaves.'

His eyes were wide. 'Are you even human, woman?'

'Oh, yes,' Zesi said. 'But you aren't. Not any more. Nor are your children, who don't even exist yet. You are as dogs to us, that we control, and we do what we like with.'

True considered this. 'I would rather die than cut your stone.' And he spat on the ground, bringing up a mouthful of bloody phlegm.

'Let me see if I can persuade you.' Shade nodded to Bark.

Bark grinned, and went over to the other captives, hefting his spear. At random he shoved the blunt end into the face of a man, who howled and went down. Shade carefully watched True's reaction. Bark struck a woman next, then another man, then aimed for another woman—

True flinched, tugging at his bonds.

'That's the one,' Shade called. 'Bring her over.' As Bark separated the woman from the group, Shade asked Zesi, 'So who is she, do you think? A lover, a sister? Well, it doesn't matter.'

Bark got a couple of the men to help. Holding the girl's limbs, they briskly cut her clothes from her and got her on the ground, laughing and coarsely fumbling at her as they did so. About the same age as True, she wasn't very pretty, Shade thought, but she had good full breasts, and a slight swelling at her belly that might be a pregnancy.

Bark laid out long hide tethers on the ground. He carefully soaked them with water from a leather pitcher, and then tied them around the woman's wrists and ankles. With the help of the hunters he pulled the tethers away so the woman was stretched out on the ground, arms and legs spread wide. The men fixed the tethers to house posts and fish racks, dragging them tight until the girl screamed, and Shade heard a joint crack.

Bark stood back and inspected what had been done. 'This is a lot easier in a forest with lots of handy trees standing around, I can tell you. But it will do, I think.'

Shade switched to the traders' tongue. 'All right, True. Let me explain what will happen now. You're going to stay there on your knees. Your lady will lie there on the ground. And in time those hide tethers will dry out. They will shrink, and cut tighter, down into the skin and the fat and the flesh, through to the bone. Very slowly. And meanwhile the long lengths that are holding her will contract too. You can imagine what will happen.' He tried to project a kind of glee. It was important to make True believe he would go through with this. 'Her body will give way where it is weakest, at the knees and the elbows. She will be jointed. Her limbs will come off, one by one.'

'No.' True raged, hauling at his ropes. 'Must I cut your stone to make you stop this?'

'Oh, no,' Zesi said. 'To save the girl . . .' She leaned close to True, who was sweating now, shuddering. 'Choose another.'

'What?'

'Choose another of your family, your friends to take her place.'

'I will not.'

'It is the only way you can save her. Do it, and you'll have her

402

back. Otherwise you will spend a day and a night and a day watching her—'

'Gentle.'

Shade snapped, 'What?'

'Take Gentle.' He turned. 'The one with the beard. Take him.'

Shade looked at the man, who looked harmless enough, but he was growing alarmed. 'Why him? No, don't answer. I don't care. Bark, free the girl and get this Gentle.'

Gentle was already screaming, cursing, struggling, for he knew what was to come. True was crying openly now, in shame and bitterness, his spirit broken, as intended. Bark cut the girl loose, and Shade saw the huge relief on her face as she folded over on herself, realising she was not going to die today.

Suddenly he was sickened.

70

The Sixteenth Year After the Great Sea: Autumn Equinox.

Dolphin was standing on the dyke across the mouth of the bay when she heard Kirike's call.

She could see him down there on the Bay Land, near a stand of willows, mature trees growing out of what had once been sea-bottom mud. He waved, his broad smile revealing a flash of white teeth.

The people around Dolphin, labouring on the dyke, looked up, distracted. They were all snailheads, most of them children, doing small jobs under the supervision of the adults. One girl grinned when she saw it was Kirike calling. You couldn't keep secrets, and everybody knew about Dolphin and Kirike.

A flood of complicated, contradictory feelings welled up in Dolphin. She'd missed him every day he'd been away on his late-summer hunting jaunt with the other boys to the southern forests. Now he had returned, but she had to share some seriously bad news with him. Besides, she felt grimy, ragged, her clothes and skin covered in dust from the Pretani sandstone she had been handling all day. It was late afternoon, and she was *tired*. Why couldn't he have come home in the morning, when she was clean and fresh?

He called again, his voice as distant as a gull's cry. She pointed north, beyond Flint Island; they had a favourite spot on the shore. He nodded, and began to jog that way.

She jabbered her apologies to the snailheads. They shrugged,

404

dirty, sweating, bored; few of them would work much longer today anyhow.

Then she walked across the dyke to its abutment at its northern end, on the island, and clambered down to the sandy beach. Her afternoon shadow stretched before her, long, oddly elegant – more elegant than she felt herself. As she walked she kicked off her boots and let the damp sand soothe her feet, which were aching after a day of cutting and hauling stone. It was almost the autumn equinox and the water was sharply cold.

At the headland she glanced back once at the dyke. The wall stood proud, defying the sea, though it wasn't nearly as spectacular as when viewed from the Bay Land side, where its whole face was exposed. It was a patchwork, with around a quarter of the original core of mud bricks and plaster now faced by sandstone slabs.

The work with the stone, with stuff that was heavy, unfamiliar and blighted by a superstitious dread, was progressing slowly. Dolphin was coming to hate the dyke, for the way it ate her life, and the lives of so many others.

She turned her back on the dyke and walked on, and was glad when she turned around the headland to the island's north shore, and the dyke was out of her sight altogether. Here wading birds, vast variegated flocks of them, worked their way along the littoral, having paused here on their way to their winter homes. There was plenty of evidence of humanity here, in the great middens, the houses standing on their mounds looking out over the ocean, even the stubs of the new dykes extending out to sea towards the Mothers' Door. But somehow, away from the great drained expanse of the Bay Land, there was more of a sense of nature, of the world as it was supposed to be.

And here came Kirike, walking along the beach to meet her. She flung away her boots and ran towards him.

They collided in a tangle of limbs, tripped each other up, and fell to the sand. His face was before hers, the skin soft under a stubble of dark beard, and she could smell his sweat, and a subtle tang of wood sap, and crushed acorns on his breath when he kissed her. 'You smell of forest,' she murmured into his mouth.

'And you smell of the sea. And of stone.'

'Ugh. Does that bother you?'

He rolled away, sat up and shrugged. 'I don't much care. Maybe that's the Pretani blood in me. Come on, shall we go up to our shell place? We'll be out of this breeze.'

She got up, brushing sand from her legs. *'Getting out of the breeze.* That's all you're concerned about, is it?'

He grinned, standing. 'For now.' He grabbed her hand so they were drawn together, arms and bodies and foreheads touching. 'Wait until we get back to the house – as long as we can get your mother out of the way.' He kissed her lightly, teasing. 'Come on.'

Then he pulled away and jogged across the sand to where she'd thrown her boots, and picked them up. He was tidy that way, with a neatness that she lacked. She mocked him for it, but it was one of the ways they fit together, the ways they worked better together than apart.

They walked along the beach, and before they reached the holy middens they clambered up into the dunes. Here there was a little hollow between one dune ripple and the next, bounded by long stalks of marram grass, just wide enough for two people to lie side by side – a spot they called their 'shell place', for it was always carpeted by broken sea shells, washed up from the beach. It was here that they had first made love, not long after returning from the midsummer Giving expedition to the World River. It was a place Dolphin liked to think was special, was theirs alone – but that was probably a dream.

Kirike lay back in the soft, dry sand, his arms tucked behind his head. 'Ah – it's good to stop moving. Believe it or not I'm pretty tired. It felt like we ran all the way to the southern forests and back.'

She grunted, not impressed. That was what you had to expect with boys and young men. She settled down beside him with her head on his shoulder. 'So how was the hunting?'

406

'The deer were shy this year. We came back with heaps of mushrooms, though. Mushrooms, and acorns. We were lousy hunters, but the squirrels won't forget us in a hurry. And how's the wall building going?'

'Dismal. Hard. Boring. Listen, Kirike, we need to talk. Ana wants to see us later. And my mother—'

He covered her hand with his. 'In a moment. I just got back. Let's not talk about that lot of old monsters, just for a while longer.' He sat up, pushing back his thick black hair from his eyes, and looked out to sea.

From here they could see the sweep of the ocean, the shadowed mass of Flint Island's single hill, the huge, empty, deep blue sky. On a rocky headland to the west Dolphin saw movement, small, fat, white shapes crawling. Baby grey seals, just born, venturing out into a new world. And in the air she saw a flight of swans leaving for the winter, their huge wings pink-white as they caught the sun's low-angled light, and waders swooping in from the east, to settle like snowflakes on the littoral.

Kirike said, 'I love this time of year, and the spring. The equinoxes, the times of change. When the birds of summer fly away, and the birds of winter come. As if the world is taking a huge breath. It's so beautiful here. Every time I go away I forget . . . Even if I don't belong here.'

'Don't say that. Listen, Kirike – my mother. She's talking about going away.'

He turned to look at her. 'Where?'

'She fears she is the last of her people – or I am. She thinks she should go back and find others. Save them, perhaps, as she was saved by Kirike, your grandfather.'

'She wants to go back over the ocean?'

'She's done it before.'

'But my grandfather Kirike is dead, and Heni who travelled with him. Without Kirike and Heni, how could she even find the way?'

'My mother thinks she might remember. There are plenty of

407

young men who say they want the adventure. Anyhow she is talking of trying.' Dolphin frowned. 'She's not happy here – not any more. She and Ana bicker a lot. There was always tension between them, because when she first came here Ana thought my mother was taking her father away from her. I think she grew close to Ana when they were recovering from the Great Sea together.'

He snorted, and spat a gob of phlegm into the sand. 'These old folk, with their ancient fights and their Great Sea. Don't you get sick of hearing about it?'

'If she goes,' Dolphin said simply, 'she wants me to go with her.'

'Oh.' He dug his fingers into the sand. 'What about us?'

'My mother doesn't want us to be together anyhow. You know that.'

'What about you? What do you want?'

His Pretani-dark eyes were on her, and she saw how important this question was to him. She didn't want to answer, she wanted their relationship to continue to be the wonderful game it had been so far. But she knew that what she told him now would shape them for ever. It must be the deepest truth.

She set her hand on his. 'How could I leave you? Our babies will be beautiful.'

He grabbed her to him. 'Beautiful, yes. Hairy, but beautiful.'

That made her laugh.

He whispered in her ear, his breath hot, 'It doesn't matter where we came from, or our parents. All that matters is who we are, and where we are. What we feel, here and now . . .' She felt his hand move down her back, strong and confident. She thrilled as he explored the cleft of her buttocks.

But she pushed him away. 'No. You were right. Too windy and cold here. And besides, Ana will be waiting.'

He pulled back, reluctant. 'All right. What shall we say to your mother?'

'Nothing.' She stood, brushing away sand from her tunic. '*We* know what we're going to do. But it's none of her business – not until she asks, or we choose to tell her. Come on. You can carry my boots, as you're so keen on them.'

They walked away down the dunes and along the beach, heading for the abutment of the dyke and the way back to Ana's house.

71

Ana's was a big house, set on top of one of the biggest mounds in Etxelur, big enough for a dozen people. This evening, when Dolphin and Kirike arrived, four people sat around the hearth. Ana herself sat on her own bed, which was piled up with skins so she looked down on the rest. She had oil lamps burning at her feet. She was thin, swathed in a cloak, and sat very still; ageless, she looked barely human, a thing made of stone.

To Ana's left Jurgi and Novu sat together, close enough for their shoulders to touch.

Ice Dreamer sat to Ana's right. When Dolphin and Kirike walked in through the door flap, defiantly hand in hand, Dreamer watched, hard and suspicious. With her proud nose and streaks of grey hair, Dolphin sometimes thought her mother was coming to look like a great and beautiful bird of prey.

Dolphin and Kirike sat together, beside Dreamer.

At last Arga pushed her way in. She looked faintly anxious, as she often did; Dolphin knew she was never truly happy away from her children. She smiled at Ana, and sat down in the gap between Dreamer and Novu. 'Sorry I'm late—'

A bundle of hair and big paws came pushing through the door flap after her. It was Thunder. The dog was excited to find all these people here, as if they had gathered especially for him. He ran around the group, wagging his tail and submitting to pats and strokes. Finally he jumped up at Ana, resting his paws on her chest. She rolled her eyes. 'You're wet, dog! Look at the marks you're making on my cloak. Oh, get away with you.' Gently, Ana pushed the dog aside. He circled, found a comfortable patch close to the hearth, and slumped down, head on his front paws.

Arga said, 'I'll take him out if you like.'

'Oh, leave him,' Jurgi said. He looked up at Ana. 'At least he's broken the silence. Shall we get on with it, whatever it is you have to say?'

Ana looked back at him, stern. 'Yes. Let's get on.' She turned to Dolphin. 'You were out on the dykes today. The work isn't going well, is it? Slower than it should. Anybody can see that.'

'The quality of the work is poor too,' Novu broke in before Dolphin could reply. 'The way the stone is being cut, the fitting. I've said how we do it in Jericho, over and over—'

'All right, Novu, we hear you.' Ana turned to Dolphin. 'Well?'

Dolphin shrugged. 'There are too few of us and too much to do. Even with the snailheads and the folk from the World River and the rest. What with all the other work we have to do just to keep alive,' she said heavily.

Ana said, 'We always need more people. But that isn't really the problem, is it?'

'It isn't?'

'If people *want* to work at something it gets done. That's one thing I've learned in life. It's clear that people just don't like working the stone. Why not?'

Dolphin shrugged. 'You know why.'

'Tell me anyway.'

'Because they fear it, I think. Or they dread it. Stone is dead. It doesn't grow like wood or reed. Flint is one thing, we have always worked flint. This Albia sandstone is the dead bones of the world. It isn't right to use it as we do.'

Arga said cautiously, 'There's been muttering . . .'

'What? Speak up, cousin.'

'Some say we are defying the little mothers.' She glanced at the priest. 'Maybe the mothers *want* the sea to cover over Etxelur, for all we know.'

Ana asked, 'And have they approached you about this, Jurgi?'

The priest nodded. 'At times. I try to reassure them—'

411

'This is one thing I want to address today. We've discussed this before. No matter how closely we work together, Jurgi and I, no matter what we say, the people always know that if they have doubts about me they can go to you. Maybe they think they can come between us, the way children can set one parent against another.'

Arga said, 'But that's the way of things. You've always had the priest on the one hand, the Giver on the other. It's just the way things are.'

Ana didn't reply.

Jurgi, watching her, said, 'I think she has a plan. Some solution to this problem she sees. And I have a feeling I'm not going to like it.'

'There's another issue too.' Ana raised her hand, and studied her own thirty-year-old flesh. 'I don't feel old. Yet I am old. There are only a handful of people on Etxelur older than me and still breathing – and several of them are in this house.' She glanced at Kirike and Dolphin. 'Our lives are so short. Even now there are people alive, adults having babies of their own, who don't remember the Great Sea. How soon before it is forgotten completely, washed away by time as the sea-bottom mud was washed away by the rain? *What will happen when I am gone?* Will the people give up, will the dykes be left to crumble, until another storm comes to smash it all to rubble and drown Etxelur for good?'

Ice Dreamer said gently, 'You'll have to let go at some point. There's a limit to how any mortal can shape the world.'

'But I have to try,' Ana said sternly, 'or it's all gone to waste. And that's where you come in again, priest.'

Jurgi's face was growing steadily more clouded, and he looked across at a confused Novu.

'I never had a child,' Ana said. 'Not until now.'

That shocked them all to silence – all save Dolphin, who to her own horror found herself bursting out laughing.

Ana turned on her. 'You think I am too old? This is another consequence of the Great Sea. It took away so many old people that kids like Dolphin here grew up not knowing about them. My own mother conceived a child when she was older than me.'

Jurgi said, 'Do I have to remind you about the tragedy that followed? She died, and so did the baby.'

'But it need not have been so. You know that, priest, as well as I do.'

Ice Dreamer studied her, fascinated. 'You are always a swirl of schemes and ambitions. What do you intend to do, Ana?'

She laid her hand on the priest's shoulder. Jurgi flinched back, as if her touch burned like a hot ember. 'To take a husband. *You, Jurgi.* And we will have a child – at least one. There. That's my plan.'

Arga, like the rest, looked astounded. 'But no priest ever married before.'

Ana shrugged. 'Nobody built a wall to keep out the sea before. But we did it anyway. I'm sure there are precedents in custom, if the priest thinks hard enough about it.'

For a heartbeat the priest seemed to consider the question as he would any other of its kind. 'Yes . . . It's happened before, so it's said . . .' He looked at Novu, who was stricken. 'This isn't about custom, Ana. You can do whatever you want – you know that. But why would you want to do this?'

'Because it solves so many problems. If we are a couple, there can be no question of a division between us. If I could become the priest myself,' she said harshly, 'I'd probably do it. But I don't think custom would bend that far, would it? Still, this is a decent second choice. And the problem disappears for ever when we have our child.'

'It disappears? How?'

'The child will be raised as the next priest. You'll see to it from birth. And meanwhile I will teach her all I know of this place and how to run it. When she grows she will combine the two of us into one, your priestly authority reinforced by my blood, and she will carry on the work into the future. Then nothing will stand in the way of the vision being fulfilled, the walls being built, the bottom lands drained. Etxelur secured against the sea for ever.' She smiled. 'Two problems solved in one. Neat, isn't it?'

'You're mad,' Arga breathed.

'Or a genius,' Ice Dreamer said.

Novu wailed, 'But what about me? What about us? Jurgi and I—'

Ana said coldly, 'Well, that's another problem solved, isn't it?'

Jurgi sat still, his face expressionless. 'And do I get a say in whether I abandon Novu, the consolation of my life – if I give you my own child to raise as your creature, driven by your dreams?'

'Ask the little mothers for guidance,' Ana said with a sneer. She stretched suddenly, her most vigorous movement since they had gathered here. 'How late is it? I'm sleepy. And I need a piss.' She got up and moved towards the door.

Suddenly Novu tumbled forward onto his knees, and plucked her cloak as she passed. 'Don't do this. I've given you everything – don't take him away from me.'

She ignored him and made for the door flap. The dog woke and padded after her, hoping she would play.

72

The Seventeenth Year After the Great Sea: Spring Equinox.

The scream of the child jolted True awake.

He rolled on his back. This Pretani-built house was dark, the only light the crimson of the banked-up hearth. There wasn't the faintest glow from the seams around the door flap. It must still be the deepest night, long before the dawn.

The Pretani men were all around him, big powerful men who slept at night in the furs they wore all day, and the house stank of meat and sweat and damp, of farts and piss. One of them was snoring – Hollow, probably, but it could have been any of them.

Beyond the house walls there was silence. The Pretani often complained about the crying of the Eel children in the night, and they would go out and throw stones at the kids in their pits until they shut up. But there was no crying tonight.

That scream, though. Had he dreamed it? His dreams had been disturbed recently, dreams of stone monsters rising up through rich, placid waters – dreams of Leafy Boys pouring through a forest canopy like monstrous birds . . .

There was a low rumble, like thunder rolling deep in the belly of the earth, and the house shook. The Pretani growled and mumbled in their own guttural tongue. True hadn't dreamed *that*.

And now there were more screams.

He rolled off his pallet, grabbed his boots and made for the door flap.

*

The night was pitch-dark, moonless and starless, the spring sky a roof of cloud. The only light came from the glow of the big communal hearth. The air was sharp, it was still some days before the spring equinox, and his breath steamed before his face.

A heap of torches had been made up by the fire, reeds tied tightly around lengths of ash branch, to allow night working. True snatched one of these and lit it quickly.

Then he ran towards the quarry workings. He glimpsed others following, Pretani. The Eel women the Pretani used peered from their own house, and True saw their pale, scared faces. Soon his booted feet ran on bare rock, where the turf and peat had been stripped away for the quarry. The three great pits were pools of darkness ahead of him. He slowed deliberately; it would do nobody any good if he fell and smashed his head. But he saw dust rising from the furthest pit, heard more screams.

He hurried that way. The screaming grew louder, the cries of children piercing his head like a flint knife.

At the lip of the pit he knelt and held out his torch. He knew every grain of the walls beneath him, every pick mark, every blood splash; in the last few months he had seen these pits dug out by his own people. He could immediately see what had happened.

The rock here came in layers, some of it the smooth, rich sandstone the Pretani preferred, and the rest a harder limestone. When all the easy stuff had been extracted from the surface they had had to break through the limestone layers, and then they had widened the pits under the limestone, working out to left and right as they drew out the precious sandstone. Now, he could see, a big chunk of the limestone shelf had broken away, crumbled and fallen into the pit, and had taken masses of the upper layers with it.

The pits were always full of people, day and night. Most of the Eel folk slept down there, save for the senior ones like himself who supervised the rest and the women favoured by the Pretani

– men, women and children huddled in pits with a bit of skin for protection from the cold. Every morning the children had to clamber up the knotted ropes to bring out the waste, the shit and the piss buckets.

He could see movement at the bottom of the pit, through the dust. Bodies moving like worms, splashed with blood, reaching for the knotted ropes. The screaming was unbearable.

'By the great oak's blight.' It was Hollow, at his side, panting from the run. He was bare to the waist; he had come out without his hide tunic. True thought he saw concern in his broad face. There were worse than Hollow.

'Here,' True said in the heroes' tongue. 'Hold this.' He handed Hollow his torch, and reached for a rope. 'I'm going down. Get more people. Bring help.' This was the only occasion True had ever dared give orders to a Pretani.

Hollow nodded, his face drawn. Holding up the torch, he turned and yelled for others to come.

True worked his way down the rope, clinging onto the knots with hands toughened by months of labour, his booted feet walking down the broken wall, his way lit only by the uncertain light of Hollow's torch. He could taste the rock dust in the air. The screaming grew louder, and now he could smell blood and shit. He felt as if he was sinking into one of his own nightmares, but this was more vivid than any dream.

He reached the end of the rope, and dropped the last short distance to the bottom of the pit. One foot landed on somebody, a child, who yelped and got out of the way. There were more torches overhead now, and he could see a little better.

People huddled against the walls. Fallen boulders, big rocks, blocked the cave they had dug out, following the seam. Clearly there were people stuck back there, behind the boulders. He could hear their screams, the yells for help.

Blood seeped from under one of the boulders, a big one by his feet.

He was frozen, unable to act. He thought he saw a faint blue glow in the night sky over the pit mouth. Dawn soon. More people gathered around the pit, men and women, both Pretani and Eel folk. The screams of the children seemed to be bringing out a common humanity.

Somebody grabbed his arm. It was Loyal, the girl he had been courting when the Pretani had come, the girl he had saved from being torn apart by the strips of hide – the girl who now warmed his bed, though whether it was for love or because she thought it gave her the best chance of staying alive he could no longer say. Now she had gashed her head, her hair was matted with blood, and pale brown dust coated her hair, her skin, her clothes.

She said, 'Help her.' He could barely hear her over the screams.

Something in him came back to life. 'Loyal—'

'I was half-awake. I heard the rocks – I rolled out of the way. If not, it would have been me under there – oh, True, you've got to help her!'

'Who?' But he already knew the answer: she meant Honest, her little sister, the only other member of her family who had survived the months under the Pretani.

She pointed to the boulder at his feet. 'True – please!'

Gently he pushed her away, and studied the rock at his feet. He saw where he could get his hands under it, where to plant his feet. He braced, bent his legs to keep his back straight, and locked his hands at the narrower end of the boulder. Then he heaved, pressing with his legs. Loyal joined him, hauling with her own callused hands. The muscles in his back tightened, and the blood rose to his face until he felt his head would burst. Yet the rock lifted, just a little, and with a final heave they pushed it aside.

As it rolled away he looked down at what he had revealed. Loyal pushed forward, but he grabbed her and held her away.

Honest had been lying on her back. Her body, loosely covered by a hide wrap, looked at peace, her legs bent slightly and resting to her left side, just as if she was sleeping; her right arm was draped over her body, covering a bone amulet. But the falling rock had caught her on the head and left shoulder, bursting her skull like a heel stamping on an overripe fruit.

'She couldn't have felt anything,' he said to Loyal. His own voice sounded strange to him, and he wondered from what deep pit he was dragging up these words of comfort. 'She must have stayed asleep, never even waking.' But he remembered the single scream that had first woken him. 'And her spirit . . .' He didn't know what to say about Honest's spirit. Their priest had died soon after the move to this place of rock and labour.

Others were coming down the ropes now, bearing torches that lit up the dust-laden air. Hollow was among them. He started to snap out orders, and the people, Pretani and Eel folk alike, began to get organised. Some of them were already hauling aside the rubble.

True pushed Loyal towards a rope. 'You go up. Try to find Resin.' The Pretani priest was a poppy-addled fool, but he had a good heart, and had been known to offer comfort to Eel folk in distress.

'Get me her amulet.'

'Loyal, just go—'

'Please.'

He braced himself, then reached past the rock with one hand and grabbed the girl's amulet. He tugged its thread hard, and to his relief it broke easily. He studied the little amulet as it lay in his hand. It was pale white, just a bit of broken deer antler, with a carving of the Great Eel wrapped around a central rod. Now it was splashed with blood, and greyish, slimy stuff. He wiped it off on his tunic and handed it to Loyal. 'Now go.'

She took the rope and began to climb.

Hollow stood beside him. 'Bad business,' he growled. 'The Etxelur folk arrive soon. Not a good way to present the quarry, all this, is it? And we'll lose whole days' work cleaning up this mess. At least we can make a start; it's not yet dawn.' But there was a fresh scream, unmistakably a child. Hollow visibly

419

flinched. He glanced at True, a kind of regret in his face, and placed his big Pretani hand on True's shoulder. 'Let's get to work.'

73

It was the sky burial platform that Arga noticed first, the morning she and Novu arrived at the Pretani quarry.

Hollow, the smooth, smiling Pretani who always accompanied the stone deliveries to Etxelur, walked with them. He wore a necklace made of flint flakes – good Etxelur flint.

And one of the worker types followed them. A slim man, wearing worn, dusty skins, he looked uncomfortable, his face oddly grey, slack, as if he wasn't quite alive. He was young, however, younger than Arga herself, she guessed.

The quarry was extraordinary. It was a patch of high open moorland that had been flayed of its turf and soil and peat, stripped down to the rocky bone. You could see where whole chunks of sandstone had been prised out of the ground. And all across this strange dug-up landscape, and even in deep pits cut into the ground, people worked, a few men, more women, many children. Coated in dust the same yellow-brown colour as the rock, some splashed with **vivid** blood from small wounds, they all looked the same: skinny **and** silent. But none of them were the dark, heavy-set Pretani; **you** could see that at a glance.

And on the sky-burial platforms that lined the bank of the nearby river, bodies had been heaped up. Most of them were children. Beyond the platforms the endless green of the oak forest rolled away.

The whole place made Arga deeply uncomfortable. Novu, short, stocky, his dark eyes gleaming, seemed fascinated.

It had been cruel of Ana, but typical of her, to send Novu away from Etxelur on this expedition to Pretani so soon after she had forced him to give up his lover Jurgi. It was one of her habits to distract possible enemies, just by getting them out of the way for a while. Arga was no enemy to Ana; she imagined she had been sent with Novu simply because Ana needed someone else from her inner circle to go with him.

But if it had been up to Arga they wouldn't be involved with the Pretani at all, no matter how good their stone was. And they certainly wouldn't be considering getting tied even more closely to them, as Hollow said he had brought them here to suggest.

Hollow, as they walked, was showing Novu the tools the slaves used to dig out their rock. 'Picks and shovels of antler, as you see. Red deer, and only the strongest, healthiest young males. This itself is brought to us by a web of trade . . .' His Etxelur tongue was smooth and fluent. He noticed Arga looking at the burial platform. 'People die here, as they do everywhere,' he said gently. 'Especially the children. At least these slaves die knowing they have achieved something with their lives – contributing to the building of Etxelur.'

Novu said, 'So tell me how you organise these people.'

Hollow gestured. 'You can see the basics. We split them half and half, roughly. The less useful half works to feed the more useful half that labours in the quarry. We use a mix of adults and children in the pits, more men than women, actually, for we need the brute strength of the bucks. And the cubs are useful for getting into the narrow spaces when we're first opening up the seams.' He made a wriggling gesture with his hands. 'In they squirm, like your Great Eel herself, True!' The man did not react. 'We change them over every so often to let minor wounds heal, that kind of thing.

'We let them sleep down in the caves because that way you need less houses on the surface. But that does have its disadvantages. We had a collapse the other night, that's why there are so many bodies on the slaves' platforms. They built them themselves. You understand we Pretani hang our dead in the trees . . .'

Slaves. Before coming on this trip Arga had only seen the stone arrive with its Pretani handlers on the boats off the shore of Etxelur. She had never thought about where it came from, who must be digging it up. She looked at the silent man walking with them. 'Who are these people?'

'They call themselves the People of the Great Eel. But there are no eels here,' Hollow said with a grin. 'Step back now, True.' He said it softly, but it was enough to make True drop back hastily and lower his head.

Novu said, 'There are some slaves in Jericho, more elsewhere. It all makes sense, Arga.' He gestured at the quarry. 'Look how much gets done!'

'And that,' Hollow said easily, 'is what I want to talk to you about.' He led them on, walking slowly around the site. 'I visit Etxelur often – you know that. I admire your great works, the dykes, the reservoirs. But the work goes so slowly! I know how difficult that is for you, Novu, for so much of it is your vision. And I know how anxious Ana is becoming, as her years slip away like grains of sand.'

'It's true, it's true.'

Arga was disturbed how much this man knew about them. He wasn't like most Pretani, who were so obsessed with their own blood-drenched honour rituals they barely noticed other people at all. Hollow knew their hungers and their fears, as a hunter knew the habits of a stalked deer.

'And,' Hollow said, 'I think, Novu, you are starting to see the solution. Just look around.'

'Yes,' Novu said, intent. 'Not the quarry – you mean *the people*.'

'Exactly. Imagine if you owned people as we own these Eel folk. Imagine how quickly the work would progress. No more arguments about who does what and when. No more relying on neighbours, their loyalty secured by the flimsy bonds of an annual Giving. With workers like this you could do what you liked, as fast as you liked – or as fast as your workers were capable of, and that would be for you to determine, not them.

It's not just stone I'm offering you now, Novu – it's people. And through people all your other problems will be solved.'

'What people?' Arga snapped. 'These? If we take away your Eel folk, who will dig the stone for you?'

'Oh, we wouldn't give you this lot. We've trained them up for this work, and half of them are worn out anyhow. No, we'd round up fresh meat. Our world-forest is full of it. We'd hand them over broken in spirit but healthy in body.'

Novu frowned. 'We'd have to discuss terms.'

'Of course.'

'But you'll do the deal, won't you?' Arga said. Since he had lost Jurgi, Novu had become even more obsessive about pursuing his great projects – as perhaps Ana, cunning, had intended all along. She hissed, 'But we don't know what the Pretani really want. How much flint can they need?'

But Novu did not respond, and Hollow led him away, around one of the pits. Hollow was gesturing, describing more aspects of the work. None of the toiling Eel folk looked up.

74

The Seventeenth Year After the Great Sea: Summer Solstice.

'I'm pregnant,' Ana said.

Her voice was so soft that Arga wasn't sure she had heard correctly. She leaned forward.

They were sitting in a circle around the hearth in Ana's house, their faces lit by the fire's dull glow, Jurgi, Novu, Arga, Ice Dreamer, and two outsiders, Knuckle of the snailheads and Qili of the World River people. As was her wont, Ana sat above the rest on a heap of skins. Beside the fire, a treat for the visitors, shellfish had been set out on the ground, covered by a kindling of sticks and dry marram grass. The kindling was burning and the shellfish were cooking; as the shells opened, spilling their juices, there were crackling sounds and delicious scents.

Ana smiled when she saw Arga's expression. 'You heard right. I'm pregnant.' She reached out and touched the hand of the priest who sat beside her. Jurgi looked faintly embarrassed. 'I'm going to announce it to everyone at the Giving in a few days' time. But you are as close to me as anybody, and I wanted you to know first.'

The Giver had never looked more human, Arga thought. Her hair was as severely cropped as ever, and she wore her tunic tight around her body and pinned at the neck. Ana would always be a serious, closed-in woman, like a house with its door flap sewn shut. But tonight she looked slightly flushed, and she smiled, her lips parted. The priest, too, though he was as grave as ever, cradled her hand as if it was as fragile as a fledgling bird.

A baby was still a baby no matter what you intended to do with it, a lover still a lover no matter for what reasons you took him into your arms. Just as a little girl who was a slave was still a little girl. Life had a funny way of breaking through, just like the weeds and wild flowers that bravely grew in cracks in Etxelur's dykes and reservoirs, and had to be cleared out every summer by the small hands of the children.

Now Qili spoke. 'This is good news. There's nothing more precious than a new life – and nothing more fragile. All our friends at the estuary will wish you well.' His Etxelur language was now fluent, but heavily accented – and his tone was oddly wistful.

Arga turned to look at him, surprised. He looked as if he'd aged; his skin was faded, and there were bags of shadowed flesh under his eyes. She'd never paid him much attention, yet she could see that something was wrong. 'Are you all right? You sound sad.'

'I'm sorry,' he said firmly. 'This is your evening, Ana, not mine.'

'Tell us,' Arga said.

He shrugged, looking away from their gazes. 'It's nothing. Or rather, it's commonplace. We lost our new baby, my wife and I. She was half a year old. She just sickened and died. There was nothing our priest could do; if she was sick, she had something he didn't recognise.'

Arga nodded. 'Sometimes the moon just takes them back.'

Ana said, 'This little girl had Heni's blood in her. All of Etxelur will grieve with you.'

'It's commonplace,' Qili said again, as if convincing himself. 'Babies die all the time. We have other children.'

'It might be commonplace,' said Jurgi. 'More than half of us die before we leave childhood. Did you know that? But it is not commonplace when it happens to you.'

Knuckle grunted. 'I too have lost children, my friend.' His harsh snailhead accent was a contrast to Qili's more fluent tones. 'I won't say it gets easier. It doesn't. But, with time, you remember the joy of the life, rather than the pain of the death. And at least you will have the comfort of knowing she can never grow up to become a slave of the Pretani.'

Everybody stiffened. Arga saw Ana draw her hands back from the priest. If she had looked briefly like a human being, now she looked like Ana again, leader of Etxelur and builder of dykes. 'No folk of the World River will ever be slaves here. And nor will snailheads, Knuckle. You know that.'

'Do I?'

'The Pretani are our allies. We have agreements—'

'Allies?' Knuckle turned his head, elaborately looking around. 'If the Pretani are your friends, why do you not invite them into your house?' Evidently he was saying what he had come here to say. 'And if they did turn on us, would you stop them, Ana? Or would you rub your hands at the idea of getting your stone walls built even quicker?'

Novu stirred. Arga thought it was typical of him to wake up when his precious building works were mentioned. 'You mustn't bring the walls into this.'

Knuckle was incredulous. 'Why not? Without the walls, no stone and slaves. And no Pretani hanging around.'

Novu closed his eyes. 'Because whatever it takes to get the walls built is justified. Because when we are dead and gone, nobody will ever know how the walls were built or who by, slave or free. Any more than we know the names of the ice giants who built the hills and carved the bays. And that is the way it should be.' He stood. 'Whenever we talk, it is always this way. Chatter about nothing – never about the work. You may talk all you like; I've had enough.'

Jurgi said plaintively, 'Oh, Novu, wait—'

'Goodnight, Ana, the rest of you.' And he swept out through the door flap.

Jurgi grinned tiredly. 'I was only trying to tell him the shell-fish smells cooked.'

Dreamer cleared away the burned-off sticks and grass, and set

427

the wide-open shells on wooden plates, with heaps of salt and crushed herbs.

Arga said, 'Do you think we should call Novu back?'

'No. Let him dream of his walls. More for us,' Knuckle said. He grinned as he took his plate and slurped down his first oyster.

75

Kirike and Dolphin walked along the northern beach of Flint Island, heading towards the Giving platforms. Thunder scampered at their feet, happy to be out on the beach.

It was a bright morning, still a few days short of the solstice. But there was a mist in the air and an unseasonably brisk bite to the wind off the sea; frothy foam blew along the littoral, and the fishing boats out at sea, grey shadows against the glittering water, were lifted by the waves. Gulls wheeled in the air, cawing, looking for food, competing for mates. To Dolphin they looked as if they were playing, and if she could fly, she thought with a deep, physical surge of joy, she would be up there playing with the best of them.

She and Kirike were still in a sleepy fug, after another long night in their own new house, the house they had built for themselves. She could smell the smoke of their fire about him, the sweet musk of his sweat. Just as every year under Ana's leadership, the latest Giving was to be more lavish than ever, and there was plenty of work for everybody in Etxelur – but as far as Dolphin was concerned this morning, all that could wait.

But in the shade of a sandstone bluff at the top of the beach, outside a slumped hut, slaves were making rope.

Dolphin slowed, curious.

Etxelur always needed rope, for hauling timbers and stone, or dragging water sleds over the hillside. Making it was simple, repetitive work that, the Pretani said, you could trust to a slave. So here were seven slaves working together in silence, one man,

429

two women, four children, the youngest of whom was only maybe five years old.

They looked up as Kirike and Dolphin stood before them, the adults incurious, the children vaguely fearful. The dog sniffed around them, tail wagging, but the people ignored him.

The women sat together on the ground, their legs crossed. They were cleaning aurochs hide with small hand-held flint scrapers, making soft repetitive rasping sounds as they cleared the last bits of fat and ligament. Dolphin could see the hide had already been cleaned of hair by scorching. The man was pushing a scraped hide into a pit, dug into the ground and lined with stone, skin and hardened mud. The pit stank of old urine. This was part of the complex process of tanning the hides. More hides lay at his feet in a heap, and Dolphin saw he had been cutting them into strips. Eventually these strips would be twisted and plaited into strong rope.

The children, meanwhile, were working on a heap of lime branches and logs. They used small flint knives to cut the bark from the wood and to divide it into strips. More pits full of water stood ready to take the bark; soaked, it would separate into long strands that could then be woven into string.

Dolphin saw that one little girl had cut the palm of her hand, for blood trickled down her arm. Her eyes were moist, but she didn't make a sound.

Their 'house' was just a slumped driftwood lean-to, heaped against the bluff. Their hearth was a shelf of pebbles scavenged from the beach, and Dolphin could see the remains of their food: offal and other scraps.

A family, working together, making rope. Slaves in Etxelur.

Kirike seemed uneasy. 'Why have we stopped?' he asked in the Etxelur tongue, a language the slaves probably wouldn't know.

'I—' Dolphin wasn't sure. She had been curious about the slaves since the first of them had been driven here by the Pretani a month ago, hauling stone.

'Let's go on,' Kirike said, uneasy.

'No, wait.' She let go of his hand and stepped forward. 'You,' she said to the man, switching to the traders' tongue. 'What's your name?'

The man looked up at her, unsmiling. He was gaunt, too thin, the joints showing in his arms like bags of hazelnuts. 'I make rope.' His accent was thick.

'You are a man, not just a rope-maker. Are you a father, a husband? What is your name?'

He didn't reply.

Kirike plucked her sleeve. 'Dolphin—'

The man's sullenness irritated her, and that reaction disturbed her. Unsure where she was going with this, she said now, 'Stand up.'

'I am working.'

She glanced around. The nearest Pretani was a fat brute of a man down at the sea's edge, squatting to shit into the sea. 'Do as I say or I'll call him over.'

Slowly, with evident reluctance, the man put down his hide and stood before her. He was shorter than she was. He had a tattoo coiled around one bare thigh, an eel with a gaping mouth. Dark, slim, not tall, he wasn't much older than she was, she realised.

The women and children bent over their work, not looking at Dolphin or Kirike.

'Tell me your name.'

'Wise,' he said at last. 'My name is Wise.'

She nodded. 'My name is Dolphin Gift. This is Kirike.'

He stared at her, and Kirike. 'What do you want?'

'Yes, what?' Kirike muttered in their own tongue.

'I don't know,' she said honestly. 'I never spoke to a slave before. *Wise*. You call yourself the People of the Great Eel.'

He was cautious in his replies. 'That is what we were.'

'Are these your children? Which of these women is their mother?'

Wise glared at her.

Kirike murmured in the Etxelur tongue, 'The Pretani ask

431

questions like this. If they know which kid is yours they can make you work harder by threatening her.'

That shocked her. 'I won't hurt you,' she said. 'Really – I'm just curious. Please, tell me about your family.'

Again he hesitated. But in the end he pointed to one of the women. 'She, my wife. The two older children, ours. And *she*, wife's sister. The two little ones, hers. Her husband died. We took her and her children in. She had four children; two of them died . . .'

It was a story that you could have heard all over Etxelur, of broken families joined together for support. All very ordinary. And yet her relationship with this Wise wasn't ordinary at all.

'Sit down,' she said.

'What?'

'Do what I tell you. Sit down.'

Kirike murmured, 'What are you doing, Dolphin?'

Wise stood still for a long heartbeat. Then, slowly, with a kind of unspoken insolence, he sat.

'Now stand up.'

Again he drew the moment out. But then he stood, unwinding his thin legs.

She said to Kirike, 'I control him in everything he does, as I control the fingers of my own hand. It's not even like a trained dog, for he is human, as we are, and can understand exactly what is asked of him. I can make him do anything. I wonder how far I could go. If I told you to take that stone knife and to start slicing away at your own flesh, would you do it, Wise?'

'Stop it, Dolphin.'

'Just imagine if everyone was your slave. You could do anything you wanted. You could rebuild the whole world! You could tear down the hills, and banish the sea.'

Kirike muttered, 'Ana seems to think she can do that already. How would you know if you gave the right commands? We aren't the little mothers. Even if we had the power, we wouldn't have their wisdom.'

'You could always ask the priest,' she said, but she giggled.

'But if _he_ was a slave, how could you trust his answers? And besides—'

'What?'

She looked down at the children. 'Having slaves around is probably all right as long as you aren't one. Look, that little one has cut her hand.' She knelt down and reached out to take the child's arm. The girl flinched away, and the women tensed. Dolphin murmured, 'It's all right. I won't hurt you. I just want to help. Oh, get your nose out, Thunder, she doesn't want you licking her!'

The wound was small but deep; the blood had smeared all down the girl's arm and over the bark she had been working. The girl was evidently terrified, and now she started to cry, though the women tried to hush her.

Dolphin said, 'This will get infected if it's not treated. The little one will get sick.' The women were scared to respond, she could see, and she wasn't sure how much they understood. She looked up at Kirike. 'Go find the priest. Bring some moss, and ask him for healing herbs – he'll know what's best – and bring cloth soaked in sea water.'

Kirike hesitated, then he nodded and jogged away.

Dolphin smiled at the girl. 'It will be all right. You'll see. I'll clean out the wound and wrap it up.'

'We have healing,' one of the women said unexpectedly. 'In home, in land of Great Eel. Not bring. Pretani. Not let us bring.'

'Well, it's stupid to stop you keeping yourselves healthy, for if you get sick you can't work, can you?'

Wise shrugged. 'Always more Eel folk. Always more children. Why are you helping us?'

'I don't know,' she said. 'Because I'm an outsider here too, and so is Kirike. Because I made you stand up and sit down, and I don't like the fact that I enjoyed it.' She probed at that bit of guilt, like a tongue exploring a broken tooth. 'I'm sorry,' she said.

'Don't say sorry to me.'

'I'm sorry anyhow. When Kirike comes back we'll fix up her hand. Later I'll bring you more healing stuff.'

'The Pretani will take it away. Punish us for having it.'

'Then we'd better make sure they don't find out, hadn't we?' She grinned. But the women looked wary, and Dolphin was reminded that this wasn't a game to these people, but a question of the lives and deaths of their children.

So she sat quietly and held the little girl's hand until Kirike came back with a satchel of medicines.

76

The Seventeenth Year After the Great Sea: Late Summer.

In the cold dawn light, Acorn and Knot approached the Leafy Boys tethered at the foot of the great old oak. Shapeless in her tunic of stiff hide, Acorn was carrying a skin food satchel. Knot, close beside her, bore a long, stout stick.

Knot felt Acorn's hand creep into his. He could feel her trembling, her small fingers clutching his. His own heart was thumping, for he had a deep gut fear of the Leafy Boys.

And he was always nervous in this place anyway. On their way to Northland, the Pretani party, led by Acorn's father, had come to the very edge of the world-forest, where there were no more trees and the skies were open. He was a forest boy who tried to hide his fundamental terror at the emptiness above.

And on top of all that the touch of Acorn's skin gave him a very complicated feeling.

He was ten years old, she was nine. Not for the first time he wished he was older, when he might understand the hot, confusing sensations that swarmed through his body when she was close. But Acorn was Shade's daughter, his only child, and the Root surely had some more suitable boy lined up to marry her when the time came – more suitable than Knot anyhow, with his slim, scrawny frame, his dead mother, and a father, Alder, who the men sneered at as more interested in mixing medicines than fighting, even when they came to him to get their wounds dressed. He had this morning with her, at least. It had been *him* she'd asked to come with her on this secret dawn jaunt – whatever it was about, and he didn't know yet.

He just wished it didn't have to involve Leafy Boys.

The Leafies lay on the ground under a weighted net, their naked bodies wrapped around each other. In the murky light Knot could see abrasions around their necks and ankles, and bruises and scars on their backs.

As they approached, the Leafies stared at Acorn and Knot, their empty gazes more animal than human. Knot could smell stale shit. One big buck fixed his gaze on Knot, challenging. Knot raised his club, and tried to think through the moves he would make if the buck tried anything.

But Acorn walked up to the Leafies without hesitation, and counted them. Their muddy limbs were so tangled up, it was hard to tell one from the other. 'Three, four, five. There's one missing. A girl.'

'Maybe the men took her.'

'Anyhow, this is the one.' Acorn was pointing to the smallest Leafy under the net, a boy, very small, thin and slight, looking no older than four or five. His eyes were huge in a skull-like head, and his ribs showed through papery flesh. Acorn made a cooing noise, as if he was a baby. 'Look at you. You're so sweet!' And, to Knot's astonishment, the small Leafy seemed to respond. He moved towards her. 'Look how little and skinny he is!'

'The Leafies snatch kids and train them to run in the canopy. There's bound to be some little ones.'

'Well, they got it wrong with this one. He's too weak – you can see that. And he's not able to feed properly. He can't fight with the others when the men bring the food.'

Knot's head spun as he worked out what was going on here. *'You're feeding him.* We're not supposed to be feeding Leafies! They're not puppies! They're killers!'

She snorted. 'Look at him. Little Shade isn't going to kill anybody. Unless they die laughing.'

He stared at her face, pale in the gathering dawn light. '*Little Shade?* You've given him a name? Your *father's* name?'

She pouted. 'Why shouldn't I give him a name?'

'He's a Leafy. Leafies don't have names.'

'He got snatched from some house, didn't he? He must have had a name there, given him by his mother, poor thing.'

'Yes, but – if your father found out—'

'Well, he won't as long as we both keep our mouths shut.'

Whatever he had come out here for it hadn't been to make her angry. 'All right, all right,' he muttered. 'Anyway if you've been feeding him already, what do you want me for?'

'Because the handlers have changed the way he's being kept. He was with other little ones before – not with these big ones. It was easier when it was just little ones. These big ones are more trouble.' She dug the food out of her pack. It was deer meat, raw, the way the Leafies preferred, and a paste of crushed hazelnuts. All the Leafies stirred at the scent. 'I thought the two of us would be all right, we could fight them off while he feeds.'

'I'd rather not fight anybody at all.'

'Let's just try.'

He had no choice. He stood at her side, and pointed his stick at the Leafies. 'We'll go in together. But stay close to me.'

Cautiously they crept in towards the net. Knot felt his heart hammer even harder. Acorn, calm and determined, made straight for Little Shade and held out a slice of meat towards him. Another Leafy girl made a grab for it, and Knot prodded his stick at her and she fell back, hissing.

Little Shade was able to reach out through the net and grab the meat. He shoved it into his mouth and chewed enthusiastically.

When he'd done, Acorn tried him with another piece. The other Leafies stirred, eyes wide, but this time the big buck growled, and the others stayed back, letting the little one take the food.

Then Acorn went in a third time. Knot kept his stick raised, ready to attack.

77

On the morning they were to enter Northland, before the rest of the camp stirred, Shade walked out of his house and into the gathering light.

He was in a broad clearing in the world-forest, here at its ragged edge. The black mounds of the Pretani tents and lean-tos, hastily erected after the march the day before, were angular shapes in the grey-blue light. The men's footprints had churned the ground to mud, and trails led off to the spring to the west, and to the south where the Leafy Boys lay in their night traps by the big old oak.

He hadn't slept well – he never slept well with Zesi in his house. Now in the uncertain light he felt disoriented, as if the boundary between the waking and sleeping worlds had become blurred. This was one reason he'd come out for an early walk; it was best to face the day with a clear head.

In the hearth at the centre of the clearing the big communal fire still smoked, though the huge fallen trunk they had hauled from the forest was disintegrating into crimson embers. Stepping towards the hearth, Shade passed a heap of spears, and a row of buckets of shit. The smell was rank, and flies buzzed in the dark. This was one of Zesi's tricks. Dip the tip of your spear in shit, and the chances were that even a grazing wound would become infected; even if you failed to kill an opponent quickly, you could do it slowly. The hunters, always proud and protective of their weapons, grumbled about the mess and the stink, and some had proposed poisons made of various herbs, but they were hard to prepare and dangerous to apply. Shit was always available, easy to apply, and safe enough to handle as long as you washed it off.

And here was Bark, squatting on his haunches by the hearth, with his stabbing spear propped before him. He might have been resting like this half the night; Shade had never known a man so patient, with leg muscles so immune to cramp. Bark had smeared soot from the fire over his bare limbs and face, the better to blend into the night's dark. When he grinned at Shade his teeth showed white, with gaps inflicted by years of fighting.

'No trouble?'

'None.' Bark pointed towards the forest wall around them; Shade could see one of the hunters Bark had posted to keep a look-out. 'I swap them around every so often.' He yawned, stretching his jaw, and shook his head. 'Keep them awake.'

'You ought to get more sleep yourself. Night after night you're out here.'

'Do you trust anybody else? I don't. Besides, plenty of time to kip when we're in Etxelur, and I'm lying back on a bed of those lovely flint nodules, with Ana's lips around my cock.'

Shade didn't react. Nobody here but Zesi knew about the tentative relationship he'd once had with Ana – certainly no Pretani left alive. He pointed east. 'I'm going to take a look from the ridge. See how the lowland lies in the dark.'

Bark was predictably reluctant. 'You want me to send some-body with you?'

Shade patted the flint axe he carried at his waist. 'I'm never alone. Anyhow you'll be busy soon enough, kicking the slug-gards out of their beds.'

Bark nodded warily.

Shade set off east, out of the clearing. The forest swallowed him up, but his eyes, open to the blackness, picked out a trail from chinks of light and the stirring of dead leaves. He remem-bered the trail from the daylight, leading towards the ridge that rose up out of the forest cover.

It was an easy walk, for him. He had grown up in the forest. It had been strange for him to learn that others feared its enclosure, like the sea-coast folk of Etxelur, or marshland dwellers like the Eel People.

He soon found the trail rising, the forest growing less dense. Then he broke out into open ground, a rising bluff on which heather grew, thick and purple and waist-high at this time of year, a month after midsummer. He was facing east towards the dawn, and a crimson glow striped the horizon.

And, on the crest of the bluff, he saw a figure standing alone – stooped, shivering from more than the faint chill of the late summer morning. Shade stopped, silent, cautious, until he recognised the man. 'Resin? It's me.'

The priest whirled, startled. But then he had always been jumpy, even before he had cut back on the poppy juice. 'Shade? That is you, isn't it? My eyes aren't so good in the dark.'

'Then what are you doing out here?'

The priest clutched his hide robe closer. Adorned with cryptic symbols and networks of lines like tree branches, the robe was old, shabby, worn, and it stank of piss. He had a mane of ragged grey hair, a face that was lined and sunken, a mouth that was often slick with drool. Resin was younger than Shade, but he looked much older, the poppies had seen to that. 'Oh, I can never sleep. Not in a house full of your hunters, Shade, with their farting and belching, and the women they take from the Eel folk – and, worse, a Leafy girl, it takes two or three of them to subdue one of those, it's like having a mad aurochs calf in the house with you.'

Shade laughed out loud. 'You've become funny since I made you give up the poppy.'

'Funny? I'm glad something good has come of it.' He held out his hand, which trembled violently. 'Look at me. I can't sleep, can't eat. Can't get it up, as your hunters never cease to point out to me.'

'You were useless under the juice,' Shade said sternly. 'I feel like I'm getting a priest back.'

'Maybe you're right. Anyhow if you hadn't stopped me the

poppies would have killed me soon enough. But you didn't come out here to talk about me, did you?'

'Walk with me.' Together they stepped forward, towards the crest of the ridge.

And from here, they looked down over Northland.

There was no obvious boundary between Albia and Northland, nothing like a river to mark off one territory from another. But standing here you could see how the nature of the country changed. Looking east from this high point the land sloped down, with forest clumps and copses dark in the grey dawn light. Beyond that the land stretched away as far as Shade could see, low and glimmering with water and folded gently into rolling hills, a plain that merged into the mist of the horizon. A flock of birds rose up in a cloud from some distant lake, their cries just audible. You could see how rich the country was just standing here, with all that standing water and the easy hills.

And all across the plain he could see the spark of fires, twinkling like orange-red stars, the people of Northland dreaming in the dark.

'It's so vast.' Resin pointed at random to a fire. 'So many of them.'

'Yes. And most probably have never even heard of Etxelur, or Pretani. And yet here we are preparing to make war.'

'Yes. And a war like no other waged before.'

'Why do we hate Northland so much, do you think?'

The priest looked at him, startled. 'That's an odd question.'

Shade was the Root, after all, and he saw that Resin wasn't sure how to answer his question safely. 'I know I have my own history with Etxelur. My brother, my father, both dead at my own hands.' He touched the scars on his forehead, his body's memory of those terrible times. 'That wouldn't have happened if not for Northlanders. And Zesi has her own grudges. Maybe we wouldn't be mounting this war if not for her. But it was easy enough to stir everybody up for the campaign, even though it's turned out to be so complicated, with the trading, the stone and

441

the slaves, all Hollow's schemes. We were ready for the war, even if we didn't know it.'

Resin nodded. 'I remember your father. He loathed Etxelur, and all Northlanders. Fat lazy rooting pigs, he called them. He always tried to stir up trouble with them.'

'Why?'

'He hated their country, for it is so easy.'

'Easy?'

'You know the stories of our gods as well as I do.' Resin rapped his head with his knuckles. 'Better, probably. How our earliest ancestors were hunters carved by the Old Gods from twigs of the World Tree. They stalked giant animals over the open plains. But then the Old Gods lost a war with the forest gods, the walking trees. The forest took over the land, and the giant animals all died, because they couldn't live in the forest. New animals were born from the leaf mulch that covered everything, the pigs and the roe deer and the aurochs, but they were small and clever creatures that were much harder to hunt. Our grandfathers survived, but had to work hard for it. Thus the Old Gods abandoned us. Maybe your father, contemplating such stories and looking down on a prospect like this, envied those who lived so easily there. Because it's like how things were for us in the olden days.'

Shade rubbed his chin. 'But I grew up here too. Why don't I think that way?'

Resin sighed. 'Because your father had a decent priest at his side. A man who would sit with him in the evenings, and chew over the old stories. Whereas you have had me, a poppy-ridden half-ghost, weak and useless and addled.'

Shade patted him on the back. 'I'm glad to be getting you back. I have a feeling I will need your wisdom in the coming months – win or lose.'

Resin looked faintly shocked. 'You're not thinking about defeat?'

'In this mortal world, nothing is impossible. But even if we win Etxelur, what then? We've come so far, fighting and conquering, all the way to the edge of Northland. If I take Etxelur, who shall I fight then – the sea, the clouds?'

'Hmm. You'd better think of something. Your hunters are used to fighting now, the rush of blood, the rewards. They need it the way I needed the poppy – and I know how bad a need like that can be.'

'And must it go on for ever?'

The priest turned to the dawn light. 'I don't know. We've changed so much, just in the months since Zesi came to us and started showing us this way of war. We were always a combative lot, brawling with each other as soon as we broke out of our mothers' wombs. But now it's different. You and Bark and Zesi have assembled the largest and most organised group of fighters in the history of the world – or if there's ever been a mightier band I've never heard of it. On this quest for Etxelur our bodies are undertaking a great journey. And so, I believe, are our spirits.'

'For better or worse,' Shade said grimly.

'Indeed. For better or worse—'

'Shade!' It was Bark's voice; they both turned.

Bark was walking up the slope towards them. Over his shoulder he had a sack of netting that contained something that squirmed and wriggled.

Behind him two children followed, half-running to keep up with Bark's powerful, impatient strides. They were Acorn, Shade saw with dismay, and Knot, Alder's son, the boy his daughter had been spending so much time with.

Resin glanced at Shade and rolled his eyes.

Bark stood before them, panting. 'I thought I'd better come to you with this.' He dumped the net sack on the floor. Inside was a Leafy Boy, a young one, small and scrawny, underfed – no use to the hunters, and probably close to death, Shade thought dispassionately. The child struggled, feebly, tangled up in the net, and he reached out skinny arms towards Acorn.

'*There's* your problem,' Bark said. 'We found it when we

443

kicked the Leafies awake this morning. Acorn wasn't far away. As soon as this one got the chance it ran across and attacked her.'

'He didn't attack me, stupid,' Acorn snapped. 'Little Shade was just frightened.'

The priest was grinning. '"Little Shade"? Well, I can see the resemblance, though the boy has better manners—'

'Oh, shut up,' Shade said tiredly.

'Your daughter's been feeding it,' Bark growled. 'Trained it to get used to her.'

Acorn said, 'What does it matter? Look how skinny he is! He's hardly big enough to fight, is he?'

'Why it matters,' Bark said heavily, 'is because it stirred up the other Leafies. Confused them, you might say. They went crazy, and had to be beaten.' He glared at Acorn. 'We were going to have a mock battle today. I'm sorry to say it, but you've wrecked the whole day.'

Acorn stared back at him, and then looked to her father for support. When none was forthcoming she burst into tears. Knot went over to her protectively, but he didn't quite have the nerve to put his arms around her, Shade saw, amused.

The storm of tears blew itself out. 'I'm sorry. I didn't know I was doing wrong. But it was wrong, wasn't it?'

Shade nodded approvingly. That was the kind of response he'd always encouraged in her. 'I think it's obvious what you have to do. This little one can't go back to the other Leafies. Can it, Bark?'

The burly man shook his head. 'She's spoiled it, and it spoils the others. Sorry, child.'

Acorn's eyes were round. 'Father, why's he sorry?'

'Because you're going to have to get rid of it.'

Her hand flew to her mouth. 'No! I can't . . . How can I kill him?'

'You have your knife.' A flint blade with a handle wrapped in thread and resin to protect her small fingers, but as sharp as any Shade owned himself. 'Don't let it out of the net. Just take it off

444

somewhere. You've killed before.' Hare, a small calf; any Pretani child had to become used to killing. 'Do it quickly and it won't suffer.'

'I can't.'

'You must,' Knot said. He looked up bravely at Shade. 'I'll help her carry it away. Am I allowed to do that? She'll have to kill it herself, of course.'

He was so young himself, but he seemed to care for Acorn. His presence would be a comfort for the girl. 'Get it done. Then come straight back to the clearing. All right?'

'Yes,' both Acorn and Knot mumbled.

'Come on,' Shade said to Resin and Bark. 'What a start to the day.' He strode off, leading the others back towards the camp. He deliberately didn't look back at his daughter.

78

The Leafy child in the sack was heavy, but it wasn't difficult for Acorn and Knot to drag him across the ridge.

The Leafy didn't fight or struggle. He seemed to be reassured by Acorn's presence. He obviously had no idea what he was being led to. It was all very sad, Knot thought.

Which made him clear in his own mind about what he was going to do.

They reached a small stand of windblown trees. They laid the child down on the leaf-strewn ground at the foot of a twisted oak, and looked at each other, panting. Acorn had been in control in front of her father, but she was angry now. 'Why are you still here? Come to make sure I do what my father told me?'

That stung him. 'No. Nothing like that. Have you got your knife?'

She dug it out from under her tunic. It was slung on her waist from a leather belt. 'I always have to carry it, my father says.'

'Can I see?'

She handed it over. He hefted it, considering. It was the best-made knife he'd ever handled. Then he crouched down and began to cut at the net, slicing through one braid after another.

Acorn was shocked. 'What are you doing?'

'Solving the problem.' He dug out his own knife, and passed hers back. 'Here. Help me. Cut over there. The sooner we can get him out of here the better.'

She stared for one heartbeat, then dropped to her knees and began to saw at the net.

Between them they soon had it cut open, and they pulled it back from the Leafy Boy. The child sat up and stared at them both. Knot made a false lunge. 'Go, go!'

The child quailed. For an instant Knot thought he might run to Acorn again. But some deeper instinct cut in, and he ran off in a blur of motion, scampering up the nearest tree like a squirrel.

Acorn laughed. Then she held her cheeks in dismay. 'What have we done? If they find out—'

'They won't.'

'But what if he goes back to find the other Leafies? When he turns up alive back in the clearing—'

'He'd have to cross open ground to get back, and a Leafy wouldn't do that.' Then he held his breath, hoping against hope that she wouldn't ask any more questions. He had no idea how this little boy was going to survive, alone. Let her work that out for herself, later; she was a year younger than he was. For now this was all he could do for the child, and for her.

She smiled, and his heart thumped. 'Thanks—'

A dead leaf crackled.

Obeying an ancient instinct he put his hand over her mouth, his finger to his lips.

Then, together, they turned, and crept silently through the little copse towards the source of the noise. It surely wasn't anything dangerous, he told himself, his heart hammering. A deer, maybe. A young calf. Maybe a squirrel making an early start on its nut cache.

But now he heard voices, male tones murmuring. People. He saw the horror on Acorn's face. Had they been followed? Was their defiance of Shade already betrayed?

He hushed Acorn again and crept further forward alone, deeper into the copse, letting his eyes adjust to the leafy shade. And there, beyond a screen of trees, he saw two men. One he recognised: it was the Eel-folk slave, True, the clever one who helped the Pretani men organise the others. The other he didn't recognise. It was a younger man with a strange tattoo on his bare belly, three circles around the navel cut through by a vertical line. They were talking urgently, but very quietly.

They were hiding, keeping some secret, just as he and Acorn were.

He waited, scarcely breathing, until they were done. At last they nodded to each other, broke away, and left the copse, True heading back towards the Pretani's clearing.

Knot came back to Acorn. She was sitting on the ground near the ruin of the net, legs folded under her. He described what he'd seen.

She frowned, a crease appearing in the perfect skin between her eyes. 'Something's wrong,' she said. 'True's a slave. He shouldn't be sneaking around like that.'

Knot said, 'We can't tell anyone.'

'We have to—'

'We can't! If we do they will come here to check, and they'll find no Leafy Boy bones. They'll know we lied!' And while Acorn might be spared by her father, he knew he would be punished severely.

'But True and the man—'

'Maybe it was nothing,' he said. 'What can one slave do to harm your father and all his hunters?' He covered her hands with his. 'Let's forget we ever saw this. Now, come and help me trap a hare or something. We should spill some blood on ourselves to make it look real.'

Subdued, barely talking, they made their way out of the little copse and back towards the clearing.

79

'Talk to me,' Dolphin snapped.

Wise just looked at her.

Barefoot, he walked in the wet sand close to the sea's shallow, lapping edge. He had a basket hung around his neck full of the cockles he'd been picking from the exposed rocks. His two wives and four children combed the beach with him, the children laden with their own small baskets. Gulls wheeled, competing for the food, but they scattered when the children clapped their hands.

It was noon, and still summer, only a couple of months after the solstice, an oppressive, colourless time of year, and though the sun was obscured by a lid of cloud the heat by the sea was intense.

One of the children splashed another, accidentally, and they giggled together, just like kids playing on a beach. But one of the women muttered a soft word in the tongue of the Eel folk, and they glanced uneasily at Dolphin, and fell silent.

Still Wise did not reply.

Dolphin snapped again, 'Talk to me, or may the little mother of the sea drown you in her wrath.'

He glanced at his family. 'Scaring children,' he said in his softly accented traders' tongue. 'Walk.' Still bending to pick cockles off the rocks, he turned and walked slowly away from the children.

She fumed, but followed. 'You wouldn't talk to a Pretani that way, would you?'

'You are not Pretani,' he said simply. 'Will talk take long?'

'What?'

He gestured at the rocks. 'Pretani don't feed us meat any more. Too many of us. We have fruits of sea. But we are hungry – we work hard – children growing. Shellfish not—' He tapped his belly, running out of words. 'They leave you hungry. We must gather many, many shells. Soon the tide will turn, rocks covered—'

'*We know.*'

He shifted the pack on his shoulder; she saw the leather strap was rubbing his bare skin raw. 'Know what?'

'What you intend.' She glanced over her shoulder at his family, who continued to work in silence. 'In Pretani there is a man called True. One of the Eel folk, like you. Perhaps you know him.'

'Many called True.'

'Just listen. The Pretani have a plan. They will come here in numbers, and attack us. This will be soon. And the Eel folk will be involved.' She stepped forward, hand on hips, glaring at him, summoning all the authority she could muster. 'You will rise up, all over Etxelur, and attack us. And when we turn to face you, the Pretani will fall on us like wolves on a lame calf. This is what True says has been planned. He says every adult of the Eel folk is prepared for it.'

'How do you know?'

'We take stone and slaves from the Pretani, in return for flints. You know this. To make the trade the Pretani come here, and some of us go to their settlements in the forest. One day True spoke to a man from Etxelur. He told him about the Pretani's plan.'

'Why would this True do that? Never been here.'

'He knows nothing of Etxelur, and cares nothing. He only knows that Etxelur is an enemy of the Pretani. And he asked our trader for favours.'

'What favours?'

'His freedom, and his family's, when the Pretani are beaten.'

Wise studied her. His face was weather-beaten, burned; many of the Eel folk, used to the milder sun of their inland lakes, had broiled in the intense light of the coast, especially the children. The darkening and tightening of Wise's skin gave him an alien, hardened look. 'Why tell me?'

'Ana is having your leaders brought to her. We're trying to do this out of sight of the Pretani. We don't want them to know what we know. Soon they will come for you. But I came first.'

'Why?'

'Because I want to understand.' Deeply hurt, betrayed, she clung to her anger. 'You aren't denying it, are you?'

He sighed. 'Why deny?'

'Even though the Pretani beat your children and rape your women, you are prepared to work for them – to kill us to further their goals?'

He shrugged. 'No choice. And besides, when the attack comes, great chaos. Perhaps we slip away.'

'But you would turn on us? What have we ever done to you? We don't beat you.'

'No. You let Pretani do that.'

'Would you have harmed *me*?' She grabbed his forearm; covered with dense grey hair, it was slick with sweat and sea spray. 'Look at me, Wise. Would you have hurt me?'

'If I had to.'

She stepped back, shocked. 'But I cared for you – your family. I brought you medicine for your sick child.'

'I depend on your kindness for life of child.' He studied her, staring at her face. 'Understand, little girl? Don't want your power over me, for good or ill.' She was horrified to see something like pity in his eyes.

She turned away and ran back up the beach.

451

80

At the end of the day, with the setting sun striping long shadows along the Etxelur beaches, Ana called her closest people to the holy middens. As Jurgi waited with her they arrived in ones and twos, Novu, Ice Dreamer, Arga, Kirike. They had to wait for Dolphin.

Jurgi thought he had never known Ana so agitated, so obviously distressed. She paced by the middens and peered out to sea, and at the great new dykes reaching out towards the drowned Mothers' Door – huge structures yet unfinished, with heaps of stone and sand at their abutments.

Arga stood by Jurgi. 'She's very worried.'

'She needs to be calm,' Jurgi said. 'To think clearly.'

'You're the priest. It's your job to soothe her, isn't it?'

'She's a troubled spirit,' he said grimly. 'But . . . I saw her grow up. She respected me, *then*. Now she's the woman who took me from my partner, and she is the mother of my unborn child, and she is the beating heart of the new Etxelur. How am I supposed to deal with such a being?'

Dolphin arrived, at last. And she had brought a slave with her, one of the Eel folk. A few years older than Dolphin, he was muscular but slim to the point of scrawny. His wrap of faded cloth was filthy and torn, and he stank of the sea, at whose edge he had probably been working most of the day. As the group stared, he simply stood before them, showing no sign of fear. He was oddly impressive.

Dolphin said the slave's name was Wise. Jurgi had never

learned any of the slaves' names. Not knowing their names made it easier for him to bear their presence.

Novu turned on Dolphin. 'I don't care what his name is. Why have you brought him here? He and his kind mean to kill us all.' With age he had become a small, angry man, plump in body and face, his dark brown eyes red-rimmed with anger. He was eaten up by his obsessions, scarred by a long-gone childhood. Jurgi believed he still loved Novu, but he had never seen him look more unappealing.

Dolphin spoke up for herself, young, angry, beautiful in her mother's striking way with her strong nose and dark hair. 'Why do you think I brought him? Because the Eel folk are at the centre of all this. If we don't hear what they have to say we're fools.'

Jurgi spoke up hastily. 'She's right. Let's not bicker. We've got some hard thinking to do, some tough decisions to make. For a start I've been trying to make sure the Pretani in Etxelur don't know that *we* know about their plan.'

Ice Dreamer asked, 'And how are you doing that?'

'Their big men are all in the dreamers' house, working their way through my store of poppies.'

Dreamer laughed throatily.

Ana spoke, for the first time. 'And what about this plan of theirs?' She glanced at Jurgi, an unusual uncertainty showing on her small, solemn face. 'Do we believe all we've been told?'

'I think we must,' Jurgi said. 'There's nothing for this man True to gain by lying. He deliberately sought out our trader to tell him about it. And the Eel folk here have admitted it.' He glanced uneasily at Wise. 'Though some of them had to be pressed.'

'Maybe it's all a bluff,' Kirike said. 'Maybe the Eel folk have been told to spin us this tale to frighten us.'

Jurgi hadn't thought of that, and he considered. 'I doubt it. We had no idea the Pretani were planning to fall on us at all. They wouldn't give away the advantage of surprise just for the sake of stirring up a bit of confusion.'

453

'Besides,' Dreamer said, 'as you should know, Kirike, you've got their blood in your veins, the Pretani aren't the subtlest of folk. This scheme of planting warriors among us is pretty smart, but is probably the limit of their ingenuity. More likely, they just weren't clever enough to imagine that one of their slaves would betray them.'

Ana said, 'So the threat is real. The question is what we do about it.'

'We fight,' Novu said immediately. 'We can't let them take our wealth, our flint. And we can't let them destroy what we've made of Etxelur.'

Jurgi glanced at Dolphin and Kirike, the young folk standing together, their hands gently touching. On impulse he asked, 'Do you two want to fight?'

Kirike considered. 'It depends what we're fighting for. Once, if the sea flooded your house, you just moved away and built another one. That was how you did things in the days before the Great Sea – that's what you tell me.'

'You didn't have slaves either,' Dolphin said now, flaring. Jurgi knew she had been helping the slaves, for she had come to him for medicines. 'You were a different people then, with different ways of thinking. Better ways, maybe. It's all changed because of you, Novu.'

'You weren't even born in the times you speak of,' Novu sneered. 'You are an outsider. Like your mother.'

'As are you—'

'What would you have us do? Run like whipped dogs?'

Kirike took a step towards him, fists clenched. 'You old people hate us, don't you? I think you wish your precious Great Sea had just washed everybody away, so you would have been spared raising ungrateful runts like us—'

'This isn't helping,' Ana said softly. 'Kirike, you're right. Once just walking way from problems was what people did. But we can't do that any more, because the sea has eaten away so much of the land. The snailheads walked away, and ended up *here*. There's nowhere left to go.' She glared at Kirike and Novu. 'But

I won't have division among us. Things are bad enough without that. Whatever we decide to do, we do it together.'

Novu turned on her, all but shouting. ' "Together." Who are you to say "together"? You who have brought this horror down on us.'

Jurgi heard gasps. He was alarmed, fearing where this direct challenge to Ana might lead. 'Novu, be careful what you say.'

'What is there to be careful about? How much more peril could we be in? Think about it. Why is the Root so determined to bring us down, determined enough to plot and scheme over months, to whip up his entire people into a war party? Because before he was the Root he was called Shade. And for Shade it's personal. It's because of her – Ana – her and her sister, the disaster they caused that ended up with Shade's brother and father both dead, at his own hands. Now he's the Root, and when he looks over Northland, what does he see? *Ana.* Ana the survivor, the Giver, the big woman of Etxelur. This is why the Pretani are coming. Shade is coming for Ana.'

Jurgi knew Novu had a point. Jurgi had been talking to Eel-folk slaves all day about their planned revolt, and had heard other rumours, spread at second or third hand from the travelling camps of the Pretani. Rumours about another presence at the camps, a woman who stayed close to Shade – a woman with hair once a vivid red but now shot through with grey, a woman once beautiful but now grown old with bitterness. He'd said nothing of this yet to Ana, unsure how to broach it. But if all this was true, if this woman was who she sounded like, the matter was indeed personal, and it really was all about Ana.

But they couldn't afford for Novu to attack Ana. Ana was all that held Etxelur together. Resented she might be at times, but she was like the knotted leather rope at the crown of a house that strapped together its timber supports. Novu was sawing away at that rope – and if Ana failed, everything might come crashing down even before the Pretani got here.

But Ana herself seemed calm. She linked her hands under her belly. 'It's always personal. Everything is. Novu, you've had it in for me since I took Jurgi away from you. Oh, don't try to deny it; our relationship soured from that day. And besides, what if it is personal, the whole Pretani attack targeted at me? What would you have me do? Would you truss me up like a pig for the spit and hand me over?'

Novu glared at her. 'If that's what it takes to save the work—'

Ice Dreamer said, 'I've always thought you were crazy, Jericho, but if you put your heaps of mud and stone ahead of the people they are supposed to protect then your mind really has gone soft.'

Ana held her hands up. 'Enough. We've worked together well in the past, Novu. When this incident is over we will work well again, I'm sure, for there is much to be done. I don't believe I will ever call you a friend again. But then, I'm not trying to make friends. I don't need friends. I need allies.'

She stepped away from Jurgi and Dreamer, away from the group, and she looked around, at the sweep of the midden, the great arms of the dykes reaching out to embrace the ocean. She was terribly lonely, Jurgi thought. Since being taken as her lover he had grown to understand that loneliness, if not to alleviate it.

She said now, 'I will always believe we had no choice but to try to save this land from the sea. It was that or run, and there was nowhere to run to. But we are doing something that has never been done before, so far as we know. And if you do something new, how can you know if you are doing it right?' She walked up to Wise. He was taller than she was, thinner; he looked down at her gravely. She switched to the traders' tongue. 'Can you understand me? Dolphin Gift is right. When I was a girl there was nobody like you in Etxelur. No slaves. There was only us, and our friends, and a few enemies. We were all the same. No wonder the Pretani were able to convince you to rise against us. *I* would rise up. Perhaps there's something of Novu in me. Perhaps I've been so intent on getting the work done I've lost sight of how we should be doing it. Well, here's a promise. If we push away the Pretani, we will continue to build our walls.

But we will do things differently. Let them have slaves in Pretani and in Jericho. Not in Etxelur.'

Jurgi heard a murmur of support, a joyful clap from Dolphin.

Ana turned back to Wise. 'You, your people, will be welcome to stay. Not as slaves.' She waved a hand. 'As friends.'

He smiled down at her. 'I think about it.'

Jurgi was amazed. 'By the mothers, man, what is there to think about?'

'Don't like sea food.'

They all laughed, save a fuming Novu.

Ana regarded the Eel man. 'Well – stay or not, you have decisions to make of your own. Will you support the Pretani?'

'Pretani worse than you. We'll fight them with you.'

'Are you sure? How can we count on you?'

'I believe your promises more than I believe the Pretani.'

'Good,' Ice Dreamer said fervently. 'But we should be clever about this. Not a word to the Pretani. Pretend you continue to side with them. Turn their ruse back on them. It will double the shock when they come to destroy us.'

'Good idea,' Ana said. 'We have much to think about – much work to do if we are to survive this, even with the help of the Eel folk. We must talk to the snailheads too, and the estuary folk. But for now – are we agreed? Are you still with me?'

There was a murmur of support. Jurgi was heartened by relieved grins on the faces of Dolphin and Kirike. After all, it was the young who mattered most, in the end, no matter what the old folk agreed among themselves.

Only Novu was scowling. But he said, 'If it will get the work done, I don't care what you do. Now – are we done here?'

81

The Seventeenth Year After the Great Sea: Autumn Equinox.

On the morning of the attack on Etxelur, the Leafies were kicked awake, as usual.

Me hunched over, protecting his face, his groin, the thick net heavy on his back. He had slept little. The strangeness of the place they had been brought to – the crisp, empty saltiness of the air, the sandy soil they had to lie on – had disturbed all the Leafy Boys profoundly.

When he opened his eyes he saw the stripe of the net, the huge shapes of the grounders standing over the Leafies. All this picked out in blue-black light. It was still dark, still long before the dawn – earlier than they normally woke. Me had learned to dread change. Change meant danger, and that somebody was going to die.

With a skill born of practice the men made a ring around the Leafies, and worked together to lift the net off. A little one got caught in the tangle, but with a couple of brisk shakes he fell down like an overripe fruit.

The Leafies moved stiffly, pissing, licking leaves on the ground for their dew. Then the men moved in on the Leafies with their knives, knotted rope and clubs, and tested the tethers attached to the loops at their necks, getting ready to move them.

Soon the men started calling to each other, big gruff bellows like bull aurochs, and they formed up into their groups.

And then they started to run, heavy in their huge leather cloaks, their faces dark with blue and black paint, the scars over their brows vivid. The Leafies had to move too, only heartbeats after they had woken, driven ahead of their handlers on their leashes.

Me could barely see what he was running into. The light, such as it was, came from the dawn sky to his right, slightly paler than the rest. It felt like a nightmare, as if he had not yet fully woken up. But as he ran his muscles warmed up, and his night-time aches started to fade, as they always did.

They came to a line of hills, low, grassy, sandy. Here the Leafy group was split in two. Some were kept back at the foot of the hills, and were taken off to the east. But Me and others were driven forward, to scramble over the soft dunes. He had no time to think about that – scarcely time to wonder if he would ever see the Leafies in that other party again.

When they got to the crest of the hills, though the light was still uncertain, Me could see the ground fall away to a shallow beach, littered with rock and mounds of some dark weed – and beyond that there was *water*, nothing but water, a great lapping lake of it that stretched off as far as he could see. Me froze in shock. This endless blank flatness could not have been a greater contrast to the enclosing green of the forest canopy where he had spent almost all of his conscious life. It was as if the world had been stripped away.

The advance broke up into chaos. All around him Leafies were crying, or standing, shocked. But the men were soon on them with their fists and spears and boots and snarls, and yanking their tethers. Me was driven on at a stumbling run.

The Leafies were sent down to the beach, and then turned to the right, towards the light of the gathering dawn. They ran and ran.

And, somewhere in the blocky dunes at the head of the beach, a point of fire flared brightly.

82

When Jurgi touched Ana's shoulder she woke slowly.

Oddly, as word had come of the Pretani's approach, she had slept as well as she had for years. Maybe it was the banishing of doubt: better to face a real enemy than to fear worse in ignorance. Or maybe these deep, dreamless sleeps were merely a rehearsal for her own imminent death.

She opened her eyes. Jurgi's face, above her, was just visible in the low glow of the house's night hearth. She reached up and cupped his cheek, feeling the priest's tattoos he had worn since he was a boy, the circular mark of Etxelur. He covered her hand with his. One last moment of tenderness.

He murmured, 'The signal fires have been seen. They come.'

'Today's the day, then.'

'I think so. The others are waiting for you.'

She nodded.

He withdrew, and hurried out of the house. She saw from the loose door flap that the dawn was not yet far advanced.

She rolled off her pallet and sat up, aware of the weight of her belly, how heavy and slow the pregnancy made her. Well, she wouldn't have to fight today, not unless all their elaborate schemes failed. She pulled on her tunic, swigging water from a hide flask as she did so. Then she squatted over the night pot, trying to ensure it caught every drop of her piss to feed the tanning pits. Of course by the time night fell even the pits might be in the hands of the Pretani. When she was done she pulled on her boots and cloak, and picked up her own fine-bladed knife and a short-handled stabbing spear.

She took one more deep breath, and glanced around. The house was tidy, the embers in the hearth dying.

Then she pushed her way out through the door.

They were waiting for her in the dawn, Arga, Dreamer, Dolphin, Kirike, Novu, Wise, a circle of grim faces, bodies hidden by heavy hide cloaks.

This house, not her own, was on the northern coast of Flint Island, set on a mound of fresh-dug earth. The holy middens were bulky shadows just paces away, and the sea lapped quietly, the rush of the waves an oddly soothing sound. Thunder was on a tether, tied up to a house post; it wasn't a day for friendly little dogs to run loose.

Cries overhead made her look up. A flock of birds swept over the sky, cool and graceful, early departures for their winter homes.

Arga saw her looking. 'Our own autumn migrants are on the way here, it seems. But we're still some days short of the autumn equinox.'

'Seven days,' said the priest, 'according to my counting sticks. Many of us had thought they would attack on the day of the equinox. Such moments in the year mean as much to the Pretani as to us.'

'Perhaps they are trying to catch us off guard,' Ana said. 'Shade is their Root. Shade was never a fool.'

Kirike said, 'They came from the south. They seem to have split into two. One group is heading inland, making for the Bay Land. The other is coming in from the west, along the coast. They must mean to use the causeway to get to Flint Island.'

Jurgi said, 'It's what we planned for. They're aiming their forces at the two targets we expected: the flint store in the Bay Land – and you, Ana, here on the coast.'

Novu grinned. 'I am no fisher. If I was, I would say the fish is nibbling at the bait.'

'I wouldn't feel so happy about it,' Jurgi said. 'Especially as

461

the "bait" is what is most precious to us. And it shows they have been watching us.'

'You should take comfort,' Ana said. 'We let the Pretani traders stay in Etxelur so they could tell Shade what we wanted him to hear. That was the whole point.'

'Maybe,' said Jurgi. 'I just don't like being at the mercy of forces I can't control.'

Wise nodded. 'And traps can fail.' His Etxelur-speak was becoming fluent. 'Our legends speak of the sky gods who set a trap for the Great Eel. The Eel swam in, took the bait, and then with a flick of his mighty tail smashed the trap to pieces. This is how the world was born, from pieces of that great cage.'

'Today we are the trap,' Ana said evenly. 'It is up to us to prove strong enough to contain the eel.'

Jurgi glanced around. 'Are we ready? Do we all know what we must do? Then let's look forward to the end of this day, when we will celebrate a great victory – and honour our dead.'

They turned and moved off, some heading for the causeway, the rest to the Bay Land.

Kirike hefted his spear and would have moved away with the rest, but Ana touched his arm. 'Stay with me.'

He looked frustrated. Dolphin glanced back, but she was pulled away by her mother. Kirike said, 'Stay here? But you're not going anywhere.' That was the plan. As a key target for the Pretani Ana was to wait by the middens, in the hope of drawing Pretani forces to her. But Kirike was sixteen years old and a slab of muscle. 'I'm supposed to go to the causeway with Jurgi and the rest. I'm ready to fight. I've been practising!' He raised his spear and jabbed it in the air.

'I know. I'm sorry. I changed my mind. Look at me – I can't fight. If the worst comes to the worst I need someone to protect me. There's no higher honour you can win today,' she added, a point the priest had advised her to make.

Kirike was confused. 'Why me?'

'Because you're family,' she said, linking his arm in hers. 'My nephew.' She patted her belly. 'Until my own child grows up,

462

who else should I rely on?' And besides, she added silently, if the rumours were true about who might have joined the Pretani and stirred up this whole war in the first place, Kirike too might be bait, even more valuable than Ana.

Kirike was visibly unhappy. But when Ana walked down from her house mound towards the beach, he followed. Full of youth and aggression, he practised spear-thrusts at crabs that scuttled out of his way.

The first sunlight was staining the sky when the Pretani force, coming from the south, reached the rim of the Bay Land. They had met no resistance. Bark stood on a last ridge of higher land, like dried-out sand dunes but far from the sea. Hollow stood with him. Behind them the Pretani warriors were ready, bristling with weapons and aggression, and the Leafies cowered at the end of the tethers held by their handlers.

And the Bay Land spread out before them, a strange place of dark soil cut by straight ditches and dotted with stands of willow. Houses stood on mounds of black earth, their hearths sending lazy trails of smoke into the sky. To the east, standing before the sea, Bark could see a pale band, the barrage of stone and mud that kept the ocean from drowning this place.

Hollow the trader knew this land as well as anybody. He pointed. 'There's the flint lode.' It was a wound in the earth, right in the middle of the Bay Land. 'But for months they've been making a stockpile of the stuff, over there beneath the dyke.' Following his finger, Bark could see a heap of yellow-brown stone that must have been as tall as a man, piled up against that strange sea wall. 'That's the easy picking today,' Hollow said. 'Tomorrow we can put the slaves to work digging out the rest from the main lode.'

'Then that's our target.' Bark sniffed, feeling oddly uneasy. 'Funny place, this. I never saw anything like it.'

'Well, this whole landscape ought to be deep under the sea. The Etxelur folk have defied their own gods to expose it to the air like this.'

'And I don't like that sea wall. The men won't like it either.'

'But that's where the good flint is,' Hollow said, unperturbed. 'Which I predict the men will like, more than they fear the wall.'

'True enough. Anyhow we have to follow the plan we worked out with the Root.' Bark glanced at the rising sun. It was time. 'Let's get on with it.' Without further discussion he jabbed his spear into the air: the signal to cut the Leafies loose from their leashes.

So it began.

Driven on with spear jabs and threats, the Leafy Boys swarmed down into the great bowl of the Bay Land, screaming, jumping and yelling. Soon people were coming out of their houses, or rising up from their early morning piss-pots, or scrambling for weapons, or just running in terror.

Like a fire sweeping over dry grassland, the Leafies with their grasping hands and meat-hungry teeth always spread confusion and chaos and fear. But Bark knew the creatures well enough by now to understand that the Leafies, pining for their green canopy world, were probably more terrified in this strange place than were the Etxelur folk.

And as always the Leafy assault soon burned itself out. A few houses had been pulled down, people were running – and a few lay dead, including a couple of the Leafy Boys. But there wasn't as much damage and mayhem as Bark had been expecting.

He turned on Hollow. 'Where are these slaves of yours that are supposed to be rising up?'

Hollow looked uneasy, but he shrugged. 'Do you need slaves to fight your battles for you?'

Bark glared. 'Don't push me, trader. You've always been too good at lying for my liking.' He looked down at the Bay Land. If he didn't act now he would lose any advantage he'd gained. 'But you're right. We don't need a bunch of ragged-arsed slaves to win our war.' He raised his spear again. 'We go in!'

The men behind him yelled, and ran forward, a mass of bloody hide and angry scars and shit-covered spears, pouring down the slope from the stranded dunes into the Bay Land.

But the ground turned out to be difficult. Around the willows and the hazel stands it was boggy, and mud clung to their boots, trapping their legs and weighing them down. Bark, frustrated, saw that the straight-line ditches Hollow said were supposed to keep the ground drained had been clogged with stones and brimmed with water, drenching the land. The advance soon slowed as the men staggered through the mud.

And now a spear flew through the air, narrowly missing Bark. He looked up to see Etxelur folk advancing, men and older boys, and women too, scared-looking but hefting spears and knives. They ran at the Pretani in little bands of two or three, not mounting a full-scale attack, but jabbing and thrusting and then retreating. Bark's warriors fought back, but one by one they fell, spilling their Pretani blood into the muddy ground.

Concern flickered. Bark hadn't expected this much resistance, not after so many days' travel with no sign of the Etxelur folk at all. But this was just how he would set a trap, he thought uneasily, if he were planning it. Draw in your prey, get him stuck in the flooded ground, and then pick him off.

But he was Pretani, not some frightened piglet. He lifted his spear arm. 'So they want a fight!' he yelled. 'I hoped they would! At them!'

The men roared in response, and surged forward anew, despite the mud.

83

Shade and Zesi followed True onto the causeway to Flint Island. The Eel-folk slave, decked out like a Pretani in hide tunic and cloak, led the way cautiously along the narrow path across the sea. Behind Shade the Pretani warriors walked, two or three abreast, moving silently, visibly uneasy.

The causeway was an arc of stone that sliced the world in two ahead of Shade, excluding the blue sea to his left from the Bay Land that stretched away to his right, several paces beneath the crest of the wall along which they walked. Shade hadn't been here in years. He was stunned by the changes that had been wrought. And he had never in his life seen anything like this wall that stood against the sea.

But today the Pretani had come to Northland. Already he could hear yells and screams drifting up from the Bay Land, see smoke drifting. Bark and his men, making their move. So they had got the timing right, with the two thrusts into the Etxelur heartland launched at the same moment. But he did not let himself be distracted by looking that way, for he had his own fight to win.

And there would be a fight, for their way was not clear, Shade saw, looking ahead. A gang of Etxelur folk had gathered at the far abutment of the causeway, where it met the island.

'We're going to have to fight our way across,' Shade said to Zesi.

At his side, she too was dressed as a Pretani warrior, lacking only the kill scars. Now she scowled at him, the lines in her face deepened by the low light of the morning sun. 'What did you expect? That Etxelur folk would just give up and let you walk in? You don't know us very well if that's your opinion, Pretani.'

He shook his head, irritated. 'Now's not the time for posturing, woman. You're sure Ana is where she's supposed to be?'

Irritated, Zesi snapped, 'My sister has been sleeping on the midden shore for months. Who knows why? Maybe she wants to be close to her grave, where she'll be lying soon enough. That's where we'll find her this morning, and that's where we'll kill her—'

There was a roar, coming from ahead of them. The band of Etxelur folk had broken into a run.

Shade had no doubt his Pretani warriors would be able to bring down these wall-builders and ditch-scrubbers in an open fight – but this wasn't an open fight, and wasn't the kind of encounter Bark had trained them for. Suspended between ocean on one hand and a steep drop on the other, with warriors closing on him, he suddenly felt extraordinarily vulnerable.

'Those aren't all Etxelur,' Zesi said now, peering ahead at the approaching warriors. 'I recognise those twisted skulls. Those are snailheads. So Etxelur is calling on its friends to fight for them.'

'We Pretani don't need friends,' Shade said.

'Just as well, as you don't have any. And, look! The man on the right – the tattoo around his thigh.'

The man, short, squat, yelling and stabbing his spear into the air, was still a good way from Shade, but he could see the tattoo. It was an eel, wrapped around the man's leg.

Furious, Shade stepped forward and punched True's shoulder. 'That man's of the Eel folk! You promised the slaves would rise against Etxelur, not fight the Pretani!'

True turned and faced Shade. Then he broke into a savage grin. 'I lied. For my children!' And he roared, raised his own stabbing spear, and drove it down with two hands into Shade's shoulder.

Shade staggered back, stunned, the spear sticking out of this shoulder, its heavy mass tearing at him, the pain coming in waves.

Zesi lunged forward and with all her strength drove her own spear up into the soft flesh beneath True's chin, through the man's skull and up into his brain. True's body fell away, shuddering in death, and slid down the wall and into the ocean water.

Shade's men supported him to keep him from falling. But the world seemed to freeze around him, the sea, the wall, all icy clear, as the pain washed out from the hot wound. Was this his last moment of life?

Without warning Zesi yanked the Eel man's spear from his shoulder. He felt his flesh rip, and he had to work hard to keep from screaming at the blistering pain.

'You'll live,' she growled. She ripped a handful of cloth from her own tunic, wadded it up and pressed it against the wound. 'Hold this. You've still got one good hand.'

'Just as well.' For the charging Etxelur warriors were about to close. Shade pushed away his support, stood alone, and braced, spear in his good hand, hunching over his injured shoulder. To Zesi he muttered, 'They were expecting us.'

'Obviously. This is a trap.' She hefted her weapons. 'But whatever it takes, however many lives I have to waste, I'm coming for you, little sister—'

'Be ready! Here they are!'

The first man to come at Shade was a heavy snailhead. Shade got his good shoulder down and used the man's own charge to shove him off the wall and into the sea. The second man stabbed but missed, and Shade managed to grab the shaft of his spear and shove him back. But then came the third, and the fourth.

And then a woman, tall and dark, called to them. 'Hello, Zesi. Remember me?'

'Ice Dreamer? Aren't you dead yet?' Zesi screamed and

468

lunged, but the woman, tall, muscular and dark, fended her off easily.

Shade, dizzy with pain and loss of blood, battling for his own life against snailheads and estuary folk and former slaves, could offer her no protection or help.

Bark led the Pretani charge across the floor of the Bay Land, heading straight for the heap of flint at the foot of the eastern barrage. When they got the chance they smashed down houses and stands on which hides cured and fish dried, and kicked over hearths to start fires. In places the Etxelur folk and their allies stood and fought, and blood yells and screams echoed across the bowl of a landscape. But mostly the Etxelur folk jabbed, fell away and scattered, to regroup further back.

Hollow was hot and already out of breath. He was a trader, not a fighter. But he seemed determined to keep up with the rest. 'Not far now. We're cutting through this Etxelur rabble like a flint knife through a calf's scrotum.'

Bark wished he had somebody more experienced with him; he wished he was at Shade's side. 'It's too easy.'

'What?'

'It's too easy! These Etxelur folk are barely putting up a fight at all.'

'They're cowards.'

'No! Think, man. Where are the children? Where are the sick, the lame, the old? They've been moved out of our way, is where they are.'

Hollow shook his head, panting as they jogged across the heavy ground. 'You're too suspicious. Just because it's easier than you thought doesn't make it any the less glorious. We're driving across this unnatural land just as tonight you'll be driving your manhood between the thighs of some Etxelur virgin – you mark my words.'

It was all a trap, Bark thought. The more he considered it, the more certain he became. But there was no point talking to

Hollow about it, for the man's head was full of greed for the flint.

And besides, there was nothing he could do about it now. Many of his men had fallen already, and lay broken or dead across the ground behind the advance. Those who survived and could still fight had the sniff of victory, as did Hollow, and were chasing down the scattered bands of Etxelur fighters. Their blood was up. Trap or not, all they could do was fight, or die.

They were almost on the flint stockpile. The sea wall towered above them, its face of Pretani stone many times the height of a warrior. They had been drawn here right across the expanse of the Bay Land, Bark saw. If the flint was bait, it had worked well.

Hollow ran to the flint, picking up rattling armfuls of nodules. 'Look at this stuff. Look at it! Enough to last a lifetime, a generation, more! Now the whole world will tremble before the singing blades of the Pretani.'

Some of the warriors joined him. They stood panting beside the flints, and fingered the nodules, or looked up at the great wall, or back the way they had come, uncertain. Some looked at Bark, hoping for guidance. What now? But he had no answers.

And there was a groan, like the branch of a giant tree straining in the wind. A scrape of stone on stone. The men looked bewildered, alarmed. Even Hollow fell silent.

The noise had come from overhead.

Bark looked up. He saw pale faces looking down at him, and glimpsed long, stripped branches being rammed into place and used as levers. And he saw the upper section of the wall tipping over, huge blocks of Pretani sandstone folding grandly. Water gushed into the air behind the blocks, breaking up into droplets, like rain.

Hollow screamed, high-pitched, like a trapped deer. The warriors, yelling, jostled to get away from the wall. Bark was knocked to the ground, face down. And he heard a yell, a single savage word in the Etxelur tongue. Raising his head he saw

470

Etxelur folk on the plain, boiling up out of nowhere, advancing with their stabbing spears to trap the fleeing Pretani.

Above him the vast blocks fell slowly, as if they were thistledown, not stone, and sea water splashed his face. In the end, the block that came for him filled the sky.

84

Watching from the midden beach, Ana saw a handful of Pretani break out of the melee by the causeway's abutment, and come running onto the island.

'Here they come,' said Kirike.

Ana took his hand. 'Walk with me. We'll go out along the ocean dyke.'

Kirike was reluctant. 'We'll be trapped out there. You go. I'll stay and fight them off.' He was scared, Ana saw, scared to his bones. He believed he was going to die. Yet he was prepared to stand to try to save her.

'No,' she said firmly. 'Stay beside me. I'm still in charge.' She pulled at his hand until he followed her.

The dykes pushed out into the ocean towards the submerged Mothers' Door. Their abutments were covered in heaps of un-used rock and timber. Ana picked her way through this to the left-hand dyke, and they walked out along its surface, until the dyke grew too narrow and ragged for them to go further safely. Looking out from here, you could see the rows of posts driven into the seabed that would become the foundation of the dyke.

And here, Ana decided, in the arms of the ocean she had been trying to tame ever since the Great Sea, she would make her stand. She gripped Kirike's hand, and they turned to face the shore.

There were five, six, seven Pretani – all that was left of the mob that had come here from their wooded country, or at least this half of them, while the rest had got bogged down in the Bay Land. The Etxelur defenders weren't far behind.

When the Pretani leader saw that Ana and Kirike had gone

472

out alone onto the dyke, he snapped quick words to his followers. And then he and one other walked cautiously out onto the dyke, following the footsteps of Ana and Kirike, both glancing down nervously at the lapping sea. Ana knew immediately who they were – and saw that the rumours about who was really behind this attack had been correct.

When her own defenders came running along the beach, the remaining Pretani turned to face them, spears raised. Ana raised both her hands, palms out. *Wait. Wait.* The Etxelur folk were clearly uncertain, but they slowed to a halt, some way short of the Pretani band.

The two warriors on the dyke saw this. A woman's voice called, in fluent Etxelur speak, 'Good, Ana. No need for anybody else to die today.'

'Nobody but us?' Ana called back.

'As long as it ends here,' called the other, a stocky man. 'One way or another.'

'Oh, it will,' Ana said. 'I promise you that.'

They stopped only ten or fifteen paces short of Kirike and Ana. The man had thick black hair, the woman pale red like Ana's though greying, and both had their hair pulled back and tied in the Pretani style. Both of them had been fighting, hard; the man had a gashed shoulder, and the woman was splashed with blood, perhaps not her own, gore smeared over her face and hands and tunic.

Kirike stared. 'Who are they?'

The man called, 'My name is Shade. I speak for the Pretani.'

And the woman said, 'You are Kirike. You have my father's name, the name I gave you. I am not Pretani. I am of Etxelur blood. My name is Zesi. I am the daughter of Kirike, and sister of Ana. Kirike, I am your mother. And this man, the Root of the Pretani – this is your father.'

'I never saw you before.'

'Not since you were too small to remember – no. You were taken away from me.'

Kirike just stared, apparently speechless.

Shade faced Ana. There was little left of the Shade Ana remembered, little of that dreamy boy in this tough, tired, competent-looking man.

'I heard you were pregnant,' he called. 'By Jurgi?'

'Yes.'

He smiled. 'A good man. I had plans to make him my own priest.'

'You could have done worse.'

'Ana, Ana – must people die each time we meet?'

'It seems so. That's why it would have been best if we had never met again.' She glanced at her sister. 'There were rumours that Zesi lived, that she had come to you.'

'Those treacherous slaves—'

'I think I would have known anyway. This whole scheme, how you worked your way into our world, into *my* head, with the stone and the labour, and then the slaves rising up against us – I knew it was too clever a plan for any Pretani. Even you, Shade.'

He grinned, and there was just a flash of the boyishness she remembered – the tender face she had longed to kiss, but never had. 'Still, it nearly worked, didn't it?'

'Why did you come back, Zesi? Why spill so much blood?'

'For the sake of the son you stole from me.' She reached out her arms towards Kirike and tried to smile. 'For you.' But she was grotesque, her hardened face smeared with the blood of dead men, more dried blood under her fingernails, and Kirike flinched back. Zesi turned on Ana. 'You took him from me.'

'He was not safe with you. None of us were safe, with you in the world.'

Zesi took another step forward, her fist closed on a bloody stabbing spear. 'Who are you? You are nothing. You are a worm beside me. All my life you got in the way. My father always favoured you—'

'That's foolish.'

'And then you took it on yourself to judge me, and to throw me out of my homeland—'

474

'If I had not you would have destroyed us all by now, as you killed the snailhead child under the reservoir you breached.'

'And for that, *you* exiled *me*! You said it must end here, Ana. Then let it be so.'

'I won't fight you.' Ana had a spear and a knife; she dropped them both.

Zesi grinned. 'If that's how you want it.' She raised her stabbing spear.

Kirike, baffled and distressed, called, 'What are you doing, Zesi – mother?'

'No,' Ana said sharply. 'Please, Kirike. Stay back—'

Zesi snarled, 'Don't stand in my way, boy.'

And Shade said, 'Enough is enough.'

His thrust was clean, the blade driving through Zesi's body from the back. For a moment more she stood, supported by the spear, an expression of outraged shock on her face.

Shade stood behind her, whispering in her ear. 'You destroyed my family. Even my mother went to her grave cursing me, because of you. You would even have killed our son, wouldn't you, to get to your sister? Now we face defeat. My men are being slaughtered. And was it for this, Zesi – your hurt pride, your hatred of your sister? I kill you, but you have killed me already.' And he thrust again. The blade punctured her heart and burst out of her ribs. She fell forward, into Ana's arms, blood spouting from her chest and mouth, already dead.

Kirike cried out, and fell on his father, but Shade easily brushed his clumsy blows aside. Then he held the boy, until he dissolved into weeping.

Shade looked over the boy's head at Ana. 'It had to be me that finished it,' he said blackly. 'Let my hands take the last of the blood, as they have the rest. I should never have come here, never have let her back into my life . . . Well. Let it end here.'

'I'm sorry,' Ana whispered, clinging to the body of her sister. 'Yes, let it end, Zesi. And if I couldn't honour you in life as you wanted, I will honour you in death.'

85

Me roamed, looking for Leafy Boys. The cut leash still dangled from his neck. He was panting, bloodied but uninjured, deeply scared, lost.

In this strange place trees grew on salty land, and fires sprouted away from the hearths where the grounders usually kept them. The world was all broken down and jumbled up. He longed for the canopy, or failing that the security of the leash and the net. But the only grounders he found lay dead or dying.

Then he found another Leafy, alive. A girl. She was feeding on a dog, its belly ripped open by a spear. The smell of blood reminded him how hungry he was. He pushed the girl aside and shoved his face into the dog's open belly, and tore away a mouthful of meat. But he hadn't eaten all day, and something about the blood trickling down his throat worked in him, and his gut ached. He crouched, and let out an enormous fart, and then a bit of shit dribbled from his bare backside.

The girl stared at him. Then she laughed.

He laughed too. He felt better. Together they pushed their faces into the dog's belly.

The food made him feel better, and he thought more clearly. He remembered the way they had come, the way the grounders had driven them here. They had come from the south and climbed down into this bowl of land. Then that was the way they must return. Maybe they would find the grounders again. Better yet, they might find their way back to the forest canopy, the endless green.

He picked up the dog. The girl fought and snapped, until she saw he did not mean to take it from her. He slung it over his shoulder, still chewing its flesh. With the girl at his side he loped off to the west, across the salty land.

FIVE

86

The Thirty-Third Year After the Great Sea: Spring Equinox.

Following the slow rise of the land, the Pretani party walked out of the forest cover and into the glare of the spring sun. It was noon, the sun was as high in the southern sky as it would get all day, and the air was heavy and windless.

Acorn, twenty-five years old and proud in her hide tunic, led steadily and strongly, Kirike thought, as befitted his half-sister's rank as the Root of the Pretani. But the handful of warriors who followed her grumbled under their breaths about how thirsty they were and the state of their feet. Warriors always grumbled.

And Old Resin, who had seen thirty-six summers, hobbled into the light, muttering and squinting. 'Wretched sun . . . Give me the forest shade any day. If we'd been meant to stumble about in the light the tree gods wouldn't have blessed us with their shadow.'

Acorn said, 'Oh, stop complaining, old man.' She dug a battered cloth cap out of Resin's pack and set it on his bald, sunburned head. 'That's enough shade for you. Mind you, from now on it's open spaces and sunlight all the way to Etxelur. What about you, Kirike? I suppose you're used to this.'

Kirike set down the bag he was carrying, turned his face up to the sun and stretched. 'But it's a long time since I made my home among you.' More than fifteen years, in fact, since he had come home with his father, Shade, to the woods of Albia. He was over thirty years old himself now. He breathed deep of the air, and he thought he detected a whiff of salt, that odd sharpness that he remembered vividly from his boyhood, so different from the damp, cloying smells of the forest. Suddenly his heavy, scratchy hide tunic felt uncomfortable, and he remembered how he had run with Dolphin Gift along the endless strands. 'I have Pretani blood, but Etxelur is in me too. Besides, even the strongest tree needs the sun.'

Resin hawked and spat. 'A nice Pretani saying for an Etxelur boy. Let me remind you of another. Saplings grow only when the great tree falls. And this old tree hasn't fallen yet. Is that bag of bones too heavy for you? If so pass it over, and let's get on.'

Kirike's sack, carried on a long shoulder strap, contained the bones of their father, Shade, dead a year now. They were making the long trek to Etxelur to fulfil his strange but firm wish that his bones should be placed in the land where the events that had shaped his whole life and the future of his people had occurred. 'No,' he said. 'My father's not heavy.' He hoisted the pack. 'Anyhow, I vaguely remember this route.'

Resin hobbled onward up the grassy slope, leaning heavily on a gnarled stick. 'So you should. This is the way we marched when we made war on Etxelur, all those years ago. And this is the place we decided to call Boundary Ridge, for it's as good as any a place to say that here Albia ends, and Northland begins . . .'

When they reached the crest of the ridge the land fell away before Kirike, the forest-choked hills of Albia giving way to a broad plain that stretched all the way to a misty, washed-out horizon. It was a land of shining water, streams and marshes and lakes reflecting the blue sky. The only trees grew in scattered clumps, probably willow and alder, water-lovers. Everywhere threads of smoke rose up from the people's fires. Off to his left-hand side, to the north, he glimpsed the ocean, a grey horizon perfectly flat.

But Northland was not as it had once been. There were ditches dead straight across the ground, cut as if by knives, and reservoirs round as cups. Some of the larger streams were dammed by pale walls, and the flow behind them was backed up into new lakes. By the ocean shore he could make out the sea walls, pale lines and arcs drawn all along the coastline. Over three decades after the disaster of the Great Sea, people had shaped the landscape. And such systems now stretched all the way along Northland's northern coast, from Albia in the west to the World River estuary and Gaira in the east.

'Remarkable,' he said now. 'It all started at Etxelur. But now it's spread across the whole country, like, like—'

'Like a pox,' Resin grunted, standing beside him. 'More to the point, look down there. There's a house, right in the middle of our trail.'

So it was, a slim cone that stood on a ledge of flat ground, halfway down the slope. Its walls were leather, unlike the kelp houses Kirike remembered from Etxelur – a tent meant for a summer's hunting inland, perhaps. A couple of hare, skinned, hung on a rack outside the house, and a hearth barely smoked, choked with ashes.

As they waited, a young man, bare to the waist, emerged from the house. When he saw the Pretani party on their ridge he waved and called into the house.

Acorn said, 'Did you see the marking on his belly? Rings and tail.'

It was a mark Kirike wore tattooed on his own body, a mark he hadn't otherwise seen in years. The mark of Etxelur. His breath caught; he was thrilled.

A young woman came out of the house, not much more than a girl, perhaps fifteen years old. She looked up at the Pretani. With a murmur to the boy she walked up the slope. Wearing a simple green smock, she was barefoot, and wore her strawberry blonde hair swept back – red and green, light and airy.

And when she got close enough for him to make out her features Kirike gasped. The small, rather serious face, the compact frame – the resemblance was unmistakable. 'You're Ana's daughter,' he said. She frowned, and he realised he had used the Pretani tongue. He made a mental effort to switch to the Etxelur language of his boyhood, and repeated what he had said.

483

'Yes. My name is Sunta, named for my mother's grandmother. And you are Kirike. My mother described you well.'

He grunted. 'I'm surprised, since I haven't seen her since she was pregnant with you.'

She laughed, and Kirike saw a row of wooden teeth in her open mouth. 'Your mother was my mother's sister,' she said, precisely, as if figuring it out. 'So we are cousins.' She glanced at his companions.

Kirike said, 'This is Resin our priest, closest companion of my father, Shade. This is Acorn, my father's daughter – my half-sister. And now the Root of the Pretani.'

Acorn smiled. 'We share no blood, Sunta. But I would like to think we are cousins of a sort.'

Sunta's grin widened. 'You speak the Etxelur tongue!'

'Kirike taught me. I hope you can forgive my slips.'

'It is all so different from how it was when your father's father was the Root, and he came to Etxelur.'

'All that was long ago. In the end my father Shade paid the price for those times.' Kirike hefted the sack. 'I think that is why he wanted his bones to rest among you. To close a too-long story.'

She nodded. 'Today is all about honour, I hope. You, Acorn, honour us by speaking our tongue. Shade honours Etxelur with his final wish. And my mother urged me to honour you by coming out here to meet you at this junction between Albia and Northland. For we knew you would come this way.'

Acorn nodded. 'And she sent her priest. I noticed your teeth. Do the priests of Etxelur still wear the teeth of wolves in their ceremonies?'

'Oh, they do,' Sunta said lightly. 'And, yes, that was why I was conceived, for my mother wanted me to be both Giver and priest. My father Jurgi took out my adult teeth when they started to grow, and he started my training. But it didn't take with me, and before he died Jurgi persuaded my mother to pick somebody else. You can imagine what a row that caused.'

484

Acorn glanced at Kirike. 'I can. Similarly, I think our father always intended Kirike to become the Root.'

'But Acorn is much better at the job than me,' Kirike said with a smile.

Resin growled, 'Kids never turn out the way you hope they will. It's the blight of humanity, and why nothing ever gets done.'

Sunta laughed. 'I never wore the wolf's jaw. Still, I'm my mother's daughter and here I am.' She gestured. 'Please, come and join us. We have food, you can see, and water, and fruit juice.'

'All I want is a bit of leafy shade,' Resin muttered, and he limped forward.

Sunta skipped forward and took his arm. Next to Resin she was like ivy wrapped around an old tree trunk. 'Then come into the house. Shall we rest for the remainder of the day, and begin our walk to Etxelur tomorrow?'

87

'Dreamer? Are you there?'

Dolphin went to Ana's pallet, set aside the piss-pots she had filled during the night, and helped Ana swivel her legs off the pallet and grab onto her stick. Ana, nearly forty-eight, was the oldest living person in Etxelur. Her eyes were filmed over with cataracts, and she could barely walk for the pain in swollen joints. And at this time of year, in the summer heat, it was extra hard work to care for her because Ana insisted on keeping a fire banked up in her stuffy house day and night, convinced that cold made her aches worse.

But here was Dolphin helping her out of her house and into the morning sunlight. Dolphin, over thirty herself and the mother of four boisterous sons, had plenty of other ways she could have used her time. But Ana, too proud even to use the second walking stick the priest had carved for her, wouldn't have anyone but Dolphin.

And, though she grumbled, it warmed Dolphin deep inside to help her. To Dolphin Ana wasn't just the visionary who had made Northland safe against the sea. Ana was the daughter of the man who had saved her own mother's life and delivered Dolphin herself – and the woman who had done so much to help Dolphin in the difficult days after she had refused to accompany her mother on her return across the ocean. So Dolphin forgave Ana her complaints, and even her odd habit of calling her by her mother's name.

With a sigh of relief Ana settled on the couch Dolphin's sons had made for her. This was the trunk of a fat oak, laboriously carved and polished. Early this morning Dolphin had loaded it with cushions stuffed with goose down. Dolphin sat cross-legged beside her and resumed her work, mending a torn tunic for her youngest boy.

Ana's latest dog, an ageing mutt called Hailstorm, was already asleep at the couch's foot. He was the son of Thunder and grandson of Lightning, and she said he was the laziest of the lot.

Ana's house still stood where it always had, when it had belonged to her long-dead grandmother Sunta, one of the Seven Houses that stood behind the line of dunes that still fringed the southern shore of Etxelur's bay – even though the bay, long drained, was now greened and thick with willows. But old Sunta would surely not have recognised this place, for the house had been rebuilt on top of a mound, its faces covered with marram grass and its base fringed by a low wall of good Pretani stone. Today the mound's slope was speckled with celandine, an early flower drawn out by the sunshine. When Dolphin absently plucked one she counted its eight perfect, spiky leaves. And, nestling in the celandine carpet, she saw the rich purple of dead-nettles, tiny, intricate flowers.

Once she was settled Ana leaned her stick against the chair where she could find it again, folded her hands in her lap, and turned her cataract-silvered eyes towards the sun. 'Ah, the light.' She rubbed her bare elbows with hands like claws. 'It's been such a long winter. Odd how the winters don't get any shorter as you get older, though the summers fly by fast as swallows . . . The sun's good for me.'

'I know, Ana.' So she did; Ana made the same sort of speech every day. But there were some who said that Ana craved the light as part of her life-long battle against her dread Other, the owl, a creature of the dark and the cold.

Noise came floating to them on the breeze – banging drums, excited cries, the squeals of children, merging into the cries of the gulls as they wheeled over the shore.

Ana turned her head. 'What's all the din?'

'Well, I don't know, sitting here, do I? But it's surely to do with the Spring Walk.'

Ana nodded. 'Just three days away.' The sunlight was making Ana's eyes water, and she wiped her face on a sleeve. 'It's all so long ago – the last time Pretani came on a Spring Walk. All that blood spilled. Hardly anybody remembers it now. The worse thing about growing old, you know, isn't setting out your friends' bodies for the sky burial, it is being the only one who remembers how it was, and *why* it was. The way we worked together – the way we fought. Novu, who died alone in his nest of bricks. Jurgi, dear Jurgi, the wisest man I ever met, who loved me, even if he never forgave me. And your mother, of course, Ice Dreamer, how I fought with her when my father brought her home! We all worked so closely together we were like the fingers of a single hand. Now they're all gone, and me left here alone.'

'You aren't alone. People know your name from Gaira to Albia. You're loved by everyone.'

Ana reached over and patted her shoulder with her bent fingers. 'It should be quite a show when they bury me in the sea wall then, shouldn't it?'

Somebody called, 'As long as it doesn't outshine what you're planning for my father.'

Ana turned her head at the new voice, her blind eyes searching. 'Who's that?'

Four people were approaching the mound, two men and a woman in the heavy hide garb of the Pretani, and Ana's daughter Sunta, barefoot in a skimpy smock. The younger Pretani man bore a heavy leather sack. Looking beyond them, Dolphin saw a few more Pretani, and a ragged bunch of Etxelur folk following. Most of them were curious children who had probably never seen a Pretani before, dancing around the warriors and pulling at their hide cloaks.

The younger Pretani was Kirike. Dolphin hadn't seen him in years. She felt her heart race.

She was still holding her ripped tunic, her needle of antler.

She put the stuff down hastily, feeling foolish, and stood. She hoped she wasn't actually blushing.

Ana, leaning heavily on her stick, was trying to stand. 'It's the Pretani, is it? We'll go down the mound and greet our guests.'

'No need.' The Pretani woman took charge. She walked up the steps cut into the side of the mound and stood before Ana. 'Giver. My father told me all about you. It's an honour to meet you.'

'Acorn?' Ana reached out with a bent finger, and stroked the woman's cheek, the line of her brow. 'You *are* Acorn. You have your father's cheekbones. I remember Shade's cheekbones . . . And now you're the Root of the Pretani. A woman!'

'Much has changed.'

'And for the better,' Ana said firmly. 'Thank you for speaking to me in my own tongue. That's respectful of you. And you've come a long way.'

'We came for our father,' said the younger man, stepping forward. He put down his bag, and Dolphin could hear a rattle of bones.

'Kirike.' Ana's face twisted into a smile and she held out her arms. Kirike came forward and embraced his aunt; he was a stocky man, built like his Pretani father, and he overwhelmed the slight, hunched woman. Ana reached back for Dolphin. 'Come to me, child. You two haven't see each other for much too long.'

So Dolphin came face to face with Kirike, the boy she'd grown to love as they grew up together, the man she'd lost in the great falling-out after the Pretani war. She felt fifteen again as the two of them stood there on the mound. 'You haven't changed.' She touched his bearded cheek. 'And yet you have. Does that make sense?'

'No.' He smiled. There were lines around his eyes and on his forehead, under a single kill scar. 'But you always did talk in riddles.'

'When we were young I thought you looked like your mother Zesi. Now you look more of a Pretani, like your father.'

'Is that a bad thing?'

'No. Because I can still see my Kirike in there, under all the years.'

He slapped his belly. 'Under all the weight, you mean.' He leaned forward, and said a few halting words in the tongue of Dolphin's mother, the tongue of the True People from across the ocean. 'You still smell of the sea.'

Dolphin laughed. 'And you of the forest. You must meet my children. Four of them. All boys.'

He grinned. 'I left my own litter at home. Three girls!'

She held his gaze for one more heartbeat. 'What might have been?'

'What indeed? But we must make the most of the world as we find it.'

'Well,' Ana barked, '*that's* an attitude I've been arguing against my whole life, I must say.' She hobbled forward to Kirike's bag, poking it with her stick. 'I take it this is the old man?'

'Let me.' Resin stepped forward, opened the bag, and picked out the Root's skull to hand to Ana.

Ana took it carefully and touched one cheekbone with a bent fingertip. 'Poor Shade! He was a good man, you know – better than the rest of you Pretani put together, and certainly better than his father and brother who were both little more than animals.'

Dolphin murmured, 'Ana—'

'No, it's true, and it has to be said. If anybody deserved to be born into a better world it was him. I always thought, you know, that if he'd been born in Etxelur he'd have made a good priest. He had the right instinct about people.' She glared at Sunta. 'Shame you never met him, child. He might have taught you a few things.' Carefully she handed the skull back to Kirike and turned her face to the sun, closing her streaming eyes. 'It's a beautiful day – best of the year so far. Why wait? Isn't it a good enough day to lay poor old Shade down for his final sleep?'

Dolphin glanced at the Pretani. 'It's not the equinox yet, Ana. We haven't arranged a proper ceremony, a procession—'

'Well, I know that. But would Shade care?' Ana turned to the Pretani. 'From what I remember of your father—'

Acorn said, 'You're right, Ana. He was a warrior who longed for peace, a leader who longed for modesty. He wouldn't want a great fuss.'

'Yes.' Ana reached out, and Acorn took her hands. 'Just us, then, his family and those who knew him. Anyhow there's time to change your mind; it will take me long enough to make my way to the Northern Barrage, curse these knees. And maybe our new earthworks will put on a show – they should be draining the barrages today.' But Dolphin could see none of the Pretani knew what that meant. 'Dolphin, child, are you still there?

Dolphin took her arm. 'This way, Ana. The first step down's just ahead of you.'

88

By the time they had reached the Northern Barrage, following Ana at her crawling pace, quite a crowd had gathered to follow them, some from Etxelur itself, and snailheads, World River folk, others who had come here for the Spring Walk – and Eel folk whose parents or grandparents had once been brought here as slaves. The children ran and played, each of them covering ten times the distance walked by the solemn adults.

One little girl, aged seven, was cheeky enough to come and walk beside Ana, trying to hold her hand. This was Zuba, granddaughter of Arga – known as a formidable swimmer, as her grandmother had once been. The world was full of children, and there always seemed to be more of them in these first bright days of every spring, playing among the first flowers. Dolphin thought of her own children, the four boys who were all but grown already, and the two others who had died young. How many of the children playing today would live to see ten years, or twenty? Let them have this brief day in the sun, and enjoy it as they could.

Having walked across the Bay Land the party climbed a line of stranded dunes, and then came upon the Northern Barrage. Stretching roughly east to west, this wall ran the length of the old tidal causeway between Flint Island and the mainland, but had been greatly extended. The southern face of smoothly worked sandstone shone in the sunlight, while the sea, excluded and tamed, lapped passively at the northern face.

Ana and her party climbed up onto the dyke from the abutment at its island end, and then walked along the stone-clad upper surface. Only Ana, Dolphin, Kirike, Acorn, Resin and Sunta walked along the wall, while those who had followed watched from below. Kirike bore the bag of bones, as he had all the way from Pretani. Ana walked with her arm linked in Dolphin's. Aside from the gull-like shouts of the playing children, the only sounds up here were the wash of the waves against the wall, and the tap-tap of Ana's stick on the stone.

Dolphin looked to her right, over the sea, where Ana's last great project, the long dykes that had been built around the site of the drowned Mothers' Door, was all but complete. This morning people were still working on the tops of the dykes, laden with sacks and ropes, and silhouetted against the sun-dazzled brilliance of the sea – but the dykes were intact enough for the long labour of excluding the sea to have begun. Today, close to the spring equinox, the tide would be exceptionally low, and Dolphin knew that the great gates could be opened in the walls to allow more water within to drain away. This was the show Ana had hoped might be fortuitously mounted to impress the Pretani, and to honour Shade.

But the bemused Pretani, staring at the earthworks, clearly understood little of what they were seeing.

The party reached the centre of the dyke's curving face and came to a halt. Here the heavy facing stones had been lifted from the upper surface of the dyke, and cists – small, stone-walled tombs – had been dug into the mud and rock of the interior.

Kirike seemed surprised to have come here. 'I wondered where we were walking, away from Flint Island . . . You would inter him here? Not in the middens?'

'We don't use the old middens any more,' Ana said. The breeze off the sea picked up, and whipped her stringy hair about her face; Acorn brushed back the greying wisps. 'Thank you, child . . . It was after the war, after your mother died in my arms, Kirike, at the hands of your father. Zesi's were the first bones I placed here, in the wall. Since then we have dismantled the middens, and we brought the bones of all the dead to this

493

place, the dyke, and to the Eastern Barrage too, across the mouth of the bay.'

She turned to Kirike, her blank eyes questing. 'This is my plan, Kirike. Let the sea walls be more than mere mounds of timber and mud and stone to our people. Let our children know that this is the resting place of their ancestors, who survived the Great Sea and built the first walls. And let them know that they are protected not just by mute, dead stone but by the last legacy of those grandmothers – their very bones.' She sniffed. 'People think this is a trick. Jurgi was always accusing me of manipulation, of twisting custom for my own needs, and inventing others where none suited. Well, what of it? Jurgi himself lies in the wall now, keeping a watchful eye on the sea. And now you too, Shade of the Pretani, will join my sister in the long sleep. You Pretani – Resin, if there's anything you want to say . . .'

'No,' Resin growled. 'All the words were said in Pretani. The gods need no more words.'

'Then get on with it.'

Kirike knelt down and opened up his bag. Reverently he unpacked the bones, and began to lay them in the shallow cist.

Ana, gripping Dolphin's arm, turned her sightless face to the northern sea. 'When I was a little girl I rarely thought of the future. What child does? Even when I was grown it seemed to me the past must have been the same as the present, and the future could be no different. Well, the Great Sea washed that away, I can tell you. And now I *know* there will be a future, for I have created it – I and Novu and Jurgi and all the rest – it is divided from the past as cleanly as this wall divides land from sea.

'But what next? That I cannot see. Knuckle's boys have dreams of their own – do you remember Knuckle? Good man, another hothead, but not all his boys are entirely foolish. The snailheads abandoned their land in the south because of the encroachment of the sea. Well, if dykes can be built here, why not *there*? And maybe it ought to be done if we don't want the sea washing up from the south to overwhelm us, just when

494

we've excluded it from the north. But that's a task for another generation, not for mine, and I won't see it done. I think I've stirred them up to do it, however.

'And then there's whatever's going on in the east.' She glanced that way, thoughtful. 'I mean the very far east, beyond the Continent where the traders walk, a world away. It's *different* where Novu was born, in Jericho, where people live in nests of stone, and don't hunt as we do but live with the cattle they feed on. Just one of them came here with a head full of strangeness, and he changed everything, for Novu's was the inspiration for building the dykes in the first place.

'What else are they up to over there? What happens when the next Novu comes here, and the next – or a whole herd of them? Well, let them come. I remember Novu said that at first he could barely see us at all, barely see Etxelur, so lightly had we touched the land. Even our houses were just heaps of seaweed to him. Let them try not to see us now . . .'

'Ana! Look at me!'

Ana turned her head towards the ocean. 'That sounds like Arga. It can't be Arga. Although she was always a good swimmer, and now she swims in the stone of the dyke . . .'

'Ana!'

Dolphin peered out to sea. The voice wasn't Arga's, but Zuba's, Arga's granddaughter. She was standing within the circle of the ocean dykes – standing on a dry surface, on a wall that curved and glistened, studded by shells and draped with seaweed.

As the water drained out through the gates in Ana's dykes, for the first time since the day of the Great Sea, the circular arcs of the Door to the Mothers' House were rising into the sunlit air.

89

For an age yet the chthonic convulsions would continue. Matters of geological chance would determine the future shape of land and sea: the release of stresses in the unburdened continental plates, the precise way the ice caps melted after their rough sculpting by the stray comet fragments. Small, random events, trivial on a planetary scale, yet with huge consequences for the humans who struggled to survive.

In Northland, as the seas rose, perhaps the flooding from north and south would continue, until the ocean broke through from north to south, separating Britain from Europe with a tongue of ocean.

Or perhaps humans could make a difference.

Time would tell.

Afterword

In 1931 a fishing trawler called the *Colinda*, working forty kilometres off the eastern coast of England, dragged up a lump of peat. Inside, the skipper found an elegantly barbed spear point made from a deer antler. Entirely unexpected, it was a relic of a country now lost beneath the ocean.

In 8000 BC sea levels were much lower than today, as vast quantities of water were still locked up in the ice caps, and around the world ocean floors were exposed. Britain was not an island. The bed of the North Sea was a vast plain now known as 'Doggerland', a country larger than modern Britain whose northern coast ran directly from England to Denmark. The present Dogger Bank was a shallow upland (called the First Mother's Ribs here), and to its south was a salt-water estuary the size of the Bristol Channel, now known as the Outer Silver Pit (and here called the Moon Sea). With twenty-four major lakes and wetlands and sixteen hundred kilometres of river courses, Doggerland was a rich, well-watered landscape that would have been very attractive to human hunters, more so than the surrounding higher land – and probably the centre of north Europe's culture at the time.

But as the last ice melted the sea levels rose, and the land itself, released from the ice's weight, rose and fell in a complex geometry of rebound. Doggerland began to drown. The sea rise may have been punctuated by sudden events such as storm surges – or even by tsunamis, as depicted here. In *c.*6200 BC a massive undersea landslip occurred off the coast of Norway at Storegga (see Bondevik et al, *Eos*, vol. 64, pp. 289–300, 2003). My earlier tsunami originates in the same undersea area.

By *c.*6000 BC Britain was severed from continental Europe, by *c.*4000 BC the last islands were submerged, and that was the end of 'Doggerland, a country that had been central to the cultural development of north-west Europe for perhaps twelve thousand years' (chapter five of *Europe's Lost World: The Rediscovery of Doggerland*, V. Gaffney et al, Council for British Archaeology, 2009). The question asked in this series is: what if this northern heartland, on the brink of the Neolithic, had *not* been lost to the ocean?

Doggerland's existence was suspected long before the *Colinda's* chance find. Observations of submerged offshore forests – 'Noah's woods' – had been recorded since the twelfth century. Geologist Clement Reid, in his *Submerged Forests* (Cambridge, 1913), was the first to speculate that a drowned landscape might once have joined Britain to the continent. A key survey was published in 1998 by Professor Bryony Coles (*Proceedings of the Prehistoric Society*, vol. 64, pp. 45–81), who coined the name 'Doggerland'. This built on data about the North Sea gathered by geologists, environmentalists, marine engineers and others. (The Northland map in this volume is based on Coles's projections.) A recent work led by the University of Birmingham utilised two decades' worth of geological data, gathered by the oil and gas companies, to produce a detailed study of a large area south of the Dogger Bank (see *Mapping Doggerland* by V. Gaffney et al, Archaeopress, 2007).

The importance of Doggerland is now recognised. Doggerland is one of the three largest preserved drowned landscapes in the world, the others being Beringia, under the Bering Strait, and Sundaland, between Indochina and Java. Archaeologists are seeking World Heritage status for the site, and there are proposals for further work with undersea archaeology and sea-bottom coring. My portrayal of Doggerland here, inspired by the excitement of the 'discovery' of this lost country, respectfully draws on the work done by these generations of researchers.

In the Netherlands people have been struggling to keep their land from the sea since before Roman times. Their earliest efforts, as in the novel, were to build artificial hills called *terpen* or *werden* in flood-affected areas, from about 500 BC. If anybody really did try to save Doggerland by building polders and dykes and drainage channels, the evidence is lost beneath the North Sea.

This book is set in Britain's Mesolithic period, *c.*10,000 BC–4,000 BC. For an overview see *Late Stone Age Hunters of the British Isles*, C. Bark, Routledge, 1992. The Mesolithic roughly corresponds culturally to the 'Archaic' period in the Americas; see *Prehistory of the Americas*, S. Fiedel, Cambridge, 1992. My Doggerland Mesolithic culture is an invention, but draws on evidence of comparable cultures around the world (see *Mesolithic Studies at the Beginning of the 21st Century* by N. Milner et al, Oxbow, 2005).

My depiction of permanent dwellings is derived in part from the archaeology of a 'house' in Howick, Northumberland, dating back to *c.*8000 BC (see *Ancient Northumberland* by C. Waddington et al, English Heritage, 2004). There is no evidence I know of regarding clothing worn in the Mesolithic. However, there is evidence of sophisticated clothing woven from vegetable fibres from much earlier epochs, even the depths of the Ice Ages (see for example, www.sciencedaily.com/releases/2000/02/000203074853.htm). Hunting people observed in the modern age have shown themselves capable of remarkable feats of medicine, including Caesarean sections, which may be anaesthetised with opium derivatives (see for example, chapters eight and nine of *Lost Civilisations of the Stone Age* by R. Rudgley, Century, 1998).

Some speculate that of languages spoken in modern Europe only Basque remains of a very ancient language super-family known as Dene-Sino-Caucasian, which was later mostly supplanted by Neolithic language groups including Uralic-Yukaghir, which includes Finnish, and the Indo-European which includes the Celtic, Germanic and Italic languages (see L. Trask, *The*

History of Basque, Routledge, 1977). This is controversial, however. And even the language group from which Basque derived must surely have been only one of many hundreds scattered across a sparsely populated Mesolithic Europe. I have respectfully borrowed or adapted some Basque words for names and place names. My name for Ana's home, 'Etxelur', is inspired by the Basque words *lur*, land, *etxe*, home. My names for Britain, 'Albia', and the British, 'Pretani', derive from records made in antiquity that appear to be based on the journey of Pytheas in the fourth century BC (see *The Extraordinary Voyage of Pytheas the Greek*, B. Cunliffe, Allen Lane, 2001).

My mythology of Northland is an invention, though it is assembled in part from fragments of Norse, Celtic and other lore.

'Rock art' based on 'cup-and-ring' circular forms is common in northern Britain and Ireland (see *British Prehistoric Rock Art* by S. Beckensall, Tempus, 1999). It is unusual in that, unlike art found in other parts of the world, it is almost all abstract. The dominant motif is a set of concentric circles with a radial 'tail', but many variants are found. The rock art is difficult to date (there is no organic component to allow carbon-dating). It is generally assumed to be Neolithic or perhaps Bronze Age, but it has been speculated that the art has Mesolithic origins.

The legend of Atlantis derives from Plato's dialogues *Timaeus* and *Critias*, written *c*.360 BC. Atlantis scholars have suggested dozens of possible locations for the lost island, including the bed of the North Sea, for example by a Professor F. Gidon in 1935. The plan of the principal city on Atlantis as described by Plato in *Critias* does indeed bear some resemblance to some examples of British rock art. However, my linking of my lost land of Etxelur with Plato's Atlantis is pure, and mischievous, invention on my part, solely intended for the fictive purpose of this novel.

Ice Dreamer comes from a remnant of the Palaeo-American culture called the 'Clovis people', with their characteristic large, fluted spear points, which was displaced by Archaic cultures – 'the Cowards' in Dreamer's language. Evidence that a cold snap at *c*.10,000 BC called the 'Younger Dryas' was triggered by a comet impact in North America was presented by researchers from the University of California to a meeting of the American Geophysical Union in May 2007 (*New Scientist*, 26 May, 2007), and additional evidence in the form of a global scatter of 'nano-diamonds', produced by the high temperatures and pressures of the impact, was presented more recently (*Science*, 2 January, 2009). The theory remains controversial (see *New Scientist*, 7 February, 2009). I have invented the detail of a secondary comet impact in northern Europe, which perturbs the complex sequence of landscape sinking and rebound.

The 'Leafy Boys', inhabitants of the forest canopy that once blanketed much of Britain, are my invention. There was surely an ecological niche to be occupied here, however, and the conditions of the forest would have made it unlikely that any fossil evidence would have been preserved.

The suggestion that Jericho's wall was not for defensive purposes but a defence against floods and mud slides was made by O. Bar-Yosef (*Current Archaeology*, vol. 27, pp.157–62, 1996). Novu and Chona, walking from Jericho, follow the natural cross-European trade routes that appear to have been used in prehistoric times (see B. Cunliffe, *Europe Between the Oceans*, Yale, 2008). The place Chona calls the 'Narrow' is based on the site known as Lepenski Vir.

This is a novel, intended as an impression of an intriguing age, and not meant to be taken as a reliable history of the Mesolithic. Many of the dates are uncertain, many key landscapes are locked under the waters of the North Sea, and even on modern dry land the peoples of the time left scant traces of their presence. However, any errors or inaccuracies are, of course, my sole responsibility.

Stephen Baxter
Northumberland
Winter Solstice, 2009

501